The Hunter's Tale

By the same author

THE NOVICE'S TALE
THE OUTLAW'S TALE
THE PRIORESS' TALE
THE SERVANT'S TALE
THE BISHOP'S TALE
THE BOY'S TALE
THE MURDERER'S TALE
THE MAIDEN'S TALE
THE REEVE'S TALE
THE SQUIRE'S TALE
THE CLERK'S TALE
THE BASTARD'S TALE

The Hunter's Tale

Margaret Frazer

ROBERT HALE · LONDON

First published in Great Britain 2004

ISBN 0 7090 7706 8

Robert Hale Limited
Clerkenwell House
Clerkenwell Green
London EC1R 0HT

2 4 6 8 10 9 7 5 3 1

Typeset in 11/14pt Classical Garamond Roman
by Derek Doyle & Associates, Liverpool.
Printed in Great Britain by
St Edmundsbury Press Ltd, Bury St Edmunds, Suffolk.
Bound by Woolnough Bookbinding Limited.

For Cheryl, because it's her fault.
And for AKC Champion Stoneybrook Brighton, FCh, SC, TT, PTF, a handsome lad who fulfills the Irish wolfhound's creed:
Gentle when stroked,
Fierce when provoked.

For in his huntyng hath he swich delit
That it is al his joye and appetit
To been hymself the grete hertes bane . . .

G. CHAUCER, *The Knight's Tale*

Chapter 1

Light trembled through the leaves, little flickers of sun and shade playing across Hugh's closed eyes where he sat with his head leaned back against the oak's deep-barked trunk, his face turned upward to the canopy of leaves and dark oak branches between him and the summer sky, listening to the whisper and sigh of leaves away into green distances, the soft sough of branches moving, the busy rustle of a squirrel passing through treetops so high the two wolfhounds – Bane's large, bony head resting on his chest and Brigand's against his hip – did not even flick an ear at it. With summer warmth all through him, Hugh let the quiet sink into him, too. Here, for a while, with manor, fields, and family – most especially family – left behind him, there was only the quiet and himself and the two hounds, with no need to speak when he'd rather be silent or feel anything when he'd rather feel nothing.

He wondered if the yelling at home had stopped yet.

His guess was that it hadn't. Sir Ralph had been at full cry and Tom ready to meet him yell for yell, a furious use of words the one thing he wholeheartedly shared with his father; and if they faltered, Miles was too often in black enough humour to start them up again. Today, when they had set to it at the midday dinner's end, Mother had risen from the table, called Lucy to her, bid Hugh fetch her spinning to her, and gone out to the arbor at the far end of her garden, not beyond sound of her husband and son's shouting in the hall but at least away from it.

Hugh had never understood whatever truce there was between his parents. Lady Anneys seemed to live somewhere beyond her husband's furious outbursts and he had never, so far as Hugh knew, ever lifted a hand against her. His sons and grandson and even Elyn once when she had backtalked him over something had, yes, all felt his fist, but Lady Anneys would simply rise and walk away, and he always let her go.

Today Hugh had escaped, too, because she had bid him come after her, and when he had fetched her distaff and basket of wool to the vine-shaded arbor, he had given them to her with a kiss on her cheek at the edge of the wimple that encircled her face framed by the stiff-starched wings of her white linen veil and said, 'I'm away then, if anyone asks.'

She had given him her small smile for answer but Lucy, being fourteen and eager for other than sitting the afternoon away, had started, 'Can I—'

'No,' her mother had said. 'You can't.'

Hugh had rubbed the top of his sister's head in the way he knew particularly irked her and left them by way of the garden's rear gate through the tall willow-woven fence, crossing over the two-plank bridge across the shallow-banked, narrow stream there to the packed earth of the cart-track running on its other side along the new-mown hayfield where the cut hay, laid out in its long windrows and turning to gold as it dried under the midsummer sun, smelled of all summer's sweetness. There had been half a dozen village women in the field this morning, turning the windrows over with their wooden rakes, the better for the hay to dry all through before it was haycocked, but they were gone to their dinners and Hugh had gone leftward along the cart-track without need to see or talk to anyone.

The way he went, the track curved behind the manor buildings, between them and the near fields, and then away to the farther fields. The other way it led to the church and village and more fields before it met the road that ran on the manor's other side and away. The manor of Woodrim had never been grand enough to warrant an enclosing wall; barn, byre, cartshed, ploughshed, dairy, poultry yard, and all else that went into making a manor's life were spread around and outward from the bare dirt yard in front of the hall in no great order. When Tom, Hugh, and Miles had all been small, the clutter of buildings had made for grand chase-and-hide games, and hiding was what Hugh had been at today, circling around to the kennel beyond the barn.

The kennel was the newest-built and best-kept place on the

manor, a high, solid fence around a wide rectangle of grass with the hounds' low, square house in the middle made with close-planked walls, a thick-thatched roof, a fireplace for warming the hounds in winter or after wet hunting, and a loft for the hound-boy to sleep.

'The dogs live better than we do,' Tom sometimes said bitterly, though not where their father would hear him.

It was Miles who said – and did not care at all if Sir Ralph heard him – that the hounds lived best of anyone on the manor because Sir Ralph cared for them more than he cared for anyone else; and Sir Ralph, hearing him, would roar, 'You have the right of that, you useless bastard. Better than I care for you, that's sure.'

Since Miles was neither useless nor a bastard, merely someone his grandfather wished had never been born, that was unfair as well as cruel, but fairness rarely mattered to Sir Ralph. Hugh doubted he knew how to be kind, except to his hounds. Hounds and the hunt were what mattered to Sir Ralph, and Hugh's good luck was that his own pleasure in hounds and hunting almost matched his father's. That had earned him something of his father's favor over the years, since the time he was ten years old and Sir Ralph had found him hiding in the kennel, crouched in the straw with his arms around Pensel's neck while Paliard licked at his wet face. His back had been aching from being beaten with Sir Ralph's leather belt for splashing wine on the cloth when serving at table during dinner and, hand to belt buckle again, Sir Ralph had stood glaring down at him, demanding, 'What in hell are you doing here, messing with my dogs?'

Angry with pain and the shame of being found in tears and certain there was another beating coming, Hugh had said back, defiant with despair, 'I'm not messing. I *like* them. I like them better than I like *you*!'

That should have earned him another whipping but Sir Ralph had eyed Paliard licking now behind Hugh's ear, the strong stroke of her tongue up-ending his hair, and had said, 'Do you, by God? Paliard, here.'

Paliard had given Hugh a final swipe with her tongue, risen with her great, gaunt, wolfhound grace, and padded to Sir Ralph's side. Fondling her ears, his father had demanded, 'What makes Paliard my best running hound?'

Hugh had promptly said, not needing to think about it, 'Lean body, small flanks, long sides. Well-slanted shoulders, straight hocks—'

He could have gone on but Sir Ralph had interrupted, 'How do you know that?'

'I've listened to you and Master Basing,' who had been hound-master and huntsman then, 'talk about it all the time.'

'Listen, do you? Come here, whelp.'

Wary of pain but knowing there would be no escaping it if his father chose to give it, Hugh had obeyed. Sir Ralph had looked him up and down, felt of his shoulders (not bothering that Hugh flinched from his fingers rough on the belt-bruises) and his arms, his hands, his legs, then held him by the chin and turned his head from side to side, checking him over as if he were a hound himself, before he let him go with a shove that staggered Hugh to the side, and said, 'You might do. Tell Master Basing you're to be his hound-boy until I say differently.'

So hound-boy he had been, with Master Basing as well as his father to whip him when he failed to do things right. But he had learned quickly more for the love of it than because of the whippings, and as his skills grew, the whippings lessened; and when he had grown enough himself that, as Sir Ralph put it, 'You're no longer so undersized that a hare could trample you into the ground, you skimp-boned whelp,' the two men had begun to teach him a hunter's skills to go with his hound ones. And three years ago, when Master Basing had fallen, clutching his chest, during a midwinter deer hunt, and died before Father Leonel could be brought to him – 'A cleaner death than a priest's mumbling could have given him anyway,' Sir Ralph had said – Sir Ralph had slapped Hugh between the shoulders and told him he was hound-master and huntsman now in Master Basing's place. 'The great lords can afford houndmasters and a blast of hunters to their pleasure, but I'm a poor knight and nothing more, and by God's teeth, at least one of my brats can finally be worth his keep.'

The main lie in that was that Sir Ralph was only a poor knight. He had started life plainly enough – though not poor – as the heir to a small manor in Leicestershire but taken himself to London, become a lawyer, married a rich merchant's daughter, and earned a goodly fortune and his knighthood there, then taken his wealth away to the country, giving up the law for hounds and hunting, his true passions. He had bought the Oxfordshire manor of Woodrim not for what profits it might make him but because of the hunting rights in the king's neighboring forest of Charlbrook Chase that went with it; and when his first wife died, he had married Lady Anneys, another merchant's daughter, for the dower of town properties that came with her and the sons she might birth for him. The properties' rents were to help to pay for his hounds and hunting. The sons were to replace the disappointing one his first wife had given him. For that, to Sir Ralph's mind, Hugh with his love of hounds and hunting had proved the best; and if Hugh had not friendship or affection from his father, at least he had less of Sir Ralph's wrath than did Tom or Miles.

Tom, being the eldest living son and therefore likely his heir, drew Sir Ralph's wrath the way a tall tree in an open field drew lightning, but – possessing much of their father's hot blood and love of yelling himself – he usually gave as good as he was given whenever he and Sir Ralph set to it, which was often enough because Tom served as his father's steward, responsible both for Woodrim and all his other properties. Today's dinnertime quarreling had come out of Tom's wanting, because of the overhot weather, to give more than the usually allotted ale to the haymakers presently working Sir Ralph's fields instead of their own, and Sir Ralph's refusing him with oaths.

With his own escape made before he was drawn into their argument, Hugh had called Bane and Brigand to him from among the twenty other hounds in the kennel yard and set out by the nearest field path across the rough pasture to the wide-cut greenway into the forest that so closely curved around two sides of the manor. If he had followed the greenway far enough, it would have taken him through Woodrim's thick-grown forest to the more open Charlbrook Chase, which was as much meadow and rough heath as woods, for all it was called a royal forest, because dense woods did not make for good galloping after deer. But neither the manor's forest nor the king's was only for hunting. Wood was taken from them for building and for fuel and for sale, and in autumns the lord's and villagers' pigs were herded in among the trees to fatten on fallen nuts before slaughtertime at Martinmas.

The grassy greenway served for passage into and through the

forest for all of that, but Hugh had followed it only a short way before turning from it into a narrow deer-path leading away among the trees. Less by thought than by long usage, he had shifted into a more careful-footed going, quiet in his soft-soled boots, barely stirring the forest's midday stillness; and Bane and Brigand, knowing they were on no hunt, had moved easily at his heels, padding as silently as he did. Before long they had come out of the green shadows into this small clearing around the tree Hugh called, to himself, the grandfather-oak because of its age and grandspreading size. It was a companionable tree, as good company in its way as were the hounds, nor was anyone likely to happen on him here by chance.

But on purpose was another matter.

Hugh opened his eyes. The silence had changed, and the two hounds lifted their heads to listen with him. Someone almost as silent-footed as he had been was coming along the deer-path. Then Bane stood up, tail swaying in a slow wag, and Hugh stayed where he was, unsurprised when Miles came into the clearing, tugged onward by Skyre, the lean, young, not-much-trained lymer-hound that was halfway to throttling herself on the leash with eagerness.

Brigand rose to join Bane in greeting her and Miles, and Hugh asked, 'How did she do?' as Miles, still holding Skyre's leash, folded his long legs and sat down in the grass beside him.

'She followed your scent as easily as if you were dragging a musk bag.'

'Me and two hounds. I should hope she could follow us.'

'No leash manners, though.'

'Did you bother trying to teach her some on the way?'

'Not my business,' Miles said.

'Not your business to have her out at all.'

'She got to pacing and whining in the hall. Sir Ralph said to take her out so I did.'

Eyes closed again, Hugh flopped one hand sideways from where it lay on his chest to hit Miles idly on the knee. 'He didn't mean this far, I warrant, you idiot. Are they still at it?'

'If there was a wind, you could probably hear them loud and clear.' Miles shifted to lean back against the oak's trunk beside Hugh. 'You'd think they'd get tired of listening to each other.'

'Don't you know the only sound sweeter to my father's ears

than his hounds baying in the hunt is his own voice baying at one of us?'

'How good for him. How unfortunate for us.' Skyre flopped down with a sigh beside him. Miles likewise sighed and added, 'Wouldn't it be good if he'd choke on his own bile and be done with it?'

Hugh said nothing; no answer was needed. The wolfhounds settled beside him again and the forest's quiet came back, with only the hum of midges in the clearing's sunlight and Brigand sometime snuffling in his sleep. For Hugh, Miles' ability to be silent was one of his virtues. That they were able to be silent together was part of their friendship, more than the fact that, close in age though they were, they were uncle and nephew because Sir Ralph – disappointed in the son he had had by his late first wife – had married Lady Anneys much about the time that disappointing son had come back from the French war with a French wife. Lady Anneys had borne Tom a year later and had Hugh a year after that, a few months before Miles was born to their half-brother, who had shortly thereafter died, leaving his wife and infant son to his father's and stepmother's care.

Miles' mother, much loathed by Sir Ralph and loathing him in return, had lived for another three years, then died, too; and Lady Anneys, with Tom and Hugh and by then a daughter of her own, had taken Miles to herself as if he were another son rather than her stepgrandson. Hugh did not know if she had quarreled with Sir Ralph over that; but then, he had never in his life seen his parents quarrel over anything. What he had equally never seen was Sir Ralph show anything like affection toward Miles. Instead, all the disgust Sir Ralph must have had against his firstborn son and the French wife had turned on Miles. And in return Miles as fully and openly loathed him.

Brigand stood up, turned around and around, and lay down again, this time dropping his head heavily onto Hugh's stomach. Jarred out of his almost-doze, Hugh ran a hand down a gray, rough-coated shoulder and said at Miles, 'You're going to be in trouble for wandering off, you know.'

'I didn't just wander off,' Miles said lazily. His hands clasped behind his head now, he was gazing idly away at nothing across the clearing. 'If anyone asks, I've been to see how the charcoal making is going at the far end of the woods.'

'*Is* there charcoal making going on at the far end of the woods?'

'No.'

'Miles,' Hugh said with feigned deep weariness, 'that's careless.' That it was also a lie was not the matter. Lying to Sir Ralph was simply the safest way to go through life.

'Old Roaring Ralph won't find out. He hardly takes enough interest in the manor to know when it's haying time, let be if there's charcoal making or not. He won't know the difference or care what I'm doing, so long as I'm "earning my keep" and not anywhere near him.'

That was all too true. Once, when they were half-grown and hiding in the hayloft nursing beaten backs for some forgotten offense, Miles had said, 'He beats you to make sure you obey him. He beats me because he wants me to break.' Had said it flatly, not so much in complaint as merely telling a truth that Hugh had not seen until then.

That they all three – he and Miles and Tom – were now grown too big to be beaten anymore only meant Sir Ralph had other ways of making sure they understood his hand was upper here, and one way was to make use of all of them. Hugh had his houndmaster and huntsman's duties, seeing to it that hounds and game were ready when Sir Ralph wanted to hunt, while Tom had had writing and arithmetic driven into him so that he could be Sir Ralph's steward. 'And any year you don't show a profit, you'd better be able to show me the reason why,' Sir Ralph had said. 'You're not so big I can't take it out of your hide if I want to.'

'You'll get what's coming to you,' Tom had snarled. 'Don't fear that.'

Sir Ralph had risen from his chair, snarling back, 'Don't loose your lip at me, boy! You haven't inherited yet. By God's teeth, you cross me and I'll leave it all to the Church. I swear I will!'

'Leave away! The day you do, you lose all hold on me and any of us and we'll be gone so fast you'll choke on the dust!'

'Good riddance to the lot of you then! Maybe I'd have a little peace around here!'

When the two of them set to one of their shouting-matches, like today, everyone who could tried simply to get out of hearing, and one good thing about Tom being steward was that he had to ride out and away to see to Sir Ralph's other properties, taking him out of shouting range for a few weeks at a time. Miles was not so fortunate. As Woodrim's forester, overseeing the manor's forest and Charlbrook Chase for the sake of the hunting and for Sir Ralph's profit, his duties took him away from the manor, yes, but never far and never for long. It was his business to see to it that the villagers took no more deadwood than they were allowed by right and custom; that timbering and coppicing were done where and when they should be to keep the trees not only from overgrowing but constantly fit for harvesting; and that new plantings were steadily made, to keep both forests fit for all their uses. It was ceaseless work, year-around in all weathers, and Miles did it well, Hugh knew. What he did not know was whether Miles had any actual care for the work or only for the excuse it gave him to be away from the manor and Sir Ralph for hours and sometimes whole days at a time. It was something Hugh had never asked, but he sometimes thought – and shied away from the thought when it came – how they all – he and Miles and Tom and everyone else – despite how much they lived together, lived so much alone, careful behind walls of silence that kept them a little safe from Sir Ralph but also shut away from each other.

So quietly that for a moment Hugh did not take in what he had said, Miles murmured, 'The wonder is that one of us hasn't killed him yet.' And after another moment's silence, 'Or that someone hasn't, if not one of us. He's crossed enough men in his life that you'd think somebody would have done for him by now.'

'Kill him?' Hugh repeated, still watching the leaves above him.

'Or beaten him bloody,' Miles went on, in the same mild voice.

Hugh pushed Brigand's head aside and propped himself up on one elbow to look at Miles, still gazing away across the clearing. 'Miles,' he said. 'Don't.'

Miles rolled his head sideways to meet his gaze. 'Don't say it or don't do it?'

'Don't do either one.'

Miles turned his face away, back to looking across the clearing. 'The pity is that I won't. I just wish someone would. His death is the only way we'll ever be cut loose from him. You have to know that. His death or ours.'

Hugh lay back down and closed his eyes. Away from Sir Ralph, he did not want even to think about him, let alone pointlessly talk about him; but feigning mildness as deliberately as Miles had, he asked, 'What thing worse than usual did he say today?'

He waited through the silence, knowing Miles would answer, and finally Miles did, still low-voiced but now openly bitter. 'In the middle of yelling at Tom over the cost of rope – you missed them moving on from ale to rope – he of a sudden pointed at me and said, "The only thing around here, Tomkin, more useless than you, is that".'

Hugh, trying for lightness, said, 'Which doubtless made Tom no happier than it made you?'

'I'd guess so, judging by how hard he threw his cup against the wall.'

'Meaning it was a good thing it was the wooden cups at dinner today?'

'A very good thing. One of the pewter ones would have holed the wall. The wooden one only broke. While Tom was yelling that Sir Ralph was wrong, the most useless thing on the manor was *him* and Sir Ralph was yelling back, I left. You don't suppose today is the day they'll finally kill each other, do you?'

Hugh doubted it would ever come to killing. They used yelling instead of blows these days. But he looked at Miles again and said, 'Just mind *you* don't go killing him, that's all. You'd be caught for it and hanged and he'd rejoice from the grave to know he'd brought you down. You don't want to make him that happy, do you?'

Miles caught Hugh's mockery and tossed it back. 'Right. I can see me standing on the scaffold with the noose around my neck and him sniggering up at me from Hell. Damn. I'll have to let him live.'

'Besides that, if you killed him, you'd go to Hell for it and have to spend eternity with him.'

Miles threw up his hands in surrender. 'Then he's surely safe from me. I'm not about to risk that.'

'Unless,' Hugh went on, 'he's left money in his will for Masses enough to send him to Heaven.'

'Ha! There aren't enough priests in the world to say that many Masses before Judgment Day.'

Hugh moved Brigand from his stomach and sat up. 'Of course,

after you killed him, you could repent of it, and then if you were hanged, you'd save your soul and be safe away to Heaven, leaving him to Hell on his own.'

'Repent?' Miles said with huge indignation. He signed himself with a large cross. 'God forgive me if I'm ever *that* much of a hypocrite!' And he and Hugh both burst into laughter. He put his hands behind his head again and, still softly chuckling, shifted to stare up into leaves in his turn while Hugh began checking the dogs' paws for thorns or cuts. A hunting dog's fate was in its paws, Master Basing had told him often enough, and yesterday he had heard himself saying to young Degory, the present hound-boy, 'A dog that can't run is good for nothing,' sounding so much like Master Basing he had almost laughed at himself.

The forest's stillness and their own companionable silence folded around him and Miles again, until the sunlight's slant through the trees told them they had been gone as long as they safely could be. There was no need to say it. When Hugh stood up, so did Miles. The three dogs rose, too, and mightily shook themselves; and in silence they all started homeward, out of the clearing into the forest path's thick shade.

Chapter 2

Dame Frevisse awoke in the dark to the whisper of rain along the roof of the nuns' dorter and smiled to herself with pleasure at the sound. This summer in the year of God's grace 1448 had thus far been all warm days and clear skies and just rain enough to keep the pastures thick-grassed for the cattle's grazing and bring the green grain tall in the village fields around St Frideswide's nunnery in northern Oxfordshire. In the wider world all rumors of trouble roiling around the king and among his lords were, since spring, faded away into the distance like a thunderstorm disappearing along the horizon, too far off to matter aught to anyone here. That rain was come again to the fields after almost a week without was a greater matter than the doings or not-doings of king and lords.

The rain's whispering kept Frevisse and St Frideswide's eight other nuns company in the thinning darkness toward dawn as they went soft-footed down from the dorter and along the roofed cloister walk to the church for Prime's prayers and psalms; and the rain was still falling when they finished the Office and passed along the walk again, around the cloister garth to breakfast in the refectory; but by the time they returned to the church for Mass, only a light pattering was left, and by midmorning, after Sext's prayers, only a dripping off the eaves under a clearing sky.

Frevisse smiled up at the cloud-streaked blue above the cloister roof as she came along the cloister walk from the infirmary with a small pot of freshly made ink. Her hope this morning was for time at her desk before Nones to go a little farther with copying out the book of Breton stories promised to a clothier's wife in Banbury by Michaelmas in return for enough black woolen cloth to make two nuns' winter gowns. If she could copy through to the end of Sir Degare's troubles today . . .

She was passing the passageway to the cloister's outer door when a knocking at it brought her to an abrupt stop. St Frideswide's was too small a nunnery to need a constant door-keeper. Whoever was nearest was expected to answer a knock when it came and there was no denying that not only was she nearest but that there was no one else in sight – either nun or servant – and reluctantly she turned and went along the passageway to open the shutter of the door's small, grilled window and look out, asking, 'Yes?'

Old Ela from the guesthall across the courtyard made a short curtsy, bobbing briefly out of view and back again before saying, 'My lady, there's someone come to see Domina Elisabeth. Master Hugh Woderove, if you please.'

'Kin to Ursula?' Frevisse asked.

'Her brother, he says, my lady.'

Careful of the inkpot, Frevisse unlatched the door one-handed and opened it. The cloister was a place men rarely and only briefly came but it was allowed when necessary, and without bothering to take clear look at the young man standing beside Ela, she bowed her head and stood aside to let him enter, thanked Ela, shut the door again, said to him, 'This way, please,' and led him into the cloister walk, where she paused to set the inkpot on the low wall between the walk and the cloister garth at its center before leading him away to the stairs up to Domina Elisabeth's parlor door. There she asked him to wait while she scratched at the door and at Domina Elisabeth's '*Benedicite*' went in to say he was here.

Both for courtesy and in matters that could not be done in chapter meetings, the prioress often received important guests or others here, and therefore her parlor was more comfortably provided than any other place in the cloister, having its own fireplace, two chairs, brightly embroidered cushions on the window seat, and a woven Spanish carpet on the table. Besides that, because she shared her nuns' copying work, Domina Elisabeth had her own slant-topped desk set near the window that overlooked the courtyard and guesthalls, where the light fell well for most of the day. She was there now but looked up from wiping a quill pen's tip clean to ask as Frevisse entered, 'Who is he? Has he said why he wants to see me?' Thereby proving that her copywork had not kept her from looking out the window to see that someone had arrived.

'He's Master Hugh Woderove, Ursula's brother,' Frevisse answered. 'I don't know why he's here.'

'To visit her, belike.' Domina Elisabeth rose from the desk's tall-legged stool and shook out her skirts. 'Bring him in, please, and stay.' Since no nun should be private with a man.

Frevisse saw Hugh Woderove in and stood aside beside the door, hands folded in front of her and head a little bowed, but not so low she could not take her first clear look at him as he crossed the room. He was a wide-shouldered, brown-haired young man in a short, dark gray houppelande slit at the sides for riding and knee-tall leather boots, well made but with many miles and probably years of use to them. His bow and his 'My lady' to Domina Elisabeth were good enough but constrained, as if he were unused to using his manners, and when Domina Elisabeth sat in her own high-backed, carven chair and bade him to the room's other, he sat uncomfortably forward on the chair's edge, hands clasped tightly around his black leather riding gloves as he said without other greeting, 'By your leave, my lady, I won't keep you long. I've only come to take my sister home.'

'Home?' Domina Elisabeth permitted quiet surprise into her voice despite she was undoubtedly – as Frevisse was – rapidly wondering why. 'So suddenly?'

Twisting the gloves in his hands, he started, 'Our father—' but stopped, interrupted by a soft scratching at the door frame.

A stranger's arrival in the cloister never went unknown for long. Frevisse's only question had been whether Dame Emma or Sister Amicia would be first, claiming to wonder if Domina Elisabeth wished food or drink brought for him. As it happened, it was Sister Amicia, panting a little from the haste she had made, who came in at Domina Elisabeth's rather sharp '*Benedicite*,' and curtsyed, taking an open, questioning look at their guest while asking, 'Does my lady wish I bring wine and something to eat?'

'Please, no,' Hugh said to Domina Elisabeth before she could answer. 'We can be home early tomorrow if we leave soon.'

Accepting his pressing need without more question, Domina Elisabeth said, 'Sister Amicia, please bring Ursula Woderove here and give order for her things to be packed.' She turned a questioning look to Ursula's brother. 'All of her things?'

'What? No. She'll be back. I hope to bring her back in a few weeks.'

'Enough of her things for a visit,' Domina Elisabeth said, and added crisply, 'Now, please,' when it seemed Sister Amicia might linger in hope of hearing more. At that, Sister Amicia made a reluctant curtsy and went and Domina Elisabeth turned her heed back to Hugh, saying, 'Your sister will be here soon. Can you tell me what the trouble is? Might our prayers help?'

'Yes. No. I mean, yes.' Hugh paused, having lost himself among answers, drew breath, and said, smoothing his gloves over his knee, 'It's our father. Sir Ralph. He's dead.'

Frevisse and Domina Elisabeth both made the sign of the cross on themselves, Frevisse murmuring a brief prayer while Domina Elisabeth asked, 'We knew nothing of him being ill. It came suddenly?'

'Yes. Suddenly,' Hugh agreed awkwardly. 'It was . . . he was killed. Someone killed him. We found him dead two days ago.'

'Not . . . an accident?' Domina Elisabeth asked. 'Not an accident, no.'

'But you don't know who . . .'

Domina Elisabeth stopped, caught between a wish to know and uncertainty of how much to ask, but Hugh answered, 'We don't know who, no. It was in the woods. He'd been hunting. Whoever did it was well away before we even knew it had happened. We made search with men and dogs but to no use.'

All of which explained the young man's unsteadiness, Frevisse thought. He had hardly had time to find his own balance and was here to tell his sister in her turn. At least he did not have to wait long; small, light footsteps were already running up the stairs, with Sister Amicia calling, 'There's no need to run, Ursula,' but too late. Ursula burst into the room. Wearing her favorite red gown, she was always startling among the nuns forever in their Benedictine black, but as Dame Claire had said last time the question had come up of dressing her in something more seemly, its boldness suited her, and besides, no one was truly willing to spoil her open pleasure in its bright color or forgo their own pleasure in seeing hers. But like her gown, she was sudden, and forgetful of manners and the courtesy due Domina Elisabeth, she cried out, 'Hugh!,' and flung herself across the room at him.

Rising from his chair, he caught her and lifted her from the floor into a great hug that she returned with her arms around his neck and hearty kissing of his cheek. He kissed her as heartily back, set her to the floor, and said the inevitable, 'You've grown!'

Ursula flashed a happy smile up at him. 'You haven't seen me since Christmastide and I turned eleven the morrow of St Mark's. Of course I've grown.' She poked at his belt buckle accusingly. 'You said you'd come at Easter but you didn't. Nobody did.'

'I only said might and it happened I couldn't. But I sent you a red ribbon for your birthday, didn't I? I did do that.'

Ursula flung her arms around his waist, as high as she could reach, and hugged him again. 'You did, you did. Just like I asked.'

'But, Ursa,' Hugh said, and the brightness was gone from his voice, warning her there was something else.

Dame Perpetua was always saying that Ursula was a quickly clever child and now she immediately read her brother's voice and pulled back from him as far as she could without letting go of him and asked, frightened, 'Has something happened to Mother?'

'Not to Mother, no. She's well.' Hugh moved to sit again, drawing Ursula to stand in front of him so they were face to face. 'It's Father. He's dead. He was killed while he was out hunting. Two days ago.'

Ursula's face went blank and her color drained away. With widened eyes, she echoed faintly, 'He's dead? He's really dead?'

'Two days ago. I'm here to take you home for the funeral.'

Belatedly Domina Elisabeth rose to her feet. 'We'll leave you together for now. Take as long as need be. Your things will be waiting for you when you're ready to leave, Ursula.'

Ursula vaguely thanked her without looking away from her brother or loosing her hold on him. Frevisse, following Domina Elisabeth out of the room, heard her ask again, 'He's really dead?' with what sounded oddly more like unbelieving hope than grief, but Frevisse rid herself of that thought by the time she reached the stairfoot, where Domina Elisabeth was sending Sister Amicia to ask Father Henry, the nunnery's priest, to meet her in the church.

'Sir Ralph Woderove was not overgenerous to us but he did send that haunch of venison when Ursula returned to us at

Christmastide, and he was her father. For her sake he shall have a Mass and prayers from us,' she said.

Frevisse agreed that would be well and, her part in it finished, retrieved her inkpot and was at her desk on the cloister walk's north side, bent over her work, when Domina Elisabeth saw Ursula and her brother out. Keeping her eyes on her copying, Frevisse did not see them actually leave but heard, when they were gone and Domina Elisabeth was come back into the cloister, the soft rush of skirts and feet along the walk and Dame Emma eagerly asking Domina Elisabeth where Ursula was going and would she be back and who was that who'd come for her and what had happened. Domina Elisabeth told her, briefly, and sent her back to whatever she should have been doing.

Frevisse missed whatever talk came after that among the other nuns, keeping at her copying through the rest of the day save for the Offices and dinner when no talking was allowed. Only in the hour's recreation allowed each day before Compline's final prayers and bed did she hear more, when the nuns went after supper to the high-walled garden behind the cloister. The fading day was warm under a sky soft with weltering sunlight, and in the usual way of things, they would have sat on the benches or strolled alone or a few together, talking and at ease, along the graveled paths between the carefully kept beds of herbs and flowers. This evening, though, while Frevisse walked slowly in company with Dame Claire, and Sister Thomasine went her usual way to the church to pray, the other nuns hurried ahead along the narrow slype that led out of the cloister walk, crowding on each other's heels into the garden and immediately clustering just inside the gateway with heads together and tongues going. There was no way for Frevisse not to hear, as she and Dame Claire made to go past them, Dame Juliana saying excitedly, 'Yes! I asked the servant who came with him.' Presently hosteler, with the duty of seeing to the nunnery's guests, Dame Juliana had plainly used her duty today as a chance to learn what she could from Hugh Woderove's servant. 'He told me everything.'

'It truly was murder?' Sister Johane asked. 'Someone did kill him?'

'They did. Very much killed him.' Dame Juliana was as eager to tell as her listeners were to hear. 'Someone bashed his head in with a stone. They'd been hunting and he went into the woods after a dog, I think, and when he didn't come back, they went looking for him and found him *dead*.'

'They don't know who did it?' Dame Emma asked.

'Well, they think it must have been a poacher and Sir Ralph surprised him and the man killed him. Whoever it was, he escaped clean away and that's why they think a poacher, because a poacher would know the woods well enough to get away and how to lose the hounds when they tried to trail him.'

Frevisse's own thought was that it must have been a singularly stupid poacher if he chose to be there in the woods when a hunt was going on, but Dame Claire asked as they moved away, neither of them interested in spending their hour in fervent talk over a murder that had nothing to do with them, 'How was it with Ursula when her brother told her, poor child?'

Cautious with her own uncertainty, Frevisse said, 'I was there only at first, before she'd had time to fully feel it, I think.'

Dame Claire bent to run her fingers through a tall clump of lavender. 'We'll have a goodly harvest of this, it seems.'

Frevisse agreed, and leaving the dead man forgotten, they strolled on.

Chapter 3

The trouble with summer days was how long they lasted, Hugh thought wearily, watching almost the last of the funeral guests ride out of sight around the far curve of the road along the woodshore beyond the church. Today had stretched out forever from sunrise until finally now when dusk had set the last guests homeward. Master and Mistress Drayton had a four-mile ride to go but twilight this near past Midsummer went on forever; they would be home before full dark. Hugh lowered his hand from a last wave after them and turned back through the gateway into the manor's foreyard, trying to hold his shoulders straight against his weariness. Long summer days and their drawn-out twilight had always been pleasure for him, but today he had found himself wanting a brief winter's day that would be done with and over, with a long night to follow when he could go to bed and not be anything except – with luck – asleep for hours upon hours and no need to say or do any of all the things he had had to do and say these past five days.

As it was, having no need for haste to be home before dark, the guests had lingered over the funeral feast. Not that there had been that many guests. 'And most of them are here simply for the pleasure of seeing him dead,' Miles had said low-voiced to Hugh as they came out of the uncrowded church after the funeral Mass. Nor was anyone there who had to take much trouble over coming except Master Wyck from Banbury and that was more because he had been Sir Ralph's attorney than for respect. Certainly there had been no great grieving from anyone, unless Elyn and Lucy's tears meant much, which Hugh doubted. That his sisters' weeping seemed more from duty – they owed it to themselves to weep – than from feeling was among the thoughts weighing on Hugh all day. Another heavy thought was that despite Sir Ralph had lived a goodly number of years, been married, had children, known a fair number of people along the way, at the end of it all he was buried with no one much caring and only duty-tears over his grave.

If anyone is going to miss him, Hugh thought as he crossed the foreyard, back toward the hall, his shadow stretching out black ahead of him, it will be me and the hounds. And I don't think we do. Except maybe Bevis. The brindled wolfhound had been Sir Ralph's present favorite, taken with him almost everywhere, even into church, where Father Leonel had frowned but not dared say anything. These days since Sir Ralph's death, Bevis had limped restlessly through the hall and foreyard or else lain beside the hall hearth, long muzzle on paws, eyes fixed on the outer door as if awaiting Sir Ralph's return. Yet when Tom had brought him to lie beside the bier, he would not, and today was tied in the kitchen yard, out of the way. Hugh had wondered before now how things would have gone that last day if Bevis had been with Sir Ralph. Assuredly not the way they had.

But Bevis had cut a forepaw on a stone the day before and the morning of the hunt Sir Ralph had rumpled his ears and said, 'Best you lie up today, old fellow. It's only hare-hunting anyway.' But a very good hare-hunting, as it happened; the best there had been that summer. Only fallow and roedeer bucks and hare were allowable to the hunt through the summer months and early autumn, between St John's Day and Holy Rood, and since Sir Ralph had hunted roedeer a few days earlier, he had been in the humour for hare-hunting, and so Hugh had been out in the green-gold dawn that day, a-foot and without dogs, to quarter the rough pastureland beyond the village fields, looking for the best place to bring the hunt. He had been glad the signs for likely best hunting looked to be in the farthest of the pastures, well away from the fields where the grain was ripening toward harvest. Sir Ralph had no care if his hounds coursed through the standing grain, but it set the villagers to fury to see their work and hope of winter bread trampled by hounds and hunters for the sake of sport. Sir Ralph's answer to their protests when they came into the manor court about it was always, 'I have to live with your poaching my game out of my forest whenever you've a mind to it and stealing my wood whenever my back is turned. You can live with my trampling a little of your fields in return. Now get out.'

A year ago Hary Gefori, the hayward's grown son and shaping well to take his father's place when the time came, had dared say angrily back, 'Aye, we poach, and when we're caught at it, we're beaten and fined for it. So, in like, when you and your hounds and horses have robbed us of our grain, why shouldn't you pay?'

Sir Ralph had half-risen from his chair, his hands gripping its arms so his knuckles stood out white, his face purpled with fury and his words almost throttled by his anger. 'Pay for what's mine? I own all this manor and everything on it, including you and every stalk of wheat and rye and barley and plain pasture grass. If anyone's going to pay, it'll be you – with half the teeth in your head and the skin off your back. Tom and you there, Duff, take him. Hugh, fetch my dog whip. I'll show . . .'

Hary had not waited to be taken or whipped but had spun on his heel and shoved his way among the men gathered to the court, with no one – including Tom – trying to stop him before he was out the door. That had earned Tom a yelling-at and every man there the fine of a penny each, including Tom, though Hugh doubted Tom ever paid it, since Tom and Father Leonel between them kept the manor accounts and Sir Ralph 'never cares what the accounts say,' Tom had raged once to their mother. 'So long as the hounds are healthy and the roof isn't falling in, he doesn't care. I could be stealing him blind and he'd never know.'

'Are you stealing him blind?' Lady Anneys had asked.

'No. The more fool me,' Tom had said bitterly.

Now everything was Tom's, and if the villagers had warily held back from outright celebration of Sir Ralph's death, Hugh did not doubt there was nonetheless hidden joy among them because Tom, for all that his anger could flare like Sir Ralph's, was far more even-handed in his dealings. He had been even more pleased than Hugh the morning of that last hunt to hear the chase would likely keep well away from the grain fields.

'It will be closer to the gathering place, too,' he had said. 'Farther for the servants but closer for us, and Mother and the girls won't mind the walk.' Which they would have to make, whether they minded or not, because last night Sir Ralph had pointed at Lady Anneys across the parlor and ordered, 'See to it there's food laid out at the spring after the hunt. We might as well make a day of it, since Sir William is bringing both Elyn and his girl.' Sir William being their near neighbor and as passionate to the hunt as Sir Ralph.

That night Miles said, while he and Hugh and Tom had been readying to bed in the chamber they shared over the kitchen at the hall's other end from Sir Ralph and Lady Anneys' own room, 'So we're to hunt in the morning, guzzle through midday, and return to the slaughter in the afternoon. I wonder if I feel a sickness coming on and must keep to my bed for the day?'

Tom had thrown a wadded shirt at him. 'If I have to be there, so do you.'

'I hate hare-hunting.'

'You hate all hunting.'

Miles threw the shirt back at him. 'Hare-hunting is worse. You can hunt the fool things twice in a day. Everything else you hunt and then go home. Red deer, roedeer, fallow deer, otter, badger, fox, boar, bear, wolf . . .'

'Boar? Bear? Wolf?' Tom had repeated cuttingly. 'When have any of us ever hunted boar or bear or wolf?'

'Never, thank St Eustace. It's been bad enough listening to Sir Ralph moaning on about lacking them. Years and years of him moaning there's no wild boar or bear or wolf left for him to slaughter. Moaning on and on . . .'

'Nephew,' Tom warned, 'if you don't shut yourself up . . .'

'. . . and on and on and . . .'

Tom and Hugh together had shoved him backward onto the bed and made to smother him with a pillow until laughter broke up their wrestling and they had all settled to sleep in the cheerfulness they so often had together when away from Sir Ralph.

In the morning Hugh had been first up and dressed and away, leaving them pulling on their heavy hunting hosen and debating whether hare was better baked in gravy in a crusted pie or roasted crisp on a spit. He had returned, more than ready for his breakfast, to find Sir William had arrived. His pair of scent hounds were in the foreyard, held on leash by Sir William's steward, Master Selenger.

Master Selenger was a man as lean and ready to the hunt as the hounds he held, and Hugh traded a few words with him before going in to tell what he had found and snatch some bread and cheese while his father and Sir William discussed which hounds they meant to use today. Sir William was not quite Sir Ralph's age nor given to anything like Sir Ralph's rages but their shared passion for hunting had made them 'as near to friends as Sir Ralph is ever likely to come,' Miles once said. Friends enough that Sir Ralph had married Elyn, his eldest daughter, to him and lately begun to talk with him of marrying Tom to Sir William's daughter, Philippa.

For a wonder, given how readily Tom quarreled with Sir Ralph over anything and everything else, he had made no protest against that. Not that there was much to protest. Besides being Sir William's only child and therefore his heir, Philippa was a pleasant-featured, pleasant-mannered girl, friends with Elyn and Lucy and so often at Woodrim that Lady Anneys, fond of her, said she was already more than halfway to belonging there. The only present complication was Sir William's marriage to Elyn two years ago. Besides that it made him Tom and Hugh's brother-in-law, it raised the likelihood he would father more children, lessening Philippa's inheritance or, if there were a son, replacing Philippa altogether. Any marriage agreement made now would have to be most carefully made to ensure she stayed worth Tom's marrying and as yet Sir Ralph and Sir William had not settled down to the task and Tom knew better than to push the matter. And since Elyn wasn't bearing yet, everything was mayhap and maybe anyway and more important that morning was the hare-hunt.

They had gone on foot to the far pasture, the hounds knowing what was coming and as eager to the business as the men. At the pasture's edge Sir Ralph had blown three glad notes on his hunting horn, and Hugh, Degory, and Master Selenger had uncoupled the six lymers – the scent hounds – who had the first work. Set forward with Hugh's cry of 'Avaunt, sire, avaunt!,' they had surged away into the pasture with Hugh's following call of, 'So howe, so howe, so howe!' to urge them onward. Not that urging was needed. Hares were cunning. As if ever-aware they might be hunted, one hare never, for choice, traveled straightforwardly but rather went one way, then back on its trail for a ways before going another way, over and over again, ten times or more and criss-crossing its own trails while it did, with sometimes a sideways leap to start a different way all over again. The lymers' challenge was to sort out the trails and thereby track a hare to its form – its resting place – and rout it out, and Somer, Sudden, Sendal, and young Skyre, along with Sir William's lymers, set to it joyfully, questing rapidly back and forth through the long grass, heads down and tails madly wagging. As always for Hugh, their intensity became his as he watched them searching, spreading apart, sweeping this way and that across the pasture to untangle the scents, while beside him and Tom, Sir Ralph, Sir William, and Master Selenger, the coursing hounds waited their chance with quivering eagerness. Miles, as always, stood a little apart, there because he had to be, but even so he was watching, smiling, the hounds' joy at their work impossible not to share.

Hugh saw Sendal start to swing too far apart from the others and called out, 'Howse, Sendal, howse!' to bring him back to the others, now closing in on a hare it seemed, to judge by how they were rushing forward, crowding together, then spreading apart and crowding forward again, all aquiver and their tails wild. As Sendal rejoined them, the hare burst up from the grass and into a run hardly three hounds' length ahead of Sudden in the lead.

'She goes!' Sir William cried. 'Ears up! She's a good one!' Because a hare that waited until the hounds saw it and ran with its ears up was confident of its strength and chance of escape. This one was as cunning in its running as it had been in laying its trail, swift in its turns and twice cutting sideways and away under the very muzzles of the hounds before Sir Ralph said, 'That's enough. Now,' and set Bertrand loose with the cry, 'Venes!' The rest of them loosed the other hounds with him and – white, and brownspotted, and brindled gray – Makarie, Melador, Bane, Brigand, and Sir William's Chandos streaked away to join the others.

The end came quickly then, and hunters trotted out to the kill-site where Melador was standing over the dead hare while the other hounds seethed around with high-waving tails, panting and pleased with themselves. Sir Ralph held the corpse high and blared the death on his horn, they went through the various ceremonies demanded at a kill, and then the hare was dismembered, bits of it mixed with blood-soaked bread and cheese and given to the hounds, but the better parts handed to a servant to carry back to the manor. Then they began again.

Two more hares were started, both of them escaping after good runs, before another one was taken. By then the morning was far enough along that Sir Ralph declared the hunting done for the while and they headed across the pastureland and along the woodshore to the greenway, men and hounds all glad of the shade under the tall-arched trees and gladder when they turned aside from the way into the wide, smooth-grassed clearing of the gathering place. At its upper end a spring bubbled out of the slope, its cold water filling a stone-built basin before flowing over and away in a shallow, broadening stream the length of the clearing and out of sight among the trees. Along the near side of the clearing wooden tabletops on trestle legs had been put up and cold chicken, new cheese, bread, and ale set out by servants waiting now to serve, while beyond the little stream Lady Anneys, Elyn, Philippa, and Lucy were seated on cushions on the grass, Philippa with her small lute on her lap, the others with their embroidery.

As usual, Hugh, Master Selenger, and Degory saw to watering the hounds, then Hugh and Master Selenger left them to Degory to tie in the shade and feed while they joined the others at the tables to eat and drink and talk over the morning's hunt. Afterward the women returned to their cushions, and the men, fed and tired and ready to rest, dropped down around them on what Lady Anneys called the hunt-cushions – large, old, not very clean cushions kept for this use. Only Miles went to sit on the wide rim of the spring's basin, dabbling his fingers in the water. The midday warmth and well-fed bellies slowed the talk and even the women sat idle, their sewing in their laps, except Philippa took up her lute again and began to stroke small, silversounding notes from its strings, simple as the sound of the water flowing and hardly more noticeable. Sir Ralph tried to pick a quarrel with Tom over a pasture that had been grazed last month instead of left rough for the summer's hunting but they were both too full and tired for it, and giving it up, Sir Ralph joined Sir William in dozing, stretched out with their heads laid on cushions and hands clasped on stomachs. Tom shifted to sit beside Philippa, watching her play. The family jest was that he had no more ear than a post for music, and when Elyn asked Philippa to sing, it was to Master Selenger that Philippa turned, asking, 'Join me?'

Lying on his side, propped up on one elbow on one of the cushions, he smilingly said, 'Gladly,' and sat up. He was Philippa's uncle, brother to Sir William's first wife, dead these dozen years, and their singing together was always everyone's pleasure. Their voices – his dark, hers light – blended around each other, wending through 'At sometime merry, at sometime sad, At sometimes well, at sometimes woe' as gracefully as dancers winding a maypole until at the end they sang exactly together, 'He is not wise, he is but mad, That after worldly wealth does go,' and then laughed at their own delight in their shared pleasure while Lady Anneys, Elyn, Tom, Hugh, and Miles lightly applauded them.

Looking back from afterward, Hugh could only think how usual it all had been. A midday gathering like uncounted others, with no warning of what would come. But what warning could there have been, Hugh wondered now, crossing the foreyard back to the hall. Almost a week was past, with time enough to remember, and he did not see what . . .

'Hugh,' his mother said quietly from the hall doorway.

He had been looking down, making no haste back to the hall, but at her call he looked up and lengthened his pace. He was tired and knew she was and he had not expected her to wait for him there after seeing the guests away. She had taken these past days quietly, the way she took everything. Not even in the first horrible surprise of Sir Ralph's death had she cried. Elyn and Lucy had shed more than enough tears and Hugh's thought was that Lady Anneys' own were dried up with comforting them, but his fear might have been that with the funeral done and the guests gone, her grieving would come over her in a storm. Except, in a carefully buried part of his mind, he doubted that she grieved at all.

But then, did any of them?

He smiled at her as he joined her at the doorway and asked, 'Will you rest now, Mother? Can I send Elyn and Lucy off to a far corner of a far field and let you be at peace for a while?'

She smiled back at him. 'Not just yet.' Against the black of her mourning gown and veil, her always fair-skinned face was even paler, the gray shadows under her eyes almost its only color. 'Master Wyck wants to speak with us all.'

'Now? Does it have to be now?'

'To have it done with,' Lady Anneys said. 'He's to spend the night with Sir William, to be that much further on his road to home come the morning with no need to come back here.'

'You're tired.' So was he, come to that. Since Sir Ralph's death there had been no pause in things to be done, beginning with the useless hunt through the woods for his murderer, looking for track of someone and not finding it, casting the hounds wide and wide again, trying to flush someone out but failing. Then there had been sending for the crowner – the king's officer charged with seeing into unexpected deaths – and when he came, his questions and demands to be answered. And then fetching Ursula from the nunnery and all the preparations for the funeral and finally today the funeral itself and the funeral feast and all that went with that, and now the lawyer wanted them.

Hugh knew he himself was faltering, doubted how much more his mother could endure, and protested more strongly, 'You're too tired for this.'

She laid her hand on his arm, briefly smiled at him, said, 'It's no matter,' and turned away, back into the hall.

Hugh, needing more time than that to gather himself, paused a moment longer on the threshold between the day's sunlight and the hall's shadows. Woodrim had never been more than a minor knight's manor and then for forty years an aged and childless widow's dower land until, after her death, Sir Ralph had bought it from a distant heir. But he had bought it for the hunting and never much bothered with anything else about it, keeping the hall as he had found it – plain, bare-raftered, not overlarge, with an open hearth in the middle and the smoke meant to escape through a penticed louver in the roof. There was not even a screen-wall here at its lower end to block the draughts when the outside door was opened and from where he stood in the doorway Hugh could see its length, past the servants clearing away the remains of the funeral feast from the long table set up along one side, in a hurry to have their own feasting in the kitchen, to the far end where the dais raised the master's table a step above the rest of the hall for whoever sat there to see and be seen by the rest of the household.

The hall's only window was there, looking out from one end of the dais onto the foreyard, tall and narrow and glassed at the top above the shutters so that even in winter or ill weather when the heavy wooden shutters were closed, there could be some light in the hall besides through the doorway or from candles or rushlights. Today in the warm afternoon the shutters stood open, letting the westering sunlight fall the dais' length across Tom, Sir William, and Master Wyck standing together behind the table there, next to Sir Ralph's tall-backed chair. Tom's chair now, Hugh reminded himself; but neither Tom nor anyone else had sat there since Sir Ralph's death. Tom would have to, sooner or later, there being only their mother's smaller chair and the benches otherwise, but presently the men were all standing, talking, a cluster of blackness in their mourning gowns and doublets. At the dais' farther end Elyn, Lucy, Ursula, and Philippa were gathered close together, Miles standing near them but somehow not with them, still in the silence that he had kept heavily around him this while since Sir Ralph's death.

'Since I can't mourn and shouldn't openly rejoice, best I just keep quiet,' he'd said when Hugh had asked how he was.

Still wishing that Master Wyck would wait with whatever he wanted to say, Hugh followed his mother up the hall. Sir William and Master Wyck bowed to her as she joined them and Tom took her by the hand to bring her to her chair beside Sir Ralph's. She sat and Sir William leaned over her, laying a hand on hers on the chair arm, saying something too low for Hugh to hear. She shook her head and said something back. At the dais' other end Miles opened the door to the parlor and stepped aside for the girls and Elyn to go in. Lucy and Ursula did, but as Lady Anneys answered Sir William, Elyn and Philippa both paused and, with Miles, looked back toward them. Then Miles said something to Elyn and she nodded and went on, but Philippa paused a moment longer, looking from Miles to her father and back to Miles until from the parlor Elyn ordered loudly, sharply, 'Philippa!'

Philippa winced. Miles ruefully shrugged at her and she ruefully shrugged back with a slight, uneven smile and followed Elyn into the parlor, Miles closing the door behind her. Hugh had sometimes wondered, in the two years since Elyn had married Sir William, how Philippa, only two years younger and often with Elyn while they were growing up, felt at having Elyn for a stepmother, wielding a stepmother's authority over her. Hugh doubted Elyn troubled herself with wondering. Elyn had welcomed marriage, been glad to become Lady Elyn and free of anyone telling her what to do except her husband, nor had she yet shown any regrets; and since there was a great deal of their father in Elyn, Hugh well supposed she probably did not care what Philippa thought or felt about any of it so long as Philippa did what she was told and made no quarrel about it.

Sir William was still speaking to Lady Anneys, now sitting with her head bowed and her hands folded on her lap, seemingly making no answer. It was Tom, standing behind her with a hand on her shoulder, who interrupted whatever Sir William was saying, saying instead to Master Wyck, 'I agree with Sir William. Why isn't this something that can wait?'

Hugh joined Miles at the end of the table. Low-voiced he asked, 'What's the trouble?'

'Master Wyck wants to talk of the will. Nobody else does.'

'Maybe it's better to have it over with?' Hugh said.

'Or better to put off knowing the worst until later,' Miles returned. There was laughter under his low-kept voice. Miles too often found laughter where no one else did, was sometimes reckless with it, and had brought Sir Ralph's wrath down on himself more than once that way. These past few days Hugh had caught glints of it behind Miles' few words and long silences that warned his outward seemliness was very thin and barely holding; but this wasn't the time to give way and Hugh punched him just hard enough in the small of his back to remind him and said, keeping his voice low, 'Easy enough for you, anyway. You already know the worst for you.'

'True,' Miles returned. 'One badly neglected and diminished manor, complete with Sir Ralph's curse because he couldn't find a way to keep it from me.'

And Sir Ralph would have kept it from him if he could. About that, Sir Ralph had always been very clear. All else that he held was his to dispose of as he chose and he had more than once goaded Tom and Hugh with, 'I can leave you no more than the clothes you stand in. You cross me once too often and that's all I will leave you. I swear it.' But the manor of Goscote in Leicestershire had come to him by right of blood and was entailed by law to pass to the eldest male heir of the blood, meaning Miles, only son of his loathed eldest son. Bitterly grudging that, Sir Ralph had taken pains over the years to take as much from the manor as he could, do as little for it as possible, and make certain Miles knew it. 'Still,' said Miles cheerfully now, 'better a broken manor without Sir Ralph than Paradise with him. Not that any place with Sir Ralph would be Paradise.'

But the rest of them – except Lady Anneys with the dower land of her marriage agreement – were not assured of anything. Despite all his talking and threats, Sir Ralph had never told them for certain what was in his will; for all any of them knew, he might have left everything to the Church or a cousin they had never heard of or 'a long-discarded mistress,' Miles had once speculated, 'who's become a nun and will pray forever for his soul.'

'I doubt it,' Tom had said. 'If he was going to do a thing like that, he'd tell us, to watch us writhe.'

With that Hugh fully agreed, so it was not to avoid something he feared to hear that Tom was delaying as he turned from Sir William and Master Wyck and said, 'Hugh, help me here. Mother doesn't need more today. She—'

Lady Anneys straightened, lifted her head, and quietly, firmly interrupted him. 'I've said that I'm ready.' She looked at Master Wyck, waiting in front of her with papers in his hand. 'If you think this time is good, then let's be done with it. Go on.'

'Lady Anneys,' Sir William said kindly, 'this may not be wise.'

Lady Anneys looked past Master Wyck and Tom to Hugh and Miles. 'Hugh. Miles. What do you say?'

Hugh hesitated. It was Miles who answered, 'If you say now, then now it should be.'

Lady Anneys returned her quiet gaze to Master Wyck. 'Now, sir, if you please.'

He made her a small bow and said to the rest of them, 'If you would care to be seated, gentlemen?'

Miles promptly hitched a hip onto the edge of the table. Hugh and Sir William sat on the benches. Tom hesitated, looked at his mother, who understood what he was silently asking and nodded at Sir Ralph's chair. 'Now, for you, too,' she said with a smile. And he sat down in it.

'Well done,' Miles said, lightly mocking. 'You fit.'

Tom shifted a little uneasily, settling himself more firmly, and turned his heed to Master Wyck.

The attorney had stayed standing, his papers at the ready. With them settled, he briefly bowed his head to them all and said, 'What

I have here is Sir Ralph's will, with his sign and seal upon it, witnessed by my clerk and Master Carrow. I think you are acquainted with Master Carrow, my lady?'

'The saddler in Banbury. Yes.'

'Another copy, likewise signed, sealed, and witnessed, is in my keeping in Banbury. The provisions of the will are much as you probably expect. If there's no objection, I will summarize, rather than read them out at length?' He paused and, when no one objected, went on, 'Of course to Master Miles Woderove goes the manor of Goscote in Leicestershire, as entailed.'

'And be damned to Sir Ralph,' Miles muttered, so low only Hugh heard him. Miles' hands, clenched one around the other, eased. He had been waiting, Hugh realized, for one final bitterness from his grandfather.

'This manor of Woodrim,' Master Wyck went on, 'goes to Master Thomas Woderove with all appurtenances and rights and so forth.' He made a general gesture with one hand. 'You are already well acquainted with what those are, I'm sure, Master Woderove. Also all other of his properties except as are otherwise given elsewhere in this will. Master Hugh Woderove is to have the hounds, all that goes with them, and his horse and his father's recommendation as a worthy and skilled huntsman and master of hounds, should he need or choose to seek other hire than with his brother.' Master Wyck paused and looked at Hugh. 'I have that recommendation in my possession, written out in his own hand, signed and sealed, against such time as you may desire it.'

Hugh made an acknowledging nod, caught between surprised pleasure and complete relief. Until now he had not dared let himself think about what might happen with him now Sir Ralph was dead. Here and the hounds were all he knew and if he had lost them . . .

'You are likewise to have such property as Sir Ralph held in Banbury and Northampton,' Master Wyck went on. 'Also ten marks in coin or else property to that amount upon such time as you marry, so long as you marry with Lady Anneys' approval and before you are thirty years of age.'

Miles insufficiently smothered a laugh. Hugh slapped the back of a hand against his leg and muttered, 'Shut up.'

Tom was trying but failing to hold in a grin. Their mother was a little frowning but whether with displeasure or disquiet Hugh could not tell.

Master Wyck continued, 'Lady Elyn, having already been provided with her dowry upon her marriage, has no further provision made for her. As is usual and as I think you knew?' he inquired of Lady Anneys and Sir William together. They both nodded that they did. Unless a daughter were also an heiress, her inheritance was usually considered complete upon her marriage. 'For his other daughters, Sir Ralph has provided as much for their marriages as was given with Lady Elyn, so long as they marry with your approval, Lady Anneys, though if Ursula chooses to become a nun she shall have five marks more than otherwise.' Master Wyck cleared his throat. 'There are a variety of other provisions made, mostly concerning Masses for his soul . . .'

Hugh kicked Miles' foot and Miles choked his laughter into a smothered cough.

'I'll leave those to Master Woderove' – he nodded respectfully to Tom – 'and the executors to read in detail. It is the matter of the executors, however, that I should like to directly address.'

Tom leaned forward. 'Is this where the bastard twists us over?'

'Tom,' Lady Anneys said.

'Three executors are appointed,' Master Wyck said. 'Lady Anneys. Sir William Trensal. Master Hugh Woderove.'

Tom looked at Hugh, his surprise matching Hugh's own, and Hugh let his discomfort and discomfiture show with a frown. He had neither expected nor wanted that duty. Tom shook his head, telling him that he didn't care, and said to Master Wyck, 'Sir William is to be main executor, I suppose?'

Master Wyck hesitated before admitting, somewhat uncomfortably, 'In truth . . . no.'

'No?' Again Tom's surprise matched Hugh's. 'Then who is?'

Master Wyck bowed his head to their mother. 'Lady Anneys.'

She drew in her breath and said, sharp with protest, 'He would never have given me that!'

'He did, my lady,' Master Wyck assured her. He cleared his throat. 'With conditions, however.'

'Ah. Conditions,' Miles said. '*This* is where the bastard twists us over.'

Chapter 4

'They are not so bad as that,' Master Wyck said stiffly. 'There are, however, certain provisions that I thought best to make known as soon as possible, particularly concerning you, my lady.'

'Please, then,' Lady Anneys said. Her face was calm, her voice was even, but her hands were clasped tightly together in her lap. 'Continue.'

Master Wyck cleared his throat again. 'It might be best if I read them out to you as they stand, so there can be no mistaking.'

'We're in for it,' Miles said, for only Hugh to hear.

Hugh jerked a fist sideways against his thigh to shut him up.

'What Sir Ralph willed is this,' Master Wyck said. ' "To my wife Lady Anneys Woderove, besides her dower lands I leave ten marks yearly, such sum to be paid from such lands as our son Thomas inherits in his name and from such heirs as follow him, for the term of her life or until she fails in such provision as here follows, namely that she live chastely, virtuously, and unmarried. Likewise, she is to have full say and rule concerning our unmarried children's marriages as given above but her rights therein to be utterly lost should she marry or prove, by the determination of her fellow executors, to have been unchaste or lived unvirtuously. Should such happen, the right and control of such of our children as are yet unmarried and the rights and profits of their marriages shall fall to my other executors, with Sir William Trensal to become chief executor with final say in all matters and the ten marks yearly that were hers to go to him in her stead. Likewise, should any child go against her wishes in the matter of their marrying or against Sir William Trensal's wishes in like matter, should she fail in her duty as above stated and her rights fall to him, their inheritance is to be utterly and finally lost, to pass to their heir as hereafter given in this will." '

Master Wyck ceased to read, looked up from his paper, and said, 'There is a clause then detailing which of his children inherits from whom in the event of one or another's death. Master Hugh is to inherit should Master Thomas die before him, but should Master Hugh die first and without heirs of his body, his inherited properties are to revert to Master Thomas. One daughter's dowry is to be increased by the other daughter's should one or the other of them die before marriage and all to be shared equally between their brothers should both daughters die unmarried.'

He finished. Around him the silence stretched out, becoming too long before Miles said very quietly, 'What it comes to, then, is that Lady Anneys has full and final decision over not only Lucy and Ursula's marriages but Tom's and Hugh's.'

'Yes.' Master Wyck's face was blank and his voice level.

'She chooses or agrees to whom Tom and Hugh and Lucy and Ursula marry,' Miles went on, 'or they lose every part of their inheritance. Even Tom.'

'Yes,' Master Wyck agreed again.

'Unless *she* marries or lives unchaste or . . . what was the other word?'

'Unvirtuously,' Master Wyck supplied.

'Unvirtuously,' Miles said. 'If she does, then Sir William is to become chief executor in her place.'

'Yes.'

'Meaning,' said Miles, 'that Sir Ralph has bound at least her and Tom almost as completely as when he lived. Neither of them has any freedom outside the narrow limits he's made for them.'

'I would hardly say the limits are so narrow as all that,' Master Wyck said stiffly.

'Only because you don't have to live inside them!' Miles snapped.

'Miles,' Lady Anneys said quietly. But Tom, having sorted everything into place, burst out, 'He's right, though! The thing is written to keep a stranglehold on both of us. Even dead, he won't let go!'

'That is commonly the way with wills,' Master Wyck pointed

out. 'The testator determines what his heirs—'

'Most testators don't try to keep their dead hands clenched around their heirs' throats,' Miles snarled. 'Do they?'

'No. No, not usually to the extent herein. No. But that does not render it less legal . . .'

'What it comes down to,' said Tom, 'is that either Mother lives exactly the way Father has willed her to or else she gets nothing and has no say in anything.'

'One can hardly say she gets nothing. Her dower land is hardly nothing,' Master Wyck protested.

'It's nothing compared to ten marks yearly. Come to that, how the hell am I going to find that much money out of what's left to me without beggaring myself anyway? And who's he to say whether she marries again or not now she's finally quit of him? How—'

'Tom,' Lady Anneys said gently. 'I have no need of those ten marks.'

'My lady,' Master Wyck said, 'you can hardly refuse—'

'I can "loan" them back to my son before he's given them to me,' Lady Anneys said, unexpectedly firm. 'There's nothing in the will against that. As for marrying or not marrying, my living chastely or unchastely, I have no intention toward either marriage or unchastity so there is no problem there either.' She looked, smiling, at Hugh and reached to touch Tom's hand gripping the arm of his chair; he turned his hand over to hold hers, and she went on, 'Nor do I think either of my sons is such a fool that I'm likely to refuse who they choose to marry.' She moved her smile to Miles. The angers that had been writhing up around them all were suddenly, simply gone. Even Miles' and even before she said, 'The most I might ask is that they help their nephew, whose inheritance has been so badly handled by their father. Is there anything else from my husband's will that we should know?'

Master Wyck fumbled, 'No. There's nothing else, I think. The minor bequests. The provision for Masses. Those are, of course, the executors' concern . . .'

Lady Anneys rose to her feet. 'We'll see to them, surely.' She looked toward the window, where the sunlight had begun to fade, the sun gone behind the forest. 'You and Sir William have a ways to ride. You'll wish to be going?'

It was a gracious dismissal and Master Wyck took it graciously, though as everyone stood up, Miles muttered in Hugh's ear, 'Probably glad to escape so easily,' before offering aloud to fetch Elyn and Philippa.

'If you would,' Lady Anneys said.

While Miles went parlorward, she moved with Sir William and Master Wyck toward the hall's outer door, making light talk and no haste, with Tom and Hugh following behind them. In the yard, while they waited for Elyn and Philippa and for their horses to be brought, Sir William took Lady Anneys by the hand and promised, 'I'll come back in a few days, my lady. We can go over matters then, to see where we stand and all when you've had time to rest.'

She thanked him gravely, thanked Master Wyck, prompted Tom to do the same, kissed both Elyn and Philippa when they came out, and stood waving to them all as they rode away, with Tom on her right and Hugh and Miles on her left, each with a hand raised in vague farewell. But when the riders were well gone, Lady Anneys' hand dropped to her side, her shoulders slumped, and her weariness was suddenly, nakedly plain. Tom put an arm around her, saying, 'It's over with, Mother. It's done. We can all have rest now.'

She leaned against him, her eyes shut, her head sideways against his shoulder. 'Rest,' she agreed on a long sigh. 'Yes. Let's all do with that.'

What surprised Hugh in the days that followed was how easily they learned to live without Sir Ralph. A few times in the first week after the funeral Lucy and Ursula went together to the churchyard to pray at his grave. No one else did and Lucy soon stopped and Ursula, so far as Hugh knew, went only once more after that and then bothered no more either.

The household remained, as always, Lady Anneys' concern, with Lucy and Ursula learning beside her as she not only gave orders to the servants but worked at such things as pastry-making in the kitchen, weeding among the cabbages in the greens garden, and sometimes scrubbing clothes in the laundry because, as she often said to Lucy's protests, 'There's no better way to know a thing than by learning to do it. Even when you have servants to do it for you, you have to know it yourself to understand whether they do it well or ill, and always there are things better done yourself than by anyone else.'

Tom went on much as he had been, ordering and overseeing things about the manor, but all went more evenly and easily without Sir Ralph there to make trouble where none had to be. Tom could even be heard whistling as he went striding from one task to another, and in the evenings he often told about his day in ways that made them all laugh aloud with him. Laughter, Hugh realized, had been scant here while Sir Ralph lived.

For Hugh there were still the hounds. If they missed Sir Ralph, they did not show it. Even Bevis had given up his restlessness and unexpectedly attached himself to Miles, following him everywhere – not entirely to Miles' pleasure – except up the steep stairs to the bedchamber. Besides that, nothing much was changed except the hounds were now all Hugh's own, any choices about them all his to make and no one else's. Not that he was making many decisions yet, willing to let things go on as they presently were. One of the smooth-coated coursing hounds, Baude, was in whelp from a breeding with Makarie and that was as much of the future as Hugh was ready to look at. For now it was enough to ride out every day, not to hunt but simply with the hounds loping beside his horse to keep them fit. His lovely hounds. *His*.

And then there was Miles. Without his anger at Sir Ralph, he sometimes seemed almost uncertain what to feel, as if thrown off balance by the void; but he joined in the laughter when it came and seemed, like Tom, to go easier about his work. It was maybe awareness that he'd be losing his work soon that made it harder for him than the rest of them to find his balance. The vague plan was that he would stay at Woodrim until the escheat of Sir Ralph's lands was done – the determining by a royal officer of what the deceased had lawfully held, to whom it lawfully went, and what fees could be had for the king from it all. Once that was settled, hopefully by Michaelmas at September's end, he would be away to his own manor and what they would do for a woodward here was undecided yet. In the meanwhile he went on as usual, often away to the woods – but never by himself these days, always with a servant or at least the wolfhound Bevis because the day after Sir Ralph's funeral Lady Anneys had asked it of him. 'Please,' she had said. 'For safety's sake, don't go alone.'

That was the nearest anyone spoke of Sir Ralph's death. Or of

Sir Ralph at all. Except that Lady Anneys continued to dress in widow-black, he might have died long ago and in an ordinary way, instead of less than a month ago and murdered, with his murderer yet unfound. Hugh wished he could leave off thinking about that day as completely as everyone had left off talking about it, but all too often his thoughts circled back to it, trying to see something, anything, that might have told how it was going to end. Something . . .

But there was nothing, even now. Philippa and her uncle had sung together. Sir Ralph and Sir William had sat up from their dozes and some chance remark by Sir William about someone they knew lately buying a hawk had set Sir Ralph to one of his favorite rages against hawking – how he would never take it up, not to save himself, no, by God's teeth he wouldn't. All that fiddling with hoods and jesses and staying up nights on end and the rot about who can have what kind. 'Gerfalcons for a king, peregrines for earls, merlins for ladies, hobys for boys. God's teeth, give me hounds and a long chase with a death at the end of it and venison on the table or a good hare pie. If I want a damned duck for my supper, I'll send to the poultry yard for one.'

The talk had gone off then to the morning's hare-hunt and somehow come around to Sir Ralph saying suddenly at Tom, 'They're pushing their plough-land out again, those peasants of yours. I swear I've lost an acre of pasture.'

From where he still sat beside Philippa, Tom had answered even-voiced, apparently not in the humour for quarreling, 'I'll see to it.'

'You damnably well will. I don't keep this manor for the peasants' pleasure. You're not to let them graze that pasture again this summer either. Cattle-cropped grass is no good for hare-hunting and you know it.'

'They have to graze somewhere.'

'They want to keep too many cattle. That's where the trouble lies.'

'They—'

'Don't quarrel with me, boy! This is my manor. I'll do as I please about it. If any of your peasants don't like it, let him pay to go free and get out of here and be damned to him.'

'It's said Clement is going to do that come Michaelmas quarter day,' Tom said bitterly.

'He's one of the ones who's been nothing but trouble at almost every manor court, isn't he? Good riddance to him.'

'He's one of the best men in the village,' Tom had said hotly. 'It's shame to lose him.'

'It's not shame to be quit of his whining over "his rights" any longer. It's bad enough I have to listen to you whine for him.'

'Then don't!' Tom had sprung to his feet. 'But don't *you* whine at me when the place goes to ruin, because when it does, it will be your doing, not mine!'

'Like hell it will!'

But Tom, red-faced and hands in fists, was striding out of the clearing toward the greenway and neither looked back nor answered. Sir Ralph spat into the grass after him and then, as if satisfied by a good day's work, lay back onto the cushions, smiling. The wary silence that always followed one of his angers ended with Lady Anneys gently pointing out a flaw in Lucy's embroidery. Elyn said something about how well her own was coming on and Miles moved from the spring's edge to sit where Tom had been, beside Philippa, asking her and Master Selenger, 'Sing something else?'

Master Selenger obligingly started the lilting, 'The Lady Fortune is friend and foe . . .' As he reached the second line, 'The poor she makes rich, the rich poor also . . .' Philippa began it over again with, 'The Lady Fortune is friend and foe . . .' and as Master Selenger reached, 'Turning woe to good and good to woe,' Miles joined in with, 'The Lady Fortune is friend and foe . . .' so that the song turned and turned around on itself as, following behind him, Master Selenger started over again.

Not about to spoil their singing by adding his own, Hugh rose and went to where Degory and the hounds were sprawled asleep in the shade beyond the spring. He stirred Degory awake with a friendly foot in the ribs and they settled together to check the hounds' paws for cuts or thorns. That Miles could sing – and sing well – for some reason always surprised Hugh, probably because Miles so rarely sang at all, but he and Philippa and Master Selenger were happily winding and warring their way through the Lady Fortune song, repeating its one verse faster and faster to see who would lose their way first, while Sir William and Elyn clapped to the beat and Lady Anneys propped up Lucy, who had fallen over with laughter.

Never given to singing or to noticeable pleasure in listening to it, Sir Ralph stood up and came over to join Hugh presently crouched beside young Skyre, seeing to a slight scrape on her ear. Despite she was nearly full-grown, she was still as scatter-brained as a puppy, with more eagerness than good sense when it came to the chase and at least twice this morning had been knocked over by Somer for being too bold among her elders and betters. But to Sir Ralph's 'How is she?,' Hugh answered, 'Taken no hurt that I can find besides this scratch and it's not much.'

'Let me see.'

Hugh had shifted a little aside without getting up, and Sir Ralph had squatted down on his heels to take hold of the young hound's head in his usual rough way, holding her hard by the muzzle while pulling her ear up for a better look.

Sir William strolled toward them, asking, 'Trouble?'

'Nothing much,' Sir Ralph had said, had let her go and stood up, turning away from her.

It was just then that something among the trees must have caught Skyre's eye – a squirrel maybe, or the bright flit of a bird among the bushes. No one ever knew what. All that Hugh – crouched beside her and rummaging in a leather bag for an ointment for the scratch – saw was her head snap up, suddenly alert. Knowing what a fool she could be, he had dropped the bag and grabbed for her collar but too late; she was away in a single long bound and gone among the trees and he was left sprawled stomach-down on the grass while above him, Sir Ralph roared out, 'Skyre!' Snarling, 'Get up, you fool,' he kicked at Hugh's hip, grabbed up a leash lying there, and whipped it across Degory's bare legs with, 'Idiot! Get after her!' Swore, 'Damned idiot!' at Hugh just scrambling up, hit him across the back with the leash for good measure, and went furiously away into the woods himself, slashing the leash at the underbrush as he went.

Within the hour he was dead.

When the body was found, they had made the hue and cry for his murderer. Law required that and fear made certain of it. The search had spread through and beyond the woods. They had tried to find a track to set the dogs on but maybe they had trammeled too much in the first horror of finding the body or there was too much blood; even Somer, best of the lymers, failed to take up a scent. Nor did Hugh with his huntsman's skills find any track to follow nor had anyone at all been seen. They had been left with nothing more to do but carry the body home and send a man to bring the crowner.

It sometimes took days for a crowner to come but Master Hampden had ridden in with his men late the next day, while Hugh was gone to fetch Ursula. He had viewed the body and where it had been found, asked questions, but received few answers because no one had many to give. By the time Hugh had returned from St Frideswide's, he was holding his inquest, where it was officially found that Sir Ralph's death was indeed murder by person or persons unknown. 'And that,' Master Hampden had apologized afterward to Lady Anneys, 'is the best I can presently give you.'

He had ridden away before the funeral, with promise that a search would be made and questions asked about likely strangers seen anywhere around there, adding a warning to keep watch themselves for anyone and anything – and as easily as that it had all been settled, tidied away into the crowner's records as tidily as Sir Ralph into his grave. Hugh wished his thoughts could be as tidily done with and put away; but aside from them – and time was dulling their edge, he found – things on the whole were very good. The summer was coming on to Lammastide with promise of a fine harvest if the weather held, and Tom had asked him what the chances were of having venison for a start-of-harvest feast he was minded to give the villagers.

Hugh had warned, 'You do this, you risk making a new custom they'll want every year,' and Tom had answered, 'Father made enough bad customs here over the years that a good new one will likely get us more than it loses.'

Therefore, tomorrow Hugh would ride out with some of the hounds to find where best to hunt a roedeer stag in a day or two; and though neither he nor Tom had said it, they both knew the fact that the hunt would be the first one since Sir Ralph's death made it all the sweeter.

But this afternoon Hugh had spent helping Degory clean out the kennel and kennel yard and spread clean straw, and he was satisfyingly tired and hardly thinking of anything at all as he bent over the washbasin set on the bench outside the hall door to scrub his face and hands before going in to supper. The late afternoon sun was warm on his back through his shirt, and when he dried his face and hands, the linen towel smelled of the rosemary bush over which it must have been draped after laundering. Inside the hall there was the thud of tabletops going onto trestles as the servants set up for supper and his stomach growled with timely hunger; but the soft thud of a horse's hoofs behind him turned him around to see Gib of the stable leading a saddled and bridled gray horse toward him across the yard.

Frowning with puzzlement rather than displeasure, Hugh said, 'That's Master Selenger's horse, isn't it?' Knowing it was.

'Aye,' Gib answered. 'The man is back again. I make that three days running he's been here.'

'It is,' Hugh agreed.

Sir William, a few days after his promised visit to see what help or comfort he might give Lady Anneys, had sent Master Selenger to ask if Tom needed help with anything and promise that he had only to ask if he did. Tom had thanked Master Selenger but said, 'It's what I've been doing for years here. The only thing that's changed is that it's all easier done without Father to tell me what's wrong with everything I do.'

Master Selenger had laughed at that, said he was likewise charged with asking after Lady Anneys, and had ended by sitting with her in her garden, talking for a somewhat while. When he came back yesterday, he had brought Elyn with him and not seen Tom at all but kept company with Lady Anneys, Elyn, Lucy, and Ursula in the garden for much of the afternoon.

And here he was back again. Without Elyn. And not to see Tom, who had gone past the kennel two hours ago on his way to the east field and not yet come back.

Hugh, frowning, turned back toward the hall and immediately smoothed the frown away to greet Master Selenger coming out.

'Hugh,' Master Selenger returned cheerfully. 'Good day. I hear there's to be a hunt.'

'We mean so,' Hugh said. 'Would you and Sir William be minded to join us for it when the time comes, do you think?'

'Surely,' Master Selenger answered and they talked hounds a

little before he made his farewell, thanked Gib, and gave him a small coin for waiting with his horse.

Watching him ride away, Gib gave the coin a toss and said, 'He's a gentleman, is that one.'

Hugh agreed to that, but while Gib tucked the coin into his belt pouch and headed back for the stable, he stood watching Master Selenger out of sight. A man much about Lady Anneys' own age. Well-featured, well-kept, pleasant-mannered.

All things Sir Ralph had not been or bothered to be.

Hugh went in search of his mother and found her in her garden, alone, standing at the gate toward the cart-track, looking outward across the field where the last of the hay, dried and carefully gathered into haycocks, was waiting to be stacked or else carted away to byres and the stable. In the weltering sunlight they looked like heaps of gold, and in their way they were – food through the winter for horses and cattle. Lady Anneys turned as Hugh neared her and said, smiling, 'I was thinking I might get a rosebush next year. When I was a girl, a neighbor had one in her garden. The flowers were more red than anything I've ever seen and smelled so beautifully. I've always wanted one of my own.'

Hugh had not known that. He had never heard her want anything at all, he realized; and wondered, with a twitch of what felt like guilt for never having wondered it before, what else she had wanted and never had. Her silence about anything she felt or wanted had been a way of hiding from Sir Ralph, he suddenly thought. They had all hidden from him in whatever ways they could. Tom had used his anger, Miles his mockery, Hugh the talk of hounds and hunting. Lady Anneys had had her silence.

But in keeping Sir Ralph shut out, they had kept shut away from each other, too. For safety's sake you left as few gaps in your wall as possible. Even banded together the way he had been with Miles and Tom against Sir Ralph, Hugh knew how much he had never said. And Lady Anneys had had no one at all. No friends because around Sir Ralph friends had been impossible to have. Not her children. She could give them her love and what comfort there was in that but not her protection and assuredly not her thoughts.

But none of that was anything he could say to her and he said instead, 'I'll find you a rosebush, come the spring. I'll ride to Northampton, Oxford, or even London to do it, if I have to.'

Lady Anneys smiled at him and said, 'That would be lovely.' But not as if she believed it would truly happen. Which goaded Hugh to ask, a little more abruptly than he might have, 'Where are Lucy and Ursula?' Had she been here alone with Master Selenger?

'I sent them in with my sewing when Master Selenger left. I was ready to be alone awhile.'

Hugh stepped back, ready to leave her, but she held out her hand and said, 'But I'd welcome your company. You're not a chattering young girl.'

Hugh returned to her side. She tucked her hand into the crook of his arm and they stood together in companionable silence, Hugh looking out at the hayfield, Lady Anneys toying with the purple flowers of whatever it was growing tall beside the gate, until in what he thought might be a safe while, Hugh asked easily, as if merely making talk, 'Was Master Selenger good company this afternoon?'

'Very good,' Lady Anneys said.

Hugh waited but she said nothing more and in another while he said, 'I wish nothing would change from how it is now.'

Lady Anneys let that lie for a few moments before she said, 'That would be good. But Tom will likely marry soon.'

'Philippa?' Hugh asked, despite he knew the answer.

Lady Anneys a little nodded. 'And Miles will go away to his manor before then. It's time and past for him to take up his own life.'

'This is his life,' Hugh said and could not keep an edge from his voice. 'Here. With us.'

Lady Anneys slightly shook her head against that. 'Miles hasn't had a life here. He's had Hell. He needs to be free of here. He needs the chance to heal as best he can from everything Sir Ralph did to ruin him.'

'Sir Ralph is gone,' Hugh said stubbornly.

'In body,' Lady Anneys answered.

And though his soul was surely gone to Hell, he lingered in other ways, Hugh bitterly, silently admitted.

'And you,' his mother went on. 'You're free to go, too, if you want.'

'There's nowhere else I want to go.' Why should there be, when everything he wanted was here? 'You, too,' he said. 'You're free, too. To stay or go.'

'I'll likely go,' she said. She must have felt him tense under her hand because she squeezed his arm and added mildly, 'Once Tom is married, Philippa should be mistress here without a mother-in-law at her back, watching her every move. I have my dower lands to go to and I will.' Her smile deepened. 'I can find you a wife and husbands for Lucy and Ursula from there as well as from here, probably. Unless you want to find your own?'

Hugh made a sound that admitted to nothing.

Lady Anneys laughed at him, squeezed his arm again, and let him go. 'There's no hurry, though. And after all, Ursula may choose the nunnery.'

'Do you think she will?'

'I don't know.'

Hugh tried to think of Ursula grown up and shut away into a nunnery but couldn't. Not that she'd be any more lost to them in the nunnery than married, he supposed. And a nunnery might be easier to visit than a brother-in-law, he half-jestingly supposed to himself, ready to let go of thought about what might come and be simply at peace in the summer-warm quiet, waiting to be called to supper.

But quietly, hardly louder than the bees humming in the beebalm in the garden bed behind her, Lady Anneys said, 'I think, when you return Ursula to St Frideswide's, I'll go with her and stay, too, for a time.'

Startled, Hugh demanded, 'Why?' More roughly than he might have if she had not taken him so much by surprise.

For a long moment she did not answer; then said only, still quietly, 'It would be best, I think,' in a way that somehow stopped him asking more.

Chapter 5

Although dawn's cobweb-gray shadows were barely gone from the cloister walk, the day was already warm and promised to be warmer and Frevisse made no more haste than the other nuns as they left the cool inside of the church after Mass to go the short way along the roofed walk to their morning chapter meeting.

St Frideswide's was neither a large nor wealthy nunnery. It maintained itself but barely more and the room used in the mornings for the daily chapter meeting, where a chapter of St Benedict's Rule was read and matters of business and discipline were discussed, was a plain place, like nearly everywhere in the nunnery, with plastered but unpainted walls, a chair for Domina Elisabeth, stools for her nuns, a small wooden worktable, and nothing more. In wet or cold weather it served for the nuns' evening hour of recreation before Compline's prayers and bed, and in winter it was their warming room, having the nunnery's only fireplace save for those in the kitchen and the prioress' parlor.

Presently, though, the hour of recreation was a long summer's day away and there was most definitely no need for warming. Instead, the door stood open and someone had already lowered the shutter from the window, letting in the soft-scented morning air and a long-slanted shaft of richly golden light from the newly risen sun. Nuns whose joint stools were in its way shifted aside and turned their backs to it with a scrape of wooden legs on stone, except Sister Thomasine went to stand directly in its brightness, her eyes shut, her face held up to the light. Sister Thomasine had always lived her nun's life more intently than most did. Given her choice, she would have been in the church praying on her knees at the altar more hours of the day and night than not. There was even sometimes whispered hope among some of the nuns that she might prove to be a saint, and Frevisse – who only slowly over the years had come to accept her as other than merely annoying – granted to herself that for Sister Thomasine the touch of the sunlight was probably like the touch of God's hand in blessing on her.

But then it *was* God's blessing, Frevisse thought. All of life was God's blessing, forget it though mankind might and ill-use it as mankind surely did. Sister Thomasine's skill – or gift – was that she did not forget but lived her life in certainty of the blessing.

It made her very hard to endure sometimes.

'Sister Thomasine, sit, please,' Domina Elisabeth said. Already seated herself in the tall-backed chair that had served all of St Frideswide's prioresses through the hundred years since the priory was founded, she did not wait to be obeyed but leaned forward to say something to Dame Claire, the priory's infirmarian, about an ache she had in her back. Sister Thomasine, with the same quietness she had given to the sunlight, sat down on the remaining stool, clasped her hands on her lap, and bowed her head to pray through the wait for Father Henry to put off his vestments and join them. Around her, the other nuns went on in steady talk. The rule of silence – that there be only necessary words within the cloister save for each evening's recreation – had slackened in the years since Frevisse had entered St Frideswide's. She missed the quiet it had enforced but saw no sign that anyone else did. Dame Emma was explaining to Sister Margrett the value of cutting the kitchen garden's green onions fine when for a salad while Sister Amicia tried to convince Dame Juliana there was no need to weed any herb bed today and Dame Perpetua and Sister Johane discussed some copying work they meant to begin.

Content to keep her own silence, Frevisse followed Sister Thomasine into prayer for the little while until Father Henry hurried in, rumpled and flushed with heat and hurry, his fair hair in unruly curls around his tonsure. In his time as the priory's priest he had grown from young manhood into middle age and a certain stoutness of girth that came with the aging of a burly body rather than from sloth or self-indulgence. He never slacked his priestly duties to the souls in his keeping but he was not a deep-minded man; Frevisse had never found any spiritual challenge in him, only the challenge of putting up with the unfailingly simple goodness he brought to everything he did, until finally experience had taught her how deeply difficult 'simple' goodness could be.

She rose to her feet with the other nuns and bowed her head willingly to receive his blessing for the day and found herself smiling to remember how she had struggled against that lesson. Humility, she too well knew, was a virtue to which she was coming only very slowly. Her smile, kept to herself by bowed head and the fall of her veil to either side of her face, went wry as she considered how much easier everything would have been if she could have started out wise and been done with it, instead of having to learn by effort and errors how far she still had to grow.

He finished the blessing.

Domina Elisabeth said, '*Dominus vobiscum.*' The Lord be with you.

They answered, '*Et cum spiritu tuo.*' And with your spirit.

They sat again, the opening prayer was made, and Father Henry read the day's chapter from St Benedict's Rule, first in Latin, then in English, followed it with a short homily easily listened to – or not, in Frevisse's case, despite her best intent. Then he blessed them and left and from there the chapter meeting went its usual way, with such complaints as any nun deemed necessary and the officers' reports and confession of faults and giving of warnings or penance as Domina Elisabeth saw fit. Sister Amicia, presently Cellarer and therefore bound to worry over food, said *someone* had eaten so carelessly at dinner yesterday that they had wastefully left bread crumbs on the refectory floor. Domina Elisabeth gave warning that *no one* should eat so carelessly again. Sister Thomasine as Sacrist murmured that the silver polish was running low; Domina Elisabeth gave leave for Dame Claire to make more. Sister Margrett confessed to nodding to sleep during Lauds last night; Domina Elisabeth bade her say twenty-five *mea culpas* on her knees in front of the altar as soon as chapter was done.

When there seemed no other business to report or deal with, Domina Elisabeth looked around at them all and asked, 'What of Lady Anneys and Ursula then? They've been with us a week and, so far as I know, have given no trouble. Is that so?'

Everyone looked at everyone else and there was a general shaking of heads that, no, neither Ursula nor her mother had been any trouble. 'In truth,' Dame Perpetua said, 'Lady Anneys has eased my work. She gives Ursula some of her lessons and has helped with the mending.' She frowned a little. 'Although Ursula's sewing has not improved.'

'She keeps to herself,' Dame Emma said. 'Lady Anneys, I mean. She comes to the Offices, of course – all but Matins and Lauds and Compline, of course, and that's understandable – and she brings Ursula with her, which is good, it spares one of the servants the task. But she doesn't talk. I've tried with her more than once but she "saves her breath to cool her fingers," as the saying goes. I don't think I've had more than ten words with her at a time . . .'

And if anyone could get away from Dame Emma with less than ten words, they had accomplished something indeed, Frevisse thought.

Domina Elisabeth raised a hand, stopping Dame Emma's present outpouring, and smiled on them all. 'I shall take it, then, that all is well there. There's nothing else? Then it's time to tell you that because today is St Swithin's holy day and because we well deserve it, too, we will have holiday this afternoon. Not merely holiday from duties either. I've provided for something altogether different for us.'

Sister Margrett forgot herself so far as to clap her hands and exclaim, 'Oh! What, my lady?' with such delight that rather than rebuke her excess, Domina Elisabeth smiled and said, 'You'll see when the time comes,' but that was all she would say.

Morning tasks were not so well attended to as they might have been and at each Office of prayer – Tierce, Sext, Nones – only Domina Elisabeth's sternest looks stopped the whispers running among Dame Emma, Sister Amicia, and Sister Margrett before the Office could begin, and when finally at their midday dinner's end Domina Elisabeth bade them gather in the cloister walk, there was an unseemly hurry of scraping benches and fluster of skirts. Dame Emma's stiffening joints kept her behind the younger nuns' rush out the refectory door, but even among the older nuns who chose to put on a front of more dignity, no one lingered. Most days in the nunnery were much like other days. The most constant change was in the Offices themselves as their prayers circled through the seasons of the Church – Whitsuntide just past, then the summer and autumn holy days, on to Advent and Christmastide, Lent and Lady Day and Easter, and around to Whitsun again. The promise of something other than the ordinary was welcomed by nearly everyone, save maybe Sister Thomasine, who had to be almost shooed ahead by Sister Johane to have her out the door quickly enough.

They found Lady Anneys and Ursula waiting in the cloister walk, Ursula bouncing a little on her toes with impatient delight. Frevisse had expected a solemn little girl to return from her father's funeral but she had not; nor had Lady Anneys shown any signs of deep grief, only a grave willingness to keep to her own and Ursula's company. Today, though, they plainly both knew something of what Domina Elisabeth purposed because they were dressed for some kind of work, their gowns plain, Lady Anneys with simply a veil pinned over her hair, and Ursula's long hair fastened up around her head instead of hanging down her back. But whatever Domina Elisabeth had in mind for them she did not yet say, merely nodded to Lady Anneys to walk beside her and, taking Ursula's hand, led the rest of them along the cloister walk and through the slype, the narrow passage leading out of the cloister toward the nuns' high-walled garden. Coming out at its far end, she turned not toward the garden's gate but leftward along the garden wall to the usually locked back-gate into the orchard. Enclosed by a steep earthen bank, the orchard was nearly as shut away from the world as the cloister, and sometimes the nuns were allowed to have their recreation among the apple, pear, and cherry trees and the peaceful unmarked graves of former nuns under the long grass; but today Domina Elisabeth led them through the fruit-burdened trees to the always-locked gate in the short length of board-made fence closing the gap between the church's north wall and the orchard's earthen bank. There, as Domina Elisabeth brought out a key, even Dame Emma's chatter stopped. Whatever else of nunnery life had eased under Domina Elisabeth's rule, she still held her nuns to strict enclosure. To go outside the cloister walls was a rare adventure for most of them, and in silence they watched her unlock the gate. Only when she started to open it did Dame Perpetua say, faint-voiced, 'We're going out, my lady?'

'We're going out,' Domina Elisabeth said and set the gate wide open.

Sister Thomasine started to drift backward and away. The times Sister Thomasine had been outside the nunnery since she had taken her vows could probably be counted on less than one hand,

and given her own choice, she would never go at all; but Domina Elisabeth pointed at her and said firmly, 'This includes you, Sister Thomasine.'

Ursula slipped away from her mother and around Dame Juliana to take hold of Sister Thomasine's sleeve, looking up at her and saying with earnest assurance, 'You can walk with me.'

One way and another, Frevisse had learned that Sister Thomasine did not lack courage to go out, merely inclination, but to Ursula it must have seemed like fear and her offer was a kindness that Sister Thomasine solemnly accepted by taking hold of her hand and following with the rest, the more eager nuns crowding to follow Domina Elisabeth and Lady Anneys through the gate into the board-fenced alley, the back way for the going and coming of carts and workers between the priory's foreyard, with its byres and barns and all the business needed to sustain the nunnery's life of prayer, and the nearer fields outside the nunnery's walls. Domina Elisabeth went right, away from the foreyard and toward altogether outside, and the other nuns' laughter and talk began to rise with excitation. Even Thomasine, drawn on by Ursula, was not last out the gate. Frevisse and Dame Claire were.

But they caught up to the others at the alley's outer end where almost everyone's eagerness faltered and they slowed and bunched together, some of them even stopping, discomfited after months of the closeness of cloister walls by the sudden distance of low-grown green fields of beans and peas stretching away to far-off hedgerows, with more sky all at once than could ever be seen above cloister roof or garden walls. But their uncertainty was only momentary. As Domina Elisabeth and Lady Anneys went on unbothered and Ursula pulled Sister Thomasine forward, everyone else's pause turned to a rush to follow them along the cart-track running there, Sister Margrett asking delightedly where they were going, Dame Emma and Sister Amicia making guesses, and Domina Elisabeth smilingly refusing any answer.

It was Ursula who could not bear her own excitement. 'Fishing!' she exclaimed. 'We're going fishing!'

'Fishing?' Sister Johane exclaimed with almost disbelief, and Domina Elisabeth said, laughing, 'Yes. Fishing.'

To meet the nunnery's constant need for fish for fast days, feast days, and every day, two square ponds had been made beyond near fields, with a stream diverted to feed them and alder planted around their banks for shade. Because their upkeep and expenses were matters discussed and dealt with in chapter meetings, all the nuns knew of them in detail, whether they had ever seen them or not, and because fishponds were part of almost every manor and therefore part of most of the nuns' lives before they entered St Frideswide's, they knew about fishing, too. More, perhaps, than Domina Elisabeth did, Frevisse thought, because early afternoon under a high summer sun was hardly the best time for catching fish.

But actually catching fish was hardly the point, she soon decided. Village boys were waiting with rods, lines, hooks, and bait in the shade among the alder trees along the first pond, and the first squealing and protests over worms on hooks from some of the nuns and laughter from most of the others led on to elbowing and nudging each other toward the water, until finally shoes and short hosen came off and skirts were hitched above ankles and soon thereafter the inevitable happened and Sister Amicia was standing in the water, grimacing at the mud between her toes and laughing at the water's coolness. Ursula, Sister Johane, Sister Margrett, and finally Dame Emma followed her, while those determined to fish went farther along the bank where their chances were hardly bettered by their flailing rods and jerking lines.

Faced with all of that, the village boys' first stiff respect crumbled, and when Sister Johane and Sister Margrett began a splashing battle against each other and anyone else in reach, Colyn, the reeve's younger son, gave up to laughter, rolling on the grass and holding his sides. So they splashed him, too.

Then Lady Anneys drew her skirts up through her belt and waded in, too, only barely avoiding her daughter's fate when Ursula, leaning to splash water at Sister Johane, overbalanced and sat down with a great splash. Lady Anneys, backing away from her, stumbled and grabbed hold of one of the boys to keep from falling, both of them laughing as Ursula rose dripping and muddied to the waist, laughing, too.

Not long after that, Sister Thomasine, finally persuaded to cast a line since she would not wade, somehow and against all likelihood hooked a fish and even – with help from the boys – landed it, a large carp. Domina Elisabeth, paying one of the boys a farthing to run it to the nunnery kitchen, said, ' 'Tis not our Lord's miracle of the loaves and fishes but assuredly a miracle nonetheless.' Which brought on more laughter.

The alders' afternoon shadows were stretching long across the water and weariness was overtaking merriment when Domina Elisabeth called an end. While the boys set to gathering the fishing gear for going home, the nuns sat on the grassy bank to put on stockings and shoes again before beginning a slow walk back toward the nunnery, a very bedraggled Ursula holding to her mother's hand and no one's tired legs able to make haste despite the time for Vespers was nearing. The church's gray-lead roof showed dully above the orchard's trees, reminder that the cloister was waiting to close them in again, and as they reached the outer gateway, Frevisse saw Sister Margrett look back across the green fields toward the deeper green of distant trees under the richly blue, high-arching sky, her young face showing a mixture of longing and puzzlement that Frevisse understood. They had taken pleasure in that world today but now were going to shut themselves away from it again, away from all its possibilities – away from the places they would never have chance to go and people they would never have chance to meet.

That was a thing a girl or woman understood when she chose to become a nun, and by the time she came to take her final vows, she understood it even better; but no one ever fully understood it until she had lived in it, year around into year after year, knowing it was for all the rest of her life. For a very few, like Sister Thomasine with her desire for nothing except God, the life absorbed them utterly. Others were content enough, accepting where they were and willing to be satisfied with it. Most, alas, were never so easily one way or the other and sometimes old longings would return, whether wanted or not. Frevisse was, mostly, past them herself, but she understood Sister Margrett's momentary longing. And then Lady Anneys, probably to help Ursula's dragging feet along, began to sing, swinging her daughter's hand, 'Hand and hand we shall us take, And joy and bliss we shall us make . . .' And in ones and twos the nuns joined in until they were all singing, some more tunefully than others but with no one's feet quite so heavy as they had been and Sister Margrett as happily as everyone else, all sign of other longing gone.

They were to the orchard gate when a boy came running along the alleyway from the priory's foreyard and Dame Juliana said, 'It's Sim from the guesthall. Sim, is there trouble?'

Flushed with hurry and the importance of bearing a message, he said, 'There's a man been waiting this while at the guesthall, my lady. My lady,' he added with a bow to Domina Elisabeth. 'Ela said to tell you he's someone come to see Lady Anneys. Ela said . . .'

Lady Anneys took a quick step forward, anxiously asking, 'One of my sons?'

'Mistress Ela said to say he's John Selenger?' the boy said questioningly.

The mingled hope and worry in Lady Anneys' face changed to something less easily read. 'Yes,' she agreed. 'John Selenger. He's our neighbor's steward.'

'You'll see him?' Domina Elisabeth asked.

'I'd best.' Though by her look she would rather not. Then she added with deliberately lightness, 'He's probably brought some word from home. That's all.'

'Bid Ela see him to the guest parlor,' Domina Elisabeth told Sim, adding as he made to dart away, 'There's no need for haste. We'll be making none.'

Nor did they. Indeed, Domina Elisabeth, having seen everyone through the gate and on their way across the orchard, followed only slowly, somewhat behind them all when Lady Anneys gave Ursula's hand to Dame Perpetua and fell back to her side to say, 'By your leave, my lady?' in a quick, low voice that Frevisse heard only because she was side by side with Dame Claire a little ahead of them.

'Yes?' Domina Elisabeth said.

'May one of your nuns be with me in the parlor while I talk with Master Selenger?'

Domina Elisabeth was quiet a moment, then began, 'If you're afraid of this man . . .'

'No,' Lady Anneys said quickly. 'Not that. I'm not afraid of him. Only I'd rather not . . . see him alone.'

Frevisse had only time to begin to wonder why not when Domina Elisabeth said, 'Dame Frevisse, come here, please you.'

Thus, simply because she had been near when Domina Elisabeth had need of someone, Frevisse went with Lady Anneys – once they were inside again and had washed hands and faces and straightened veils – around the cloister walk with Lady Anneys to the small, bare room near the outer door where nuns met any visitors they might have; and while they went, Lady Anneys said, 'This man. This Master Selenger. I've nothing against him. But . . . since my husband's death he's . . . shown interest in me. I don't want his interest. That's . . . why I want someone with me.'

'Of course,' Frevisse murmured, readily able to suppose that in all likelihood this Master Selenger was too old or too young or too ill-favored or too obviously intent on Lady Anneys' dower properties, and that Lady Anneys had yet to find a way to turn him away without giving offense; but when she followed Lady Anneys into the parlor, the man standing there in the middle of the room was neither aged nor ill-favored and his deep bow to them was both graceful and gracious.

That left only the likelihood that he was ambitious rather than amorous, Frevisse thought dryly, as Lady Anneys answered his questioning look with, 'It's hardly suitable I talk alone with a man inside the cloister, Master Selenger.'

Since Lady Anneys was under no vows, that was not true, nor had there been any reason except her own choice for not seeing him in the guesthall, and by his slight frown Frevisse guessed Master Selenger knew as much. But then, very likely, Lady Anneys had known he knew it and this was simply her quiet way of saying she did not want to see him alone while leaving him no choice but to accept that or else to argue with her. He chose to accept it, slightly bowing his head to Frevisse, who bowed hers in return while Lady Anneys asked, 'Is everyone well at home? You've brought no ill news?'

'Everyone's well. There's no ill news, my lady. Will you sit?'

The room had only a small square table, a bench, and three stools. Master Selenger gestured toward the bench. Lady Anneys refused with a curt shake of her head and insisted, 'Everything's well?'

Her curtness was just barely short of unmannerly but Master Selenger kept his smile and assured her, 'Very well, save that Lady Elyn and Lucy don't go on as well together as they might.'

Lady Anneys gave a tight laugh. 'They haven't gone on well together since Lucy was born. I only insisted she stay with Elyn because she'd trouble her brothers even worse. Has there been any word from the crowner?'

Her change from Elyn and Lucy left Master Selenger behind her. 'The crowner?' he repeated blankly, then caught up with, 'No, no word. Nothing has been found out.'

'Nor anyone?' Lady Anneys said.

'Nor anyone.'

'Nor any word when the escheater will come?'

'No word of that either. There won't be any trouble over it, whenever it's held, though.'

'I'm not supposing there will be. Haven't you brought me any messages from anyone?'

Master Selenger paused at his answer before finally saying, 'I didn't tell anyone I was coming here.'

Lady Anneys stared at him in surprise and coldly, and said nothing.

Master Selenger ended the uncomfortable silence with, 'You could ask me how I come to be here.'

'I could,' Lady Anneys answered, cold as her look. 'I presumed you had business this way.'

Master Selenger hesitated, his eyes flickering toward Frevisse still standing in the doorway. She had deliberately taken her 'I'm not here' stand beside the doorway, her hands tucked out of sight into her opposite sleeves and her head bowed – though not so far that she could not see, with a little upward look through her lashes, everything happening there. She saw Master Selenger make up his mind and return his gaze to Lady Anneys to say, 'My only business this way was with you.'

His directness gave Lady Anneys pause. She might even have wavered, between one heartbeat and another, in her sharpness at him; but if she did, it was for no longer than that and she said, still sharply, 'My thanks for letting me know that all's well and may you fare well on your ride home. Dame Frevisse and I have to ready for Vespers now. God go with you.'

She was drawing back from him, turning toward the door as she spoke. Master Selenger put out a hand to stop her, protesting, 'My lady . . .'

Lady Anneys kept going, repeating more firmly, without looking back, 'God go with you, Master Selenger.'

As taken aback by the suddenness as Master Selenger was, Frevisse stepped aside, out of her way. Master Selenger moved as if to follow her out the door but with a quick gathering of her wits Frevisse stepped back into his way and said, 'I'll see you out, sir, if you will.'

He stopped, looking past her with confusion and an edge of understandable anger, but Lady Anneys was already out of sight, heading along the cloister walk toward the room she shared with Ursula; and he gathered himself and answered Frevisse with at least outward good grace over whatever else he was thinking, 'If you would be so good, my lady, yes, I'll go now.'

Frevisse led him in silence to the door to the guesthall yard. Only as she opened it for him did she ask, very mildly, 'You'll stay the night and leave in the morning?'

Gone somewhere in his own thoughts, her question seemed to take him by surprise and he answered with something of Lady Anneys' sharpness. 'What? Yes.' He recovered and said more evenly, 'Yes. I suppose so. In the morning. Thank you, my lady,' and went out.

And yet the next morning at Tierce, when he might have been supposed to be well on his way homeward, he was still there.

Frevisse, intent on readying her mind for the Office as the nuns settled into their choir stalls, half to either side, facing each other across the choir, would not have known it except Sister Johane whispered rather too loudly to Sister Amicia, 'He's there again. I told you he would be. Look. He's watching her.'

A slight clearing of Domina Elisabeth's throat stopped anything Sister Amicia might have answered, but Frevisse slightly turned her already bowed head and slid her eyes sideways to look past the edge of her veil down the length of the church. The nuns had mentioned among themselves at chapter meeting that neither Lady Anneys nor Ursula had been at Prime or Mass this morning. Frevisse, after supposing to herself that Lady Anneys had probably chosen not to chance meeting Master Selenger again before he left, had forgotten it. Now her careful look told her both Lady Anneys and Ursula were there in the nave, standing not far beyond the choir with the few of the nunnery servants that came now and again to Offices. And that Master Selenger was standing not far behind them.

Domina Elisabeth set the Office firmly on its way by saying in her clear, determined voice, '*Pater noster, qui es in caelis* . . .' – Our father, you who are in heaven . . . – and her nuns obediently followed her into the prayer.

Domina Elisabeth took a workmanlike approach to the Offices and every other service due to God and his saints, believing – as nearly as Frevisse could tell – that God and his saints would in return see to the priory's well-being – fair pay for fair work, as it were – and indeed St Frideswide's was prospering compared to what it had been; but there were still times when Frevisse greatly missed Domina Edith, prioress when she first entered St Frideswide's. For Domina Edith, the Offices' beauty and passion had been a way to deepen her own and her nuns' devotion, a way to bring them nearer to God. There had been none of the 'I give you thus and you give me so in return' that seemed to be Domina Elisabeth's way. Instead Domina Edith had tried for as full a giving of herself as was possible, in the hope of growing to be worthy of God's great love.

Much of what Frevisse understood of nunhood had come from her, but Domina Edith had been dead these twelve years, and at least it could be said that under Domina Elisabeth's careful governance no one was allowed to scant their prayers. The chant rose, '*Nunc, Sancte, nobis, Spiritus, Unum Patri cum Filio* . . .' – Now, Holy Spirit, one with the Father, with the Son . . . – and Frevisse gave her full heed to that and for the while forgot all else, until at the ending *Amen* Domina Elisabeth promptly closed her breviary and rose to her feet.

Her nuns did likewise and, two by two, made procession from the choir and out the church's side door into the cloister walk in a busy bustle. There Domina Elisabeth briefly blessed them and left them to scatter to whatever tasks they might do in the while before Sext. The day was bright and dry and warm again, and minded to work at her copying, Frevisse went the little way along the walk to the desk she used among the five set endwise there to the church's wall for the sake of the best light. The half-filled page she had been working on before Tierce was waiting for her, but rather than sitting down, she stood looking back to the church door, waiting to see Lady Anneys come out.

The servants came. And Ursula, led by Malde from the kitchen, whose grip on her hand was just short of an open struggle as Ursula twisted to pull free.

'Malde,' Frevisse said. 'What's the matter?'

Not letting go of Ursula, Malde stopped and started to say something. But Ursula said fiercely past her, still pulling to be loose, 'He gave her money and told her to take me away so he could talk to Mother. Mother doesn't want to talk to him. Let me go.'

She wrenched hard and it might have turned to tussling but Frevisse said, moving toward them, 'I'll see to it, Ursula. Go on with Malde. Malde, I'll talk with you later about this.'

Malde looked suddenly uncertain she had been paid enough for that, but Frevisse went past her and Ursula to the door still standing open into the church. Yesterday Lady Anneys had made it plain to Master Selenger she had no wish to talk with him anymore. If she had changed her mind today, then Frevisse would discreetly withdraw but . . .

She was not even a single pace inside the door before she knew Lady Anneys had not changed her mind. Standing much where she had been during Tierce, she was turning away from whatever Master Selenger had said to keep her there, saying at him angrily, 'There's no use to this. Leave me alone.'

He reached out and caught her by the arm. 'Lady Anneys, listen . . .'

'Sir?' Frevisse said, bland as if blind to what was happening. 'My lady?'

Master Selenger let go his hold so suddenly that Lady Anneys, still pulling back from him, stumbled. He caught her arm again to steady her, but as fierce as Ursula had been against Malde, she jerked free again, turned her back on him, and said with open anger to Frevisse, 'Master Selenger was just making his good-byes. He's leaving now.'

'I'm certain he is,' Frevisse agreed, staring coldly at him as she moved forward to Lady Anneys' side. 'The Lord's blessing on your going, sir.'

She made that more of a command than a blessing, and Master Selenger's face was flamingly red and stiff with things unsaid as he bowed rigidly first to her, then to Lady Anneys' back still turned firmly to him. He opened his mouth as if to speak, decided against it, swung around, and left, going at a swift walk down the nave and out the church's west door to the guesthall yard without looking back.

Frevisse and Lady Anneys stayed where they were. Only when the heavy door had thudded shut behind him and the church was safely empty did Lady Anneys turn to Frevisse. A tear was sliding down one cheek and her voice shook a little as she said, 'This mustn't be talked about. I pray you, Dame Frevisse, say nothing about it to anyone. If anyone – *anyone* – asks if anything passed between Master Selenger and me, tell them what you saw. That he wanted to keep me here against my will and I was trying to leave. That yesterday I encouraged him to nothing.'

'I will,' Frevisse promised, since all that was nothing more than the truth.

Lady Anneys wiped at the tear, seeming angry it was there; shut her eyes and pressed her fingers to them to stop more from coming.

Carefully, Frevisse said, 'Cry if need be. There's no one here to mind.'

Lady Anneys dropped her hands and opened her dry eyes, refusing both the offer and more tears. '*I* would mind.'

'It's sometimes best to cry and be done with it.'

'If once I started,' Lady Anneys said, 'I might never be done. There are too many in me that I never shed. My late, damned husband would have treasured every one he ever forced from me, so even now I won't give them to him.'

Frevisse had long since judged that Lady Anneys was hardly in mourning for her husband, but the hatred naked in Lady Anneys' words and voice surprised her enough she showed her surprise, and Lady Anneys said bitterly, 'Oh, yes, I hate him. I didn't dare while he was alive, but now that he's dead and I'm free of him, I hate him very, very much. That's one of the reasons I needed to be here, away from everything. I need this time to pray and purge myself of him.'

She had said 'one of the reasons,' Frevisse noted but did not ask the others, only offered, 'Do you want I should leave to your prayers now?'

Lady Anneys looked uneasily the way Master Selenger had gone.

'I'll see that he's left or that it's understood he's to go before I do anything else,' Frevisse said. Under St Benedict's Rule, the priory was required to receive such guests as God might send them. That did not mean they had to put up with those who spoiled their own welcome by making trouble.

'Yes,' Lady Anneys said. 'Yes. Thank you. If I know he's gone . . . yes, I'd like to pray for a while. But . . .' She hesitated, then asked, 'No questions? No wanting to know anything else?'

'I may want to know,' Frevisse said in all honesty, 'but I don't think you want to tell me.'

That surprised a half-unwilling laugh from Lady Anneys. 'I don't, no. Thank you.'

'But if sometime you do, I'll listen. And still not ask questions if you don't want them.'

Lady Anneys regarded her in searching silence for a moment, then slightly bowed her head in thanks again. 'If the time comes, I'll remember.' She drew back a step, looking toward the altar. 'For now, though, I think prayer will suffice. By your leave, my lady.'

Chapter 6

The bright, late summer days had turned from warm to hot, and Tom, Hugh, and Miles were lingering in the shadowy hall after midday dinner, none of them in haste to be about their afternoon work. Hugh had spent the early morning riding out to exercise the dogs while the day was still somewhat cool and then he and Degory had rather uselessly worked with Skyre, who was seeming less and less likely to ever be a usable scent-hound after all. In the alarm after Sir Ralph was found, no one had remembered her save Degory, and when they carried Sir Ralph's body back to the manor, he had stayed behind, searched for her, found her, 'Cowering under a bush close by where *he* was,' he told Hugh when he went to ask his help. 'She maybe saw it or something. It's like she's witless. I've brought her in. She won't stop shaking.' Nor did she until Hugh had wrapped her in a blanket, tightly swaddling her almost the way a nurse would do a howling baby to quiet it. But Skyre had not howled, only trembled, and even now still trembled and cringed at any sudden noise or movement. Still, she had been too promising a hound to let go without he tried to save her, but it had made for a discouraging morning and because he had nothing particularly planned for this afternoon, he was simply sitting on the dais step with Baude between his knees, stroking a brush down her back and sides not so much because she needed the grooming as for the pleasure it gave them both.

Tom, with seemingly no more ambition toward the rest of the day than Hugh had, was leaned back in his chair behind the table, legs stretched out in front of him, his eyes shut although – if anyone had asked him – he would have said he was not sleeping, only not ready to move. He had spent the morning walking the fields with Lucas, the reeve, overseeing the start of the barley harvest, and once he bestirred himself he'd be out again all the afternoon.

Miles had his head down on his crossed arms on the table, and under the table Bevis was stretched out with his chin resting on Miles' foot. When Hugh had laughingly goaded him at first about the hound's unwanted devotion, Miles had grumbled, 'Can't you kennel him with the rest of the hounds?'

'He's too used to being with Sir Ralph. I doubt he'd do anything but make trouble if put with the other hounds.'

'Instead, he's making trouble for *me*,' Miles had muttered. But lately, except when he remembered to complain, he had begun to seem as content in Bevis' company as the hound was in his; he had not, Hugh noted, moved his foot since Bevis' chin came to rest on it.

Miles and Bevis had been out about woodward duties from not much after dawn today, away to Skippitt Coppice to see where best to start the autumn cutting. Most times lately when Miles went out, George from the village went with him and, 'I think he might do well enough in my place the while until you find someone else,' Miles had told Tom over dinner. 'He knows what he's seeing when he looks at it.'

That would be something to tell Mother when she came home, Hugh thought. What they would do for a woodward was one of the things she had talked of when he was taking her and Ursula to St Frideswide's. He had taken the chance to ask her then when she thought to come home and been relieved when she said, 'Before Miles leaves us, surely.'

He had been half-afraid she was thinking of nunhood for herself. It would be the most straightforward way to fulfill Sir Ralph's order that she live a virtuous, unmarried life, and almost Hugh could want it to be that simple for her. Almost but not quite.

Nor did he want it for Ursula, he had admitted to himself. She had been quiet out of the ordinary on the ride to St Frideswide's. Once, to Hugh's pleasure, she had started to whistle back to a linnet in a hedgerow as they rode past, but Lady Anneys had reminded her that whistling was unladylike and Ursula had fallen quiet again, until – outside the cloister door in St Frideswide's guesthall courtyard when Hugh had lifted her up for a better embrace good-bye – she had clung to him and whispered in his ear,

'I wish I was going home with you.'

He had whispered back, 'I wish you were, too,' but had set her down and let the waiting nun take her hand as he turned to embrace his mother, too.

She had said nothing, only when she drew back from him had looked deeply into his eyes as if searching for something before briefly touching his cheek and turning away. He had stood there in the courtyard, watching as she and Ursula went inside, until the door was closed behind them, shutting them in and him out, and then he had ridden away, as oddly bereft as if that door would never open to let either of them out again.

To the good, he was not bereft by Lucy being gone to stay with Elyn. That was merely pleasant; but along with missing Lady Anneys and Ursula, he missed Tom sharing the loft with him and Miles. Before she had left, Lady Anneys had told Tom he should move into the lord of the manor's bedchamber above the parlor when she was gone. 'It's yours,' she had said. 'You may as well grow used to it.'

'But where will you sleep?' Tom had protested.

'Not there again, if I can help it,' she had said. 'In the girls' chamber with Lucy, probably.'

But it was odd to have Tom gone from their own chamber. 'It's not that we miss your snoring,' Miles had told Tom the first morning after he had shifted. 'It's just hard getting used to the quiet.' They had been standing in the hall, breaking their morning fast, and Tom had thrown a heavy-crusted chunk of bread at him. Miles had ducked out of the way and Bevis had seized the crust for his own.

Now Miles gave a wide yawn and sat up.

'Don't,' said Tom without opening his eyes. 'If you start moving, I'll have to.'

'All right,' Miles said and put his head down again.

Hugh, still stroking the brush down Baude's back, said, 'I'm thinking to hare-hunt tomorrow morning. Helinor,' the manor's cook, 'says she wouldn't mind some fresh meat for the pot. Either of you interested in coming?'

Tom stretched and said, 'Yes. Good. I'll come.'

Miles mumbled into the crook of his arm, 'Not me.'

They sat in silence a little longer, until Miles said, still without lifting his head, 'Did you know there's a copy of Sir William's will in Sir Ralph's strong-chest, Tom?'

'Um-hum,' Tom murmured. His eyes were closed again. 'There's Sir William's will, and deeds, and rent statements, and papers that look left over from Sir Ralph's lawyer-days. I'm still reading through them. It's killing me.'

Idly, Hugh asked, 'What were you doing in the strongchest, Miles?' The iron-bound, padlocked box was kept under Sir Ralph's . . . under Tom's bed, to hold what ready money there was and whatever deeds, charters, and suchlike as were worth safe-guarding.

'I had him fetch me some pence yesterday,' Tom answered, rather than Miles. 'To pay old Wat for turfing that place where the stream bank had started to slide. He made good work of it. Wat, I mean.'

'Sir William's will was lying right on top of everything else,' Miles said, 'and I was curious.'

'You were snooping,' Tom said lazily and not as if he minded.

Miles sat up, stretched his back and crooked his neck as if they were stiff, and asked, 'What did you think of the will?'

'I thought it read pretty much like Father's.' Tom sounded not in the least interested. 'He'll have to make a new one, now Sir Ralph is dead and can't be his executor. But if Philippa and I are married soon enough, he won't have to bother with deciding who's to oversee her marriage in his place.'

'You're thinking you'll marry soon?' Hugh asked.

Tom rolled his shoulders in a lazy shrug. 'Might as well, since we're going to do it sooner or later anyway and none of us are much interested in a year's mourning for Sir Ralph anyway, are we?'

'If Sir Ralph had a copy of Sir William's will in his safekeeping,' Miles said, 'don't you suppose Sir William has a copy of Sir Ralph's?'

'I suppose.' Tom did not sound like he was supposing it very hard.

'Then he must have known everything that was in it long before Master Wyck told us. Just as Sir Ralph must have known what was in his will, too,' Miles persisted.

Still lazily, Tom granted again, 'I suppose.'

Hugh looked up, frowning warily. Miles was going somewhere with this.

Miles reached over and shook Tom's knee. 'But remember how Sir William tried to put off Master Wyck telling us about it?'

'He thought it was too soon to be burdening Mother with it,' Tom said. 'That's all.'

'Was it?' Miles demanded. 'What about Selenger?'

Tom finally drew himself up straight in his chair. 'What about him?'

'Mind how he was here so often before she went away? Always coming to see her? Keeping her company for half an afternoon at a time?'

'Yes,' Tom granted.

'I half-thought . . .' Hugh started, thought better of saying it but knew there was no going back, and finished slowly, 'I've half-thought she went with Ursula to be away from him.'

Tom was deeply frowning now. 'She never said that, did she?'

'No. It was just something I . . . felt.'

Carefully, as if he had considered the words for quite a while, Miles said, 'He's been to the nunnery to see her.'

'To see Mother? Don't be witless,' Tom protested. 'Why would he go without telling us he was? Or else, when he came back, tell us how she is?'

Miles held silent, waiting for them to figure it out for themselves. Tom took hardly longer than Hugh did to see where Miles was going; but while Hugh said nothing, Tom protested more strongly, 'Miles, don't try that one. He's not angling for her, if that's what you're going around the bush to say.'

'Then why did he go?' Miles said.

'I don't know.' Tom was impatient about it. 'A letter from Elyn. Complaints from Lucy. Sir William wanting to ask her something. I don't know.'

'Why not ask if we had any word to send her?' Miles demanded. 'That would be courtesy.'

Tom made an impatient gesture at him. 'Give it over, Miles. He's not fool enough to be after her if that's what you're on about. She won't marry again. Why would she? She's too old to want another husband, anyway.' He stood up and stretched his arms wide to the sides. 'It's too hot for this much thinking. I'm away to see how far they're likely to get with Pollard Field today. Time you shifted yourself, too.'

Miles waved a lazy hand at him, saying nothing. Nor did Hugh. Tom left, and when he was gone, Miles stood up, still saying nothing, and left, too, with Bevis at his heels. Hugh stayed a little longer where he was, stroking Baude with his hand now, considering everything Miles had said and some of the things he had not, before finally rising to his feet. Baude, who was beginning to feel the weight of her whelping, rose more grudgingly, and he told her, 'You stay here.' He pointed at the hall's cool stone floor. 'Stay.'

With a whoof that Hugh took for gratitude, Baude lay down again, and he went in search of Miles.

He found him in the stable, sitting on a manger's edge feeding carrot bits to Lanval, the squat roan gelding with carthorse in its ancestry that Sir Ralph had said was good enough for him. Bevis, lying flat on his side under the manger, opened an eye at Hugh, decided he was no problem, and shut it again. Hugh leaned a shoulder against the post outside the stall to show he meant to stay awhile and asked, 'Where did you get the carrots? And why's Lanval in stable rather than pasture?'

'I'm riding out again this afternoon. There's a stretch of timber over Ashstock way that's ready for thinning, I think, but it's been a while since I've had a look at it. As for the carrots, they're from the kitchen garden, of course.'

Raiding the kitchen garden had been a favored pastime with them and Tom when they were small. Helinor would have let them have what they wanted for the asking but the skulking and 'stealing' had been better sport, and Helinor had obliged by calling dire threats after them whenever she saw them at it. She never complained of them to Lady Anneys, though, and always had some treat for them when they ventured into the kitchen itself.

Hugh grinned. 'Nobody saw you?'

'Well, yes, but only Alson.' The kitchen maid. 'I gave her a kiss to keep her quiet.'

'You would,' said Hugh. For years he and Miles and Tom had jested at each other's alleged passion for Alson, who was somewhat old enough to be their grandmother. But this time Miles let the jest lie and Hugh did not keep it up. Lanval crunched carrots and swept his tail at flies whose lazy buzzing was the only other sound in the stable. The other horses were in pasture or at work, and Gib, like everyone else on the manor who could be spared, was out to the barley harvest. There was no one there, no one to overhear, and in a while Hugh asked, 'How did you know Master Selenger went to St Frideswide's of late?'

Miles slowly drew his hand down Lanval's long face before saying, seemingly to the gelding's forelock, 'Philippa told me.'

Carefully, because so far as he knew none of them had been near Sir William's manor in a week, Hugh asked, 'When did you talk with Philippa?'

Miles looked at him, saying nothing at all.

Hugh looked back at him and did not ask again but said instead, very, very quietly, 'She's meant for Tom.'

Miles turned away, ducking under Lanval's neck to the other side of the stall. 'We know,' he said.

'If you know . . .'

'We *know.*' Miles pulled his saddle from the stall wall and slung it over Lanval's back.

Hugh tried again. 'Miles . . .'

Miles began fastening up the girths. 'How long have you known about us?'

'I haven't known.' Nor could he say how long he had been working hard not to know it. 'I've only thought it . . . possible. Miles, it's no good.'

Miles paused in drawing up the rear girth and looked at him across Lanval's back. 'No,' he agreed. 'It isn't any good. Nor is it well-witted of us. And no, it isn't safe either. We know all that. And no, I'm not going to take Philippa from Tom. We're neither of us fools, Philippa and I. It will be years, if ever, before I can afford a wife, before my ruin of a manor – a manor I've never even seen, mind you – is worth anything again.'

'But you and Philippa . . .'

'Know we have no hope of each other. That she's all but promised elsewhere. That I can't give her anything worth having. We sometimes see each other, yes. That's all. We see each other and take what comfort there is in that, for this little while until we won't be able to see each other anymore.'

Miles' sharp bitterness warned Hugh to let that be the end of it, but more than the bitterness, Hugh heard the pain behind the words – he had always been too able to hear Miles' pain – and found himself saying against good sense, 'Even if Elyn bears Sir William children, Philippa will still have a goodly dowry. Enough to make a good start toward bringing your manor back.'

Miles finished with the girth, heaved a sigh heavy with patience, and hands clasped, leaned his arms across Lanval's back. 'Do you really think,' he said, 'that Sir William will give her much of a dowry – if any at all – if she marries against his wish?'

No answer was needed to that, and Miles turned away from Hugh's silence to take down his bridle from the peg where it hung at the end of the stall. But as he turned back, Hugh asked, 'About Master Selenger. You really think there's something to worry about him?'

Slipping the bit into Lanval's mouth, Miles said evenly, 'I think his interest in Lady Anneys is very sudden.'

'It might not be. He might have . . . been interested for a long time. He'd hardly have let it be known while Sir Ralph was alive.'

'I'd be willing to have a go at believing that, save for how hard Sir William tried to delay her knowing Sir Ralph's will.'

'He feared Mother was too tired for it just then. That's all.'

Miles paused in buckling the bridle's throat lash to look at him. 'Hugh, you can think better than that. You just don't bother.'

Hugh crossed his arms and glared at him, refusing to be drawn.

That did not stop Miles, who went on, 'In truth, most of the time, you'd rather not think further than your hounds if you could help it.'

'I think enough to know you're trying to goad me into an argument.'

Miles grinned. 'See? You can think when you're forced to it.'

'You want an argument so I'll be forced to think about the possibility that Sir William maybe wanted Mother not to know how the will bound her because he wanted Master Selenger to have better chance of . . . something . . . with her.'

'Or ruining her,' Miles said curtly. 'She doesn't even have to marry again, remember. She only has to be "unvirtuous" for her to lose her control of everything and Sir William gain it. And what's "unvirtuous" can be almost anything, depending on who's deciding. Which means Sir William.'

'And me. I'm executor with him.'

'Making you an executor was a jest and you know it. Sir Ralph never expected you'd do aught but leave everything to Lady Anneys and Sir William.'

Yes, Hugh knew that. Had known it from the first.

It had not bothered him until now.

But his bother was not the point at present and he said, 'Miles, we don't even know that Sir William knows Master Selenger is giving her such heed, let alone that he's behind it.'

'How does Selenger get away from Denhill so often and easily, if not with Sir William's leave?'

'How does Philippa get away to see you?'

'She doesn't. We meet at the far end of the orchard, beyond the hedge and very rarely. Leave that. Listen. If Selenger brings Lady Anneys to marriage or anything else or even the seeming of anything else, it's you who are going to be in as much trouble as Tom. It won't be Lady Anneys but Sir William who has the say over who you and Tom and Lucy and Ursula marry. It will be Sir William who'll have the profit from selling you all to the highest bidders, whoever they are, and never mind how any of you feel about it. If any of you refuse his choice, you lose your inheritance.'

'I know all that, but—'

'Think about the possibilities. Because I'll warrant Sir William has.'

'Tom is to marry Philippa . . .'

'There's no betrothal yet. Nothing that seals and sets it to happen. Let's suppose Sir William decides instead to find someone else for Tom. Someone who'll pay Sir William a goodly amount to marry a daughter to the well-propertied young man that Tom now is.'

'Then Tom will have her for a wife instead of Philippa.'

'And Sir William will still have Philippa to marry off profitably to someone else altogether. That's double profit for him. Well and good and all very reasonable, as such things go. But suppose whoever he finds for Tom is so ghastly that Tom can only refuse the marriage? Then everything – this manor and everything else that are Tom's – goes to you. Whose marriage Sir William likewise controls. You're now in possession of Tom's inheritance as well as your own and very well worth marrying to Philippa, who thereby gains more than she would have if Sir William had settled for merely marrying her to Tom. Or he may play the same game on you he played Tom, finds you a bride you have to refuse. Then everything goes to Lucy, and can you imagine what someone is likely to pay him to marry a son to her at that point? He can—'

'Miles!' Hugh said harshly. 'Stop it!'

Bevis stood up uneasily under the manger and Lanval tossed his head. Miles caught the gelding by the bridle and stroked his face, speaking to him soothingly. Hugh, regaining control of his anger, said, trying to be reasonable, 'None of that's happened yet and nothing says it's going to.'

'It hasn't happened yet,' Miles agreed very quietly. 'And it may not. But it's possible.'

'Not very,' Hugh insisted.

Miles straightened and began to back Lanval from the stall.

'Wait,' Hugh said. 'Is George going with you or only Bevis?'

'Only Bevis. George is gone to the harvesting.'

'Then I'll come with you, if you'll wait while I fetch Foix and saddle him.' His tall-legged bay palfrey. Because he suddenly did not want Miles to ride out alone with himself this afternoon. Not alone with his dark thoughts anyway. 'I haven't been toward Ashstock for a while either and ought to see how the hunting seems that way.'

Miles did not frown against the thought, only looked momentarily surprised before – surprisingly – he smiled and said, 'Hurry up, then. The day won't last forever.'

Despite of that, they made no haste on their ride, let the horses set their own easy, head-bobbing walk along one of the lesser trails through the forest's green quiet, and did not talk at all themselves, the only sounds around them the soft fall of the horses' hoofs on the trail's bare earth and the softer whispering of the trees among the sunlight-flecked green shadows. And when they reached the Ashstock woods and talked a little, it was only about the five well-grown ash trees and an oak that Miles judged ready for cutting and how many trees could be planted to replace them. Hugh found out enough signs of deer to show there would likely be good hunting this way, and then in companionable silence they started homeward, still making no haste, so that by the time they rode out of the woods above the manor, the sun had slid from sight, leaving the green twilight sky feathered by a few high clouds turned gold from the vanished sun, and smoke from supper fires was rising lazily above the hall and village roofs. Home and supper, and afterward a quiet evening, and then bed. That, Hugh thought, was the way every day should end.

He remembered that day afterward, because, in its way, it was the last of the good ones.

Chapter 7

The morrow started as fair a summer's day as could be hoped for, warm and clear-skied and the hounds ready to run. The hare-hunt went well. The hares gave fine sport, both the ones that were caught and the ones that escaped – sometimes especially the ones that escaped. At the hunt's end Tom sent the smallest hare away to old Goditha in the village who was ailing. 'It's old age and she won't get over that,' he said blithely, 'but meat in the cooking pot will make her daughter-in-law better resigned to having care of her.'

The rest of the dead hares were handed over to Degory to take to Helinor in the kitchen. 'Tell her to make as many hare pies as she can from them. Two for the hall at supper tonight, the rest for the harvest-folk at their noontide break tomorrow,' he said and Degory trotted away happy at the likelihood of hare pie tonight and maybe tomorrow, too, because when he was not needed for the hounds, he had been at the harvest.

Not ready to end the morning, Hugh and Tom saw the hounds back to the kennel together and helped Degory, back from the kitchen, to settle the hounds to a well-earned, well-fed rest. They made easy talk while they did and while they headed to the hall to wash before dinner, beginning to feel their tiredness now but laughing as they went, reminding each other how one of the young hounds had leaned too far over in turning after a hare and gone down in a flail of legs and humiliation. By the time he had untangled himself and stood up, Bane had been standing with the dead hare in her mouth and a distainful look at him.

'Baseot's young,' Hugh said in his defense. 'He hasn't learned to match eagerness to balance yet.'

'I'll warrant he remembers after today!' Tom laughed.

They came from between the stable and byre into the sideyard where the wide-trunked elm that must have been young when the manor was, spread welcome shade and found Miles there, sitting on the bench beneath it, doing nothing.

'Very grand,' Tom said. 'Wish I had that kind of lazying time.'

Standing up, ignoring the jibe, Miles said, 'One of Sir William's men is here to see you. I thought you'd want to know before you saw him.'

'What's he want?' Tom asked.

'To see you. That's all I know.'

'And thought to warn me so I'd be ready, in case there's an ambush in it?' Tom scorned. 'Give it over, Miles.'

They rounded the corner of the hall into the foreyard and Sir William's man rose from the bench beside the door where the late morning shadow still lay and it was cooler than inside the hall. Someone had properly given him a cup of ale and he had probably been happy enough in his waiting, but leaving the cup on the bench, he came to meet them, bowed, and said to Tom, 'Sir, Sir William asks you come to see him.'

'When?' Tom asked.

'Now, please you.'

'Now? For what?'

'I don't know, sir.'

'Well, I'm not going now. I want to wash, sit down awhile, and have my dinner. When all that's done, then I'll go to Sir William.'

He moved to go on, into the halt. The man said, 'Please, sir, I think he meant you to come directly back with me and I've been waiting awhile.'

Tom stopped, turned back to the man, and smiled on him, not unkindly but not yielding either. 'I don't care what Sir William meant. I'm dirty and tired and starting to be hungry. When I've taken care of all that, then I'll go to Sir William. You're welcome to ride back and tell him so, or you can wait, eat with us, and ride with me.'

Looking as if neither choice made him comfortable, the man bowed. 'I think I'd best go back. To let him know you're coming.'

'As you choose,' Tom said and went past him into the hall, leaving the man to bow to his back and tossing over his shoulder as he went, 'If he'd had the courtesy to say what he wanted me for, I might be more willing to oblige, but since all he did was order me to come, he can damn all wait until I'm ready.'

The man was staring, startled, at Tom's back as Hugh and Miles went past him, too. Hugh could only hope the man had wit enough not to pass that along to Sir William with the rest of the message and that dinner would take the edge off Tom's sudden ill-humour. He had sounded exactly the way he had when readying to do battle with Sir Ralph, and Miles must have thought so, too, because he said, low-voiced for Tom not to hear, 'You better go with him, Hugh.'

'Hah,' said Hugh. 'You think I can stop him if he gets hot-humoured?'

'If worse comes to worse, you can throw yourself between him and Sir William.'

'If you're keen on throwing, you go.'

'Have you ever known me to be a soothing presence when there's trouble?'

'A point well-made,' Hugh said. 'I'll go.'

Washed and in clean hosen and shirts, they fed well on a plain dinner of new-baked bread, fresh cheese, cold pork tarts, and garden greens – lettuce, borage, cress, parsley, fennel, and young onions mixed and dressed with vinegar and salt. Afterward, leaving Miles still comfortably at the table, Tom and Hugh grudgingly shrugged into their good doublets that were unfortunately – considering the day was now moving into its midday heat – of wool. Deep crimson for Tom and forest green for Hugh. Tom, who had begun to mellow over dinner, began to unmellow, grumbling while fastening the stiffly standing upright collar high under his chin, 'I've probably already irked Sir William enough by not being there before now that I doubt making pretty for him is going to help.'

Not any happier about it himself, Hugh said, 'It can't hurt.'

'It's hurting me. I'm roasting.'

'I like the way your face matches your doublet,' Miles offered.

'Remind me to wrap you in a blanket and set you by the kitchen fire when we get home,' Tom returned.

They rode at an easy walk, making no haste. Sir William's manor was barely two miles away and the day too warm for hurry. Once past Woodrim's church, the road to Denhill curved between this year's fallow field sloping green up to the woodshore on one side and a grassy verge, thick hedge, and golden-standing wheatfield ready to the harvest when its turn came. Because presently the work was farther off, in Pollard Field, here was strangely unpeopled, and there was not even the usual distant calling back and forth because all the harvest-folk were still at their midday rest, stretched out in the shade of the hedge and trees along Pollard Field and the stream there. The day was drowsing. Gay blue chicory, bright yellow yarrow, and bold red poppies still bloomed in the tall summer-growing grasses along the road; and if the grasses' greens were beginning to dull with the year's turn toward autumn, the sky was clear, high-arched, and deeply blue, and contentedly Tom said, 'It's going to be a good year for the harvest. Everything is the best I've ever seen it.'

'There looks to be deer in plenty, too,' Hugh said. 'The hunting should be good all winter.'

'Praise St Eustace. Not so much salt meat.' Tom had never cared much for salt-kept meat, no matter how it was cooked.

They rode beyond their own fields and for a while were quiet, easy-swaying in their saddles to their horses' even stride, until Tom said out of wherever his thoughts had been, 'You don't mean to leave, do you, Hugh? I mean, you can if you want, but all in all I'd rather you stayed.'

Hugh had been gazing aside at the green roll of countryside, the land sloping away just here to a long view of fields and woods familiar to him all his life. They were as part of him as his own arms or legs – or heart – and no, he did not want to go away. Not now, not ever, and he turned his head toward Tom and answered as quietly as Tom had asked it, 'No. I'm not wanting to leave.'

'Good.' Tom suddenly held out his hand. Hugh without hesitation reached for him in return, but better than only a handshake, they gripped each other's arms near the elbow, forearm to forearm in promise that their friendship would go on. Then, just as suddenly, they both felt foolish for showing so much feeling and let each other go and Hugh said, for the sake of saying something, 'Of course your wife may want me out from underfoot when the time comes.'

'Philippa? Not likely. She's as used to you being underfoot as the rest of us are.'

'Do you think it's about your marriage Sir William wants to see you?'

'Probably.'

'Are you ready to talk about it?'

'Why not? We're getting no younger, Philippa and I. If Sir William and I can make our agreement soon enough, then the banns can be said, we can be wed by maybe Michaelmas, and I'll have someone warm in my bed come winter.'

'And Philippa?' Hugh asked despite himself.

'She'll have someone warm in bed, too, you dolt.'

That had not been what Hugh meant but he let it go, because after all, Tom probably had the right of it. There was small use in wondering what Philippa thought of the marriage when she was going to have no choice about it.

They were riding through Sir William's manor now, the land that would someday be Tom's if he married Philippa. And if Elyn birthed no sons, Hugh silently added. Ahead, as the road rolled over another lift of low hill, the manor hall and its surrounding buildings came into sight, settled tightly in a curve of land below a hill, gardens and orchard flanking it before the fields began, with an arm of forest stretched behind it, hedged from the rest. That made it easy for Miles to come unseen to the orchard's end to meet with Philippa, Hugh thought; and wished he had not.

'Father kept too much of Woodrim for hunting,' Tom said. 'Sir William has more in fields. If I can put Woodrim and Denhill together someday, it will make a manor well worth the having.'

'Do you know,' he added as they neared the manor yard, 'I think I'd prefer to live here when the time comes that Sir William is no more. You can have Woodrim for a hunting lodge and all the hounds you can fit into it.'

'I have been thinking . . .' Hugh started, but stopped, unsure how to say what had only lately begun to shape itself in his mind.

'Go on,' Tom encouraged.

Hesitantly, Hugh said, 'I've thought of maybe setting to breed and train hounds for more than my own use. To sell, you know. We have two good lines already. If I worked at it . . .'

He stopped because it sounded overbold when said aloud; but Tom reached over to punch him lightly in the arm, saying, 'Good. Good for you. Do it. I'll breed sons and you can breed hounds.

And sons of your own, too, when the time comes. Once I'm married, we'll find you a wife.'

Two servants came out from the hall to meet them as they rode into the manor foreyard, one to lead them inside, the other to take their horses away to the stable. Sir William greeted them in the great hall, not with the – at best – simmering rage Sir Ralph would have had for Tom not coming immediately, but merely courtesy as he led them into the parlor. It was larger and more comfortable than anything at Woodrim. There was a fireplace, for one thing, with a long, cushioned settle in front of it, and everything – polished wooden table, short-backed chairs, close-woven reed matting – was better-made and better-kept. It was more comfortably lived in, too. At Woodrim there was a barrenness still there from all the years of no one daring to show much of themselves to Sir Ralph, hiding from him by having very little of their own for him to attack, either by word or, in his angers, by deed. Here, there were Elyn's tapestry frame beside a chair with the wall-hanging she had been working at for a year and more; an untidy sewing basket at one end of the settle that was surely Lucy's; Philippa's lute lying on the end of the seat below the window that looked out into the garden.

Besides that, there was a wooden chest standing open along one wall, scrolls and papers inside it. More writing-covered papers, an inkpot, several clean quills, and a penknife with a knotwork pattern carved around its wooden hilt were on the table where Sir William's chair waited at one side and a tall-legged joint stool at the end. Gesturing Tom to the stool and seating himself in the chair, Sir William said, continuing his jest, 'It's a wife you need, Tom, to stir you up in the morning and set you going.'

Left to sit where he chose, Hugh went to the window bench. A brief look into the garden showed him Elyn, Philippa, and Lucy sitting together on the turf-topped seat in the slight shade cast by a trellised vine at the garden's far end before he turned back to the room as Tom answered Sir William with an easy smile, 'That's what we're to talk about, isn't it? Marriage?'

Sir William, shuffling the papers on the table in front of him, said, 'That's why you're here, yes. Your marriage to Philippa.'

A maidservant came in with a pitcher and three pewter goblets. Sir William bade her set them at the table's other end and waved her out. 'Hugh, if you would?' he asked, and Hugh rose, went, and poured the dark wine for them and for himself while Tom said, 'What sort of agreement were you and Father shaping before he died?'

'Well.' Sir William settled comfortably back in his chair. 'Things have changed since then. You're no longer your father's heir but lord of the manor. That puts a stronger front on things for you.'

Hugh returned to the window seat with his wine and sat down. Tom had already set his goblet aside and was leaning toward Sir William, saying, 'It doesn't change that you're married to a young wife who'll likely give you other heirs. For all I know, Elyn is bearing right now.'

Sir William slightly flushed. 'She's not.'

'That's not to say she won't,' Tom insisted. 'If she does, there goes much if not most of Philippa's inheritance. A daughter would mean Philippa's inheritance is cut by half. A son would mean Philippa loses almost everything. Any marriage settlement we make has to allow for both those chances.'

'You're the son of my best friend. He and I meant from the very first for our children to marry. It was his hope.' Sir William spread his hands in a gesture of open-heartedness. 'It's still mine.'

'My father's main hope was to make everyone closest to him as miserable as possible,' Tom said curtly. 'Now that he's dead, I don't have to oblige him anymore. We know what Philippa will get if she remains your heir. The question, then, is what do you have to offer in compensation for everything she loses if you have a son to replace her?'

Sir William rapped the tabletop with his knuckles. 'Tom. Let's not take a harsh line with this. We're here to talk it out . . .'

'That doesn't mean I lie down and roll over and take what I'm given. Because Sir Ralph wanted me to marry Philippa doesn't mean I *have* to marry Philippa and no more than gamble that I'll gain more than I lose by it.'

Sir William took a deep drink of his wine, maybe hoping to wash down the anger tightening his face. Hugh guessed he had not counted on argument from Tom, while Tom was suddenly feeling the freedom Sir Ralph's death had given him; and Hugh said, hoping to forestall trouble, 'Wouldn't this better wait until Mother is here to have say in it?'

Sir William dismissed that with a flick of one hand. 'We don't need a woman's dealing in this. Besides, she's put herself away into that nunnery.'

'Not forever,' Hugh said. 'She—'

'She'll accept what I decide,' Tom cut in impatiently.

Sir William looked back and forth between them and – to give himself somewhere else to look, Hugh guessed – restlessly picked up the small-bladed penknife and one of the untrimmed quills lying on the table and began to work a point onto it, saying while he did, 'Besides, it's doubtful she'll much longer have any say at all in these matters, what with this uncommon interest she's taking in John Selenger. Not that he isn't worth her interest but—'

'It's Selenger who's shown uncommon interest in her,' Hugh said. 'She went into the nunnery to get away from him.'

Tom gave him a surprised look. He clearly had never connected the two, despite what Miles had said yesterday.

With a slight and maybe scornful smile at one corner of his mouth, Sir William said, trimming more intently at the quill, 'It's odd, then, that she sent him a letter asking for him to come see her there.' He looked up, first at Hugh, now as surprised as Tom, and then at Tom. 'Or didn't you know that? Sent for him and was not at all ungiving of her . . . company, shall we say?'

Tom and Hugh traded looks. Hugh shook his head, not believing it. Nor did Tom, who said angrily at Sir William, 'I doubt both the letter and that she welcomed him. I think Miles is right. I think you've set him on to her.'

'John needs no "setting on" to have interest in a comely woman. And why shouldn't she have an interest in him? Their marrying would give her protection and the pleasures of a husband and—'

'And give him her property to use as he chooses,' Tom snapped, 'while she loses all say in my marriage and in Hugh's and the girls'. *You'd* have say over all our marriages. You'd make them to suit yourself and take the profits of them for good measure. You knew what was in Sir Ralph's will. You wanted to keep it from us long enough for Selenger to have a clear run at her.' Tom swung around to Hugh. 'Miles was right!'

Red-faced with open anger, still clutching the quill in one hand, Sir William pointed at Tom with the penknife and said furiously, 'Miles has nothing to do with this. Now listen, Tom . . .'

Tom stood up so sharply he knocked over the stool behind him. 'If Selenger wants a wife, he can have Lucy. She's ready for marriage and it'll save the bother of searching out someone else for her. But if all he wants is to make trouble for Mother so you can have the profit of it, then be damned to you both!'

The quill bent and broke in Sir William's grasp. He drew in breath for an angry answer but Tom stepped around the corner of the table and leaned over him, one hand on the table, the other braced on the back of Sir William's chair. Thrusting his face close at Sir William, he said, 'As for Philippa, the next time you want to talk marriage with me . . .'

Sir William, crowded back into his chair, swept a hand at him like warding off a fly too close to his face. Tom jerked away, enough that Sir William was able to shove himself out of his chair and swing around to put it between them, saying angrily, 'Listen, you young fool . . .'

But by then Hugh was across the room and gripping Tom by the arm, pleading, 'Tom. Let it go. Let's go home. You're both too angry for this. Let's go.' Tom shook him off. Hugh moved in front of him, between him and Sir William, insisting, 'It's wrong, Tom. Let it go for now. The day's too hot for talking. This isn't the time. Let's go home for now. We can all talk later.' Spilling words the way he would have spilled water on a fire to stop it.

And Tom fell back a step and then another, threw up his hands in surrender, and said, 'Yes. Fine. Good enough.' Forcing himself back from his anger, he slapped the side of Hugh's shoulder. 'You're right. Let's go.' And before Hugh could answer that, he swung around and stalked from the room.

Still churned with the suddenness of it all, Hugh turned around to Sir William, trying desperately to think of some apology that was not betrayal of Tom, saying, 'He'll settle. I'm sorry. We'll be back. Or you can come to Woodrim next time.'

'Supposing there is a next time,' Sir William snapped; but like Tom, he was forcing his anger back into control and said a little less tersely, 'Yes. Next time I'll come to Woodrim maybe. I'm sorry, too.'

He made to lay the penknife still clutched in his fist onto the table beside him, then went rigid, staring at it so that Hugh looked, too. And saw the short, sharp blade was bloodied. He and Sir

William raised their eyes from it together, looking at each other with mutual unbelief before Sir William half-whispered, 'I forgot I was even holding it.'

'You must have . . . when you swung at him . . . you must have . . .'

'I didn't feel it. I didn't feel anything. I didn't know . . . I didn't mean . . .'

'He didn't know either.' Hugh was already away from the table, leaving. 'It's so sharp he must not even have felt it.' And with the high, crimson collar of his doublet and no one looking for blood . . .

By the time he was out of the parlor, Hugh was running. Running, he passed through the great hall without seeing it, ran out of it into the yard where no one was, and crossed it, still at a run, into the stableyard, where a stableman leading Hugh's unsaddled and unbridled Foix away from the watering trough startled to a stop, staring.

'My brother,' Hugh demanded. 'Where is he?'

'Gone,' the man said. 'Stormed in and rode out. He's gone.'

'You couldn't have saddled his horse in the time.'

'I hadn't unsaddled it yet. I was tending to this one. I'd just finished wiping him down and was coming out for the other one. It was tied there.' He nodded to a ring in the stable wall. 'Sir William said you'd be here a longish while so I was making no hurry about it . . .'

Hugh grabbed the lead rope from him. 'My bridle. Get it. Fast.'

The man went – not fast enough – into the stable and came out with both saddle and bridle. Hugh grabbed the bridle from him, flung a rein around Foix's neck to hold him where he was, stripped off the halter, and bridled Foix as fast as his suddenly clumsy fingers would let him. Foix shook his head and tried to back away and Hugh cursed him. The stableman, still not fast enough, made to throw the saddle on Foix but Hugh said, 'No, I haven't time,' and flung himself up and astride Foix's bare back, gathered the reins, swung him around, and set him into a gallop out of the yard.

Tom couldn't be far ahead. He'd know by now he was bleeding. He'd have stopped to deal with it. Over the first rise of the road he'd surely be in sight.

He wasn't. And beyond the rise the road curved and the forest came down to its edge, cutting off longer view, and Hugh, leaned low over Foix's neck, dug his heels harder into the horse's sides to set him faster. But Tom must have ridden with an anger that more than equaled Hugh's desperation because it was beyond there, after another rise of the road, that Hugh finally saw . . .

. . . not Tom. His horse. A bay, like Hugh's. Riderless. Grazing on the grassy verge beside Woodrim's wheatfield near a spreading oak tree that in harvest served the workers for shade when they broke for their dinner or rest times. But it was barley harvest now. There was no one in sight here. Not even Tom. Only his bay horse.

Confused, Hugh drew rein, bringing Foix to a halt beside the other horse. And only then saw Tom. Lying on his stomach in the long grass at the edge of the oak's deep shade, his head pillowed on one arm as if he might be sleeping, his face turned away from Hugh, who suddenly wanted to go no nearer.

But he slid from Foix's back and went toward him, saying unsteadily, 'Tom? What are you doing?'

He knelt and touched Tom's shoulder; said, 'Tom?' again; and then – all unwillingly – took hold of his shoulder and started to turn him over.

And knew by the body's utter slackness, even before he saw the dulled, empty-staring eyes, that Tom was no longer there.

Chapter 8

In the warm, clear-skied evening the nuns were come into the walled garden for their hour of recreation before Compline and bed. The sun was not yet set, Frevisse supposed, but it was gone below the cloister's roofs, leaving the garden in gentle evening shadows, the day's warmth lingering with the mingled scents of the summer fields beyond the nunnery walls and the garden's herbs and flowers.

Most of the younger nuns and Dame Emma were clustered on the turf benches near one another, heads together in busy talk. Dame Juliana, ever in love with flowers, was drifting from bed to bed, humming happily under her breath, touching her more treasured blooms, stooping now and again to smell one or another, sometimes plucking out a daring, doomed weed.

Dame Claire as infirmarian cared more for the herbs from which she made the nunnery's medicines than for merely flowers but this evening she was simply walking slowly, alone, back and forth along the path beside their beds, a sprig of some plant between her fingers and a thoughtful look on her face. She had been in talk with Margery, the village herbwife, today, Frevisse knew, and was maybe considering something newly learned from her. The powdered cinnamon and pepper mixed with honey they had tried last year against Dame Emma's toothache had not been a success but a vervain poultice they had devised two winters ago had worked well against an ulcerating sore on a villager's leg.

Tired from a day spent mostly at her copying work, Frevisse was pacing quietly back and forth along a different path, at the garden's far end and well away from the talking, Dame Juliana, and even Dame Claire. Oddly, Sister Thomasine was there, too, pacing the same path rather than at her prayers in the church, her pace and Frevisse's so nearly the same that they passed each other at almost the same point every time, never speaking or ever looking at one another. Over the years, Frevisse had come to trust Sister Thomasine's silences. Like Frevisse, she had no need for constant talk to reassure herself that she was real. Her intense piety was more than Frevisse could match, but for Frevisse the quiet of her own thoughts was company enough for now. Some people withdrew from the world into nunnery or monastery because either they had no other choices or they could not face what choices they had. Frevisse had become a nun not so much in withdrawal from the world as in a glad going toward God.

What had surprised her was how much, even in the nunnery, a day's necessities and duties got in the way of that going. She found herself, sometimes, regretting she did not have Sister Thomasine's gift for making a prayer of almost everything she did, but at least in little whiles like this, when she was alone and silent, she could go a small way toward where she wanted to be in her mind and heart.

The evening's quiet was stirred – not disturbed – by Ursula's laughter from the orchard beyond the garden's wall. Domina Elisabeth only sometimes spent the recreation hour in her nuns' company, preferring to be in solitude for the one hour of the day when no one was likely to need her for anything; but this evening, as often of late, she was with Lady Anneys and Ursula, and whatever their pastime in the orchard was, Ursula was very happy with it. Indeed, as the days had drawn on since Master Selenger's visit, Lady Anneys seemed happier, and a few times her own laughter rose from the orchard.

But in the garden, at its other end from Frevisse, the nuns' talk stopped and heads turned at sound of someone coming at a hurry along the slype from the cloister. A servant surely, but this far toward the day's end, with all business done, they were almost surely bringing trouble, and Sister Amicia and Sister Margrett sprang up and ran to the gate to meet whoever was there. By the uneven pad of the footsteps Frevisse had guessed it was lame Ela from the guesthall and was not surprised to see her at the gateway; but she only briefly asked something of Sister Amicia and Sister Margrett and immediately disappeared again. The rap a moment later on the orchard's gate told where she had gone, and Sister

Amicia turned back to the other nuns to say, disappointed, 'Just old Ela wanting Domina Elisabeth. Probably somebody's arrived she ought to know about.' But no one likely to divert them, her disappointment said.

Not needing to be diverted, Frevisse continued her slow pacing, content with her own thoughts about nothing in particular until the bell rang to Compline.

It was at next morning's chapter meeting they learned that, after all, it had been trouble that brought Ela into the cloister. After Father Henry had given his blessing and left them, Domina Elisabeth said with no other beginning, 'There was ill news came to Lady Anneys yesterday evening. Her older son was killed two days ago.'

While making the sign of the cross and murmuring a quick prayer for his soul, Frevisse tried to remember if the son she had met had been the older or younger one. Or had she ever known which he was?

'Her younger son brought word of it,' Domina Elisabeth was going on. 'He's here to take her and Ursula home again today.'

'How was he killed?' Dame Emma asked, more eagerly than seemly.

Domina Elisabeth fixed her with a look that warned her to silence, said crisply, 'That is something for later, dame,' and returned to the rest of them. 'They would be gone already except Lady Anneys has asked for one of us to go with her. That being the only comfort besides our prayers that we can offer her, I've agreed. Dame Frevisse, it was you she asked for. Sister Johane will go with you.' Because no nun should go from the nunnery uncompanioned by another nun. 'You are both excused to ready what you'll need and meet Lady Anneys in the guesthall yard in as few minutes as possible. Sister Johane, be guided by Dame Frevisse in this and on your journeying.'

Sister Johane, already eagerly on her feet, bobbed a deep, quick curtsy, ready to be out the door and not minding the hard looks turned her way by Sister Amicia and Sister Margrett, who probably felt that if Domina Elisabeth wanted a younger nun to go, they might equally well – nay, better – have been chosen. Frevisse, nothing like so ready to go out into the world for whatever reason, rose more slowly, her eyes down to keep her prioress from reading her unwillingness, and curtsied as deeply.

Domina Elisabeth made the sign of the cross toward them and said, 'My blessing on you both. Father Henry and I will be in the yard to see you away.'

Despite bishops' best efforts that nuns be kept strictly enclosed, they were not. Now and again some family matter or other reason – even simply fishing – would take them out of their cloister. As lately as last Martinmas Sister Margrett had gone, companioned with Dame Emma, to her sister's lying-in with a fourth child, stayed for the christening because she was to be godmother, and returned to St Frideswide's barely in time for Advent. Now, safely out of Domina Elisabeth's sight, Sister Johane all but bounced up the stairs to the dorter ahead of Frevisse. Only the sad reason for their going out probably kept her from outright singing, Frevisse suspected, while they gathered a change of clothing and what little else they would need; and she remembered to be at least outwardly subdued when she followed Frevisse out the cloister door into the guesthall's cobbled yard and with lowered eyes gave her bag to a servant to be strapped behind the saddle of one of the nunnery horses waiting for them.

Lady Anneys and Ursula were already on theirs, ready to leave, and Frevisse, giving over her bag in turn, saw with relief that the young man waiting with them was the same son who had come for Ursula those few weeks ago. The death of either of Lady Anneys' sons was a sorrow, but Frevisse knew this one a little while the dead man was no one to her, without even a face she could put to him in her prayers unless the chance came to see him unshrouded in his coffin. With no particular feelings of her own about him, no burden of personal sorrow, she would be more free to pay heed to curbing Sister Johane – should it come to that – and in giving what comfort she could to Lady Anneys and Ursula, she supposed. Just now, though, they both looked beyond comforting, and Hugh – that was his name, Frevisse remembered – looked no better. Ursula was mounted behind him, leaning against his back, the side of her face pressed to him, her arms tightly around his waist. Lady Anneys had her own horse but was close enough to her son that they were reached out to each other, holding hands as if that were their last hold on life. They had both been crying, that was plain, and Ursula still was, her eyes red and swollen, her cheeks shiny with tears. All the grief that Frevisse had not seen in Lady Anneys or her for their husband and father was terribly there now. That death had not hurt. This one did, and Frevisse foresaw that despite the golden sunshine of yet another perfect summer's day, today's riding was going to be dark with their pain.

She and Sister Johane had just swung astride their horses and were settling their skirts, neither of them interested in fashionable side-riding in box saddles, when Domina Elisabeth and Father Henry came from the cloister into the yard. The priest went to say something to Lady Anneys and the others. Domina Elisabeth came instead to Sister Johane, spoke too low to her for Frevisse to hear, then handed her a fair-sized, cloth-wrapped parcel that Sister Johane, nodding agreement to something, turned to tuck into the bag tied behind her saddle. Coming to Frevisse, Domina Elisabeth said, still in a low voice, 'I've given some herbs to Sister Johane that Dame Claire thought might be useful if Lady Anneys or anyone is too uncalm to sleep or rest.'

Domina Elisabeth's choice of Sister Johane to come with her suddenly made sense to Frevisse. All of the nuns helped Dame Claire, turn and turn again, at her infirmarian tasks, but of them all, Sister Johane had so far proved the most apt to the work. Very probably the comfort she could offer by way of soothing herbs would be worth as much or more than Frevisse's these following days, and Frevisse nodded to Domina Elisabeth with brisk understanding.

Domina Elisabeth gave a brisk nod in return and stepped back as Father Henry raised his hand to bless their journeying.

It proved to be a long, hard day's journeying. Frevisse remembered that when Hugh had come for Ursula, he had said that by rights it should take a day and a little more of reasonable riding to reach their manor. Today they did not ride reasonably. Rather than an easy, steady pace of no great haste, they went at trot or even canter more than half the time, easing the horses only when necessary and themselves hardly at all.

The choice did not seem to be Hugh's. More than a few times Frevisse saw him speak to Lady Anneys with concern on his face, but each time Lady Anneys shook her head against whatever he was asking her. Even when they stopped for a midday meal of sorts at some village's alehouse, Frevisse thought Lady Anneys would have stayed in the saddle to eat, except her son dismounted, lifted Ursula down, and came to help her so firmly that, although she hesitated, she did not refuse and, when she was dismounted, let him lead her to a bench in the shade by the alehouse door.

But if Lady Anneys did not want the respite, Frevisse most definitely did. She rode well but not often enough to be ready for this kind of riding and was willing to admit that her years were telling on her. It was only pride that kept her from groaning even more than Sister Johane did at the effort of pulling themselves back into their saddles when time came to ride on.

They rode through the afternoon and into the long, pale twilight, paused for a slight supper at another alehouse, then rode on into the darkening blue of evening. A rising moon gave light enough they hardly slowed their pace, but the servant who had come with Hugh rode on ahead to warn of their coming, and when they finally rode into the manor yard, there were people waiting and lighted torches flaring in the darkness. Hugh had long since moved Ursula to ride in front of him, cradled in the curve of his arm, and she must have been asleep because as the torchlight fell on her face, she startled upright with a small cry. Hugh said something to her and she answered, 'Home?,' then leaned against him, softly crying again.

A young man, who had gone first to Lady Anneys, turned to them and took Ursula from Hugh into his own arms. In the torchlight and Frevisse's tiredness, he looked so much like Hugh that he could have been his brother. But Lady Anneys had only two sons and one of them was dead, she thought a little confusedly. But whoever he was, Ursula clung to him as readily as she had to Hugh as he carried her away, into the house, leaving Hugh to dismount and help Lady Anneys from her saddle while two girls – as dressed in black as Lady Anneys and crying – hovered close, waiting only until Hugh stepped aside before they flung themselves at her, crying harder.

More daughters, Frevisse supposed.

Wearily, she dragged herself from her own saddle, lowering herself carefully to the ground and not letting go of the horse until she had convinced her legs that they not only had to hold her up but were going to walk, too. But now, please God, this day was nearly ended and soon there would be somewhere she could lie down and sleep.

As she followed Sister Johane following a servant toward the hall, she heard Lady Anneys say to someone in a tired and aching voice, 'Where's Tom? I want to see him.'

Chapter 9

In the morning Frevisse remembered, as she awoke, where she was and wished herself asleep again. She and Sister Johane had shared a truckle bed rolled from under Lady Anneys' own in an upper bedchamber, and although she had stayed awake and upright long enough to undress down to her undergown and fold her clothing onto a nearby stool, she had noticed nothing beyond that, simply lain down and fallen to sleep. She had awakened when Lady Anneys came in with her daughters but only enough to realize that beyond the bedchamber there was a room that must be theirs. Then she had slept again. Now it was morning, with nothing she looked forward to about the day.

Wary of her aches and stiffness, she sat up. Lady Anneys' bed had been slept in but she was not there now, and to judge by the open door and the quiet from the farther room, the girls were gone, too. That she had not heard them at all, as well as slept through her usual hours of prayer, told Frevisse how tired and deeply sleeping she must have been. Beside her, Sister Johane was still deeply sleeping and Frevisse took the chance to see better where they were. Someone had unshuttered the bedchamber's one, unglassed window before they left, letting in the gray light of an overcast day, letting her see not only the wide bed that nearly filled the room but its faded, plain green curtains and the two large, flat-topped chests set along one wall with a hunting dagger in its sheath lying on one of them. There was a small table beside the door with a pottery pitcher and basin and a white towel on it. A man's brown doublet and white shirt hung somewhat carelessly over the single wall-pole. Her own and Sister Johane's travel bags were leaning against the wall beside the truckle bed. That was all.

It was not so much a bare room, Frevisse thought, as a barren room. As if someone had been here but not lived in it. Except for the man's clothing and the dagger – the dead son's, she realized; he would have slept here as the manor's new lord, when his mother was gone – it was a room curiously empty of anyone. Even empty, a room usually carried some sense of who lived in it. This room was no one's. Admittedly the young man had maybe had too little time to make it fully his own, but even though Lady Anneys must have lived and slept here for years and very probably birthed her children here, there was nothing of her either and there should be. Embroidered cushions on the chests for softer sitting. A plant on the windowsill. Bright painted patterns on the plaster walls or on the roof beams. A woven mat on the floor. Something that said someone belonged here. But there was nothing. As if she had never been here at all.

Frevisse made to crawl out of the bed, deliberately clumsy at it so that Sister Johane awoke, mumbled, rolled over, awoke a little more, enough to open her eyes and say, pleased, 'We slept in. Wonderful. If we haven't missed breakfast.'

'We're late for Prime,' Frevisse answered.

'This morning?' Sister Johane protested. 'Now?'

'Now,' Frevisse said.

Sister Johane sighed heavily but made no other protest. They dressed and took their breviaries from their bags and, kneeling on either side of the truckle bed, set to the shortened Office that was allowed to nuns when traveling. Sister Johane, despite Frevisse's attempt to hold to a reasonable pace, rushed at the prayers and psalms, shortening the Offices more, reached the end with, '*Et fidelium animae per misericordiam Dei requiescant in pace. Amen*' – And the souls of the faithful through the mercy of God rest in peace – in a burst of speed, slapped her breviary closed, and was climbing stiffly to her feet before Frevisse had finished saying that final *Amen*. Another time Frevisse would have been irked into snapping at her for her haste – or, better, gently rebuked her – but just now the effort was too much and Frevisse let it go. Working her way to her own feet was trouble enough; but when Sister Johane headed for the stairs down to the hall while Frevisse was still slipping on her shoes, Frevisse said, 'Sister,' just quellingly enough that Sister Johane stopped, abashed, and waited, as was proper, for Frevisse to lead.

The overcast sky made judging the time difficult but there had been sounds enough, both from outside and downstairs, for Frevisse to think the morning was well begun. She found, upon opening the door at the stairfoot, that indeed breakfast had already happened for some, but a pitcher and the ample remains of a cold meat pie still waited at one end of the high table, and Lady Anneys, Ursula, and the two girls Frevisse presumed were her other daughters were standing nearby it. The gray day, the hall in its shadows, and their mourning dresses – that they had begun to wear for one death and now would wear for two – made for more gloom. But presently, mercifully, no one was crying.

Frevisse admitted the ungraciousness of that thought even as she had it. She was still weary from yesterday's ride, did not want to be here, did not know what was expected of her, and was altogether far from happy about anything. Was she supposed to give comfort to Lady Anneys? The woman had a son and three daughters who were surely better suited to that than a nun she barely knew. On yesterday's long ride, Frevisse had considered that she was maybe meant to be a guard for Lady Anneys against that man who had troubled her at the nunnery. But surely he wouldn't be so much a fool as to plague her with his attentions for this while.

There were no servants in sight but Ursula moved immediately to pour ale from the pitcher into two waiting cups while Lady Anneys said, weary-voiced but with attempted graciousness, 'My ladies, good morrow.' Though 'good' was probably the last thing the day seemed to her. She was pale and holding herself in the way of someone determined to go on despite a wound whose pain was almost overwhelming them. 'Would you please to meet my other daughters?' She gestured to the older of the girls. 'Lady Elyn.' Who was not so young as Frevisse had thought her by torchlight last night. She was not a girl but a young woman, and as she briefly curtsied, her mother said, 'She's wed to our neighbor Sir William Trensal.'

At mention of her husband, Lady Elyn turned away, stifling a sob.

'And this is Lucy,' said Lady Anneys.

A round-faced, half-grown girl who might have dimples when she smiled, Lucy made a curtsy and sniffed on tears that were not far from being shed.

Ursula, bringing the ale to Frevisse and Sister Johane, asked, 'Would you like some of the hare pie, my ladies?'

When they said they would, she returned to the table to cut it, and Frevisse asked Lady Anneys, 'How does it go with you this morning, my lady?'

'Not very well,' Lady Anneys answered quietly. 'And it will go worse. I have to warn you the crowner will be here shortly. He arrived late yesterday and stayed the night with our priest in the village. He'll hold his inquest here this morning, when he's viewed Tom's . . .' Her steadiness faltered. She took hold on it again and went on, '. . . when he's viewed Tom's body and the jurors have come.'

It was something that could not be avoided. A crowner's inquiry must always come after any unexpected or violent death, to determine where guilt lay or if there was guilt at all; and who, if anyone, should be arrested; and whether the sheriff must needs be called in; and what fines were due to the king. All that would be far too familiar here already this summer, Frevisse thought. To go through it again was surely nightmare added to nightmare for Lady Anneys. But she also thought, as she thanked Ursula for the thick wedge of pie the girl now handed to her, that by hearing the inquest she would learn everything about this Tom's death without need to ask questions of her own and that would be to the good, both for her curiosity's sake and as help in giving better comfort to Lady Anneys afterward.

Lucy was rubbing at her eyes, murmuring that they hurt. They were red and swollen and probably salt-scalded with tears and Lady Elyn pressed her fingers to the outer corners of her own eyes, which looked no better, and said, 'So do mine. We'll look dreadful for the inquest.' Trembling toward a new siege of weeping, Lucy nodded agreement with that.

The unkind thought crossed Frevisse's mind that besides their very real grief, they both were feeling very sorry for themselves at being so unhappy.

She was instantly sorry for that thought. Each person had to grieve in their own way, as best or worst, greatest or least they could; and very possibly their way was better than Lady Anneys' stiff, braced quiet, as if she hardly dared move for fear of the hurt in her despite it would come no matter what she did or did not do.

Sister Johane, putting down her emptied ale cup and her partly eaten piece of pie, said, 'Yes, your poor eyes. I have something that might help. An ointment that I brought. It's meant exactly for soothing sore eyes. I have it with my things. If you'll come to the bedchamber?'

Lucy nodded readily and Lady Elyn said, 'Oh, please, yes,' and Frevisse felt even more contrite. Sister Johane offered needed help, while all she had were unkind thoughts that were no use to anyone.

'Mother, you'll come, too?' Lady Elyn said as she and Lucy started toward the stairs with Sister Johane.

'Miles is here,' Lady Anneys said. 'He probably has something to tell me. You go on.'

They did; and with a word of apology to Frevisse, Lady Anneys went the other way, Ursula following her like a small shadow afraid of being lost, down the hall toward a man who had just come in, the one who looked so much like Hugh, with a tall, brindled wolfhound at his side. Frevisse, quite abruptly left to herself, took her first chance to look freely around her while finishing her breakfast. The hall was a plain one, bare-raftered and small, paved with plain stone and without even a screens passage at the far end, just the door to the yard at one side and another door opposite it, presumably to the kitchen and whatever rest of the house there might be. Just as in the bedchamber, everything was plain and well-worn, including the aged and ordinary high-backed chair meant for the lord of the manor here at the high table. The only thing beyond bare necessity was a rather poorly painted tapestry on the wall behind the table, with hunters and hounds striding stiff-legged across a green field strewn with flowers after an oddly proportioned deer leaping away from them toward a grove of scrawny trees.

Servants had come into the hall now. One of them was heading toward the high table, probably to clear the breakfast things away. The others were starting to shift benches from along the walls into rows across the middle of the hall, facing the table. Finished eating and not minded either to sit or return upstairs or join Lady Anneys still in talk at the hall's far end, Frevisse set down her cup for the servant to take and moved away toward the tall window at one end of the dais, out of everyone's way.

The shutters were open, letting in air soft with coming rain. It seemed they had been fortunate in fair weather for their traveling yesterday. She stood looking out at the manor's foreyard, still wishing she were elsewhere, until behind her someone said, 'My lady?'

She turned around to find it was the young man who had been in talk with Lady Anneys, his hound still with him. Seen close to and by daylight, he was leaner than Hugh and perhaps a little taller but with the same brown hair and eyes and general look about him, she thought, as he bowed and said, 'I'm Miles Woderove, Lady Anneys' stepgrandson. She's gone to be sure all's going well in the kitchen. She asked me to ask if there's anything you need or I could do for you.'

She looked at him, trying to decide if she dared ask what she wanted to know. He seemed the most calm, least grieved, of any of the family she had so far met, but as he looked steadily back at her, she took in the tight-drawn lines around his eyes, the thin line of his mouth, and judged that his calm was a shield he was barely keeping between himself and the world. So he was someone both controlled and deeply caring, and she said, though she had not thought it out beforehand, 'Tell me what you can of how things are here, if you please.'

His eyes flickered. Stiffly he asked, 'About Tom's death, you mean?'

'No. I'll hear enough and more than enough about that at the inquest. What I need to know . . . If I'm to help Lady Anneys at all, I need to have some thought of how things are, how they've been for her here.'

Either puzzled over what she meant or considering whether he should answer, Miles looked down at the dog beside him. From what little Frevisse knew of dogs, this was a very fine wolfhound, lean and long-legged like his master, alertly looking at her with dark, intelligent eyes, and so tall that Miles' hand rested on his head without effort.

'I've gathered,' Frevisse said carefully, feeling her way, 'that Lady Anneys doesn't much grieve for her husband's death.'

Miles' head snapped up. The calm was gone. 'Nobody grieves for Sir Ralph's death,' he said curtly. 'Even his own dog doesn't grieve for him. You want to help Lady Anneys? Help her forget my late, unlamented grandfather ever existed.'

Frevisse had not expected that much of an answer. Falling back on the obvious, she said, 'He wasn't a good man?'

Miles made a sound too harsh to be laughter. 'He was the human equivalent of something you'd scrape off the bottom of your shoe.'

Frevisse was so startled that she said, 'He's dead, and you still hate him that badly?'

'That badly and three times worse, my lady.'

If he could be so open, so could she. 'Why?'

'Why? Because he had pleasure in only two things. Hunting and being cruel to everyone around him. Now that he's gone, *I* enjoy being cruel about *him*.'

Frevisse had recovered enough balance by now to ask without showing particular feeling about it, 'You've come back here on visit, now that he's dead?'

Bitter laughter bent the corners of Miles' mouth upward into what could not be called a smile. 'I've never left, my lady. I tried. Twice. Once, when I was ten or so, I took off into the woods. He tracked me with hounds and beat me and brought me back. I tried again when I was fifteen and made a better go of it. That time he took three days to find me but brought men with him to hold me while he beat me. He said I was his heir and, by God's teeth, I was going to stay where he could see to me.' He shrugged, maybe to shrug off the memory and the anger, looked down at the hound, and said, his smile all bitterly twisted to one side, 'You shouldn't have set me on to this.'

She maybe should not have, but now that she had, she said, 'I thought Hugh's brother Tom was the heir.'

'To everything Sir Ralph had purchased with his ill-taken fortune from his lawyer days in London, yes. All of that except what Sir Ralph left to Hugh and the girls went to Tom. But there's a Leicestershire manor entailed from eldest son to eldest son to eldest son. That's me, the only son of Sir Ralph's only son by his first wife. Sir Ralph hated him, too.'

'Your mother is dead?'

'Long ago. Lady Anneys raised me.' Miles' voice and smile lost their bitterness when he named her.

It was good to know his hatred did not reach to everyone

around him and Frevisse asked, 'Was Sir Ralph cruel to her, too?'

Miles slightly frowned, almost as if considering a riddle. 'Sir Ralph would hit anyone else in his reach, even the girls – though rarely them and not Tom or Hugh or I since we grew big enough to hit back hard enough to make it count. But none of us ever saw him raise a hand against her. No, he never struck her. He never had much to do with her at all. She left him alone and he left her.'

But there were other ways than blows to hurt and ways of 'leaving alone' that could cut to the heart, Frevisse thought. Aloud, she only asked, 'There's been no word of who killed him?'

'None,' Miles said sharply. 'Nor no more searching either, I think. I hope they never catch who did it.'

'What about Tom? Was he like his father?'

'No.' Miles harshly refused that. 'Tom hated him, too. We all did. But Tom . . .' Miles broke off. There seemed easily enough hatred in him to include the man who had inherited so much that might have been his if Sir Ralph had been other than he was, but rather than anger, it was grief that twisted Miles' voice as he recovered and said, 'After Hugh, Tom was my best friend. I could strangle Sir William with my own hands for killing him.'

'Sir William?' She had just heard of a Sir William here, she thought.

Miles' spasm of grief was gone, the bitterness and anger back. 'Our near neighbor. Lady Elyn's husband.'

Yesterday, on the long ride to here, there had been no talk about Tom's death. Frevisse had supposed everything had been said the night before between Lady Anneys and Hugh and to Ursula, leaving them with only the grim need to reach home. Faced with that, neither she nor Sister Johane had asked anything. Now Frevisse wished they had, because there seemed to be far too many things she ought to know – and no chance to ask them because Miles was turning away from her to look out the window into the yard where harness-jangle and the thudding of hoofs warned riders had arrived. Three men and a girl, Frevisse saw when she looked out, too, as Miles drew in a hissing breath and stepped back, saying, 'St Anne help us. He's brought Philippa. My lady, *that* is Sir William and I doubt he has the good grace to wait in the yard until the crowner comes. Pray, excuse me.'

With a curt bow and not waiting for Frevisse's answer, he went away toward the outer door, the hound beside him. Left on her own, Frevisse watched the newcomers, more accepting of Lady Elyn's tears if her husband was indeed her brother's murderer but wondering why, if he was known to be Tom Woderove's murderer, this Sir William was riding free.

At least she could easily tell which of the three men he was. If his richer clothing – a long, high-collared, black houppelande and dark blue, brimless hat with a glinting, silver-set jewel pinned to it – and better horse – a black palfrey – had not told her, the speed with which one of the men with him, servant-dressed in simple doublet and hosen, dismounted and went to hold his bridle would have. And the girl, who must be Philippa, would be his daughter, Frevisse guessed. Not someone's wife, anyway, because her long, fair hair was bound back but covered by only a black veil pinned to a small hat's padded roll. A married woman or a widow like Lady Anneys would have worn a wimple that circled her face and hid her hair and been finished with a starched veil.

But the next moment Frevisse's heed went from the girl to the man now lifting her down from her side-saddle. The other man who had ridden in with Sir William.

Master Selenger.

What did Master Selenger have to do with Sir William? He looked to be in attendance on Philippa but was too well dressed to be only servant.

Frevisse was suddenly deeply annoyed to be so ignorant of everything and everyone here.

The newcomers' horses were being led away toward the stables and Master Selenger had led Philippa to Sir William, who was saying something to her. Though Frevisse could not see the doorway from where she stood, she guessed Miles was standing there, in their way, instead of going out to them, but if he meant some challenge to Sir William, he was forestalled by a half dozen more horsemen riding into the yard. Frevisse immediately judged them likely to be the crowner with his clerk and men, all dressed in a plain business way with loose surcoats over doublets and hosen and riding boots, and was disappointed that none of them was the one Oxfordshire crowner she knew. It would have been good to have a friend here.

Sir William and Master Selenger moved to meet them as they

dismounted; or rather, they moved to meet the man who dismounted and stepped forward from among them, leaving his horse for someone else to hold. He wore authority as openly as he wore his fullsomely cut surcoat of deep-dyed dark green and seemed to greet both Sir William and Master Selenger familiarly.

Philippa had stayed where she was, standing alone; but now Miles came into sight, likewise crossing the yard toward the crowner and his men, and he paused by her to say something. His anger toward Sir William seemed not to include her. Whatever he said, she answered with a nod, and when he reached to touch her shoulder briefly, she briefly raised her own hand to touch his before Miles went onward to the men and Philippa toward the hall.

Having seen how much anger was in Miles, his gentleness toward the girl surprised Frevisse, and surprised her the more because it was toward someone linked to the loathed Sir William. But Hugh had appeared from somewhere beyond the hall, crossing the yard to join the crowner and Sir William, reaching them at the same time as Miles and putting himself with what looked like purpose between Miles and Sir William as they all greeted the crowner. It might have been by chance but Frevisse thought it was deliberate. From where she stood she could not tell if Hugh had the same anger toward Sir William that Miles did, though Miles' rigid back was clear enough even from here.

The men spoke together for a few moments, then walked on toward the hall. Frevisse moved away from the window. Sister Johane, Lady Elyn, and Lucy were just returning to the hall. At its far end Lady Anneys, with Ursula still beside her, was in talk with a maidservant but finished and dismissed her as her daughters and Sister Johane approached her, Frevisse following behind them. But it was to Frevisse and Sister Johane she said, 'My ladies, you'd do well to take a place on one of the benches before more people come, I think. Besides our own folk there'll be neighbors surely, and whoever Sir William has brought, and the crowner's men and jurors. There are to be ten jurors, I'm told. Five men of ours and five from Sir William's manor. But . . .' Her flood of words suddenly stopped. She paused, bewildered, seemingly trying to remember why she had been saying any of that and why it mattered.

Frevisse, understanding the need to flee from overwhelming grief by clinging to practical things and how easy it was to stumble in that flight and be overtaken, hoped there was a strong quieting draught included in whatever Dame Claire had provided Sister Johane and that Lady Anneys could be persuaded to take it when this day was done; but for now she only said, 'There's no need to think about us, my lady. We'll do well,' and went away with Sister Johane to the last of the three bench-rows facing the dais. For the ease of whoever came later, she and Sister Johane sat in the middle of the bench they chose so it could fill in to either side of them. Two other long benches – for the jurors, Frevisse supposed – had been set at an angle between the dais with its high table and the bench-rows, and presently two manservants were wrestling a long settle through a door behind the dais that Frevisse presumed led to the parlor since the other door there led to the stairs to the bedchambers. Once through the door, the men brought the settle down from the dais, lurching a little with its weight, and set it behind the jurors' benches, facing the high table where the crowner would sit. That would be for Lady Anneys and her daughters, Frevisse guessed.

Not interested in benches, Sister Johane had twisted around to watch the outer door and said excitedly, 'Someone's arrived.'

'Sir William and the crowner,' Frevisse said. 'I saw them from the window.'

Sister Johane twisted back to say low-voiced and close to her, 'He's Lady Elyn's husband, did you know? Sir William, I mean. They've been married about two years and his daughter Philippa was going to marry this Tom who's dead. That's why he was at Sir William's. To talk about the marriage. Only they quarreled and Sir William killed him by mistake, Lady Elyn says.'

'Is that why Lady Elyn is here instead of with her husband? Because he killed her brother?'

'Oh, no, not at all. She says nobody blames Sir William. It was a mistake. She's here because, well, she was needed here more than there, with her mother being gone and all.' Sister Johane broke off and twisted around again to see what was happening.

Frevisse somewhat turned, too. The crowner, companioned with Miles, was greeting Lady Anneys where she stood with her daughters beside her not far inside the hall door. She gave him her hand and he bowed over it and spoke briefly to her before going on toward the dais with Miles, followed by a man who was probably his clerk, carrying a leather bundle of probably papers.

Sir William had come in behind them and now stepped forward, his hands held out to Lady Anneys, his voice carrying as he said, 'Lady Anneys, I'm sorry beyond words for this. It was all . . .'

Lady Anneys, rigid, snatched her hands away from him and pressed them together over her heart. Sir William, his own hands still out, pleaded, 'Lady Anneys, please. For Elyn's sake if nothing else, don't turn this to a quarrel between us. I never meant—'

She interrupted, her voice carrying as clearly as his. 'It isn't a quarrel between us, Sir William. All the anger in this world won't bring Tom back to me. But I can't . . . I won't take the hand that held the knife that killed my son.'

Sir William looked down at his out-held right hand with the surprise of a man seeing a thing in a way he never had until now. Then he withdrew it, took a step back from her, and stiffly bowed. Lady Anneys as stiffly bowed her head to him in return and stood staring over his shoulder at nothing, waiting for him to go away. He looked at Lady Elyn and held out his hand to her. After a bare moment of hesitation and a flicker of her eyes toward her mother, she took it and he led her up the hall to the front bench.

In Frevisse's ear, Sister Johane whispered, 'Lady Elyn said her mother told her she must go with Sir William when the time came. She said Lady Anneys said there wasn't choice to make between her husband and family. That they were wed and that was what she had to do.'

To Frevisse that spoke well of Lady Anneys, but now she was faced by Master Selenger and the girl Philippa, come in together behind Sir William. Master Selenger looked ready to speak to Lady Anneys but Philippa was hesitating, uncertain whether she should do that or go immediately after her father. Lady Anneys, paying Master Selenger no heed at all, held out both her hands to the girl and said tenderly and smiling, 'Philippa,' and with a grateful gasp Philippa moved quickly to take her hands, holding tightly to them and saying something too low to be heard. Lady Anneys answered quietly, too, then let her go, with a crisp nod and nothing else at Master Selenger, letting him know to keep his distance. He bowed silently and moved off with Philippa, taking her to sit on her father's other side from her stepmother before seating himself on the bench directly behind them.

Since Sister Johane seemed to have learned a great deal in the while she was tending to Lady Elyn and Lucy, Frevisse whispered to her, 'Who is Master Selenger?'

'Who?'

'The man who came in with Philippa just now?'

'Oh. I don't know.'

'What does Lady Elyn say about having a stepdaughter not much younger than she is?'

'Not anything to me. They all grew up together, I think. Philippa and Lady Elyn and the others. So they know each other and all.'

Frevisse wondered whether that would make it harder or easier among them. And how difficult was it for Philippa to sit there beside her father, who had killed the man she was supposed to marry?

'The two families were close until now?' she asked.

'I gather so. Sir William and Sir Ralph were friends, from what Lucy was saying. They both loved hunting. Sir William and Lady Anneys are both executors of her husband's will and that makes all this even worse because how are they ever going to deal together now?' She broke off as Hugh entered beside a shuffling old man in a priest's black gown, then said, 'That will be Father Leonel. Lady Elyn says he's useless as a priest but that was what her father wanted, not somebody who'd try to change him. Lucy said she shouldn't talk like that about their father or priests but Elyn said it's the truth and she'll say it if she wants to.'

Miles returned to Lady Anneys from seeing the crowner to the dais just as Hugh and the priest joined her. They all spoke low-voiced together and seemed to agree on something before Hugh went back outside and Miles, with Lady Anneys, Lucy, and Ursula following, led Father Leonel to the end of a bench near the settle. While the priest seated himself with the carefulness of stiff joints, Lady Anneys took her place on the settle with Lucy on one side of her and Ursula on the other and Miles took his place standing at the settle's end, looking ready to do whatever Lady Anneys might need but also able from there to see whatever else went on in the hall.

Hugh and one of the crowner's men came in with ten men. The inquest's jurors. Five men from each manor, Lady Anneys said. They were all solemn and well-scrubbed, well-combed, and wearing their best clothes – plain, belted tunics in dull reds, blues, greens, browns, and loose hosen. They bowed to the crowner seated behind the high table where his clerk was laying out papers in front of him, and took their places on the benches set for them. Watching them, Frevisse saw there was no mistaking which five went together against the other five. Cold shoulders and wary looks told more than enough and for the first time Frevisse thought beyond the grief of the young man's family to the raw possibility of open enmity between one manor's folk and the other's because of it. It was not usual for lesser folk to serve on a jury against someone like Sir William but here it might well be best because a decision reached among them would more likely be accepted on both manors.

Once they were sitting, however grudgingly with each other, the crowner looked down the hall and nodded to someone and a moment later people in quantity began to enter. They must have been gathering in the yard ever since Frevisse left the window. Neighbors, she judged – other gentry like Sir William and the Woderoves; mostly men, a few women. They filled the benches quickly. Two men with polite bows took the place to Frevisse's right; a husband and wife sat to Sister Johane's left. Later comers were directed by some of the crowner's men to places along the side of the hall across from Lady Anneys and her daughters, and then the common folk were let in. They crowded quietly in, filling the hall's end behind the benches. Manor folk, Frevisse decided with a quick look back at them. There were both sorrow and inheld anger in their faces. They were here to know for certain what had happened to their young lord and ready to make trouble over his death if things came to that. And that told Frevisse much more about Tom Woderove than the little she knew, because while it was one thing for his family to grieve his death, it was something more for people whose lives had been under his rule for ill or good to grieve for him, too.

From what she had so far heard, she doubted they had grieved for his father.

The crowner's clerk, a solid, middle-aged man, stood up at the end of the high table and announced the inquest would now begin, bowed to the crowner with 'Master Hampden,' sat down, took up a quill pen, and waited with it poised over an inkpot, paper ready in front of him.

The inquest went the usual way, with statements as to where it was and why and whose death was in question. It was established that Sir William Trensal and Hugh Woderove – now Master Woderove since his brother's death – were the only witnesses, besides the deceased, to the actual occasion of the death. Master Hampden averred that he had viewed the body and that the only wound on it was a small cut to the right side of the neck that had been sufficient to sever a blood vessel. The deceased had then bled to death.

Lady Anneys, her head already bowed, shuddered. Ursula buried her face against her mother's shoulder and Lucy openly sobbed. Lady Anneys put her arms around them.

There were no other marks or wounds upon the body, Master Hampden said, and Hugh was called forward to describe what had happened.

Frevisse, listening while Hugh told what had passed between his brother and Sir William, watched Lady Anneys and her daughters listening, too, and ached with how pointless the death had been. Pointless and, it would seem, never intended.

'You believe, from what you saw,' Master Hampden asked when Hugh had told of seeing the blood on Sir William's penknife, 'that Sir William was surprised to see the blood? That he had had no knowledge until then that he had stabbed your brother?'

'I believe that, yes,' Hugh said. 'He looked surprised to find he was still holding the knife. Nor did he stab Tom. He . . .' Hugh made a gesture. 'He just swept a hand at him like that. To make him back off.'

'Which Master Woderove did.'

'Yes. '

'Did he show any sign of knowing he was hurt?'

'No.'

'You saw no blood on him at the time?'

'No. He was wearing a dark red doublet. It must have hid that he was bleeding, and I was standing on the other side of him anyway. And he wasn't there long. He said an angry thing or two more at Sir William and stormed out.'

'What happened then?'

'Sir William and I said a few things at each other. Then he saw the blood on his penknife and I knew Tom was hurt and went after him.'

'You overtook him before he reached home?'

'I saw his horse grazing at the roadside maybe a quarter mile from the yard here.'

'And your brother? When did you see him?'

'Not until I was nearly to him. He was stretched out in the shade of a tree there. He was lying down, face down, his head resting on one crooked arm. I thought he was sleeping. I thought . . .' For the first time the young man's stiff attempt to say what he knew but feel nothing while he said it broke down. 'I don't know . . . what I thought,' he fumbled. 'Then I turned him over and saw he was . . . dead.'

Lady Elyn broke into open sobs. Lucy in the circle of her mother's arm and Ursula huddled against Lady Anneys' other side could cry no harder than they were, but Lady Anneys sat with lifted head, looking dry-eyed at her son. Only the pleading in her haunted eyes begged for it to be over soon. Frevisse saw Master Hampden glance toward her before going on to ask what Hugh had done next.

'I cried out. I stood up and I shouted for help.'

'Who were you shouting to?'

'No one. Anyone who could hear me.'

'There was no one there who might have seen your brother fall?'

'I didn't see anybody.'

'But somebody came?'

'Finally. From one of the further fields where they were barley-harvesting. Somebody heard me and some of the men came and we carried Tom home.'

'But they hadn't heard or seen anything before then?'

'No.'

'Are those men here?'

Hugh moved one hand toward the jurors. 'There. In front.'

The five men on the nearest bench acknowledged that with nods.

'So you were first-finder of the body but they came immediately afterwards.'

'Yes.'

'What did you do then?'

The questions and answering went on, through sending one of the men running for Father Leonel while the others carried the body to the hall, to sending one of the manor men to Sir William to tell him Tom was dead and to bring Lucy and Lady Elyn back to Woodrim to sending another manor man away to find out and tell the crowner he was needed.

'You didn't send or go yourself to seize Sir William,' Master Hampden said. 'Why?'

Hugh had to have known that question would come. By law and under penalty of fine, the first-finder of a body, when the murderer was known, had to raise the hue and cry and, joined by everyone who heard him, pursue the murderer. If taken, the murderer was then to be held until the crowner came and claimed him into custody. But firmly Hugh said, 'I saw no likelihood Sir William would seek escape. He knew and I knew that he never meant harm to Tom. It was chance and nothing else that Tom . . . died.' He choked on the word and for the first time bent his head, tears thick in his voice.

Master Hampden drew a penknife from under the papers in front of him, laid it on the open palm of his hand, and held it out for Hugh to see. 'Is this the penknife you saw in Sir William's hand when your brother was wounded?'

Hugh raised his head and looked. 'Yes.'

Master Hampden asked the jurors if they had any questions of their own for him. They did not and Master Hampden thanked him and bade him sit down.

Sir William was next. He was solemn, as well he should be, but he carried himself assuredly. To the crowner's questions he said much the same things as Hugh had. That he had asked Master Woderove to come to him in order to discuss the planned marriage. That they had somehow fallen into a quarrel, Sir William was not sure how. 'One nothing thing leading to another. That was all. He had his father's hot humour and Sir Ralph could go into a fury over things most men would not.'

There was general head-nodding agreement from the Woodrim

manor men of the jury and among the onlookers. Master Hampden noted it. It was his task to learn as much as he could about what had happened and where blame should be laid, if blame there should be, and because he had the right of inquest, he had the power to ask all the questions he could think to ask and to expect answers for them under oath; but he was also expected to make use of anyone who best knew the accused and victim, to better understand what might lie behind and around the actual crime itself. So the jury was made of local men and a competent crowner gave them heed.

Frevisse had known a crowner who, unless forced to it, never bothered with more than his own opinion of who the guilty should be. He had been a dangerous man in his narrow way and she was thankful to find that Master Hampden was a different sort.

He was come now to the moment Sir William had struck at Tom. 'He leaned toward you and you swept your hand with the penknife in it at him. Is that what you say?'

'And that I'd forgotten I was holding the knife, yes.'

'Were you frightened at that moment? Did you fear he was going to attack you?'

'No, sir, I was not frightened. He was angry, he was leaning too close, I wanted him to stand back. That was all. I never meant even to touch him. I didn't know I had.'

'But you admit that you did?'

'I must have but I was unaware of it at the time.'

Outside the day had grown grayer and the rain begun to fall, soft as weary weeping. The questioning went on. Sir William readily admitted the penknife was his own, the one he had had that day, and agreed that, yes, it was very sharp; penknives had to be able to trim tough quills to usable points.

'What did you do after Master Woderove and then his brother left you?' Master Hampden asked.

'I called one of my servants to saddle my horse and set out after them both, to find out how badly Tom . . . Master Woderove was hurt. I meant to apologize, before the matter could fester into something worse.'

'You were not angry?'

'I was irked it had come to this. A petty quarreling for no good reason except he was young and hotheaded. But I was not angry. I simply wanted to end it before it worsened.'

'In regard to Master Woderove's death, what would you say you're guilty of?'

'Of misadventure,' Sir William replied firmly. 'I didn't strike at him with intent to hurt, much less to kill. I didn't mean to strike him at all.'

Master Hampden gave the jurors their turn to ask whatever questions they might have, but they had few and Sir William was permitted to sit again. They asked to see and handle the penknife and then talked among themselves, twisted around on the benches, heads close together, and Frevisse noted the stiff wariness among them was gone. When they had finished and all faced forward again, Master Hampden asked if they had come to a conclusion and one of the Woodrim men stood up to say that to all their minds Master Woderove's death had been by misadventure. The other jurors all nodded their agreement and after that everything was nearly done. Master Hampden asked if there were three men here who would stand bond for Sir William to appear at the next county court. Five men among the onlookers stood up. Master Hampden accepted all five, told them to speak to his clerk, and declared the court ended.

People who had been standing began shifting from where they stood. Those who had been sitting began to stand up, Sir William among them. He turned to say something to the men behind him. He would almost surely be found guilty of lesser manslaughter at the county court and somewhat fined for it, but from everything that had been said here, he had no great guilt in Master Woderove's death. So far as the law was concerned, the matter was all but done. All that was left, Frevisse thought as she stood up along with everyone else, was for the two families to come somehow to peace with each other and to terms with their grief. If there had been outright murder done, there would have been a harsh sundering of one kind or another – outright rage at Sir William and maybe crude satisfaction for his punishment – but because it had been mischance, not murder, somehow, for the sake of everyone, there would be healing.

At least Frevisse, watching Lady Elyn rise and go to her mother, prayed there would be.

Chapter 10

The crowd thinned as the manor folk shifted out the door. The rain was still lightly falling, barely enough to dampen anyone or harm the harvest-ready crops, but there would have been no work in the fields today even without the inquest and the manor folk were not heading out to work again, merely removing themselves now that they were satisfied about their lord's death. Some of the neighbors and others who had come were in talk with Sir William; others were going to Hugh; the five men who had offered to stand bond for Sir William were with the crowner's clerk at the high table; most of the women were gathering toward Lady Anneys.

Beside Frevisse, Sister Johane said, 'At least it's over.'

The inquest was, Frevisse thought; but nothing else. 'When will the funeral be?' she asked.

'I think we're meant to go from here to the church for it.' Sister Johane lowered her voice and leaned close to say, 'It's been four days.' As if it were a secret that burial now would be best since no body would keep for long in this warm weather.

Frevisse made no answer. She was watching Sir William excuse himself from the men with whom he had been in talk and went toward Lady Anneys. Miles, seeing him, too, moved to Lady Anneys' side. Frevisse, finding herself very interested in what would be said among the three of them, went, with Sister Johane following her, to join the cluster of people drawing away to either side to let Sir William reach Lady Anneys, who stood stiffly looking at him, saying nothing when he stopped in front of her.

'Lady Anneys,' he said, holding out his hand as he had before, 'let it end here?'

'Let what end here?' she said back at him. 'My son's death?'

Sir William did not withdraw his hand. 'I'm acquitted of guilt in that.'

'You're acquitted of willful guilt,' Lady Anneys said quietly. 'You never purposed Tom's death. I accept and believe that. I hope in return you'll accept that my pain is still too new for me to be willing toward peace with you.' She looked down at his out-held hand. 'And that is still the hand that killed my son.'

Sir William had begun to redden above his collar. He drew his hand back. 'We can't ignore each other. By Sir Ralph's will you and I must—'

'Work together. I know. But not for this while. Not soon.'

Sir William's color deepened. Frevisse suspected he was not used to being interrupted or refused, and Lady Anneys had just done both.

At Lady Anneys' side, Miles said – as quietly as Lady Anneys but with warning below the words, 'Leave it, Sir William.'

Sir William's eyes narrowed with the anger he had been holding back from Lady Anneys, but Hugh slipped between people to his side and said calmly, respectfully, 'Master Hampden asks leave to speak with you, if you please, Sir William.'

Sir William turned his head, looking as ready to snap at Hugh as at Miles, except that Hugh added, 'And Philippa would like to speak with my mother, if she may.'

As Lady Anneys said with warm affection, 'Of course she may speak with me,' Sir William's angry look went to Philippa standing just behind Hugh, then shifted quickly back and forth between them, his anger giving way to some other thought, and with a curt bow of his head to Lady Anneys, he stepped from Philippa's way and went toward the crowner at the high table. A look passed between Hugh and Miles, agreeing on something before Hugh followed Sir William, and Miles turned to talk with several men nearby. Lady Anneys, keeping one arm around Ursula, took Philippa by the hand with her other hand and drew her close so they could talk with their heads close together, leaving Lady Elyn and Lucy to the other women come to offer their comfort and regrets. Sister Johane shifted to join them, but Frevisse drifted away in Sir William and Hugh's wake with some vague purpose of speaking at least briefly to the crowner.

That proved easier than she had supposed it might. Whatever

Master Hampden had to say to Sir William was short. Well before Frevisse was near, Sir William had gone on along the table to where the five men who were to stand his bond were signing papers for the clerk and pressing their seals to wax. Hugh in his turn said something to Master Hampden, who answered him and then Hugh went away, too, toward the hall's outer door where Father Leonel was waiting for him.

Taking her chance, Frevisse stepped onto the dais across the table from Master Hampden, who was now gathering together his papers. He looked up, gave a slight bow in answer to the respectful bending of her head to him, and asked, 'May I help you, my lady?'

'I'm Dame Frevisse of St Frideswide's priory.'

'I know of it. A worthy house. You're here as comforter to Lady Anneys, I believe.'

She slightly bent her head to him again, admitting that but saying, 'I met one of your fellow crowners a few years ago. Master Christopher Montfort. I wondered if you could tell me how he does?'

Master Hampden smiled. 'Young Christopher. Yes. I saw him two weeks or so ago. He was in fine health and doing well. He's to be married close on to St Edward's Day, I hear.'

Frevisse expressed her pleasure at that and said, before Master Hampden could excuse himself or else his clerk come to rescue him, 'I'm here because Lady Anneys was visiting her youngest daughter at the priory when word came of her son's death. As you said, Sister Johane and I hope to give what help and comfort we can. Our trouble is that we hardly know the family and fear we're as likely to say the wrong thing as the right in trying to comfort her. We don't want to pry among the servants to learn more and know no one else to ask. Could you, as someone outside it all, tell me something about Lady Anneys' husband's death and how things seem to you here, so we'd have a better chance of giving help instead of hurt?'

Master Hampden considered that with a slight, not unfriendly frown. Farther along the table Sir William and the other men had finished their business with the clerk and were going away. The clerk, gathering up his papers, pens, and ink, was watching with a careful eye to see if Master Hampden wanted rescuing or not, and with a small lift of one hand, Master Hampden let him know no rescue was needed yet before saying to Frevisse, 'I can willingly tell you everything that's generally known. Come aside and we'll talk.'

They went along their opposite sides of the table, Master Hampden pausing to say a few words to his clerk before meeting Frevisse at the window, much where she had stood in talk with Miles. By then Master Hampden had a question of his own and asked, 'How much do you know, or understand, about the Woderove family?'

'I've gathered that Sir Ralph was its head. Miles is his grandson and heir by a first son long dead, by a first wife also long dead. Lady Anneys is Sir Ralph's second wife and by her he had two sons and three daughters that I know of. The eldest daughter is married to Sir William. Sir Ralph was murdered earlier this summer, no one knows by whom. All I've heard is that he was killed while hunting. What I know about Tom Woderove's death I heard here, just now, but he seems mourned by everyone while no one seems grieved for Sir Ralph at all.'

She stopped and waited and Master Hampden said, 'You have all of that right, especially about Sir Ralph. The inquest on his death was very different from this one. You can see the grief there is for Master Woderove. I don't think anyone at all minded Sir Ralph was dead. The suddenness of his death had them thrown off balance but there was no grief.'

'Why?' Although, after talk with Miles, she had some thought about that.

'He seems to have been a brutal man. As part of finding out who might have wanted him dead I asked about him elsewhere as well as here. There was no good report to be had of him anywhere except somewhat from Sir William, who was as near to a friend as he had, I gather. They had both been lawyers and shared a love for hunting. Aside from that, the only other person Sir Ralph even somewhat got on with was his son Hugh – Master Woderove as he is now that his brother is dead. He served as his father's huntsman and saw to his hounds. He inherited them at his father's death, I believe. For the most part, though, Sir Ralph was careless about people. Or maybe he was deliberately cruel. I think "cruel" is the correct word in his case. I only ever met him in passing and have had mostly to go by what I gather from other people. Either way, there was no mourning for him here. In helping Lady Anneys, it's only her son's death you need worry for and about that you know as much as everyone.'

Her son's death, yes, Frevisse silently agreed; but there were surely also years-old wounds left by a man careless of everybody but himself. Lady Anneys had hardly had chance to begin to heal from those before this new wound came. And not only Lady Anneys. From even the little Frevisse had so far seen and heard here, she could guess that still-raw hurts ran deep in probably everyone ever in Sir Ralph's reach. It wasn't only her own pain with which Lady Anneys had to deal, but her broken family's, worse broken now with Tom Woderove's death just when there had been hope of healing.

Quickly, because Master Hampden was readying to make his excuse to be done with her, Frevisse asked, 'Sir Ralph, then, was well disliked outside his family as well as in?'

'He was disliked by almost anyone who ever had to deal with him, yes.'

'And outright hated by some?'

Master Hampden hesitated before answering carefully, 'I'd say so, yes.'

'But you've no one to suspect more than another for his death?'

'Not yet, no. There was a man driven off the manor by Sir Ralph a year ago. I was told he was in no danger of Sir Ralph bothering to find him and force him back, but we found him out anyway, on the chance he'd come back for revenge.'

'Had he?'

'He's found work in an inn's stable off Kettering way, looks likely to marry the owner's daughter, and blesses the day he left here. Nor could my man find that he'd been away for even a day this summer, let be the time he'd need to come back here and lie in wait on the chance of finding Sir Ralph alone. Now, if you'll pardon me, my clerk wants me for something.'

He parted from her graciously but firmly nor did she try to keep him. She gave him thanks and let him go and stood alone, looking out the window and thinking. Lady Anneys' husband had been disliked to the point of hatred. By his grandson certainly and by others undoubtedly, so many that the crowner had no one in particular to suspect of his death. What did she remember hearing about how he had died? That he had been found dead in the woods, his head smashed in? Was that what someone had said at the nunnery? If that was all, it told her almost nothing. He had been hunting, been separated from others who had been hunting with him, and found dead. Had he happened to be alone or had he been on purpose, maybe secretly to meet someone who had then killed him? Or had someone been lurking in the woods, hoping for the chance to kill him and taking the chance when it came their way? Or had it been pure happenstance – someone had happened on him when he was alone and killed him because the chance was suddenly there? Surely the crowner had tried to learn of any recent quarrel that could have brought someone to murder. Or did Sir Ralph have so many quarrels there was no way to point at one before another as possibly the cause?

And what business was it of hers?

It wasn't. Except that she was here and she doubted, knowing herself, that she would let go of it so long as there was chance of having an answer.

She looked down the hall at the gathering of family, manor folk, and neighbors and knew it was not simply curiosity in her. Very probably a wound or wounds given by Sir Ralph had festered in someone's mind into murder and as with any wound that festered and went bad there would be no healing until the wound was cleansed, which in this would be by finding out the murderer.

Even if, as was all too likely, the murderer was someone here.

The rain fell lightly, steadily, all through the funeral and the afternoon, and Hugh felt much like the weather – gray and weeping, despite he had no outward tears. Partly his lack of outward grieving was simply that he was tired almost past thinking. Tom's death, followed by two days of hard riding to bring Mother and Ursula back from the priory, then keeping the vigil beside Tom's body all last night because Miles had kept it the night before and one of them at least should sleep . . . With all of that, the best he could do with his howling grief was keep it buried until there was time and place to give way to it. But time and place wouldn't come today, and all through today, from somewhere aside from it all, he had watched himself doing what needed to be done, heard himself being a comfort to his mother and sisters and grateful to everyone who offered their consolations; had listened to himself making needed decisions and saw himself move with apparent purpose through the hours of a day five times longer than any day he could remember.

But finally it was done. Everyone who was not staying was gone and he was standing alone at the hall's tall window, watching a watery yellow sun slide below thinning gray clouds toward a damp sunset. It was all over.

Except it would never be over.

Tom was never coming back.

By the soft footfall he knew it was Ursula behind him and he did not turn around but waited until she slipped her small hand into his before he looked down at her and tried a smile. It was a smile as thin and damp as the sunset, but so was hers and neither of them said anything as she leaned against him, clinging to his hand with both of hers and rubbing her face on his sleeve, the silence maybe as comforting to her as it was to him.

It could not last. Comforts so rarely did, and much too soon Ursula said, 'Mother wants to see you, Hugh. She's in her garden.'

'Now?' With evening coming on at the end of a wet day, a dripping garden was hardly the best of places, surely. But even as he questioned it, Hugh knew why she was there. Her garden was her place of comforting. He could not remember his father going into it even once, just as she had never, in Hugh's memory, ever gone on any hunt.

But it was still no place to be when night vapors would soon be rising and he kissed the top of Ursula's head and said, 'I'll bring her in. Where are you going to be? Where's Lucy?'

'In the parlor with the nuns. We're going to have a cold supper there.'

'That's good. I'll bring Mother.'

He found Lady Anneys standing at the garden's rear gate, looking out across the cart-track and the stubbled hayfield where the cattle would be turned to graze come frost time. He joined her without a word, and much the way Ursula had done, she took his hand. She was not crying nor did she lean against him like Ursula but stayed standing straight and gazing outward. Dark was coming quickly on, bringing chill with it, but despite what he had told Ursula, Hugh did not try to draw her inside. He guessed that, like his little while in the hall, this was her pause before taking up life again in its new, unwanted shape, and he was willing to wait as long as she needed until she was ready – or able – to say why she had sent for him.

But what she said when finally she spoke was, quietly, 'At this hour three days ago I had just lately finished praying at Vespers for my children's safety and good health. That day and all the next I was thinking of Tom as alive and he was already dead.'

Not knowing what to say, not trusting his voice, Hugh held silent.

His mother looked at him with a smile both tender and bleak. 'I haven't been able to pray. Nothing beyond "God keep his soul" and a rather desperate thanks that I still have you and Miles.'

'And the girls.'

'And the girls. But I'm thinking of sons just now.'

Her eyes were fixed on his face, as if to be certain of it past ever forgetting. He looked away, out into the gray-blue mist and evening shadows now hiding the far end of the hayfield. 'I can't pray at all,' he said. 'Not even as much as you've done.'

She squeezed his hand. 'It will come back. Even feeling will come back, though I think I'd rather it didn't. I don't think I want to feel again.'

Hugh made a small, assenting sound. The fierceness of his first grief had torn him into shreds with pain. After that, dealing with necessities had brought on a numbness he feared to lose despite he knew it would not last.

Lady Anneys was still looking at him. He went on gazing into the gathering darkness, willing her to say nothing else, to leave them where they were for just a little longer.

'You're Master Woderove now,' she said.

Hugh hoped his shudder – as if someone had walked on his grave – did not show. 'People kept calling me that all day. I kept thinking they were somehow talking to Tom.'

'Tom's place is yours now.'

'I *know*.' Hugh kept the words muted but not the anguish in them. He snatched his hand from hers, put both his hands to his face, and rubbed at the pain behind his eyes. 'I know, and I would to God it wasn't.'

His mother's only reply was to lay a hand on his shoulder. For a time they stood in silence, his face hidden behind his hands. Only finally did he drop one to his side and put the other on his mother's still resting on his shoulder. Keeping his voice even but fooling neither of them, he said, 'The rain today wasn't enough to hurt the fields. Tomorrow looks to be fair. Maybe we can get on with the harvest by afternoon.'

Chapter 11

Through the next few days Frevisse found herself oddly more alone in the midst of Woodrim's household bustle than ever she was able to be in St Frideswide's cloister. At St Frideswide's she had place and duties. Here she had neither, except to keep Lady Anneys company, and even that seemed purposeless because Lady Anneys, with a household to bring back into balance and order, hardly seemed in need of company besides her own people here and her children. She had no idle time to fill nor did she seem in want of comforting talk. If she had, Father Leonel could probably have given it as well as anyone. He made daily visits to the hall, and from what she saw of him, Frevisse judged that, elderly and slow a-foot though he certainly was, he was not feeble of mind. But Lady Anneys never made more than ordinary talk with him. The while he was there each evening was spent with Hugh, showing him how the manor's accounts were ordered.

It was hard going for both of them. Frevisse gathered from what she heard around her that the dead Sir Ralph had given all his time and heed to hunting, while his elder son had had the running of the manor and his younger son had seen to the hounds and huntsman's duties. Now Father Leonel was trying to show Hugh in short order all that his brother had learned and known over years, and Hugh did not seem happy at it.

Things were easier, Frevisse supposed, for Miles. As woodward, overseeing the forest both for the hunting there and for what profits could be had from it, his duties were not changed at all and he and his hound were away into the forest early and for most of every day, so that Frevisse had seen very little of him since the inquest. He sometimes returned to the hall for midday dinner but usually was only there in time for supper and afterward stayed near Hugh and Father Leonel while they worked in a corner of the parlor and Lady Anneys made Lucy leave them alone.

'Master Woderove really doesn't want to be lord here, does he?' Sister Johane said as she and Frevisse walked back from Mass in the village church their fourth morning at the manor. 'Lucy says Lady Anneys says he's well-witted and that Father Leonel worked the accounts for years with Tom and will show him all he needs to know. But he doesn't even like to be called Master Woderove. Have you noted that?'

Frevisse had. In truth, Hugh all but flinched when called Master Woderove, and Father Leonel, from forgetfulness or kindness, mostly said 'Master Hugh' when they worked together.

But Sister Johane, pleased to have so much new to talk about after the small, same things of the nunnery, was going on, 'Lucy hopes her mother will make a marriage for her soon. She says it's impossible having Lady Elyn for a sister now Lady Elyn is married and all. She has all the power to settle her children's marriages. Lady Anneys, I mean. Her husband gave it to her in his will. Even her sons' marriages. Well, just Master Woderove's now, of course.'

'Not Miles'?' Frevisse asked, no more than mildly curious.

'Not Miles'. Lucy says she thinks Sir Ralph just hoped Miles would rot. She says . . .'

Lucy seemed to say a great deal, but despite the haste of Sister Johane's tongue, Frevisse did not hurry their walk. At least the weather, after the funeral day's rain, was turned dry and late-summer warm, as perfect as could be wished for the harvest, now moved on to the wheatfield, Frevisse understood. They were nearly to the foreyard and she was wondering rather longingly how the harvest was going at St Frideswide's when Sister Johane chatted brightly, 'Everything is much better here since Sir Ralph died, you know. Everyone is sorry about Tom being dead but everybody's glad about Sir Ralph, even if he was murdered.'

Frevisse stopped short and faced her. 'Did Lucy say that about her father? That plainly?'

Sister Johane had the grace to turn pink within the white circle of her wimple around her face and she dropped her gaze to the dusty road at her feet. 'One of the maidservants did,' she murmured; then added with unwilling honesty, 'Two of the maidservants.'

'When were you talking with the servants?'

Still toward the road, Sister Johane said, 'When I was in the kitchen yesterday, making the eyebright and clary poultice for Lucy's eyes. There's a lovely lot of clary in Lady Anneys' garden.'

There were so many objections to falling into light talk with servants that Frevisse did not know where to start, nor did she mean to be turned from her disapproval by a surfeit of herbs; but a second's more thought told her there was small point to saying any of the objections since Sister Johane surely knew them already. Instead, surprising herself, Frevisse said, 'Dame Claire would be pleased at how much you've helped Lucy with her sore eyes. Whatever you've given Lady Anneys to help her sleep has surely helped her, too, these past two nights.'

Sister Johane looked up, openly startled at praise when she had expected rebuke. 'It's only . . . it's all very simple,' she fumbled.

'When something makes the difference between suffering and not-suffering, it's more than "only." '

Sister Johane brightened with pleasure and said, 'Thank you,' in a way that made Frevisse think that maybe she should find more things for which to praise Sister Johane, both because she deserved it and in the hope that encouraging her skills might serve to draw her away from talk with servants and a silly girl.

The morning passed in what were become usual ways, spent in the garden when Lady Anneys had finished giving to the servants what orders were needed for the day. Sometimes she worked among her flowers and herbs, teaching Lucy and Ursula and asking Sister Johane for all she knew about such medicinal things as she had growing here. Other times, like today, they sat in the arbor, Lady Anneys spinning thread from this season's flax, her spindle's whorl twisting as she worked the thin strands into fine thread, while the girls and Sister Johane sewed at the white linen shirts they had begun yesterday for Miles and Hugh, and Frevisse – because her sewing skill reached no further than hemming – read aloud to them of John Mandeville's travels to the far reaches of the world. It was the only book on the manor besides Lady Anneys' prayer book, unless Father Leonel had some others and Frevisse had not yet asked him, putting off her disappointment if he did not.

When the times came for each of the Offices, she and Sister

Johane went inside and up to Lady Anneys' bedchamber to say them. At first Frevisse had half-expected Lady Anneys would ask them to stay in the garden for the Offices and join in with her daughters, the way she and Ursula had done at St Frideswide's, but Lady Anneys never did. Her interest in prayers – even in going to morning Mass – had gone, nor did anyone else in her family show inclination that way. Frevisse had considered speaking with Father Leonel, to find if there were anything she might do to help, but so far had put it off. There were too many hurts here, both old and new, for her to begin carelessly probing at them, she thought.

Because most of the house servants were gone to the fields to help with the harvest instead of here for the cooking, the midday meal was no more than herb fritters, a cold cheese and onion tart, and fruit. Miles did not appear, but Hugh was there, sitting in the lord's chair where he looked so ill at ease. Lady Anneys was on his left, with Lucy and Ursula beyond her, while Frevisse and Sister Johane were on his right and the hound bitch Baude, round-bellied in whelp, lay on the floor behind the chair.

Talk was small, merely about Hugh's morning spent seeing how the harvest work was going. 'Gefori says the weather will hold a few more days for sure before there's chance of rain again,' he said, wiping the rim of the goblet he shared with his mother and passing it to her.

'Then it will,' Lady Anneys said. 'He always knows.'

'How?' Ursula asked.

'Reads the signs, he says,' answered Hugh.

'What signs?' Ursula persisted.

'I've never asked him.'

Ursula gave her brother a disgusted look. He made a face back at her and said, 'Ask him yourself if you're so interested.'

'I will.'

'After harvest,' Lady Anneys said. 'He doesn't need distracting now.'

As they finished the pears baked with spices, Hugh said, 'I'm away to Charlbrook Chase this afternoon. We're closing fast on Holy Rood Day.' When the mercy-time on game ended. 'I want to see how the hunting looks likely to be that way.'

'You're not taking Baude, are you?' Lady Anneys asked.

Hearing her name, the bitch raised her head. Hugh reached

back and scratched between her ears, saying, 'She's too close to whelping. That's another reason to go today rather than some other. I want to be here when she does.' He stood up to leave.

'You're going alone?' Lady Anneys asked, her worry ill-concealed.

Hugh bent and kissed her cheek. 'I'm not going alone. I'm taking Bane and Brigand. I might meet up with Miles, too.'

He bade them all good afternoon; and Frevisse, watching Lady Anneys watch him stride away toward the hall door, Baude following him, saw her lips move, silently bidding him, 'Be careful.' At the door he stopped to pet the hound, ordered her to stay, then left. Baude lingered in the doorway, still hoping, before giving in to disappointment and going to lie beside the cold hearth.

Lady Anneys rose and led her daughters, Frevisse, and Sister Johane out to the garden again and the tasks they had left in the arbor's shade when called to dinner. One shirt was ready for hemming, and Frevisse worked at that rather than any more reading aloud because Lady Anneys had brought out one of the household accounts scrolls to lesson Lucy on how the accounts could be used to plan the autumn buying of what would be needed to see the manor through the winter.

'You set how much salt we have on hand now against how much we bought a year ago, on the chance we overbought last year and can do with buying less this year,' Lady Anneys was saying. 'But against that you must needs allow for how well the calving went this spring, and the summer's haying, to judge whether there will be less or more beef to salt down at this autumn's slaughtering. If it's been a poor year for cattle, you'll need less salt because there'll be less meat to cure. Or if it was a good year for cattle but a poor one for hay and there'll have to be a greater slaughtering of cattle we can't over winter, you'll need much more salt for the curing. You see?'

Lucy nodded but looked closer to napping than thinking in the afternoon's drowsy warmth until Ursula raised her head from her sewing and said, 'Someone's coming.' Her younger ears must have heard footfall or something because the arbor was set so that, from inside of it, the house was out of sight. Lucy instantly said, 'I'll see who!' and sprang up to lean out of the arbor.

Probably no one but Frevisse saw Lady Anneys' hands clutch the account roll on her lap and her eyes widen with the unthinking fear of someone always afraid that anything sudden meant news of trouble; or saw her relief when Lucy said, 'It's Elyn!,' so that she was smiling when her daughter came into the arbor, dressed in a plain blue gown for riding and smiling, too. She exchanged quick kisses with her sisters and mother, bent her head with a respectful, 'Good day, my ladies,' to Frevisse and Sister Johane, and sat down beside Lady Anneys where Lucy had been, saying as she pulled off her riding gloves, 'My, isn't it hot today?' They all agreed on that before Lady Anneys asked, 'Isn't Philippa with you?'

'I left her home. She's my stepdaughter, not my dog. She doesn't have to go everywhere with me,' Lady Elyn laughed.

'You didn't ride alone?'

'Sawnder came with me. I left him in the yard with the horses. I can't stay long.'

'What's the matter?' Lady Anneys asked.

It was a reasonable question. Lady Elyn was sitting on the edge of the seat, looking ready to spring up again, holding her riding gloves in one hand and drawing them again and again through the other. But she was discomposed to be so readily found out, looked quickly around at everyone, and said as if she could not hold it in a moment longer, 'Mother, can I talk with you alone a little?'

Lady Anneys stiffened but said with seeming ease, 'Of course. Sister Johane, would you be so good as to take Lucy and Ursula for a walk? Perhaps along the stream toward the village.' Well away from hearing anything that might be said in the arbor.

Sister Johane stood up readily, Lucy and Ursula less readily and looking the protest they did not make, but when Frevisse stood up, too, Lady Anneys said, 'I'd have you stay, please, Dame Frevisse.'

Frevisse sat down again, as unwilling to stay as Lucy and Ursula were to go, and Lady Elyn started to protest, 'Oh, Mother . . .' but Lady Anneys silenced her with a look, but waiting until Sister Johane had led the others away toward the garden's back gate before she said, 'Dame Frevisse is here to advise and help me. You needn't worry about what you say for her to hear.' While Frevisse kept her surprise at that to herself, Lady Anneys laid a quieting hand on her daughter's restless ones and said, 'Now, what is it? Do you think you're with child?'

'Oh, Mother. No.' Lady Elyn shook her head impatiently. 'That isn't it. It's Hugh. No. It's Sir William. It's what Sir William is saying about Hugh.'

Lady Anneys' hand tightened on her daughter's and her voice was strained, for all that she kept it low as she asked, 'What's Sir William saying?'

'And to whom,' Frevisse said.

Lady Anneys cast her a sharp, agreeing glance and added, 'And to whom?'

'To Master Wyck today. I don't know if he's ever said it to anyone else.'

'To Master Wyck?' Lady Anneys repeated. 'Today? Why was he at Denhill?'

'I don't know. Sir William doesn't tell me things. About his will maybe, or some property. I don't know. They were in the parlor. I was going to go in to see if they needed more wine or wanted aught to eat. I supposed they were talking business and it would be better if I went in than a servant. The way you taught me, Mother.'

'And Sir William said something while you were there.'

'Not while I was really there. It was just as I was about to knock. I heard Tom's name and tears came up in my eyes and I stopped to dry them. Sir William doesn't like tears.' New tears welled in her eyes as she said it, but with more indignation than grief she said, 'He doesn't care how I feel. I swear it. All he wants is not to be bothered.'

'Men are cowards that way,' Lady Anneys said evenly. 'It doesn't matter if you're in pain, whether of mind or body. What matters is that you don't trouble them with it. I warned you of that when you married.'

Frevisse had now and again known men with courage enough to care and to show their care, but she could easily guess Sir Ralph had not been one and Sir William must be no better; but Lady Anneys was taking Lady Elyn back to the point, saying, 'It was while you were drying your eyes that you heard something.'

'I heard Sir William say . . .' Lady Elyn wiped more tears away, drew a deep breath, and said it all at a rush. 'He said it was as well Hugh didn't try to make trouble at the inquest, because if Hugh had, he would have pointed out that when Tom left Denhill, he was alive and that when he was next seen by anyone besides Hugh, he was dead and maybe someone should take closer look at that.'

Lady Anneys drew in a sharp breath. 'He said that?'

Lady Elyn now could not tumble the words out fast enough. 'He said he'd point out that maybe Hugh took advantage of the quarrel to make it seem Tom's death was Sir William's fault but wasn't it more likely Hugh killed him for the sake of having everything for himself?'

Angrily, Lady Anneys said, 'There was nothing that showed anything like that. There was no sign Tom's death was anything but accident and ill chance. How could he even think to blame Hugh?'

'Master Wyck said that, too. That there was no proof that way at all. But Sir William said proof didn't matter and he didn't want to have Hugh into true trouble. He would have said it just to draw trouble off from himself if Hugh had tried to make it. I was so angry I didn't even dare go in. I just went away and . . . and came here because I had to tell someone!' Lady Elyn sniffed on her dried tears. Having shifted some of her upset's burden onto someone else, she was beginning to calm. 'At least it never came to him really saying it to anyone, so I suppose it's all right. But I thought it was a vile thing for him to think of.'

'It was,' Lady Anneys said, the words flat and hard.

'Do you think Hugh should know?'

'He should not.' Lady Anneys was sharply certain of that. 'No one should know it. And you must never, ever, speak of it again to anyone. Even me. *Ever*, Elyn. Do you understand?'

Startled by her mother's vehemence, Lady Elyn fumbled, 'Well . . . yes.' She looked aside at Frevisse. 'But . . .'

'Dame Frevisse will never speak of it either. None of us will. Even the slightest whisper of something as ugly as that can fly into full-blown rumor clear across the county before you can turn around. Do you understand?'

'Yes.' Lady Elyn was impatient at having to say it again. 'But what am *I* going to do? How am I even going to look at Sir William, knowing he thought such a thing about Hugh?'

Lady Anneys' fierceness was suddenly gone. Or . . . not gone, Frevisse thought, but drawn back out of sight, into wherever she kept it. Her face was returned to its usual smooth quietness as she let go Lady Elyn's hands, patted them gently, and said, 'You'll find a way. We all have to find our ways.' She took her hands back into her own lap, looking at them rather than Lady Elyn as she added, sounding just as she had when lessoning Lucy over the account roll, 'Accept him as he is. Submit to what he asks of you. Be dutiful. Demand nothing.'

Lady Elyn gave an impatient sigh. 'But it makes me so *angry* he even thought of it.'

'Feel whatever you need to feel,' Lady Anneys said, 'but never let Sir William know it.'

Lady Elyn gave another sigh, heavy this time, and stood up. 'I have to go back.'

Lady Anneys stood up, too, embraced her gently and, as they drew apart touched her cheek lovingly and said, 'St Anne be with you.'

'And with you, Mother,' Lady Elyn said.

Frevisse watched Lady Anneys watch her daughter leave and did not try to hide what she was thinking when Lady Anneys turned around and looked at her.

'You don't agree with what I told her,' Lady Anneys said.

'You know her husband better than I do. You know whether your advice was good.'

Lady Anneys sat down, took up the account roll, put it down again, took up Ursula's sewing, searched out the needle thrust into the cloth, and began to stitch the gathering of a sleeve into a cuff, before she said, wearily defiant, 'It was at least necessary advice, if she's to live in anything like peace. Sir William won't be changed.' She laid the sewing on her lap and met Frevisse's gaze. 'You understand that it was a lie? What Elyn said Sir William threatened to say about Hugh? Hugh never harmed his brother.'

Slowly, measuring her thoughts and words, Frevisse said, 'I think, from what I heard at the crowner's inquest, that the right verdict was given. Your son's death was by mischance.' She paused, thinking to leave it there, but after all went on. 'What I don't see is why Sir William would think Hugh might try to use his brother's death against him.'

She made that a statement, not a question, and waited. Lady Anneys took up the sewing again, stitched a single, jerky stitch, put the shirt down, and said to her lap, 'In his will, my late husband made me his chief executor and left me considerable property beyond simply my dower lands. Enough that I could live very well rather than merely in bare comfort. He also gave me control of all our children's marriages and of our daughters until they marry, with disinheritance for any of them who refuses my choice.'

'He must have thought well of you to trust you that far,' said Frevisse carefully.

'It wasn't trust. It was bribe.' Anger and bitterness sharpened Lady Anneys' voice. 'In order to have that property and to keep control of my children's marriages, I have to live chastely and unmarried. If I'm unchaste or if I marry again, I lose it all, save for my dower land. The property is no matter. If that were all that stood between me and being finally, fully free of Sir Ralph, I'd spit on his will and let it go. But if I forfeit my say in my children's lives, Sir William takes my place. If I fail Sir Ralph's strictures against me, the girls' marriages and Hugh's all become Sir William's to control and profit from as he pleases.'

'And you don't trust him?' Frevisse asked, still very carefully choosing her words.

'I trust him no more,' Lady Anneys said coldly and precisely, 'than I would have trusted my cur of a husband.'

She held Frevisse's eyes in a long look that Frevisse met, letting Lady Anneys see that she understood. And Lady Anneys drew a shaken breath and said, 'It helps to say it.' She looked at her hands lying on the shirt across her lap and went on, 'And while I'm saying so much, I have to warn you that any day now Master Selenger will begin to visit me here.'

'The man who came to see you at the nunnery.'

'Him. Yes.'

'He was at your son's inquest and funeral but kept his distance. He was with Sir William, I thought.'

'He's Sir William's steward and Philippa's uncle.' Lady Anneys lowered her gaze and began to smooth the shirt across her lap. 'He began coming to see me after my husband's death. He says . . . he said once, when he had the chance to do out of anyone else's hearing, that he's long loved and wanted me.'

'Wanted you,' Frevisse repeated, keeping the words as empty of meaning as she could.

'For his wife. He claims.'

'You don't believe him?'

'He's Sir William's brother-in-law and his steward. How likely do you think it is that he doesn't know about the will and how much power would come into Sir William's hands if I marry again or am unchaste?'

'It isn't open knowledge?'

'We agreed among ourselves – Tom, Hugh, Miles, Sir William, and I – that no one else needed to know.'

'Your daughters don't know?'

'Not even Lady Elyn. Of that I'm sure because if she knew she'd talk of it. Discretion is not her better part, unless she's frightened. The way she was frightened by what she overheard today because she has wit enough to know what trouble that kind of talk could make.'

'But you think Sir William has told Master Selenger?'

'I don't know. But if Master Selenger does know and hasn't said, then I have to fear he's working to Sir William's purpose, to bring me to forfeit my place in the will, giving everything over to Sir William.'

'Is it the kind of thing Sir William would undertake? Is Master Selenger the kind of man who would do it?'

'I haven't enough trust left toward men to say Master Selenger wouldn't do it. As for Sir William, look what he would have done to Hugh if he'd felt threatened at the inquest. With rumor creeping about that Hugh might have killed his brother, who would be eager to marry their daughter to him? Only Sir William. He and Sir Ralph were set on Philippa marrying Tom . . .'

'Were Tom and Philippa set on it?'

'There was no reason for them not to be. They knew each other and there was nothing against either one.'

'But she'll marry Hugh instead?'

'The marriage is a good one for all the reasons there were before and no reasons against it. It's what Sir William would do with the girls' marriages that I worry over.'

Frevisse sat silent, considering, and finally asked, 'What if Master Selenger *isn't* working to Sir William's purpose?'

'You mean what if he does truly desire me?' Lady Anneys shoved the shirt aside, onto Lucy's sewing basket again. 'Then I have only myself to fear. No.' She made a sharp dismissing movement of one hand. 'That's wrong. I doubt there's enough womanhood left in me to rouse to any desire. What I'm afraid is that somehow some *seeming* might happen that could be used against me.' She dropped her voice to a strained whisper, sounding almost ashamed to say it. 'What I fear is that if he can't seduce me to marriage, Master Selenger may simply claim we've done . . . wrong together. That would be enough to serve Sir William's purpose.'

Frevisse briefly wondered whether Lady Anneys were grown so cold as she said. At a guess, she was hardly to forty years and the body's fires were rarely burned out by then, however weary the heart and mind might be.

But that same weariness could lessen the guard against the body's lusts and maybe, whether she admitted it to herself or not, Lady Anneys did well to fear, if only her own body's possible treachery. But if she were right in her suspicions against Sir William and Master Selenger . . . *if* she were right . . . then she had much more than that to fear, and slowly Frevisse said, 'So you wanted me here to stand guard of you against Master Selenger, the way I did at St Frideswide's. But you have family and servants here who could do that.'

'I don't dare let Hugh or Miles know of this! If ever they suspected such a thing . . .' She made a taut gesture of helpless fear of their anger and what might come of it. 'And the girls are too young and any servant's word not enough. Your oath that I'd done nothing wrong would have weight, if it comes to that, but yes, I want you to stand guard between me and Master Selenger.'

Rather than immediately answering, Frevisse looked away from her, stared out of the arbor to the bright sunlight on the garden path while inwardly seeing the layers of Lady Anneys' fears – of Sir William and Master Selenger, who possibly intended ill against her; for what Hugh and Miles might do in anger; for her daughters if she lost the care of them. If Master Selenger and Sir William were indeed sporting with Lady Anneys' life the way she feared, then she needed whatever help Frevisse could give. But . . .

Frevisse returned her gaze to Lady Anneys and said, 'We can't stay here forever, Sister Johane and I.'

'I know. I just need . . .' Lady Anneys shook her head, impatient at being unable to find the words. 'When Hugh came for me, to tell me Tom was dead, I didn't have time to think anything through. Tom . . .' Tears flooded her eyes. She fought them, steadied her voice, and said, 'I couldn't think of anything but that he was dead and I had to be back here and I was afraid. I needed . . . needed . . .'

'Someone to somewhat guard you until you're certain of things again. Until you have chance to find your balance,' Frevisse offered.

'Yes.' Lady Anneys put a world of heartsick weariness into the word. 'Yes. That.' Relieved to have someone say it for her.

Voices warned that Sister Johane, Lucy, and Ursula were returning, and Lady Anneys straightened her back, wiped her eyes free of tears, and smoothed her face to calm again, so that to outward seeming there might have been nothing but the day's quietness in her. But her gaze sought Frevisse's, asking, and quietly to her quietness Frevisse said, 'I'll do all that I can.'

Chapter 12

Hugh made no haste homeward despite the day was wearing out and suppertime was near. The small excuse he would give if asked what kept him so long was that in the afternoon's heat neither he nor the hounds had felt like hurrying. That was somewhat true enough; Bane and Brigand, pacing patiently beside Foix, were lightly panting and he had taken off his doublet and untied his shirt at the throat. But the true reason he was making no haste – the reason he hardly admitted to himself, let be to anyone else – was that he did not want to be home. Away from the manor, he could almost believe things were as they had been those few weeks after his father's death. Could almost believe that when he reached the manor he would see to the hounds, talk with Degory awhile, wander to the hall, and wash off the day's dirt while listening to Tom complain over some village disagreement he had probably enjoyed settling. Miles would be leaning easily on an end of the high table, teasing Lucy or Ursula. Mother would be coming from the kitchen, having seen that supper was nearly ready and tucking a stray strand of hair back under her wimple. Hugh could not remember her hair ever straying loose while Sir Ralph was alive.

Those had been good days, with Tom happy to have all his own way with the manor, Miles not constantly ready to be angry, Mother content and smiling, no one wary with waiting for Sir Ralph's next anger. Even when Mother and Ursula were gone to the nunnery and Lucy to stay with Elyn, the days had gone on being good.

And now they were not.

He did not mean to turn aside from the greenway as he came through the woods. He had not been to the gathering place since the day Sir Ralph had died and had no thought to go there now, but as they reached the side-trail that went to it, Brigand lagged, looked up at him, and whined, letting Hugh know he was thirsty and saw no reason he should wait until the kennel when water was close here. Hugh hesitated but suddenly wanted a drink, too, and why not of fresh, cold spring water? It was hardly as if Sir Ralph had died there. And without admitting to his thought that he would now be even later reaching home, he turned Foix into the side-trail.

Bane and Brigand went eagerly ahead of him. It was their tails stirring into a pleased wagging that told him someone was in the clearing, someone they knew, and so he was only half-surprised to see Miles sitting sideways on the wall around the spring, staring down into water, so far into whatever he was seeing or thinking that, with the water's soft burbling over the pool's edge to cover any small sounds of their coming, his first warning he was not alone was Bevis standing up from the grass beside him. He put a hand on the hound's shoulder and twisted a little around to quirk half a smile at Hugh dismounting at the clearing's edge. 'Caught me doing nothing,' he said.

'There's two of us then.' Hugh wrapped his reins over a branch low enough that Foix could reach the grass and went to sit on the low wall across the spring from Miles. The hounds, having circled with Bevis a few times and decided they were all still friends, were lapping busily from the stream, and Hugh leaned over to splash water up into his face before drinking from his cupped hands.

When he straightened up, Miles was watching him with a shut, unreadable look.

'Hot, isn't it?' Hugh said for the sake of saying something.

'Hot enough.' Miles dropped his gaze and plucked up a handful of grass. The hounds, having finished their lapping, collapsed on the grass with sighs of pleasure, and Miles began to drop the grass blades one by one into the pool, watching one swirl away over the edge before dropping in the next. The forest's late afternoon quiet closed around them, and Hugh, lulled by the stream's burble and chuckle, slipped into a small measure of welcome unthinking until Miles said, 'You'll agree soon with Sir William over marrying Philippa?'

'What? Philippa? She . . .' Almost Hugh blurted out 'She's meant for Tom' but stopped himself and said instead, even-voiced,

'I can't marry her. You want her. She wants you.'

Miles shrugged.

'Doesn't she?' Hugh persisted.

Miles shrugged again. 'It doesn't matter, does it?' He dropped another grass blade, with great care, into the very middle of the pool. 'With Tom dead, Sir William will be looking for you to marry her.'

'I don't want to marry her.'

He said it maybe more strongly than need be but he hated when Miles went distant like this. Hated it worse when Miles finally looked at him blank-faced and said with no feeling at all in his voice, 'You had better. Because I won't.'

Hugh glared at him across the pool and demanded, 'Why not?'

Miles went back to dropping grass blades into the water. 'She'd lose everything and gain nearly nothing.'

'She'd gain you.'

'As I said. Nearly nothing.'

There was no point in trying to reason with Miles in his black humour but Hugh said, setting his stubbornness against Miles', 'You might as well marry her because, come what may, I'm not going to.'

Miles did not answer that, only went on dropping grass blades. One. Two. Three. Then said quietly, barely above the sound of the flowing water, 'Remember how we used to plot that we'd run off if ever we saw the chance? Join a cry of players or else cattle drovers, maybe? Anything to get away from here forever.'

'I remember. You even tried to go. Twice.'

'Only to be hauled back both times, beaten and bloody.'

'At least you tried.' Guilt stirred in Hugh. 'I never did.'

'Because you had the sense to know he'd never let us go. Not even me.'

'It wasn't more sense. I wasn't as desperate.'

'Desperate, or else mad to think there was ever escape.'

There was a bleakness in Miles' voice that Hugh could not answer and silence came back between them, Hugh watching the water flow, hoping they were done with talk, until Miles said, even more quietly, 'Marry Philippa.'

Hugh jerked up his head too sharply, hurting his neck. Sharp with the pain, he said, 'No! Not if you—'

'Marry her,' Miles said, still quietly, not looking up, watching his last grass blade swirl away out of the pool. 'If you don't, who knows what kind of man Sir William will marry her to. Marry her so she'll be safe.'

Staring at the top of Miles' head, Hugh looked for some answer but found none, and said finally, bitterly, 'I'm glad Sir Ralph is dead.'

'The pity,' Miles said, 'is that it didn't happen sooner.' He sprang to his feet, startling the hounds, who all sat up, looking around for whatever the trouble was. 'Come on. Let's go home. I'm hungry.'

He seemed to have shaken off whatever humour had been on him, but they said little as they walked together, Hugh leading Foix and the hounds ranging around them. They left Bane and Brigand at the kennel with Degory, who was just back from helping with the harvest and said all was going well, and took Foix to the stable, where Gib was just back, too. With Bevis still at Miles' side, they headed for the hall then, their shadows long across the foreyard ahead of them, and were met by Lucas, the village reeve, coming out of the hall doorway. He gave Hugh a deep bow and Miles a brief one and said, 'I was come to find you, sir. This was something you needed to know as soon as might be.' He held out a sickle in two pieces, the metal blade broken off from the wooden handle. 'It's the metal broke, not the handle,' Lucas said. 'I'd not say it was Hal's fault it broke but it's the manor's sickle, not his, and he's all tied up in fits that you'll make him pay for it or have it out of his hide.'

Hugh's insides turned sickly over with the thought that with Tom dead he now had the kind of power that could make people afraid of him that way, and maybe too quickly he said, 'I won't do that. Let me see it.'

Lucas gave the pieces to him and he easily saw for himself how worn thin the haft was where it had gone into the handle. He remembered Tom had been at Sir Ralph early in the summer about the need to remake some of the sickles before harvest-time. Sir Ralph had refused, grudging the cost because the manor had no smith and the work would have had to be taken elsewhere. Once he was lord, Tom had probably meant to see to it but had not had time before . . .

'So we're a sickle short,' Hugh said. And therefore a worker short. How much would that set back the harvest, he wondered.

'Nay,' Lucas said. 'As it happens, Master Woderove bought a new one that time he went to Banbury about Whitsuntide. So all's well there. But this one needs remaking and there's always chance another one may go, so I thought you'd best know.'

'A new one?' Hugh echoed. Where had Tom found the money for that? But aloud he only said, 'Yes. Thank you. I'll see to having it done.'

Lucas bowed, took a step toward leaving, but stopped and said, 'Begging your pardon if I speak out of turn, but you might want to talk a bit to Father Leonel. He might be able, like, to tell you things.'

'Tell me things?'

'About sickle blades and such like.'

Before Hugh had sorted himself to ask another question, Lucas quickly made another bow and left. Hugh watched him go, looked down at the broken scythe in his hands, looked after the now-vanished Lucas, and finally looked at Miles in hope of an answer from him.

Miles shrugged and said, 'You'd best talk to Father Leonel, I guess.'

'What am I supposed to say? "Father, have you anything to confess to me?" '

'That's as good a way as any.' Miles grinned, the task not being his, and went inside.

Hugh stared broodingly at the white-plastered wall beside the doorway, knowing yet again how little he liked being lord of the manor. But there was no use putting off what was probably better done sooner than later and he went, first, to find Lady Anneys, to ask if it would be no trouble to have Father Leonel to supper, then sent Lucy to ask if he would come.

The priest returned with Lucy as they were readying to sit down. He took his place on Hugh's other side from Lady Anneys, Lucy, and Ursula, with the nuns sitting beyond him and Miles sitting between them, being courteous to both. Uncourteous though Sir Ralph had been, he had forced courtesy at table on everyone else. 'I'll not have you disgracing me in front of others,' he had said. A sure way to goad at least Miles into rampant discourtesy; but because Lady Anneys had asked it, too, and taught them, he had learned and this evening gracefully served the nuns the roast chicken in black sauce and a barley frumenty set before them and asked about their day. Lady Anneys talked with Father Leonel about a village woman who had badly cut her foot on a stone just before harvest started while Hugh, passing a small piece of chicken to Baude lying behind his chair, wondered what he could ask Father Leonel.

The day's last sunlight, slanted across the far end of the hall's east wall and banded with shadow from the tall, unglassed window's wooden mullions, was slipping upward as the sun sank downward. Dusk thickened in the hall but there was light enough by which to finish the meal and talk, with no need for candles. Afterward, for the while until bedtime, they would probably go into Lady Anneys' garden or else to the parlor, and Hugh wished that was all he need think about this evening; but when the fish in a green tart and the carrots roasted in herbs, oil, and vinegar had been served, Lady Anneys claimed Frevisse's attention with a question about what flax was grown at St Frideswide's, Sister Johane was talking to Miles, and Hugh took the chance to ask Father Leonel, 'Ivetta's foot is healing then?'

'The poultice Lady Anneys recommended seems to be drawing the poison out,' the priest said. 'The cut is so deep, though, she likely won't be walking well before Martinmas. She's worried less about her foot, though, than that she can't do her boon work this harvest. She fears you'll either demand rent money she can't pay or else force her out.'

'Force her out?' Hugh repeated, bewildered. 'Because she's hurt?'

'Because she can't do her share of the fieldwork she owes you and can't pay you for either,' Father Leonel said patiently. 'You'd be within your rights, as lord of the manor.'

Hugh gave intent heed to spearing a piece of carrot on his knife point, giving himself time to stop his insides' turning before he finally said, 'Weren't you saying with Mother that she could help here in the kitchen until her foot is healed? In place of her field-work?'

'That would need your agreement,' Father Leonel said in the careful way he would have said it to Sir Ralph.

Hugh held back an urge to smash his knife down on the table and yell, 'Don't talk to me like that!' Instead, because lord of the manor was a thing he was, whether he liked it or not, he laid his knife down quietly, spread his hands flat on the tabletop to either side of his bread trencher, and said, 'Tell me about her.'

Father Leonel did – how Ivetta had never given trouble or failed in her duty before now, nor had her late husband, and that their son kept his holding well and never failed of his rent or boon work. 'A good family. First and last, a good family. It would be shame to—'

He broke off abruptly. Hugh knew well enough that he was thinking how it had always been ill to tell Sir Ralph what he should or should not do – and said, hating anyone could think he might be like his father that way, 'It would be shame to repay them with unkindness in her need. She's welcome to work in the kitchen this while for her boon work. Would it help if I sent a cart for her every day, so she doesn't have to walk here?'

The relief that swept over Father Leonel's face was even better payment than his quick thanks; and on Hugh's other side Lady Anneys briefly laid a hand over his own, telling Hugh that despite she was still in talk with Dame Frevisse, she had heard and approved his answer, too. On the warmth of that, Hugh waited while Alson from the kitchen served out the meal's final dish – apple pudding sprinkled with nutmeg – in wooden bowls to each of them, and said when Alson was gone, 'This afternoon Lucas said I should maybe talk to you about some things, Father.'

'Anything in particular?' Father Leonel asked lightly, openly much eased now the matter of Ivetta was settled.

'Sickle blades and suchlike, he said.' From the side of his eye Hugh saw the priest's hand, about to dip his spoon into the cream, cease to move. Trying to seem he had not seen that, Hugh went on, 'He was here to tell me that an old sickle blade had broken and that it was a good thing Tom had bought a new one at Whitsuntide. Then, as he was going, he said you might be able to "tell me things." '

Father Leonel set down his spoon, drew back his hands, and folded them together on the edge of the table. 'Now?' he said, very softly.

Hugh put down his own spoon, knowing food would not go

past his throat's sudden tightness even if he did pretend to eat. He turned in his chair toward the priest and said, 'Now would likely be good.' Wishing he had not chosen now to ask, here with everyone to hear. He had thought it would be easier, done friendliwise over a meal. Instead he was suddenly afraid it was something he was going to wish he had never done at all. 'Unless we should go apart,' he said hurriedly and too late. The change in their voices and in Father Leonel had drawn Lady Anneys' heed toward them and now everyone else along the table was looking, too.

'No.' Father Leonel pushed back his shoulders, straightening his bent back as much as might be, and faced Hugh squarely – an old man whose body was failing him but not his courage. And that startled Hugh because 'courage' was not a word he had ever put to Father Leonel shambling about the manor in his old priest's gown and worn shoes, always worried about one person or another. He had come to the manor when Hugh was small, had never had interest in hunting and had therefore been despised by Sir Ralph; but he had gently taught all the boys and the girls their reading, writing, and numbers and had kept the manor accounts for Sir Ralph until Tom was old enough to have a hand in them and after that he and Tom had kept them together. A kindly, useful man and that was all, Hugh would have said if there had been need to say anything about him at all, until now he faced Hugh and said firmly, 'There's no need to go apart. It's not a thing of shame. What Lucas meant was that Tom and I had been deceiving Sir Ralph with the manor accounts for years. I did it when I kept them by myself. When Sir Ralph set Tom to be steward and I had to show him the accounts, Tom saw almost at the first, without my telling him, what I had been doing. From then on we did it together.'

The silence along the table was complete and stunned, until Lady Anneys breathed, 'Sir Ralph would have all but killed you if he'd found out.'

The priest smiled at her. 'I trusted to God's mercy that he'd not find out.' He sobered. 'But likewise I was willing to pay the price if he did.'

'But why?' Hugh asked. Then answered for himself. 'So there would be money for such things as spare sickle blades.'

Father Leonel smiled the way he had when Hugh had been especially apt at some lesson. 'For such things as that, yes, and sometimes we'd write that someone had paid a fine when they had not, if Tom and I thought the fine unjust or someone was unable to pay it for good reason. Things like that. Never much. We only did it because there were always needs but Sir Ralph never cared for anything but himself and . . .'

Father Leonel stopped, not because his courage failed him there, Hugh saw, but out of pity. That pity hurt worse than anger could have and Hugh finished for him, not able to keep bitterness out of the words, 'For anything but himself and his hounds and hunting. It was always everything for his hounds and hunting.'

'And to hell with the rest of us,' said Miles.

Hugh shoved his chair roughly back from the table – careful not to hit Baude lying there – and stood up. 'And you're afraid I'll be the same,' he said. It was a struggle to speak evenly but somehow he did. 'Tomorrow morning you can show me what you and Tom have done. After that we'll make it so there's no more need for deceiving anymore. No,' he said as everyone started to rise with him, and ordered Baude struggling to pull herself to her feet, 'Stay,' before swinging around, away from his chair and through the nearest doorway, into the parlor, shutting the door hard behind him.

But that was not far enough away and he crossed to the room's one window, its shutters standing open to the warm evening, and swung himself over the sill and out. If he had been younger, there were places enough where he could have gone to hide, but he was too old for that and only went to his usual refuge, the kennel. Degory was scrubbing out the dogs' feeding dishes after their supper and welcomed him much the same way the hounds did without surprise or need to talk. He went on with his work and Hugh squatted on his heels just inside the gate, welcoming one hound after another as they ambled over to snuffle at him and be briefly petted. Only the lymer Somer stayed with him, flopping down with a hearty sigh in front of him, and Hugh was absently fondling her ears when Miles appeared, leaned on the gate with deliberant ease, and said nothing.

Neither did Hugh. Degory finished with the dishes, judged their silence with a wary look, and slipped out through the kennel door, away on some business of his own. The silence drew out until Hugh gave way and said, half-bitterly, half-bewildered, 'If it's been secret all this long, why did Lucas set me on to Father Leonel like that?'

Miles did not answer for an uncomfortably long time. Though the west was still ablaze with orange from the vanished sun, the shadows were gathered deeply blue in the kennel-yard and Hugh could read Miles' face no better than Miles could probably read his; he had to wait for answer until finally Miles said with the gentleness that – coming from him – was always surprising, 'Maybe the folk are as tired of walking wary as the rest of us are. Maybe Lucas wanted it settled what kind of lord you're going to be.'

Hugh stood up, startling Somer. 'Walking wary?' he protested fiercely. 'You know me. You know I'm not Sir Ralph.'

'You're not Tom either,' Miles pointed out kindly. 'What you've been is Sir Ralph's huntsman. Hounds, hunting, Sir Ralph, and you. That's what the folk here have known. What are Lucas and everyone else to think but that they'll matter less to you than the hounds and hunting? Just like with Sir Ralph.'

'What do *you* think?' Hugh asked harshly.

Slowly, seeming to make sure of the words as he went, Miles said, 'Sir Ralph used every spare penny – and sometimes pennies that weren't to spare – for his hounds and hunting and be-damned to the rest of us. I don't see you ever be-damning.'

Somer had left, offended. Bounder, one of the younger hounds, wandered to Hugh, tail swaying behind him, and Hugh absently took his great head between his hands, stroking the broad forehead while saying slowly to Miles, 'No. I don't think I'm any good at be-damning.'

'And pleased the manor folk will be to learn it,' Miles said. 'But they'll have to learn it. You're going to have to show them.'

'Can I show them?' Hugh had never said it aloud, never even let himself clearly think it until now. 'How good am I going to be at this? I won't be-damn like Sir Ralph, but I'm not Tom. There's nothing to say I won't be damned bad no matter how I try.'

Offensively cheerful, Miles said, 'We'll find out, won't we?'

Even knowing that the cheerfulness was meant deliberately to goad him into cheerfulness himself, Hugh wanted to throw something at him. Unfortunately, a clean-kept kennel-yard offered little to throw besides straw and dogs, and before Hugh came up with at least some words to throw, Miles shifted aside for Degory to lean on the gate, too, carrying a slice of the fish tart in one hand and a thick piece of bread folded around other things for the rest of his supper in the other. The hounds gathered to the fence, too well trained to grab and snatch but assuring him of their coming gratitude if he cared to share with them.

'I don't eat your suppers,' Degory told them, then said to Hugh over their backs and waving tails, 'That Master Selenger is here again. He'll be going home by moonlight, won't he?'

Chapter 13

It was that evening Frevisse could no longer hide from knowing how wrong things were at Woodrim. After Hugh's leaving, supper finished in a stiff silence and eyes kept to bowls and table-top until Lady Anneys asked Father Leonel to give the final grace. That done, Ursula hurriedly slid off the bench and went to open the parlor door too quickly for her mother to say more than 'Leave him be . . .' before Ursula said from the doorway, 'He's gone,' all disappointment and worry.

'He's gone to the kennel then,' said Lady Anneys. 'Miles.'

Miles rose quickly, gave her a slight smile, a brief bow, and left.

Calmly, Lady Anneys invited Father Leonel to join her in the garden for a while but he declined. 'Not because I don't want to talk about . . .' He made a vague gesture of distress, to include all there might be to talk – or not to talk – about.

Lady Anneys caught his hand and held it, saying affectionately, 'I wasn't going to ask you anything. I only wanted your company.'

He clasped her hand in both of his. 'Bless you, my lady. But I'm promised this evening to Roberd and Mariote. He's Lucas' younger son, you remember? They're planning to marry just after Michaelmas. We're to set when the banns will be and decide other things tonight.'

'That I'll not keep you from,' Lady Anneys said. 'Be sure to let me know with what I can best gift them when the time comes.'

'I will, my lady.'

Father Leonel blessed her with a quickly sketched cross in the air between them. He was making another in a general way at Frevisse, Sister Johane, Lucy, and Ursula scattered along the table, when Lucy exclaimed, 'Someone is coming,' and dashed to the window, looked out, and swung around to say with a glowing look at her mother, 'It's Master Selenger!' She dashed back to catch Ursula by the hand. 'Come on. Let's walk Father Leonel to the village. Are you coming, Father? Sister Johane, Dame Frevisse, you'll come with us, too?'

Even if she had wanted a different choice, Ursula was given no chance for it. Lucy was already dragging her toward the outer door, Father Leonel following, smiling, and after the barest hesitation and a look at Frevisse, who refused with a small shake of her head, Sister Johane went, too.

'Dame Frevisse!' Lucy insisted from the hall's far end.

'No,' Lady Anneys said, too low for anyone but Frevisse to hear, all her smiling ease of a few moments ago gone.

Frevisse waved the others onward. They met Master Selenger at the door, their brief exchange of greetings among them all giving her chance to say to Lady Anneys, 'It might go easier if your daughters knew you didn't want to be left alone with him.'

'They're the least burdened by everything that's happened,' Lady Anneys said. 'I'd like to keep them that way as long as possible. Ursula is still so young.'

Remembering how Ursula had taken the news of her father's death with relief rather than grief, Frevisse doubted Ursula was so young as her mother thought her. Grief had come only with her brother's death and surely left her even less young than she had been before it. But this was hardly the time to take that up with Lady Anneys, who was moving from behind the table, down from the dais to meet Master Selenger coming up the hall toward her. Frevisse, tucking her hands into her opposite sleeves, followed her, eyes lowered in the seeming of quiet nunhood but not so far she could not see Master Selenger meet Lady Anneys with, 'Good evening, my lady,' and a bow and a hand held out to take one of hers.

Seeming not to see his hand, keeping her own folded at her waist, one over the other, Lady Anneys said with no particular feeling to the words, 'Good evening to you, too, Master Selenger. What brings you here?'

By then Frevisse was beside her, and Master Selenger, his hand returned to his side, made her a bow while answering, 'Hope for the pleasure of your company and to ask about Lady Elyn.'

Alarm sharpened Lady Anneys' voice. 'She left here hours ago. Isn't she home yet?'

'Yes! Oh, yes,' Master Selenger said with instant, matching alarm. 'I'm sorry. I didn't mean to fright you. She's home and safe. But . . .'

He cast a meaningful look at the servants now coming to clear supper's remains from the table. 'We'll be cooler in the garden, don't you think?' he asked.

Lady Anneys murmured unwilling agreement but added, 'Dame Frevisse, you'll come, too?'

Frevisse accepted with a slight bow of her head.

What Master Selenger thought he kept to himself nor, when they were in the garden, did he offer his hand to Lady Anneys again even while they walked side by side along the path. He could take an unspoken suggestion when it was given, Frevisse thought, following behind them. Except he as yet refused to understand that Lady Anneys did not want his company.

The garden was in deepening twilight but not much cooled by the slight wind beginning to stir the evening air. The day's warm scents of flowers and herbs still lingered and a last few bees were bumbling in the bee-flowers, late at going hive-ward. Lady Anneys paused near the door to break off stems of fern-leaved tansy for herself and Frevisse to keep off whatever evening midges might seek them out, but left Master Selenger to pluck his own, which he did. Since leaving the hall, none of them had spoken. Lady Anneys led the way to the long, wood-sided, turf-topped bench along one side of the garden's wall and sat down, leaving room for Frevisse between herself and one end of the bench and nodding Master Selenger toward the bench's far end, well away from her.

He somewhat took the hint, sitting not altogether to the bench's end but an arm's length and a little more away as Lady Anneys demanded, 'What about Lady Elyn, then?'

'She came to see you this afternoon.'

'She did.' Lady Anneys said the words flatly and let them lie there, leaving it to Master Selenger to make of them what he would. She was looking not at him but across the path and down at a cluster of red gillyflowers so that the soft fall of her veil on either side of her face served to hide her from him and Frevisse both.

'Why?' he asked.

'To see me. Isn't that reason enough?'

'She seemed unhappy when she returned.'

'Sir William sent you to find out why from me, rather than ask her himself?'

'He asked. She said she wanted to see her mother.'

'Why wasn't that enough?'

Master Selenger very slightly smiled. 'Because of the way she sniffled while she did it and wouldn't look at him. He's worried there's something wrong that he should know.' Master Selenger paused, then added, subdued and apologizing, 'Besides what's obviously wrong, of course. He would have come himself but won't until he's asked. Besides, he knew I' – Master Selenger's voice was very low – 'would not mind the chance.'

Lady Anneys still had not looked at him, nor did her voice give anything away as she said mildly, 'I'm grateful for Sir William's concern and consideration, but since she was unhappy when she came here, the reason for it would be better sought there than here.'

'Save that she might have spoken to you more freely than she would to Sir William and you could advise him of what best he might do.'

Lady Anneys drew a long breath and sat up straighter, still without looking at him. 'That would be somewhat betraying my daughter's trust.'

'If, truly, it's something Sir William can't help, then of course you won't tell it,' Master Selenger said.

'Such as "women's problems," ' Lady Anneys said, still mildly but probably fully aware that Master Selenger instantly shifted uneasily. There were few things so sure as 'women's problems' to set a man back.

'Um,' he said. 'Yes.'

'Or,' said Lady Anneys, still mildly and toward the gillyflowers across the path, 'Sir William may be worried that I'm trying to turn her against him because of her brother's death.'

Master Selenger went very still and in the blue gathering dusk Frevisse could see his eyes searching for some clue in Lady Anneys' faceless stillness to her seriousness in that.

She answered his unasked question, 'I'm not.'

Master Selenger went on looking at her with a worry Frevisse could not quite read. Then he reached a hand toward Lady Anneys' lying quietly together in her lap; but her shoulder nearest him jerked forward, warning him away, and he took his hand back and after a moment tried, even more gently than he had been speaking, 'Lady Anneys—'

Her own voice suddenly crisp, she interrupted him. 'I'll tell you this much.' She raised her head and finally looked at him; Frevisse wished she could see her face. 'Lady Elyn came to me with a woman's worry. I advised her just as my mother advised me before ever I married – that a wife's duty is to submit and accept. So I advised her and so I hope she will do. Will that satisfy Sir William?'

Uncertainly Master Selenger said, 'It should.'

Lady Anneys nodded once and looked away again, letting him see she was waiting for him to leave; but he went on sitting there, still looking at her and silent as she was. In the quiet, small birds were twittering and settling for the night among the vine leaves over the arbor and from somewhere, faintly carried on the small wind, came distant laughter. From the village, Frevisse supposed; she did not think she had heard anyone here at the hall laugh since she had come, save maybe Miles, and darkness ran under his laughter.

But then darkness seemed to run under and behind everything and everyone here.

And from more than Tom Woderove's death.

Why that thought should come to her so clearly here in the garden's quiet, Frevisse did not know, nor did she fully understand what it meant, but she followed it, to find where it would go. Sir Ralph was the core of it, she thought. Assuredly he seemed to have created darkness enough in his life that it still lay over everyone here. Tom Woderove's death had only added to it. But there was some shadow more than that. Something sharper, newer. There was . . . fear?

Frevisse moved carefully around the edge of that thought, looking more closely at it. Lady Anneys was afraid, surely, and admitted as much. She was afraid of Master Selenger because of the trouble he could bring on her; and of Sir William because if she was right about him, he was the cause of that trouble; and for her children – afraid not only of losing more of them but of how amiss their lives might go. But those were fears every parent had, and her worry over Sir William and Master Selenger was reasonable, too; but both those fears had shape and boundaries. It was her fear beyond that that Frevisse did not understand. There was a ceaseless wariness in Lady Anneys, a ceaseless waiting for something *more* to happen, as if some other, deeper, secret fear were feeding her more open, reasonable ones.

And though to say Hugh or Miles or Ursula were afraid might be to say too much, still, there was something . . . There was a wariness in them, too. The sense of a guard being kept. Against what?

Master Selenger stirred and said slowly, as if he regretted the need, 'There's something else, my lady.'

For the first time Lady Anneys let impatience into her voice. 'What?'

Both looking and sounding on the edge of apology, Master Selenger said, 'Sir William asked me to speak to you about Hugh's marriage to Philippa.'

Lady Anneys lifted her head and faced him again, said nothing, then said, with each word carefully separated from the others, 'Hugh's marriage to Philippa?'

'My lady—' Master Selenger began.

Lady Anneys interrupted him with cold anger. 'You can tell Sir William that he'll be told when anyone here is ready to discuss marriage and that until then I do not want to hear about it from him or anyone else.'

'You can tell him, too,' Hugh said over the rear gate, 'that when and *if* the time comes to talk marriage, I will be the one to talk to.' He shoved open the gate and came in with Miles behind him. 'Not my mother. She has grief and troubles enough without having to deal about that or with Sir William. Especially now.'

Master Selenger stood up. 'Hugh. Miles. Lady Anneys and I were—'

'We heard,' Hugh said. The arbor and the evening's shadows had hidden his and Miles' coming along the cart-track until they were at the gate. There was no knowing how much they had heard, but like his mother, Hugh was angry. Unlike her, he was not cold and sounded ready to include Master Selenger in his anger.

Lady Anneys stood up, too, saying quickly, 'Master Selenger was only asking because Sir William told him to.'

'Then Master Selenger can take our message back to him that no one here is ready to talk marriage yet,' Hugh answered, his look fixed on Master Selenger.

Master Selenger accepted that with a small bow and started, 'Sir William only thought that—'

'Sir William can keep his thoughts to himself,' Hugh said tersely.

'—that the marriage would reassure everyone that there's peace between the families.'

'They can be reassured by the fact that we're not openly fighting.'

'*Is* there peace?' Master Selenger persisted.

'Yes. There's peace,' Hugh snapped.

'Simply not ease,' Miles put in quietly. 'Ease will take longer than peace.'

'Tell Sir William we need time,' Lady Anneys said. 'That's all. He's simply too soon with it.'

Frevisse saw Master Selenger's swift look from her face to Hugh's and Miles' before he bowed to her and said, 'I'll tell him so, my lady. He'll understand.'

He held out his hand for hers. It was a reasonable courtesy but unreasonable here and now since she had so lately refused it. But after only the barest pause and probably for the sake of keeping up a seeming of courtesy in front of Hugh and Miles, she gave her hand to him in return. He bowed over it, did not make so bold as to kiss it but, when he straightened, held it a moment overlong, taking the chance to gaze into her eyes. Only the instant before she would have snatched her hand away did he let her go, smoothly turning to bow to Frevisse and bend his head to Hugh and then to Miles, who said, 'I'll keep you company to the yard,' in a way that warned he would see him out of the yard and well away, too.

While they left, silence except for the settling rustle of the birds in the arbor vine filled in the garden. Not until they were gone did Hugh ask, 'Is that all he came for? To talk about Philippa's marriage?'

Again Lady Anneys paused, barely, before answering, 'He asked first why Elyn came here today.'

Hugh frowned, puzzled. 'Why shouldn't Elyn come here?'

'She was upset about something. Sir William was worried for

her because she wouldn't say why. I told Master Selenger that we talked and that I reassured her.'

'Is she with child?'

'No. It was a woman trouble.'

That put Hugh off that track as thoroughly as it had Master Selenger, but he went to, 'What about this marriage business?'

'Nothing beyond the ordinary. Philippa's marriage to Tom had been purposed for years. You know that and why.'

'Because adding Sir William's manor to ours is sensible. But not as sensible as it was before Father married Elyn to Sir William.'

'Sir William was thinking to marry again. Sir Ralph offered Elyn to him as a way to double-guard our interest. Nor was Elyn unwilling.'

'Of course Elyn wasn't unwilling,' Hugh said, sounding impatient at being told what he knew too well. 'And even if Elyn does bear a child or children, Philippa has enough inheritance from her mother that her marriage to Tom would still have been a profitable thing. I know all that. I suppose what Sir William wants is assurance I'll marry her in Tom's place. The trouble with that is—'

Either catching his impatience or else giving way to the anger she had not dared show Master Selenger, Lady Anneys said sharply, 'The trouble is that no one ever seems to wonder what Philippa might feel or want in the way of marriage. That's the trouble and the pity. You've never thought about what she might want in the matter, have you? Of course you haven't. No man ever does. All that's ever asked of women is to submit and accept. That's what I told Elyn today. Submit and accept. Just like every woman has to do.'

Frevisse had not found, over the years, that simple submission and plain acceptance were all that common among women, whether maidens, wives, widows, or nuns. For some women, yes, for some women, no, with most women living somewhere between, sometimes yes and very often no. Just as most men lived in between what was expected from them in their lives and what they truly wanted. Most men but not men like Sir Ralph – and Frevisse had known women like him, too – who demanded and forced and took what they wanted and left the pain and scars of it on others. The way the pain and scars were left on Lady Anneys, who said now with deep-scored bitterness, 'That's how I survived your father. By submitting and accepting, accepting and submitting.' She spat the words. 'And wished him dead so many times, so badly wanted him dead . . .'

Frevisse was unable to see her face, but Hugh's was raw with pain. He tried to speak but Lady Anneys cut him off again with, 'Do you know how I stopped him from hitting me? You never saw him hit me, did you? You know how I did that? I was six months married when I found I was with child. With Tom.' Her voice threatened to break on his name but she pulled back into her anger and went on, 'I was so afraid Sir Ralph would do something to me and I'd lose my baby that I told him I'd see to it I'd never bear him any child at all if he ever, *ever* laid hand, fist, or whip on me again.'

'Again?' Hugh said hoarsely. 'He'd already hit you?'

'Already? Better to ask how often. I spent that first half-year of my marriage being hit whenever he felt like it. After all, I wasn't one of his hounds, to be gently handled and cherished. I was his brood mare, to give him sons to replace Miles' father, his disappointing firstborn. So I told him that if he ever struck me again, there'd be no sons at all, only a long, barren marriage. I made him believe there'd be no children if he ever hit me. Later, when we'd had children enough, he'd ceased noting me enough for me to be worth hitting. But the threat to never bear him children at all was how I won free of him.'

'Could you have done it?' Hugh asked, sounding half-frightened of the answer.

'Yes.' Her voice was flat with certainty but bitterly weary as she went on, 'Only I never found a way, after you all were born, to save any of you from him. I could only save myself.' She sank down on the bench beside Frevisse, all the anger and strength gone suddenly out of her. 'And now I'm worn out. Childbirths and all those years of never showing weakness to Sir Ralph – of never showing *anything* to Sir Ralph – have left nothing of me except tiredness.'

She made to stand up but might have failed if Frevisse had not hurriedly stood up, too, to help her. Hugh, too, took her by one arm and helped to steady her when she was on her feet; but it was on Frevisse she leaned and to Frevisse she said, hardly above a whisper and on the edge of tears, 'I want to go inside now. I want to go to bed and never get up again. Please.'

Chapter 14

Hugh let his mother and Dame Frevisse leave him standing there beside the bench in the gathering darkness. He was not needed by them nor did he know where to go or what to do, and when they were gone, he sat down on the bench again, leaned forward with his elbows on his knees and his head in his hands, and waited to feel something else besides sick with the weariness of worry. Too many things were too wrong in too many ways, with no way he saw to make anything better.

When Degory had said Master Selenger was here again, he had been angry – and been angrier when he saw how badly troubled by him Lady Anneys was. Did she guess the same thing Miles guessed about Selenger's attention to her? Or should she be warned? He didn't know. There were so many things he didn't know – didn't know what to think, didn't know what to do, was beginning not to know even what to feel.

And now there was what his mother had just said.

That she could have kept him, Tom, the girls from ever being at all.

He had never even thought much about being or not being until lately, and that was strange, because death was such a close part of life. There were always, in the usual way of things, the deaths of manor folk or neighbors and every autumn the slaughter of whatever cattle and pigs could not be kept through the winter and sometimes the need to put down hounds that were too hurt or sick to live, let be that he had hunted enough animals to the death for sport and food.

But Sir Ralph's death . . .

That had been different.

. . . his head all splintered bone and blood and gray brain matter . . .

And then Tom's death.

Tom lying there so . . . empty.

Gone past ever having back.

And now their mother said she could have made it so they never were at all . . .

Hugh gripped his head more tightly, wishing he could stop his thoughts. Any and all of his thoughts. Everything was become so tangled out of sense and shape, the whole world unraveling around him, with nothing left to his life but rough, torn, unmendable edges . . .

'Hugh?' Ursula asked softly.

He lifted his head. He had not realized it was grown so late; she was only a shadow-shape among the other garden shadows, and he said, 'Come looking for me? I'm sorry,' and made to rise.

But she asked, 'Could we just stay awhile? It's quiet here,' sat down beside him when he nodded, took his hand between her own small ones, and leaned against him. Her head came just to his shoulder.

Content to stay if she was, Hugh asked with feigned lightness, 'Is someone fighting again? Is that why you came for me?'

'They're just talking. Lucy is. She always does and then everybody else has to talk, too.'

'Words get to be heavy after a while, don't they? They wear you down.'

She nodded against his shoulder but did not say anything and neither did he, only slipped his near hand free of hers and put his arm around her waist, cuddling her to him the way he might have a lonely hound. He guessed they were both in need, himself and her, of someone to hold to and be held by; so he held to her and she held to him and they sat there in the garden quiet, neither of them saying anything while the last afterglow of the sunset faded behind the hall's roof and the stars thickened across the sky.

The green-gold morning was already warm when Frevisse and Sister Johane came out of the church after Mass next day. Such manor servants as had been there headed back to their morning duties at the hall and the villager folk went away to whatever work they could do about their own places while they waited for the dew to dry so harvest could go on. Lady Anneys, as was usual, had not come, nor Miles, but Frevisse had seen him at Mass only the one Sunday since she had come to Woodrim, and Hugh had been no better until this morning. Today he had accompanied his sisters, which made it easier at the Mass' end, when Frevisse said that she and Sister Johane were going to stay at the church awhile, for them to go happily away with him, back to the hall.

She had told Sister Johane on their way to church that she wanted to stay '. . . to talk a little with Father Leonel. He knows everyone here far better than we yet can. If he can help us understand more, perhaps we can help more.'

Sister Johane had readily accepted that. Only while they waited in the churchyard for him to come out did Frevisse suggest she should talk with him alone. 'He might be easier with only one of us, rather than two,' she said.

'He might be, yes,' Sister Johane agreed, possibly a little doubtfully, but she sat down, seemingly content to wait as long as need be, on the mounting block at the churchyard gate while Frevisse went back to the church door. Until last night she had not considered consulting the priest; he had seemed only an old man enduring a thankless place by being and seeing as little as he could. The exchange at supper last night had changed her mind about that and now she wanted to know not only what he knew but what he thought, and that, indeed, he would probably better say to one person than to two.

Father Leonel seemed surprised but not unwelcoming to find her there when he came out, but when she asked if she might speak with him, he only asked, 'Inside or out here, my lady?'

'Out here, if it please you. The day is so fair.'

'It is indeed. But I pray you pardon my aged body and let us sit.'

There was a bench made of a roughly flattened log pegged a-top two sawn-off stumps of wood beside the low churchyard wall well away from the gateway. Father Leonel led her there across the sheep-cropped grass of the churchyard's grave mounds and hollows, sat down with stiff carefulness, and said, 'Oddly enough, hot, damp days bother my aches more than cold ones do. It's a sorry thing when one has to be grateful for winter.' He settled himself, rested his gnarl-knuckled hands on his knees, and asked as

Frevisse sat down beside him, 'Is it spiritual counsel you want or help to deal with the Woderoves?'

Frevisse gave a small, surprised laugh. 'The Woderoves,' she said, returning the favor of his directness. 'Sister Johane and I want to give comfort and be a help but there's so much pain here that we don't understand.'

'I can give so little of the so much comfort that's needed that any comfort you can give will be most welcome. But where to start.' Father Leonel drew and released a deep breath. 'To begin, let it be said straight out that we're all the better for being rid of Sir Ralph.'

'I've gathered that,' Frevisse agreed. Though she had hardly expected him to say it out so bluntly.

'You've probably gathered enough that I need say nothing else about him?' He looked at her questioningly and she nodded that that was true. 'What have you determined about Lady Anneys in the while you've known her?' he asked.

'That she's endured by burying herself so deeply it will be a wonder if she ever finds herself again.'

Father Leonel's gaze at her became considering. 'That's well seen,' he said slowly. 'Very well seen.' He thought about something for a moment, then said, 'My hope is that enough of the strength she used to bury herself remains for her to bring herself back to life. Her children are going to need her.'

'And Miles.'

'Miles is a son to her in all but blood, but yes, perhaps Miles most especially. And Ursula.'

'Ursula? Was Sir Ralph particularly cruel to her?'

'It was Miles he was particularly cruel to, having come to hate the boy's father so greatly and despising his mother.'

'Why?'

'Sir Ralph hated Miles' father, his son, because the young man went against his wishes in everything. He hated Miles' mother because, as Sir Ralph often said – often enough that I remember the words – "The woman is French. What in the devil's name is there to like about her?" Besides, like his son, she fought Sir Ralph almost every day she knew him. Then, like his son, she died, and that left only their son for Sir Ralph to pay back for the both of them.'

Frevisse considered the ugliness of soul a man had to have to keep up that cruelty for year after year against a boy who had done nothing but be born.

'As for Ursula,' Father Leonel sighed, 'her trouble has been that she was her father's favorite. Can you imagine being the favored, petted, well-beloved child of a man who was a monster to everyone else around you?'

Barely, Frevisse could and said with muted horror, 'Blessed St Nicholas.' The patron saint of children.

Father Leonel nodded in dark agreement. 'Yes. A person might well turn either into a monster or, if their heart is good enough to resist that, live constantly trying not to cringe from him. Happily, Ursula's heart is good.'

'But if she was his favorite, how did he come to send her away to the nunnery?'

Father Leonel rubbed at one hand with the other. 'I think he saw it as a way to keep her for himself forever. Rather than give her up to a worldly husband, he intended she should become a nun and spend her life in prayer for him.'

'And Lady Elyn's marriage was because Sir William was his friend?'

'Partly, but mostly as a way to keep up hope of his properties and Sir William's being someday joined, if not in this generation, then perhaps a later. Sir William's only child, Philippa, had always been intended to marry Tom as Sir Ralph's heir. When Sir William began to think of marrying again, meaning he might have a son to replace Philippa as his heir, Sir Ralph reckoned to bring Sir Ralph's lands his way by marrying Elyn to Sir William. That way any more children Sir William had would be his grandchildren.'

'But now that Tom is dead?'

'I expect the expectation is for Master Hugh to marry her.'

It very surely was, but, 'Will he?'

'Very probably. He favors no one else so far as I know. They get on well enough together and all the reasons for marriage between Sir William's and Sir Ralph's heirs remain.'

'I gather Hugh got on better with his father than anyone else did?'

'He got on best with Sir Ralph, yes. Hugh is quiet-spirited enough he would rather oblige than quarrel, and their shared love of hounds and hunting meant he had some use and value to his father.'

'And Tom?'

'Tom,' Father Leonel said with a smile and softened voice that showed who had been his favorite. 'Tom had something of his father's quick angers but a better heart. A far better heart.' The old man's voice twisted with grief. 'He's a loss beyond measure.'

Frevisse paused for his grief, then said gently, 'It must have been more than only hard for you to see all this and be able to do so little. At least I suppose, from what I hear of Sir Ralph, there was little to be done with him?'

Father Leonel's aged face and voice hardened. 'There was nothing anybody could do with Sir Ralph except endure him, and yes, it was very bitter being priest to a man whom nothing could touch. Not guilt or pity. And never love.'

'But you stayed. Was there never chance to go? Plead your age and be given an easier parish?'

'I was needed here,' Father Leonel said simply. 'By everyone else if not by Sir Ralph. At least I could give comfort to some, shelter to others, and keep from quarreling with the man. Another priest might have given way to quarreling and, believe me, that would have done far more harm than good. To cross Sir Ralph in anything was merely to make the matter worse.'

'How did he come to die? I know he was killed in the forest but nothing else.'

Father Leonel sighed from far down inside himself and turned his head away to stare toward the forest's edge dark along the rising ground beyond the manor; stared for a long while before he said at last, his gaze still away, 'There had been a hunt that day. Only hare-coursing since it was nigh to high summer. There's a place not far inside the wood where they often gather before or during or after a day's hunting to rest and eat. A clearing with a spring and a small stream. They were there that day for the midday meal and resting afterwards, meaning to hunt again in the afternoon. I understand what happened was that one of the young hounds ran off into the woods and Sir Ralph and some of the others went after it. A while later, still searching for the dog, Hugh found Sir Ralph instead. Very dead. He had been savagely attacked, struck on the head with a rock. Struck many times. No one let Lady Anneys see the body. Nor his daughters. All was bad enough as it was. By the time I was brought, Lady Elyn was screaming and crying so that her mother had to be comforting her when it should have been the other way around.'

'Lady Elyn was there?'

'What? Oh, yes. They all were. Sir William, Lady Elyn, Philippa, Master Selenger. Lucy, too.'

'Sir William's steward was there?'

'He's Philippa's uncle, too. Brother to Sir William's first wife. As much family as steward, you see.'

'Was that usual, for them all to be here?'

'Oh, yes. Sir Ralph and Sir William shared a passion for hunting. They often hunted together.'

Frevisse hesitated over what she wanted most to ask: Did he have any thought of who might have killed Sir Ralph? She had claimed her questions were for the sake of understanding more so she could comfort better, and she had already ranged somewhat far from that – far enough that another straying question would make small difference, she decided and asked, 'There's no talk about who might have killed Sir Ralph?'

'Talk?' Father Leonel pulled himself straight as if his back ached. 'Alas, there's always talk.' He braced his hands on the bench to either side of himself and began the slow work of pushing himself to his feet. Frevisse quickly helped with a careful hold on his arm. On his feet at last, Father Leonel thanked her and began a stiff shuffle back toward the gate. She matched her steps to his but asked nothing more. They went in silence until, almost to the gate, he added, 'The only surety is that whoever did it must be far away by now, escaped from the law's judgment maybe, if not from God's.'

There was a second surety, too, Frevisse thought suddenly – that everyone *wanted* Sir Ralph's murderer to be someone long gone.

And that, unwillingly, made her wonder if he was.

At the gate she thanked Father Leonel for his time and help. He blessed both her and Sister Johane and was shuffling back toward his church as they went their way away toward the hall. Taken up with her own thoughts, Frevisse did not notice Sister Johane's silence until, almost to the manor yard, she asked, 'Was he able to help?'

Nearly, Frevisse said, 'Very little,' before she remembered the reason she had given for wanting to talk with him and said instead, 'Lady Anneys' husband was something of a monster. You've spent most time with the girls. Have they talked about him?'

'So very little that I've been wondering about him. They talk about their brother Tom but almost never about their father.'

'He seems to have cared for nothing much beyond himself and his dogs. Everyone lived afraid of his anger. Even Father Leonel, I think.'

'Nobody seems to mind he's dead, that's certain,' Sister Johane said. 'It's their brother that Lucy and Ursula are mourning, not him at all.'

'Everyone seems to mourn Tom. Everyone seems to have liked him and thought things would go well with him as lord of the manor.'

'Well, Master Hugh seems a good young man, too. He's kind to his sisters and his mother, certainly.'

'What do you think of Miles?'

Sister Johane was silent a time before she answered, 'He makes the girls laugh and I think he's Master Hugh's good friend, but he always seems like he's about to be angry at something.'

'By what Father Leonel says, Sir Ralph was worse to him than to anybody else.'

'Well, I'm just glad he can make Lucy laugh. He was the first one to give her something else to do besides cry.' Sister Johane wrinkled her forehead thoughtfully. 'Though she would have stopped sooner or later. You can only cry so long before you begin to bore even yourself.'

Surprised, because she had not thought Sister Johane saw things that sharply, Frevisse said, 'True,' so warmly that Sister Johane looked at her with answering surprise, making Frevisse wonder why. But something more had come into her mind while she and Sister Johane talked: they had both said 'seems' again and again. Now that she thought of it, it was a word she had been using often, if only to herself, since coming to Woodrim, and she thought on it harder as she and Sister Johane went on across the foreyard. So many things 'seemed' here at Woodrim. Why? And if so much 'seemed,' what truly was?

If so much was seeming here – if so many were holding up a

mask of themselves between their truth and what they wanted others to see of them – then what were they hiding? Or hiding from? Not from Sir Ralph anymore. That only left that they were hiding from each other.

Or hiding something they didn't want known.

Or else hiding from each other what they knew and did not want to know.

Or else were hiding to keep from knowing something more than they did. Because if you buried yourself deeply enough, you could keep from knowing almost anything.

Let them alone, she told herself. Leave things as they are. Let these people piece their lives back together and heal as best they could. It was no business of hers nor did she want to make it her business.

But buried things had a tendency to rot.

And what else had her questions to Father Leonel been except the beginning of making it her business? Something was deeply wrong here. She knew it, and she knew herself well enough to know that, once begun, she would not stop her seeking to know what.

They were nearly to the hall door but she said, 'Shall we go see the kennel and dogs we keep hearing about?'

'Yes!' Sister Johane said instantly, then added more hesitantly, 'Well, yes, but wouldn't it be better to ask Master Hugh to go with us?'

Because it was not to Hugh she wanted to talk, Frevisse said, 'Do we really want to hear that much about dogs?'

Sister Johane smiled at that, then a little frowned and looked vaguely around. 'Do we know where the kennel is?'

Frevisse pointed vaguely away to their left. 'I've seen Master Hugh go that way sometimes,' she said.

They found their way well enough, past a large elm tree beyond the hall and by way of the stableyard to finally the kennels, where the dog-boy was leaning at ease on the kennel-yard's gate, scratching under the chin of a young wolfhound standing on its hind legs, its forepaws on the gate top, its head towering above him. About a dozen other hounds of various sizes and kinds – rough-coated, smooth-coated, brindled, plain, and spotted brown and black – lay in the early morning sunlight or paced around the yard, and if the dog-boy was idle now, it was because he had already done his morning work; the kennel-yard was clean and the water in the well-scrubbed wooden trough unslobbered yet. He straightened from the fence and bowed low as Frevisse and Sister Johane approached, and Frevisse saw his eyes shift past them, expecting Hugh to be there.

'We thought we'd like to see the dogs without troubling Master Woderove,' she said before he could say anything. 'We thought surely you could tell us enough about them.'

The boy showed doubtful but willing. 'That I can, probably.' He looked past them again, maybe still hoping Hugh would somehow be there after all. 'You don't know where Master Hugh is, do you? He usually comes of a morning to see things.'

'He walked his sisters home from Mass,' Frevisse said. 'I don't know where he is now.'

The boy grimaced. 'Likely he's shut up with papers and ink again. There's too much of that when you're lord, looks to me.'

'I doubt he likes it any better,' Sister Johane said, kindly. 'What's your name?'

'Nay, I don't suppose he does,' the boy sadly agreed. 'Degory, my lady.'

'You keep a fine kennel, Degory. It reminds me of my father's. He keeps about thirty hounds. Or did when I was last at home.'

'Does he?' Degory's deference slid into eagerness. 'We've but fifteen. But they're good ones.'

'And beautifully kept. You do all the work yourself?' Sister Johane asked.

'Master Hugh and me, we did it between us. It's mostly me now, he's so taken up with other things. But I don't mind,' he added hurriedly. 'He comes when he can.'

'You're breeding here, too, aren't you? How many lines do you have?' Sister Johane asked.

Frevisse had been wondering how to set about putting the boy at ease enough to answer the questions she wanted to ask him. Sister Johane with her unexpected interest was solving that and Frevisse left her to it until in a while, when Sister Johane and Degory were talking of the training of hounds, Sister Johane said, 'My father won't have whip or stick used on his hounds. How is it with Master Woderove?'

'He's the same. He never hits at all. It was Sir Ralph used to hit all the time.'

'The dogs?' Frevisse put quickly in.

'Me mostly. He liked the hounds best, see, and Master Hugh and I, we train 'em well. There's never cause for hitting them.'

'With dogs this big, you want them well-trained, I suppose,' Frevisse said.

'Aye, well, they're quiet-minded anyway, by nature,' Degory said. 'You wouldn't want hounds that big wanting to fight you all the time on everything. They're quiet-natured but then we train them, too.'

'But one of them ran off the day Sir Ralph was killed,' Frevisse said, with a carefully concerned frown. 'That's what I've heard, anyway.'

'Oh, aye. That was Skyre, the silly bitch. She's young and hadn't learned better. That's her there.' Degory pointed to a smooth-coated, yellow hound lying alone in a corner of the yard, muzzle on paws but round, dark eyes fixed on the unknown women at the fence as if worried they were dangerous. 'She was shaping to be a good lymer but likely she's ruined, Master Woderove says. Whatever happened with Sir Ralph there in the woods, by the time I found her she was frighted silly out of her wits and doesn't look to be getting over it. Twitchy all the time, see. So maybe we'll keep her for a litter or two, if she breeds well, and then see what can be done with her.'

'What did happen in the woods with Sir Ralph?' Frevisse said, meaning to sound no more curious than anyone might be who lacked the courtesy not to ask at all. 'No one ever quite says and we don't like to ask Master Hugh. He found his father, didn't he?'

Degory's shudder looked a little practiced, as if maybe he had done it too often and hardly meant it anymore; and he answered readily enough, 'It was terrible. There's none of us will forget it.'

'Skyre had run off and Sir Ralph had gone after her?' Frevisse prompted.

'Aye. Silly bitch,' Degory said again, looking at the disgraced dog with pity and disgust. 'Saw a squirrel on the ground or something and took off after it. Sir Ralph yelled and that didn't help. Then he hit me and he hit Master Hugh and said to get after her and took off himself after her, too. That was the last we saw him. Until he was dead.'

'But you and Master Hugh went after her, too.'

'Oh, aye. Wouldn't dare otherwise once Sir Ralph said to.'

'Together?'

'No. Could cover more going separate, see.'

'And everyone else stayed where they were.'

'Master Tom wasn't there anymore. He'd fought with Sir Ralph already and gone home. I guess Sir William after a while tired of waiting and told Master Selenger they could look, too. Master Selenger was there at Sir Ralph's body even afore me when Master Hugh started yelling for help after he'd found Sir Ralph. Daft that was – all of us out looking for her. More likely to scare her off than not.' Degory lowered his voice but did not keep his satisfaction out of it. 'Sir William isn't so good with hounds as he likes to think he is. They're just things to hunt with, that's all, to him.'

'I've known dogs with finer feelings than any person,' said Sister Johane. 'There was one my father had . . .'

Frevisse let her and the boy talk on awhile longer before drawing Sister Johane off by suggesting they would be missed by now. Sister Johane gave way unwillingly, told Degory again that he kept a fine kennel, and talked happily all the way back to the hall about dogs she had known. Grateful for the unwitting help she had been, Frevisse let her.

Chapter 15

Since coming to Woodrim, Frevisse had tried to keep the Offices of prayer at something like their proper times. This morning they were late about it because of her time with Father Leonel and the dog-boy, and while they were going back to the hall, Sister Johane said a little hopefully, 'We've missed Tierce. We could simply forgo it and do only Sext.'

'Or we could do both,' Frevisse said in a way that said they *were* going to do both.

Sister Johane sighed but made no protest. There were servant-sounds from kitchenward as they crossed the hall toward the stairs but the hall was empty, and the bedchamber, too. Breviaries in hand, they sat together on one of the chests and began. The familiar web of prayers and psalms – *Et posuit in ore meo canticum novum, carmen Deo nostro . . . Beatus vir, qui posuit in Domino spem suam.* And he put in my mouth a new song, a song to our God . . . Happy man, who puts in the Lord his hope – quickly drew Frevisse away from all the ways her thoughts had been twisting since yesterday. That was the pleasure and much of the blessing of the Offices: they were reminder that there was more than only here and this brief now; that there were other passions than the passing ones of the body; that there was Love beyond love and Joy beyond the world's so easily lost happinesses.

There were surely lost happinesses enough here at Woodrim. Nor had Sir Ralph's death purged the ugliness he had made of his life. *Exstingue flammas litium.* Put out the flames of quarrel. *Aufer calorem noxium, Confer salutem corporum, Veramque pacem cordium.* Take away guilty love, Give health to the body, And true peace to the soul.

But there wasn't peace here. There was a shadow through everything, like blight through a field of grain, sickening and blackening what should have been well and fine.

From what did the shadow come? And how many people knew of it?

Most here might well be living in it without knowing that they were, or else, like herself, they knew there was a darkness without knowing what it was. But it was here, subtly eating at hearts and minds.

Or maybe not so subtly, for some.

Was it suspicion that cast the shadow, she suddenly wondered. She had her own suspicion, surely, and it was a dark one – that Sir Ralph's murderer was not someone long gone; that he was still here. And very probably she was not the only one who suspected that. Suspicion without certainty – that was a darkness very hard to live in. Or – worse – not suspicion but certainty the murderer was still here without knowing who he was. That would cast a darkness deep enough to make the shadow she felt here.

But worse yet was her guess that no one wanted Sir Ralph's murderer caught. That they would rather, given the choice, live in the shadow.

When the Office ended, she would have sat quietly awhile longer, but Sister Johane closed her prayer book with a satisfied sigh and stood up, ready for whatever came next. Frevisse set aside a stir of impatience, looked up at her, and said, kindly rather than accusing, 'You're enjoying being here.'

With open pleasure, Sister Johane said, 'I am. It makes such a change, being around people who aren't nuns.'

With effort Frevisse kept hidden her worry at that, but Sister Johane said next, with a small, thoughtful frown, 'It helps me remember how good it is to be a nun. It's not as if being a nun is easy.' She was frowning harder, staring at the wall above Frevisse's head with concentration, her breviary held to her breast. 'But so many of the problems are inward. They can be made all right if I look at them hard enough, grow enough so I can understand them and change myself. Not like poor Lady Anneys, who's had so many things happen *to* her she can't find her balance at all. Or like Lucy, who doesn't even try to think about things, just feels them as hard as she can.'

Sister Johane suddenly realized she was saying all that aloud and maybe read the surprise open on Frevisse's face as disapproval because she ducked her head and said hurriedly, 'It's not that I don't like Lucy. I do. She's just so . . . so . . .'

'So very young?' Frevisse supplied, with a silent laugh at herself because, to her, Sister Johane was very young; but Sister Johane had taken her vows when she was hardly older than Lucy was and had been a nun almost ten years.

'Yes,' Sister Johane said, encouraged. 'She's very young.'

'And Ursula?' Frevisse asked, finding for the first time that she was interested in what Sister Johane thought about something.

Sister Johane a little frowned again. 'I don't know about Ursula. She reminds me of her brother, the way she keeps herself to herself. Or do I mean she reminds me of Miles? No, she doesn't have Miles' anger. She just has Hugh's quietness. Is she going to be a nun, do you think?'

'I don't know,' Frevisse answered, thoughtful in her turn because Sister Johane was right: Ursula did not show herself.

She considered that as she and Sister Johane put away their breviaries and went downstairs. Despite Ursula seemed an open child and Hugh an open young man, Frevisse's talk with Father Leonel had shown her there were very likely deeply hidden places in them both, places where they had hidden from their father. Nor were they probably the only ones. Lady Anneys, assuredly. Tom very probably. Even Father Leonel, elderly and crippled, had kept hidden his secret reworking of the manor accounts. Oddly enough, Miles in his way was probably the most open of any of them. His hatred for Sir Ralph had never been hidden, she had gathered, and his pleasure that Sir Ralph was dead was completely open.

Or did he have other things hidden so deep there was no hint of them for anyone to see?

When her thinking turned that far around on its own track, with nothing to feed on but itself, Frevisse knew to be done with it for a time and she was glad to find Lady Anneys, Lucy, and Ursula in the garden, weeding one of the herb beds. All three of them were lightly dressed in simple linen gowns over their underdresses, with sleeves pushed up and only Lady Anneys bothering with shoes though they all wore broad-brimmed straw hats against the sun riding high now, the day bright and warm.

They all straightened to greet Frevisse and Sister Johane, with

Lucy asking, 'Aren't you too hot, wearing all that and your wimples and veils and all? I'm simply roasting. Can't you take some of it off?'

'We're used to it,' said Sister Johane. She sounded faintly surprised, though perhaps not at Lucy so much as at herself, maybe only just realizing how completely her nun's clothing was part of her. Frevisse well remembered the moment, well into her own nunhood, when she had realized how used she was to her nun's clothing, how unnatural she would have felt wearing anything else or even less of it.

'Besides,' said Ursula at her sister, scornfully, 'they *have* to wear it.'

Lucy wiped at her forehead. 'Then there's another reason I'll never be a nun.'

Lady Anneys wiped at her forehead, too, then pressed her hand to it, her eyes closed. For coolness' sake, she wore only a loose veil over her hair and no wimple at all, but her face was an odd shade of white and Frevisse asked, thinking the day's warmth was too much for her, 'My lady, are you ill?'

'One of my headaches,' Lady Anneys said.

'It isn't better?' Ursula asked, then said to Sister Johane, 'She took fennel and that usually helps.'

'It hasn't this time,' Lady Anneys said. 'It's that the day's so warm, I think.' Her voice wavered, as if thinking were difficult. 'It's worsening. Do you have something stronger that might help, Sister?'

'Yes, but you'd best come inside, out of the sun, and lie down while I ready it.' Sister Johane sounded very much like Dame Claire in one of her brisker moments. 'Ursula, please pick me some balm and bring it after us. I'll be in the kitchen after I've seen your mother to her bed.'

Lady Anneys and Sister Johane went away together, Ursula picked a goodly handful of the balm and hurried out of the garden after them, and Frevisse asked Lucy, 'What can I do? If you point me to what a weed looks like, I can try to pull out nothing else.'

'I'm tired of weeds,' Lucy said. 'Let's head the basil for a while.'

Frevisse was willing to that. Whereas one green plant looked much like another to her, making her a peril in the garden when it came to weeding, she could tell a plain leaf from a flower and plucking off the flower stems from basil plants, to keep the herb usable for longer, was well within her ability. Besides, the spicey scent of the basil in the warm sunshine and on her fingers was pleasant and soothing and she was willing to be soothed just now. Even Lucy's talk was undisturbing, since so little thought needed be given to it, Lucy giving so little to it herself. She started with mourning her mother's headache, went on to say she liked the smell of basil, and, 'Sister Johane is so clever about herbs. She made my eyes stop being red after I'd cried so much for Tom. She's given me something to bathe them with when I've been crying again. I don't know what it is, though.'

'Eyebright,' Frevisse murmured.

'That might be it. There can hardly be anything more useful than knowing how to do things like that, don't you think? I mean to have her teach me things like that while she's here. When there's less going on.'

Frevisse kept to herself that thought that Lucy was probably someone who often meant to do things, only to be satisfied that the intent was as good as the deed and did nothing. Working far more slowly from plant to plant than Frevisse was – despite Frevisse was making no haste – Lucy had talked her way around to how she hoped Ursula didn't go back to the nunnery, she was better at reading aloud than Lucy was and so Lucy didn't have to do it if Ursula was home – 'Besides, I like listening better than having to read' – by the time Sister Johane came back into the garden, her own sleeves rolled up now and worry on her face. Interrupting Lucy as if she knew that were the best way to get a word in, she said, 'Dame Frevisse, I know it's almost time for Nones but I'm in the midst of mixing the drink for Lady Anneys and I'd like to sit with her after she's taken it. Might I miss prayers this time?'

'There are more ways than one to pray,' Frevisse said. 'What you're doing can be prayer in its way. And it's certainly a mercy. Of course go on with it.'

Lucy watched Sister Johane hurry out of the garden and said as if the two had no business together, 'She's quite pretty. Why did she ever become a nun?'

Frevisse settled for, 'Her aunt was our prioress at the time,' and that was sufficient to satisfy Lucy, who shifted to talking happily of her hope that Hugh would see to arranging her marriage soon.

'Though he'll probably marry Philippa before he sees to mine, and that will have to wait until we've done the mourning time for Tom.'

Frevisse had been about to excuse herself to say Nones but asked instead, 'Does Philippa mind she's to marry Hugh, not Tom?'

'Oh, I don't know she liked Tom better than she likes Hugh so it's much the same to her, I should think.' Lucy gave another sigh, this one just short of tears. 'It's Tom I feel sorry for. I do so miss Tom. Everything is so wrong without him.'

'Wrong?'

'Not the same. I was already used to Father being gone, and Master Selenger had been coming to see Mother all the time and that was so sweet – except she went away and I don't understand why, except it was too soon after Father died for her to be interested in Master Selenger, I suppose – and Tom was going to marry Philippa. Everything was *good* and now it isn't. I hardly get to see Elyn or Philippa, and Master Selenger isn't welcome here anymore and Hugh is unhappy . . .'

'More unhappy than after your father's death?'

'Oh, much more unhappy. He loved Tom.' She lowered her voice. 'He doesn't want to be lord of the manor. He just wants to be with his dogs and go hunting.' She tossed her head. 'But that's just too bad for him. He's just going to have to make the best of it and that's all there is to it.'

Frevisse had long since ceased to be surprised that 'that's all there is to it' always applied to other people and rarely to the person saying it. She knew she should go aside to her prayers now, but since Lucy was so ready to talk and another chance with her alone might not come so easily, Frevisse quelled her conscience and said, 'If Hugh's badly missing his father and brother, that makes it all harder for him.'

'If anyone is missing Father, it's Hugh,' Lucy granted. 'They both liked the hounds and hunting. Now there's just Hugh likes the hunting. Until we can be friends with Sir William again, I suppose.'

'Don't you like the hunting?'

Lucy shrugged a shoulder. They had finished with the basil but she was too happy with talking to move on to something else. 'Not much. Noise and blood. That's all it is.'

'But you were there on the hunt the day your father died, weren't you?'

'There for the hare-hunting? Never.' Lucy found the thought displeasing. 'You can't imagine how stupid that is. No, Mother and Philippa and I were at the gathering place with the food and servants, that's all. That's the only good part about the hunting. We eat and sit on cushions by the stream and talk. That day we sang, too. Philippa and her uncle sing lovely together. And Miles,' she added, as if surprised. 'He can sing, too, when he wants to. But he hardly ever wants to.' She giggled. 'He did that day, though, because Philippa was.' She leaned toward Frevisse and lowered her voice, as if imparting a choice secret. 'I think he's fond of her. You know?'

'Ah,' Frevisse said, trying to sound only lightly interested. 'And is she fond of him?'

Lucy frowned. 'She *likes* him but I can't get her to say it's more than that, no matter how I push her to.'

Frevisse held back from pointing out that if Philippa was to marry Hugh, trying to make her admit to caring for Miles was hardly kind. Instead, while she looked for a way to lead on to anything about Sir Ralph's murder, Lucy went on, 'They went off together that day. That's all I know. And they didn't hurry back even when the shouting started. When Hugh found Father's body, there was so much shouting, you know.'

'They went off together? Miles and Philippa? Looking for the dog that ran off, you mean?'

Lucy laughed. 'Hardly! Father went, and Hugh and Degory, and they were no more than gone when Sir William said he might as well look, too, as sit there, and he and Master Selenger went off, too. I asked Miles if he wasn't going to go. He said he wasn't, but Philippa said she was tired of sitting and wanted him to walk with her.'

'So the forest is fairly open there?' Most forests – especially those kept for hunting – were less trees than open ground, with large clearings and little undergrowth. It was something Frevisse only now considered about Sir Ralph's death. How had he been so away from the others that he could be killed and no one either see or hear it happen or catch sight of his murderer?

But Lucy said, 'Oh, no. It's not open at all. The king's forest – the royal chase that Father has right . . . had right to – that's clear and open, of course, but Father always kept our woods thicker. For coverts, you know. If the deer had places to hide, they'd stay nearer, that's what he said. He only let the villagers use it a little, for fattening the pigs on acorns in the autumn and hardly at all to gather wood. He and Tom used to quarrel over that. Tom said it wasn't fair people had to go so far for wood – there's another bit of woodland at a far end of the manor – and Father said he didn't care. I remember once Tom yelled at him, "If you didn't like pork, you probably wouldn't even let the pigs in to fatten," and Father yelled back, "You're damnably right I wouldn't!" ' Lucy laughed, then lowered her voice again, though Frevisse didn't know who else was likely to hear her. 'But I think the villagers took more wood from there than Father knew about and I think Tom let them. He just kept quiet and never fined anyone unless Father caught them at it himself.'

'But Philippa wanted to walk there?'

Lucy shrugged her shoulder again. 'There are paths. They went off along one of those.' She lowered her voice to almost a whisper and leaned toward Frevisse. 'I don't think Mother or Elyn liked it but I asked Elyn something and kept her talking to me until they were gone.'

And they had not come quickly back even when the shouting over Sir Ralph's body began. Frevisse, not worried Lucy would make too much of any questions – the girl enjoyed talking too much to pause for thinking – asked, 'So you and your mother and Lady Elyn were alone, still at the gathering place, when Sir Ralph's body was found? What did you do?'

Lucy's eyes grew big. 'We didn't know *what* to do. We didn't even know what the shouting was about.' Whatever horror there had been that day had been, for her, replaced by the pleasure of being horrified by it all over again. 'Nobody else knew either. Sir William came crashing back into the clearing, wanting to know what was happening, were we all right, told us to stay there, then ran off toward the shouting. The dogs all started barking and we tried to quiet them and then Degory came, with a great, bleeding scratch down one side of his face, and he was crying and said Sir

Ralph was dead and he had to fetch Tom and Father Leonel. After that Mother and Elyn and I just stood there, holding on to each other, not even crying, just waiting to find out what had happened, not believing it could be that bad. It was forever before Tom and Father Leonel came and of course they didn't know anything either, but then Master Selenger came back to us and he knew. Sir William had sent him and he told us all that someone had killed Sir Ralph and that Father Leonel and Tom had better come see the body because they couldn't leave it there for the crowner, but Mother and Elyn and Philippa and I had better go back to the manor. It was terrible.'

'When did Philippa and Miles come back to you?'

'Oh, sometime then, while all that was happening. We told them what Degory had said and Miles went off to join the rest of them.' Lucy lowered her voice again. 'We were never even let to see Father's body when they brought it back. Did you know that? Not even Mother. Isn't that awful?'

Frevisse agreed it was, tried to think what else she might get out of Lucy, but decided to excuse herself at last to say Nones. 'I'll just go into the arbor if that won't bother you.'

'Oh no, of course it won't. But don't you need your book?'

'It's in the bedchamber and I won't chance disturbing Lady Anneys. I know it mostly by heart.'

'By heart,' Lucy said with awe. 'Oh, my. I mean to learn some of my prayers that way sometime. I mean, besides the paternoster and ave.'

Frevisse granted that would be a good thing and went to settle to Nones in the arbor, leaving the girl poking among the feverfew for weeds.

Chapter 16

Lady Anneys was not at dinner but, 'I gave her something to help her to sleep as well as ease her headache,' Sister Johane said to Hugh's question.

Nor was Miles there, and when Ursula asked about him, Hugh answered, 'He said at breakfast he was going off to Beech Heath. That's too far for being back by now.'

'He's always gone somewhere,' Ursula complained. 'Even more than before.'

'He'll be gone altogether after Michaelmas,' said Lucy. She leaned forward to say past Hugh to Frevisse and Sister Johane, 'That's when he means to go to his own manor in Leicestershire.' She sat back and added to Ursula, goading older sister to younger, 'We'll probably never see him again after that.'

'Of course we'll see him,' said Hugh impatiently, shoving the cheese tart to her instead of politely serving her.

Lucy stared indignantly first at the tart, then at him, but Ursula reached for it and willingly helped herself while insisting, 'He doesn't have to go. Father hardly ever went. He could just stay here like always.'

'He'll want to marry, you goose,' Lucy said. 'His wife won't want to be here with all of us. Whoever she is,' she added, trying to sound meaningful about it.

No one chose to take a meaning from it; or if they did, they kept it to themselves in a thick silence that made Frevisse wonder if some besides Lucy had thoughts about Miles and Philippa. Did Hugh suspect he might have a rival for his proposed wife? The day of the inquest, when everyone had been here and she might have noted something, Frevisse had known too little about anyone to be much judging what she saw. Had she seen anything particular between Miles and Philippa then? Or between Hugh and Philippa, come to that. She remembered nothing, but it had hardly been the time or place for something that way, anyway. But what if Lucy was not merely making trouble when she talked of Miles and Philippa? What would happen if that was real and they were foolish?

In the while she had been here, it had become plain to her that there was friendship between Hugh and Miles. That made her think better of Miles than she might have. With his bitter edge and sharp tongue, friendship with him could not have come easily; that it was there between him and Hugh meant there must be more to him than she had so far seen. And judging by the tender way Lady Anneys had leaned from her chair and stroked Miles' hair back from his hot forehead the other evening, when he had been sitting on the parlor floor playing at jackstraws with Ursula, and how he had paused to smile up at her, he was – as Father Leonel had said – a son in all but blood, as dear as Hugh and her daughters openly were. Frevisse guessed that despite all that Sir Ralph had done to ruin these people – when they might have chosen to be as savage to each other as he was to all of them – they had all banded together instead, made a hard knot of family against him and guarded each other as best they could. And that, Frevisse suspected, was Lady Anneys' doing more than anyone's. She had outwardly submitted to Sir Ralph because she had to and must have kept much of herself buried beyond his reach through the years of her marriage; but she had never surrendered. She had loved and sheltered her sons and Miles and her daughters as best she could and now if she could have peace for a while and a chance to heal – maybe she could become herself, instead of Sir Ralph's wife, just as they all had chance to live as themselves now Sir Ralph was dead.

And yet . . .

Listening without heed to Lucy trying to persuade Hugh that they all needed to go to Banbury market next week – 'For something different to do!' she pleaded – and him telling her, 'Not while harvest is on,' and eating without noting the pottage of broad beans fried with onions and sage set before her, Frevisse probed at the uneasy edge of her thoughts. And yet . . . what?

Behind the affection among them all and beyond the relief of Sir Ralph's death and the still-raw grief for Tom there was something else.

She put a word to it.

Wariness.

Not that wariness was unreasonable, given the hell Sir Ralph seemed to have kept them in while he lived.

But he was dead now.

Was it simply that it was too soon after his death to leave behind all the old ways of feeling? Lucy seemed to have done so; Frevisse felt no undercurrents or shut doors in her. But from the others . . . even Ursula . . . there was that sense of wariness, of being guarded. Against what?

The meal was ended. As they rose from their places, Ursula asked, 'Can you keep us company awhile, Hugh?'

He tweaked one of her long, braided plaits. 'I fear not. I'm going out with Father Leonel to see how the harvest is coming on.'

'The way Tom used to,' Lucy said, all mournful.

Hugh sent her a glance of dislike. 'Yes. Like Tom used to,' he snapped, then said to Ursula, more kindly, 'I want to see how much longer it's likely to be before we need to hunt a deer for the harvest-home feast.'

'Kill two this year,' said Lucy. 'So there'll be enough for us afterwards.'

'Greedy,' he said, not meaning it, and bowed to Frevisse and Sister Johane. 'By your leave, my ladies.'

They bent their heads to him in return and he left, leaving them with all the afternoon ahead of them. Sister Johane went to be sure Lady Anneys was sleeping quietly while Ursula and Lucy fetched their sewing and Mandeville's *Travels* from the parlor, and when Sister Johane came down, the four of them went out to the arbor's shade. This warm middle of the day, the quiet there was as thick as the sunlight save for the hum of bees. Frevisse would have willingly joined the quiet or else read, but when the girls had opened their sewing baskets and set to work on Hugh's and Miles' shirts again, Lucy began to talk of how she meant to persuade her mother to buy her some red cloth to make her a new gown this autumn.

'Something very, very bright, but I don't know yet whether I want crimson or scarlet,' she said.

'You won't be able to wear it for almost a year,' Ursula pointed out.

'I won't have to hurry at making it, then, will I? And I'll have it waiting for me when I don't have to be in mourning anymore, while you'll have to go back to wearing your same old gowns then.'

'By then Ursula will probably have outgrown anything that fits her now and need a new gown, too,' Sister Johane said, maybe trying to head off trouble.

But well able to see to her sister herself, Ursula retorted at Lucy, '*You'll* probably be too fat by this time next year to fit into anything you make now.'

'Fat?' Lucy protested. 'I won't be!'

'Fat*ter*,' Ursula said with great and insulting precision.

'Shall I read?' said Frevisse, taking up the book at the same moment that Sister Johane said, 'Would you like me to stitch this neckband together for you, Lucy?,' picking up the pieces of cloth from the sewing basket between them.

The distraction worked. While Lucy showed how wide a seam the neckband should have, Frevisse opened the book at the ribbon marking her place and began to read aloud about the court of the Great Khan in Cathay, her voice pitched low to match the garden's quiet. She was reading of the Tartars' round houses when Sister Johane cried out, 'Oh!' with such sharp dismay that Frevisse, Lucy, and Ursula all looked at her. She stared back, wide-eyed with alarm. 'I forgot! Lady Anneys asked if I'd make certain Helinor in the kitchen had sent the boon-ale to the field.' The lord of the manor's expected daily gift to his people during harvest.

'The workers won't like it if she hasn't,' Lucy said. 'Even Father never dared stop their boon-ale. He wanted to, though.'

'Helinor wouldn't forget,' Ursula said scornfully.

Sister Johane started to lay her sewing aside. 'But I told Lady Anneys I'd make certain.'

'I'll go,' said Frevisse. She placed the ribbon where she had left off, closed the book, and stood up before Sister Johane could. 'You go on with your sewing.'

Sister Johane accepted that with willing thanks that gave some ease to Frevisse's slight guilt, because she had offered not to be helpful but because she saw suddenly a chance to talk unsuspiciously with whoever was at work in the kitchen this afternoon.

When she had gone inside and through the pantry into the kitchen, she found it a square and high-roofed room with a deep stone fireplace along one wall, flanked with racks of pans, kettles, grill, and skillet and hanging long-handled spoons, ladles, and forks. A long, narrow table ran along the wall beside the door from the pantry, for setting out readied dishes to be carried into the hall during a meal, while the middle of the room was filled by the solid bulk of a worktable where three people could work side by side without touching elbows and broad enough a person would have to stretch to set a bowl across it to the far edge. To Frevisse's regret, though, there was only one person presently at work there, an aproned woman of late middle-years briskly slicing a young onion's long green leaves to small pieces on a well-scrubbed cutting board at the table's far end.

She stopped when Frevisse entered and, with the knife poised over her work, gave her a quick curtsy while asking, 'May I help you, my lady?'

The Woderove household was not large but Frevisse knew more than a lone woman was needed in the kitchen and asked in return, surprised, 'Where's everyone else?' Then immediately answered her own question. 'Gone to fields for the harvest, of course.'

'That's right,' the woman agreed.

She still stood with the knife ready over the onion and Frevisse said, 'Go on, please,' looked at the basket sitting beside the cutting board, heaped with more onions and clean, slender carrots, and said, 'You've more than enough for one woman to be doing alone, if that's to be for supper.'

'Aye.' The woman went back to slicing, deft and quick about it. She was not unfriendly, just very busy. 'Alson will be back in time to help finish it all off, though.'

'May I help?'

The woman gave her a quick, doubting glance.

'I often do it at the nunnery,' Frevisse said. St Frideswide's was not so prosperous it could afford many servants nor so large that any nun could be allowed to stand on her dignity; they all had turns at what work needed to be done, including in the kitchen.

'If you like, then, it would be a help, aye,' the woman said without pausing at her work. 'There's more knives there.'

She nodded to the rack fastened to the table's end and Frevisse took one, saying while reaching for a carrot, 'I came to ask if Helinor had seen to the boon-ale going to the field. Are you Helinor?'

'I'm Helinor and the ale has gone. I'd not be allowed to forget for long, that's sure. Somebody would be at the kitchen door asking.'

The kitchen door stood open to a garden far less well-kept than Lady Anneys' but flourishing with all the different greens of herbs and summer vegetables useful to cooking. Frevisse complimented it as a way to starting talk with Helinor, who said cheerfully, 'Oh, aye. It's been a good-growing summer.'

'The harvest looks to be fine, from all I've heard.'

'Very fine. It's going to be a happy harvest-home when it comes.'

'Will it be much of a harvest-home, what with the mourning and all?'

'Aye, there's that,' Helinor said soberly. 'Master Tom is going to be missed. He loved harvest-home, he did. Every year he worked hard as anyone to make it happen. He would have been a good lord to have. He'll be kindly remembered. There's been more than a few candles lighted in the church for him.'

'But not for Sir Ralph?'

Helinor hacked with sudden, unnecessary savagery at a defenseless onion she had just put on the cutting board. 'Any candles lighted will be in thanks to whoever did for the old bastard. Begging your pardon for speaking out,' she added.

'No pardon needed,' Frevisse said easily, to show she was willing to hear more. 'From what I've heard, he needed killing.'

'He did that.' The onion, having suffered enough, was swept aside with the knife blade to join the growing pile of its predecessors. 'At birth, if you ask me.' Helinor began on another onion with no more mercy than she had shown the last one. 'The wonder is he lasted so long as he did.'

Working less viciously at a carrot, Frevisse ventured, 'I don't think anyone even cares who did it.'

'They don't that. Not in the least. Except maybe we'd like to thank him. Only there's so many likely to have done it, we'll never know. My own guess is it was one of the men he'd driven off from here, come back to do for him and long gone again.'

'He'd forced a great many men away?'

'More than his fair share.' The pieces of the onion were swept aside and another took its place. 'He didn't care about people at all, or their rights. The manor and its folk were here long before he came, but he acted like nobody mattered aught but him and what he wanted. We weren't even supposed to keep the deer out of the fields. They come out of the woods into the fields to graze and we were supposed to let them, because then they'd be near to hand for hunting. "Eaten by the deer" is what we say about someone when they can't bear it anymore and leave. Half a dozen men in the past ten years. And women, too. It's been bad.'

'What sort of lord do you think Master Hugh will be?'

Helinor paused to consider that, then set at the onion again. 'Not so bad as Sir Ralph, that's sure. He has a kinder heart.'

'No one's afraid he'll be like his father about the deer?'

'He's let Master Tom's order stand that we could keep them out of the fields this year. That's enough to satisfy everyone for now.'

Finishing one carrot and starting another, Frevisse said thoughtfully, 'What I've found odd is that no one ever says how Sir Ralph died. They say he was found dead in the forest but not how he was killed. It must have been terrible?'

'Terrible enough that nobody will ever talk of it around Lady Anneys or her daughters if they've any kindness toward them at all.'

'You saw his body?' Frevisse prompted.

'Ha. I was one of them that had to clean it and ready it for burial. Nobody was going to let Lady Anneys see it, let alone do any of that. His head was all smashed in. Someone took a rock to it and smashed it to bits.'

Because it was expected of her, Frevisse made a wordless sound of horror.

'Aye, it was bad.' Memory of it subdued even Helinor. She paused, staring down at the half-chopped onion on the cutting board. 'His head was broken so bad I don't even know if all the pieces were there. We had to wrap it in waxed cloth to hold together what there was, then pad it around with more cloth to give it a head-shape before we wrapped it in the shroud. So it would look right.' She shook her head and started cutting again. 'It was bad, aye.'

'There weren't any other wounds on the body? Just his head all smashed?'

'That's all. He'd not been stabbed or beaten or anything else. Just his head smashed to bone-bits and bloody pulp. That's why I say it was someone he'd wronged and they'd come back to do for him. It was revenge, not simple killing, if you see what I mean.'

Frevisse saw and went back to carefully slicing the carrot she had in hand before she said, 'Well, Lady Anneys is better off, from all I hear.'

'She is that. But Master Tom's death is a grief she didn't need. Nor none of us. Still, she's rid of Sir Ralph and that's more than a little to the good. I just hope she doesn't make haste over marrying that Master Selenger.'

'Is she likely to? Are people saying it's likely?'

'Well, he's here as often as not, isn't he? Started a few days after Sir Ralph was buried and it's not for the sake of anyone else's company he comes.' Helinor smiled at her present onion, going at it less brutally with her knife. 'He's a good-looking man and well-mannered. He could do with a wife and she could do worse. Besides, what's she to do with herself after Lady Philippa marries Master Hugh? She's too good a lady to think there can be two mistresses in one house or want to keep Master Hugh's wife from her rights.'

So the provisions of Sir Ralph's will concerning Lady Anneys' remarrying were still as secret as Lady Anneys supposed, Frevisse thought, and there seemed to be no suspicions about Hugh marrying Philippa. Knowing she must go back to the garden soon but hoping for more, she said mildly, 'Things will be different around here when all that has happened. Master Miles will be leaving soon, too, I gather.'

'So we hear. Poor lad. It's time he had a life of his own but he's going to be lonely at it, I fear.'

'He could well marry, now he had his own manor.'

'Not from what I hear about that manor. Run-down and neglected. He'd need a wife who'd bring money with her, and what woman with money would marry someone with no more to offer than a ruined manor?' Helinor had finished the last onion and began on the carrots, their pile already much lessened by Frevisse. 'But you have the right of it about things here. They'll be different and God be praised for that. The sorry thing is that it was hardest on Master Miles, maybe, when that old devil Sir Ralph was alive, but now that everything's changed, it's still Master Miles who's going to have it hardest. Those three boys were good at guarding each other's backs. They worked together and now Master Hugh has the manor and will have a wife, while Master Miles must go off on his own to somewhere he's never been before and make a whole new life for himself. That's going to be hard for him. Hard, too, for Master Hugh,' she added after a thoughtful moment. 'Being left alone when for so long there's been the three of them.'

Frevisse thought the same, now she came to think of it at all. But she was also thinking of what else Helinor had said. Hugh, Miles, and Tom had worked together; but Hugh hadn't known about Tom's and Father Leonel's twisting of the accounts. Had Miles? Who had been keeping secrets from whom? And what other secrets might there be?

And then there were the provisions against Lady Anneys remarrying. Both Hugh and Miles knew about those but neither her daughters nor the servants did. Come to that, Lady Anneys did not know whether Master Selenger did or not, and on that hung the question of whether or not Sir William was playing some sort of double game of marriage – his daughter's and Lady Anneys' – to his own advantage.

How many layers of secrets were here? Frevisse wondered. When she had first come to Woodrim, she had assumed that with a family torn by the grief of two deaths, there would be sorrow in plenty but a straightforward sorrow, straightly dealt with. Instead, she was finding almost nothing was straightforward here at all.

She worked awhile longer, leading Helinor to talk about Lucy, Ursula, and Lady Elyn but learning nothing she did not already know except that, 'Oh, aye, Elyn was ready to be married, she was. Couldn't wait to be Lady Elyn and away from here. Took to that marriage from the moment it was offered her and who could blame her?' Helinor said. 'Anything to be away from here. Another one on the run from Sir Ralph.'

'She wanted it more to be away from Sir Ralph than for love of

Sir William, you mean?'

'Very much more.' About that Helinor had no doubts.

'But now Sir Ralph is dead and no one was counting on that.'

'She took her chance when it came,' Helinor said, unconcerned. 'She made her bed and must go on lying in it, just like everyone else does.'

Chapter 17

As Frevisse passed through the garden, returning to the arbor, she saw over the garden's back gate a manservant sitting on the grassy edge of the far side of the cart-track, holding the reins of two grazing horses. She knew neither the man nor the horses and for a moment did not know the girl, either, seated in the arbor between Lucy and Ursula, turning the pages of Mandeville's *Travels*, then realized she was Sir William's daughter, the talked-of Philippa, as the girl stood up and curtsied to her, saying, 'My lady.'

Frevisse bent her head in return and they both sat, Frevisse beside Sister Johane on the bench facing her and taking the chance for a long look as Lucy went on saying, '. . . didn't come with you only because it's too hot? She's feeling well, isn't she? She's not, um, not . . .'

'Breeding?' Ursula asked brightly, looking up from her sewing.

'*Ursula*,' Lucy said, sending quick looks toward Sister Johane and Frevisse, probably to warn against talking about such things in front of nuns.

But Ursula had spent enough time among nuns not to think their living out of the world meant they were unworldly, and said, still brightly, 'But that's what we all want to know, isn't it? Is Elyn going to have a baby and spoil Philippa's chance to marry Hugh?'

'That won't spoil her chance to marry Hugh. She just won't bring as much to the marriage,' Lucy snapped.

'How far have you gone with Mandeville?' Philippa asked somewhat quickly, opening the book again. She was an even-featured girl, nothing particular about her and her hair simply brown, but she knew when and how to change the course of a conversation. 'I like the part about the dog-headed people the best. What about you, Lucy?'

'There are too many dog-heads around here as it is,' said Lucy. 'I like to hear about all the riches in Cathay. When is Master Selenger coming to visit Mother again?'

'I don't know,' Philippa said with a lightness that failed to ring completely true to Frevisse. 'He probably wouldn't be good company if he did. He had angry words with Father this morning.'

'About what?' Lucy asked eagerly.

'*Lucy*,' Ursula said.

But Philippa answered, 'I don't know. I could hear that they were angry, but not about what.'

'It's because of Mother,' said Lucy certainly. 'He's pining and angry because she won't say she'll marry him.'

'Lucy, why would that make my father angry at him?' Philippa said patiently. 'Besides, Uncle John isn't that unsensible, to expect Lady Anneys to be ready to marry again so soon.'

'How is your father?' Sister Johane asked, taking the talk a different way. Deliberately, Frevisse thought, but this time regretted it. She would have liked to hear more about Selenger. And if Philippa had come visiting to forget troubles at home, no one was helping her do it.

'He's still unsettled by . . . all of it,' Philippa answered. 'And that Lady Anneys won't have anything to do with him.'

'It's early days yet,' Sister Johane said comfortingly. 'Lady Anneys only needs time until she can face him again.'

'Besides,' Lucy said cheerily, 'you and Hugh can't be married for probably a year anyway. There's plenty of time yet.'

'Lucy, you don't care who marries who,' Ursula said impatiently, 'just so long as somebody is marrying somebody.'

At the opening of the arbor Miles said, 'If Hugh is wise, he'll find a husband for you, Lucy, before he does anything else and get you out of here.'

'Miles!' Ursula exclaimed happily while Lucy complained, 'I wish he would,' and Miles laughed at her. He was still in the rough, dark green tunic, hosen, and soft-soled leather boots he wore to the forest and his hound was beside him.

'Oh, Miles, not Bevis,' Lucy protested. 'Not here.'

Ignoring her, he made a half-bow to Philippa and said, 'I saw your horse and man and thought I'd find you here. You look well, my lady.'

'As do you, good sir,' she answered as lightly.

'Where's Lady Anneys?'

'Gone to bed with a headache,' said Lucy, 'and Hugh is gone off with Father Leonel, so you might as well join us. Here. But do leave Bevis there.' She started to shift sideways to make room between her and Philippa.

'By your leave,' Miles said, coming only a single pace into the arbor's shade before he folded his legs and sank down cross-legged on the ground. 'Here will suit me better, where I can look on all your lovely faces.' The hound Bevis lay down beside him with a heavy huff. 'How go things at home, Philippa?'

'Well,' she said, then amended, 'Well enough.'

'What you mean is that Sir William is still glooming because Lady Anneys doesn't want to talk him just now, and that your Uncle John is glooming because she doesn't want him wooing her. And you're glooming because you have to wait a year to marry Hugh?' Just barely he turned the last into a question and put a stinging edge to it.

Lucy protested, 'Oh, Miles, don't be mean!'

But Philippa laughed and tossed his challenge back at him with, 'And Elyn is glooming because everyone else is. I came here so I could gloom somewhere else for a change, yes.'

Miles laughed, too, and with mocking regret said, 'It seems Father Leonel will have to give us a sermon on the virtue of patience some Sunday soon.'

'And on how blessed it is to have a cheerful heart in the face of adversity,' Philippa returned.

'And about the sin of gloom,' Miles said.

'And the sin of sloth,' Philippa retorted.

'Sloth?' Miles protested. 'Where does sloth come into it?'

'Sloth in pursuing the virtue of patience. Sloth in avoiding the sin of gloom.' Philippa paused in counting them off on her fingers to say, 'Though I've never heard gloom listed among the sins. And *your* sloth in not giving up tormenting your sisters and me.'

Miles and Ursula laughed, while Lucy looked back and forth between him and Philippa and said, 'Oh, you two. You're so strange.'

'Strange and stranger,' Miles agreed. 'So, as long as we're talking of gloom and marrying, who do you want to marry, Lucy?'

Frevisse immediately guessed it was a question to which they all knew the answer, because Ursula rolled her eyes upward and took up her sewing again and Philippa sat back with smothered laughter while Lucy unhesitatingly launched into telling how she wanted a husband who was wealthy, not too old, and certainly not ugly, and lived in a town because she was so tired of living in the country and never seeing anything, and for her wedding dress she wanted . . .

Frevisse watched the others listening to her and wondered what angry things Sir William and Master Selenger had been saying to each other. Philippa had seemed unsure her uncle's anger this morning was from disappointment over Lady Anneys, but even if it had been, why would that bring him to angry words with Sir William? Because Sir William disapproved of his interest? Or because Lady Anneys was right – Sir William had set Master Selenger onto her for Sir William's own ends? If that was it, then both Sir William's and Master Selenger's anger could have been not at each other but at Lady Anneys for forestalling them. Or Sir William might be angry at Master Selenger for, thus far, failing in his purpose. Or just possibly Master Selenger was unwilling to the work and angry at having to do it.

Or this morning might have had nothing to do with Lady Anneys at all.

And possibly Master Selenger was only what he outwardly seemed – a man honestly drawn to a woman.

But what was the likelihood that Sir William had indeed ordered Master Selenger at her, the way Lady Anneys feared? Uncomfortably, Frevisse had to admit that, from what she had been told, Lady Anneys was the one hindrance between him and the profitable control of Hugh's, Lucy's, and Ursula's marriages. If he had ambitions that way, Lady Anneys was the obstacle he needed to remove.

Once Sir Ralph was out of the way.

Which brought her back to the question at the heart of everything here. Who had killed Sir Ralph?

Miles was telling Lucy that however rich a husband she married, she would undoubtedly use up all his money within a year. Lucy was telling him he was mean and Philippa was saying that they simply needed to marry Lucy to someone so rich she couldn't possibly use up all his money in a mere year.

No one more than barely noticed when Frevisse stood up and, with a murmur that she would walk awhile, left the arbor.

The garden was drowsy in the afternoon's warmth and sunshine. Hands quietly clasped in front of her, Frevisse moved along the paths. The beds enclosed in their low wattle fencing were full as could be with the end-of-summer flourish of flowers and herbs. Blue scabious and borage, feverfew with its flood of yellow and white flowers, tall and golden St John's Wort, towering scarlet hollyhocks, thick-growing low thyme and marjorem, others that Frevisse did not know by name. Pleasures for the eye, ease for the mind, healing for the body. But her thoughts came with her and the garden's loveliness did not keep her from turning them over and over with the care she would have given to coals she feared were hot enough to burn.

Everyone said Sir Ralph must have been murdered by someone now long gone and never likely to be found out. They all said it . . . but how many of them believed it?

Some of them might. Others might doubt but were willing, Frevisse thought, to ignore their doubt. What she feared was that someone here knew for certain it was a lie. Because if the murderer was not long gone away, he was still here.

And there had to be those among the doubters who feared it, too.

Feared . . . but refused to face it: would rather live with the murderer still among them than find out who he was.

Whoever had killed Sir Ralph that savagely, beating his head in even after it had to be clear he was dead, had to have hated him. Unhappily, that hardly limited who might have done it. To guess from all she had heard, there were surely villagers in plenty who hated him; and certainly no one in his family loved him. And all of his family had been in the woods that day when he was killed, except for Ursula.

And Tom, Frevisse amended. He had quarreled with his father and gone back to the manor before the dog ran off.

But had he gone back to the manor? He wouldn't have purposefully lain in wait for Sir Ralph since they were hare-hunting that day and Sir Ralph unlikely to be alone in the forest. But what if he had stayed in the woods to walk off his anger, rather than going back to the manor, and had happened on his father and, still in a fury at him, killed him?

That was possible. Someone had told her it had taken a long time to find and bring Father Leonel and Tom after Sir Ralph's body was found. Although how long 'a long time' was to someone frantically looking for someone would be difficult to determine.

And besides his immediate anger, Tom could have been afraid his cheating on the accounts with Father Leonel was about to be found out. Had Sir Ralph lately been growing suspicious? If so, Tom had better reason than a quarrel to want him dead and better reason to kill him if he suddenly had the chance.

Who else had immediate reason or need to have Sir Ralph dead? Hugh? Had he stood to gain anything from his father's death? Unless he had simply been unable to bear his father any longer, he had already had all he seemed to want – the hounds and hunting. Or was there more he wanted that she had yet to see? Tom had stood between him and inheriting the manor and now Tom was dead, too; but nothing about Hugh told Frevisse he had wanted the manor at all, let alone wanted it badly enough to kill for it. The only other thing that would come to him because of Tom's death was Philippa. Did he want her that badly? Frevisse had no way to know.

For what it was worth, Lucy claimed it was Miles, not Hugh, who was something more than only friendly with Philippa. From what Frevisse had just seen of them together, they did accord well together; but accord and love were two different things and neither one was enough for murder. Or rather, love could be used as a reason to kill but only by the most desperate or foolish, and Miles did not seem to be either. Not for the kind of murder that had been done on Sir Ralph. Hatred, though, was another matter, and Miles did not in the slightest hide his hatred of Sir Ralph or his pleasure that he was dead. Besides, with Sir Ralph's death he gained his freedom. Lucy had said he and Philippa were together when Sir Ralph was killed, but if there was love between them, she might well lie for him. But could she lie well enough? And keep up the lie? And if she could, then what sort of person was she, to see murder like that done and not only hold quiet about it afterward, but stay a laughing friend with the murderer?

That was, of course, supposing she had not killed Sir Ralph herself. But the objection to that was the same Frevisse already had against Lady Anneys or Lady Elyn or Lucy doing it: a woman repeatedly smashing a man's skull could not have avoided such a splashing and spattering of blood onto her skirts as would have been afterward seen and questioned.

For that matter, a man would not have escaped being bloodied either but after a morning spent hunting there had likely been blood on more than one of them already. If no one noted Sir Ralph's when it was fresh, later it would simply be dried blood along with other dried blood and unremarkable.

Her pacing of the garden had brought her past the arbor again and Sister Johane said, 'You won't come back into the shade and sit?'

Frevisse made a smile whose worth she doubted and said, 'No,' and walked on, wishing she had not seen that Miles had shifted onto the bench facing Philippa and was leaning toward her with one hand out to hold a fold of her skirt while she leaned toward him, a hand resting on his knee, the two of them laughing together over something. But she had seen it and she put it with the rest.

The rest of what? What, altogether, did she have? There was Tom, who might have killed his father to protect himself. And Hugh, who maybe wanted either the manor or Philippa or both badly enough to kill for them not once but twice, meaning Tom's death was not by chance after all. And Miles, who openly hated Sir Ralph and had gained freedom by his death but not Philippa. To have Philippa, if he did want her, which was not certain, he needed both Tom and Hugh out of his way and, true, Tom was dead, but not by Miles' doing. So far as anyone had yet said, Miles had been altogether somewhere else when it happened.

But they weren't the only possibilities in Sir Ralph's death. There were Sir William and Master Selenger, too. Master Selenger could have wanted him dead, to clear his way to Lady Anneys if his interest in her was real rather than a thing made up between him and Sir William for their profit. And for Sir William himself, of course, there was the obvious reason that Sir Ralph's death put him in reach of profitable control of the Woderove marriages. That did not explain the savagery of the killing, though.

Of course, Sir William might have had an entire other reason for needing or wanting Sir Ralph dead, and the control of the marriages be only an afterthought. Come to that, Master Selenger might have other reason of his own, too. Some old anger or wrong only finally avenged.

If that were it, Frevisse had no thought on how she might find it out, but what did she know about them that day at least? Lucy had said they left the clearing together but that Sir William had come back alone. If he and Master Selenger had separated in the woods, one of them could have come on Sir Ralph and killed him. Or they could have killed him together and then separated. Either way, Master Selenger was Sir William's man. If Lady Anneys was right in believing his wooing of her was at Sir William's bidding, it could be supposed he might equally well lie to keep Sir William clear of murder.

Or Sir William could be lying for him.

About what had they been angry and arguing today?

She swiped an impatient hand at a tall borage plant as she passed. All she had were guesses and questions and no thought on how to find answers. Someone had murdered Sir Ralph. That was one certainty. Another was that he had been well-hated by many people, while some of them and too many others stood to profit by his death. Set the question of 'who' to the side, then, since it was so wide. What about 'why then' and 'why there'? Why that time and place for his death?

Those questions told her something anyway – that his killing hadn't been planned. There had been no way to know the dog would run off and Sir Ralph go after it, no reason to expect he would be alone at all that day. That meant the chance to kill him had merely happened and someone had taken it, probably without thought of afterward. And very likely only blind luck, rather than forethought, had kept whoever it was from being caught at it or found out soon afterward.

Frevisse paused to rub thyme leaves between her fingers, releasing the scent into the warm air. A chance murder, yes. But had it been someone taking the chance when it came or someone forced to it then and there? There was still the possibility that it had been nothing more than Sir Ralph catching someone where they should not have been – someone poaching or a peasant taking wood.

Though how could someone have been fool enough to be anywhere near where Sir Ralph was hunting when it was known he favored that place in the woods for his midday rest she did not know.

Hunting. The dog-boy Degory. She had forgotten him but he had been there. He had even said that Sir Ralph had hit him when the dog ran off. Had it been one blow too many?

He had also said Sir Ralph had hit Hugh then, too. Had *that* been one blow too many?

Frevisse found she had stopped and was standing over the same cluster of red gillyflowers that Lady Anneys had looked at so long last evening. They seemed such simple flowers until one not only looked but truly *saw* them; then, with their finely veined, delicately fringed petals, their careful stems and leaves, their rich and subtle coloring, they were not simple at all. Beauty, at its heart, was rarely simple, and yet the world held so much of it, and what Frevisse found forever hard to understand was why mankind so often chose ugliness when beauty was so readily, amply there.

Was it because the ugliness was easier? Because it let a person feel powerful without the cost of being anything but selfish?

She walked on. Sir Ralph, by all that she had so far heard of him, had been that kind of petty, small-hearted man, his life a blight on everyone around him. The pity was that the blight had not been cleansed by his death. It was still here, a blood-tainted shadowing in minds and hearts.

She came to the garden's rear gate and stopped there to gaze out across the field stubbled yellow from the summer-harvested hay. Come autumn, the cattle would be turned out there to feed and in the spring it would be ploughed and planted, to be harvested when another autumn came and after that left fallow, to be hay again another year.

Year went around into year, the pattern of them repeating and yet never the same. This year had brought murder here. She wished she could forget that. Wished she would let the matter lie, for someone else to take up or leave, as they would. She could do that, she told herself – could just leave it all alone. Guilt and justice were the crowner's and sheriff's business, not hers. If the crowner was satisfied and everyone here content, shouldn't she be, too?

But she couldn't be. Someone here was a murderer, and even

though no one might know who he was, enough of them knew he was here that their denial, their willed unknowing, was a rot at the heart of things – and rot, left to itself, only spread, rotting everything around it.

Chapter 18

The afternoon had drawn on while Frevisse walked and the others talked. She was thinking she should rejoin them when Sister Johane joined her at the gate, leaned on it beside her, and said, 'In spite of Dame Emma and Sister Amicia, I'm not used to this much talking. I'm going to see how Lady Anneys does. Should we do Vespers after that?'

Pleased that for once she need not remind Sister Johane about an Office, Frevisse said, 'I'll come with you and save you coming back.'

As they crossed the silent, empty hall, the hound Baude – stretched out on the cool floor-tiles near the empty hearth – opened one eye as they passed but did not bother to raise her head. Upstairs, they found Lady Anneys just awakened, sitting on the side of her bed trying to pin up her hair. Still slow with sleep, she was not doing well and Sister Johane went to take comb and hair-pins from her, asking, 'How do you feel, my lady?'

Lady Anneys gave a soft half-laugh. 'I'm not sure I'm awake enough yet to know. But my headache is gone. Thank you for that.'

'You can have the sleeping draught again tonight if you like. It's a mild one. Having it twice in one day this once will do no harm.'

'I should like that, I think.' Lady Anneys sighed and moved her neck from side to side as if she were stiff. 'It's so tiring when even going to sleep takes effort.'

Still eased from her sleep and maybe from the quieting aftereffects of whatever Sister Johane had given her for the headache, Lady Anneys unprotestingly let Sister Johane finish her hair and then pin on her veil for her. 'But not my wimple,' she said. 'I know as a properly grieving widow I should go wimpled, veiled, and all but invisible, but the day is hot and I'm not properly grieving and we have no guests to be offended. So just the veil.'

'Lady Philippa is here,' Frevisse said.

'Philippa is family, not guest.' Lady Anneys made to rise, found herself a little unsteady at it, and thanked Sister Johane for a steadying hand to her back. On her feet, she straightened her shoulders with a visible effort and asked, 'Is Elyn here, too?'

'Only Lady Philippa,' Frevisse said.

'Where is everyone?'

'In the garden, except Master Hugh, who went to see how the harvest does.'

Lady Anneys was both fully awake and had her balance now and said as she started for the door, 'I'll go to the parlor then. I don't want all Lucy's chatter just yet. But could you ask Philippa to come to me, Dame Frevisse?'

Frevisse took the errand willingly. By the mingle of voices from the kitchen as she passed, she guessed someone was back from the field and readying supper, and in the garden she found Hugh had returned, too, and was sitting beside Ursula, pretending to find fault with her sewing. Philippa had moved to the other bench, while Miles had shifted back to the ground and was leaning with his back against the wooden wall of the bench near her, his hound stretched out beside him, chin resting on his knee, his hand on its shoulder. Frevisse gave her message. Philippa said she would come in a few moments, and after returning to tell that to Lady Anneys in the parlor, Frevisse went thankfully up to the bedchamber with Sister Johane again.

Vespers was supposed to draw the day's work to an end in prayer that left the heart and mind free of whatever burdens the day had held. In the nunnery there would be supper afterward, the nuns silent while someone read aloud from a suitable book, then the hour of recreation followed by Compline's brief prayers and bed in good time for a few hours' sleep before Matins and Lauds in the middle of the night. But today Frevisse could not settle her mind to the Office. Vespers' comfort did not come and she was merely grateful when at last she and Sister Johane ended, '*Fidelium animae per misericordiam Dei requiescant in pace. Amen*' – The souls of the faithful through the mercy of God rest in peace – and could cross themselves and stand up.

She made herself wait, though, until they had put their breviaries away before she said, 'Shall we see if Lady Anneys wants our company?' Because this might be her chance to talk with Philippa apart from the others.

Her restlessness must have showed despite herself or else she had betrayed herself in some other way, because rather than immediately answering, Sister Johane gave her a long look and finally said, 'You're doing it again, aren't you?'

Frevisse was surprised into asking, 'I'm doing what again?'

'We talk about it sometimes. What you do. Finding out murderers. You're trying to find out who murdered Sir Ralph, aren't you?'

Frevisse opened her mouth, closed it again, and at last answered, 'Yes.'

'Is it wise?' Sister Johane asked seriously.

Again Frevisse hesitated before saying with matching seriousness, 'I don't know.'

'You can't just let it go?'

That at least she could answer without hesitation. 'I can't, no.'

Now Sister Johane paused, before finally saying, simply, 'If you need any help, I'll give it.'

The simple steadiness of that took Frevisse by more surprise. She had to will herself to remember that, after all, Dame Claire trusted this girl – this woman – and that said much for her, before she could bring herself to say, 'Just listen for anyone saying anything about the day Sir Ralph was killed. Or anything that's said that's . . . not right to your mind.'

Sister Johane gave a small nod. 'I understand.'

'But don't ask anything. Don't let anyone know you've any interest. I'd have you promise me that.'

Steadily, Sister Johane said, 'I promise.'

Frevisse stared at her a moment longer. Sister Johane levelly returned her gaze in a way that satisfied Frevisse, she understood the danger there could be, the odd thing being that until now Frevisse had not clearly considered the danger that someone who had killed once might well kill again to protect himself. But there was no going back from it now and she only said, 'I'd like to see Lady Anneys and Philippa alone. Would you go back to the garden without me?'

Sister Johane agreed to that with a nod. They went down to the hall and parted and outside the partly open parlor door Frevisse forwent the temptation to pause and listen, instead scratched lightly at the doorframe and, at Lady Anneys' bidding, went in. Lady Anneys and Philippa were seated on the long chest under the open window to catch whatever breeze might come that way, both of them leaning on the windowsill, Philippa with her head bowed and resting in one elbow-propped hand, Lady Anneys with her arm lying along the sill, her hand touching the girl's arm. By the look of it, Philippa had been crying, and although she was recovering from it, she turned her face away without lifting her head, hiding behind her hand, as Frevisse entered. Contrariwise, Lady Anneys was calm-faced and asked in an even voice, 'Where's Sister Johane?'

'Gone back to the others in the garden.'

'Please, sit, if you like.' Lady Anneys nodded toward a carved joint stool near them and went on as Frevisse crossed to it, 'Philippa has been warning me of exactly what I feared.'

Philippa raised her head, began a protest. Lady Anneys briefly, tenderly squeezed her arm and said, 'I've already talked about the will and Sir William and your uncle with Dame Frevisse. She knows enough there's no harm in her knowing more. Please, tell her what you told me.'

Philippa let out her breath on an unsteady half-sob but obediently straightened up, folded her hands into her lap, and faced Frevisse. Dry-throated from her crying and her voice not so even as Lady Anneys', she said, 'You heard me saying my father and uncle were angry at each other this morning. What I didn't tell was why.' She looked down at her hands in her lap and said, pacing the words like something learned by rote, 'Father wants Lady Anneys married or unchaste so he can take over Hugh and Lucy and Ursula's marriages. He's set my uncle on to do it and is impatient because it hasn't happened yet. This morning he was saying he wants it done sooner rather than later, before she does anything on her own about the marriages. About Hugh's marriage especially. Father is afraid she won't agree to me marrying him.'

Frevisse looked at Lady Anneys. 'You're thinking against it now?'

'My lady,' Lady Anneys said wearily, 'Sir William is ahead of me on this by a long ways. I'm too tired and hurting, heart and mind both, to think about any marriages. Left to myself, I'd leave at least theirs to Hugh and Philippa's choice anyway.'

'That's one of the things that worries Father,' said Philippa, her head still bowed. 'He doesn't want it left to our choice.'

'Because he thinks you or Hugh will refuse the marriage?' Frevisse quickly asked.

Philippa finally looked up. 'He thinks Hugh is too cool toward it. He's afraid Lady Anneys will influence Hugh against it. Because of Tom.'

'And you? Is he afraid you're cool toward it?'

Philippa looked down at her lap again. 'He expects me to do what I'm told to do.'

'And will you?' Frevisse asked.

'Yes.' Flat and without feeling.

'What about Miles?'

Philippa jerked up her head and stared at Frevisse, eyes frightened wide and not answering.

It was Lady Anneys who asked, puzzled, 'Philippa?'

Philippa turned her head to stare at her, still making no answer.

Carefully, making no mention of Lucy's tattling talk, Frevisse said to her in a meaningful way, 'I watched you together today.'

She did not add that she had seen nothing that truly betrayed them, but Philippa gave a small gasp and covered her face with both hands.

Beginning to be alarmed, Lady Anneys asked, 'Philippa?'

Philippa dropped her hands into her lap again and lifted her head. She was flushed but not crying, and said, somewhere toward defiant, 'Miles and I. Yes. If I had my choice, I'd choose Miles. Only he won't let me. Because we know there's no hope in it. Father will never let it happen.' She gave a brief, unhappy laugh. 'Nor will Miles. He says I'd lose too much by marrying him. He says he won't do that to me.'

Gently Frevisse asked, 'Does Sir William know what's between you?'

'If he did, I doubt I'd be let out of the house again until safely married to Hugh.'

'Does Elyn know of it?' Lady Anneys asked.

'No. Nor even suspect. She'd surely tell Father if she did.'

'But when you went alone with Miles, didn't that make her wonder?' Frevisse asked.

'How do you know I've been alone with Miles?' Philippa asked with sudden fear. 'Who else knows we've been meeting?'

'Oh, Philippa,' Lady Anneys said, sharp with worry. 'You've not been meeting secretly?'

'A few times. That's all. Just a poor, few times. But no one else is supposed to know about it at all. Who's seen us?' she demanded of Frevisse, half-angry as well as frightened. 'Who told you?'

Quickly, deliberately mildly, to soothe her, Frevisse said, 'All I know is that someone said that the day of Sir Ralph's death you and Miles went walking together while the others were searching for the dog.'

Philippa put a hand over her mouth, realizing she had said things she could have left unsaid; but an instant later she dropped her hand and said, 'Miles and I went off on our own that day, yes. There was nothing wrong about it. Lady Anneys was there. She saw us and said nothing.'

'Because I thought it was simply that you and Miles couldn't bear Lucy's and Elyn's nattering any longer. There seemed less harm in your walking together than in Miles knocking their heads together. I never thought . . .' Lady Anneys shook her head. 'I never thought you and Miles . . .'

Or maybe she had unknowingly chosen not to think it, Frevisse thought. Among the things Lady Anneys had not needed in her life then, any more than now, was one more trouble. She might have unknowingly chosen not to see that one.

'It doesn't matter anyway,' said Philippa. 'Nothing can come of what we want. It's Father is the trouble. And Uncle John.' Whose treachery – to judge by her voice – hurt her worse than her father's did.

'He's completely willing to do Sir William's bidding in this?' Lady Anneys asked bitterly.

'I . . . I gather so. What he seemed angry at was being pushed too hard at it. Father wants it done now and he says it can't be.'

'Is he supposed to go so far as to marry me? Or will ruining my reputation be enough?'

'I don't know,' whispered Philippa.

'Or why not do both?' Miles asked angrily from the doorway.

He and Hugh stood together there, both of them darkfaced with matching anger, and again Frevisse was struck by how much like brothers they looked. But it was Miles who came forward ahead of Hugh, saying at Lady Anneys, 'Why shouldn't Selenger ruin your reputation for Sir William's behalf, then marry you for his own? That way both of them will have something out of it.'

Behind him Hugh said warningly, 'Miles.'

Miles, halfway across the room, swung around and said at him, 'For years, because of Sir Ralph, we've always talked around things, never straight at them. Where has it put us? Anywhere we want to be?'

'In that, you're right,' Lady Anneys said before Hugh could answer. 'So let's talk straight at them now. But let's not have anger in place of silence. Sit down. You and Hugh both.'

It was an order more than a request, and Hugh came forward to sit on a joint stool. Miles held back, on the edge of rebellion for a moment, then went to lean his hips against the table edge, arms folded across his breast.

'First,' said Lady Anneys to both of them, 'Philippa came here today to warn me about Sir William and Master Selenger. Dame Frevisse and Hugh both know I already feared it. Miles, did you?'

'Yes. From almost the first day Selenger came here after Sir Ralph's death.'

'Well, now there's no more need to fear because now that we know for certain and I don't have to worry you'll find out, I won't let him near me again. It's finished. That leaves us with you, Miles. You and Philippa.'

She must have seen as clearly as Frevisse did the look that flashed between Miles and Hugh because she asked quickly, 'Hugh knows?'

For once Miles was less than assured, his glance at Philippa uncertain as he answered, 'We've talked some of Philippa and me, yes, but this isn't the time to—'

'You said you were tired of talking carefully around things,' Lady Anneys pointed out. 'So am I. Philippa has already given away more of what's between you than she meant to, so Dame Frevisse and I know. I take it Hugh knows, too?'

Grudging and uncomfortable, looking aside rather than at any of them, Miles said, 'I've told him, yes.'

'Hugh? What have you thought of it?'

Hugh looked as if he were thinking he'd like very much to be somewhere else just then but met his mother's gaze and said, 'I favor it.'

Philippa stood quickly up and went to Miles. Laying her hands on his folded arms, she said gladly, 'You see?'

'Except,' Hugh said with a wary look from his mother to them and back again, 'he keeps saying I should marry her.'

Philippa looked unbelievingly from Miles to him to Miles again, stepped back, and said fiercely, 'You idiot!'

Miles tried to catch her hands but she did not let him and he spread out his own, half-entreating, half-insisting, 'We've talked of the hopelessness of it often enough. What can I give you except trouble? It's better that you're safe with Hugh than ruined with me.'

'Idiot!' she said again, still fiercely.

Lady Anneys laughed, startling them, maybe startling herself; but she pointed a finger at Miles and said, 'I don't know much of love, but when a woman calls you "idiot" in that way, my guess is she's much too much in love with you to reason about it.'

Stubbornly Miles said, 'It doesn't solve anything.' But even as he said it, one of his hands reached toward Philippa, who moved close to him and took it.

'No,' Lady Anneys agreed. 'But with it in the open among us, it makes one less secret.'

For her part, Frevisse was watching Hugh. He had been tensely silent until, when Miles reached out to Philippa, his face lightened into a smile of relief and pleasure, telling her he had meant it when he said he favored Philippa for Miles rather than for himself. The friendship between them was that true. But because she was unlikely to have better chance than this, she asked, 'Miles, when you and Philippa were away together the day Sir Ralph was killed, did you hear anything – any angry voices, a quarrel, someone moving in the woods who shouldn't have been there . . .'

At mention of Sir Ralph, Philippa pressed close to Miles and hid her face against his shoulder. Putting his arm around her, Miles answered, 'If we had, we would have said so.'

'Except maybe you were afraid of Sir William learning you'd been away together?' Frevisse asked.

'I don't want to hear or ever think about that day again,' Philippa said, her face still to Miles' shoulder. Lady Anneys, her own head bowed over her hands now clenched together in her lap, nodded sharp agreement. Hugh made no answer at all except to turn his head away from all of them. Only Miles met Frevisse's gaze and said steadily, 'It was murder. We would have said if we'd heard or seen anything, Sir William or no.'

Hugh turned back. 'That's one thing. We none of us heard anything. There was no shouting.'

'And Sir Ralph was a famous shouter,' Miles said drily.

'The crowner asked the same thing,' Hugh said, 'but whoever it was must have taken him by surprise. They must have been lying in wait and taken him by surprise.'

Philippa stepped back from Miles. 'I'd best go home now.'

Miles moved as if to see her out, but Lady Anneys said, 'Let Hugh go with her, Miles. He'd be expected to and for now we might do best not to bother giving anyone other thoughts.'

Hugh and Miles exchanged looks and matching wry smiles before Miles nodded. Philippa, missing none of that, smiled much the same, curtsied to Frevisse and Lady Anneys while Hugh bowed, and then left easily with him, except as they went out the door she pushed his arm and said, 'He told you about us?'

Miles, as if abruptly weary, sank down on the joint stool Hugh had left. Lady Anneys rose and went to him, leaned down, and kissed his forehead before laying a hand on his shoulder and saying quietly, 'Heed me in this, Miles. Don't lose or ruin what there is between you and Philippa. You can only guess at how much hurt there'll be for her if she marries someone she doesn't want, but I know, and I say that whatever she loses from Sir William is nothing when set against it.'

Miles stood abruptly up and without a word or even a bow went out of the room.

Lady Anneys watched him go, then turned back to the window, sat again on the chest, and said, 'I would never be so young again for all the world.'

'Nor I,' Frevisse agreed. She went to sit at the chest's other end. There were heartaches of one kind and another all through life but those of one's young years, even looked back on, seemed to cut with a sharper edge than almost any later ones, simply – or not so simply – because one had not yet learned any defense against them. And that, in time, like all things, they passed. But slowly, feeling her way through the thought as it came to her, Frevisse said, 'I would never have thought, seeing Philippa in the garden this afternoon, that she was as deeply upset as she showed here about what she'd overheard between her father and uncle.'

Lady Anneys looked out the window into the dusty sideyard where the broad-trunked, thickly green-leaved elm tree spread its branches to half-hide the back of the stable and byre and slowly said, 'We've all learned not to show our thoughts or what we feel. We hide almost everything from one another. Around men like Sir Ralph and Sir William, that's safest, but sometimes we even hide ourselves from ourselves, I think.'

She was calm rather than bitter about it. But she was calm about most things, Frevisse had found. Except now Frevisse was coming to think it was not so much calm as the smoothness of old, old scars over deep wounds. The kind of scars that ache when the weather is wrong and sometimes hurt with shadow of their old pain. Gently, and again because she could not be sure she would have such another chance, she said, 'Neither you nor anyone else cares at all that your husband is dead, do they?'

Lady Anneys paused before answering, then said, 'If by "cares," you mean "grieves," no. No one grieves for him. His death lessened, not increased, our grief here.'

'No one even cares that his murderer goes unknown.'

Again the pause. Then, 'Whether we care or not makes no difference. His murderer is long gone from here and there's an end of it.'

'And you're content with that?'

'I'm content *because* of that.'

From the hall came the sounds of the tables being set up for supper and servants' voices. The girls and Sister Johane would come in from the garden soon, or Hugh come back from seeing Philippa away, and Frevisse considered quickly asking who else had left the clearing the day Sir Ralph died and what Lady Anneys might have noticed about anyone when they came back there after his death. But those questions were too open; Lady Anneys would understand too readily why she asked; and unable to think of anything else to say, Frevisse let the silence lie between them, looking out the window at the elm tree's leaves hanging unmoving in the still, hot air.

It was Lady Anneys who stirred and spoke first, answering something that had not been asked. 'My husband was murdered. My son died by mischance. But that mischance came because of all the wrongs and ugliness my husband made while he lived. Those are deaths and griefs enough. I only want it all to be done with and forgotten and the rest of us left free to go on with our lives. I want to remember Tom and forget my husband as completely as if he had never lived.'

And could there be worse epitaph than that for anyone, Frevisse thought. To be so hated that someone wished to forget that you had ever been at all.

Chapter 19

Hugh awoke too early, when only the first bird was twittering outside the loft's small window, and lay in the darkness too long with only his thoughts and the even sound of Miles' breathing for company. When finally the black square of the window lightened to the dark blue of dawn's beginning and there were the sounds of the servants who slept in the kitchen below him getting up, he could no longer bear it and rolled off his bed, gathered up his clothes from on and around the stool where he had tossed them as he undressed last night, and groped his way to the ladder-steep stairs.

Miles mumbled a question. Hugh answered, 'Out,' and creaked down the steps into the passage between hall and kitchen. Bevis, lying on an old blanket put along the wall for him there, raised his great head but did not bother to rise. Hugh touched him briefly, silently letting him know everything was well, and went along the passage to let himself out the rear door into his mother's garden. He stopped there to dress. The birds were in full choir now and the world was brightening from blue shadows into colors. By the time he went, fully dressed, out the garden gate in the already warm half-light of dawn, he could hear Helinor in the kitchen threatening Alson over something and, from above, at the far end of the hall, Lucy complaining to Ursula in their room that Ursula's bad dreams had kept her awake in the night.

With no particular purpose except to be away from all that household busyness beginning the day, he went to the kennel where the hounds, strewn in long-legged sprawls around the yard, lifted their heads to look at him, but only Bane rose and ambled to the fence. Degory, burrowed into sleep with an arm around Skyre's neck on a heap of straw in a corner of the yard, stirred less readily and asked, not fully awake, 'What is it?'

'Nothing. I just came to see the hounds.' He stroked Bane's long head. 'I don't see them enough anymore.'

Yawning, Degory sat up with straw in his hair. Skyre sat up, too, and licked his face.

'Is she doing better?' Hugh asked.

Degory climbed to his feet, scratching. 'Better, but I doubt she'll ever be right.' He ambled to the fence much the way Bane had. 'We're going to be short on lymers without her.'

'Not if she breeds true. I'm thinking to try her with Makarie when the time comes.'

'Aye, that might do. How is it with Baude? Are you going to bring her back here to whelp?'

'I mean to, yes.'

'I've her place ready for her. She can't be long off it now.'

They made comfortable dog-talk for a time, daylight growing around them and the manor coming well awake. The hounds roused and wandered around their yard, came to be petted, wandered off again. 'What about old Bevis, then?' Degory asked. 'Still following Master Miles everywhere?'

'Except into the loft to sleep with us.'

'Odd, that,' Degory said on a yawn. 'Him being so much Sir Ralph's dog but taking to Master Miles like this.'

Hugh kept back from saying that it showed Sir Ralph had not been worth even a dog's loyalty, but offered, 'Come to that, it's just as odd that Miles has taken to him.'

'That's true enough. Master Miles never much cared for dogs that I ever saw.'

'Maybe he'll be one of us yet. What do you say? Are you and the pack up to some hunting tomorrow?'

'That we are!' Degory exclaimed, then added hopefully, 'A hart maybe?'

'I can't take any men off the harvest to make a hart-hunt. It will have to be hare again, but I'm thinking we'll go all the way off to Beech Heath. We haven't coursed there since spring and Miles said he saw signs of hare in plenty of late.'

'They'll be fat and lazy by this time,' Degory said happily. 'Ready for the hounds to tickle them up they'll be. We'll have to be off early though, to be ahead of the heat. Is it staying this hot?'

'Gefori says there'll be rain in a day or two.'

'Too much for the harvest?'

'He doesn't know.'

'St Peter bless us,' Degory said. He slipped the latch on the gate and came out of the yard, pushed several hopeful muzzles back inside, and fastened the gate. 'I'm to breakfast. You?'

'No. I'll linger here a time. You go on.'

Degory left and Hugh stayed where he was, a hand out to stroke heads and receive licks. The sun edged into sight over the horizon, sharpening the day to long-thrown shadows and molten gold. Hugh wished he felt that bright about the day. His heart had lightened with talk of hounds and hunting and the thought that tomorrow he'd not be bound to the manor by one duty and another but away and rid of everything save the needs of the hunt. But that was tomorrow. There was still today and then the days after tomorrow and him tethered here at the manor for most of them. Tom had had everything in hand and ready for the harvest, and the reeve saw to most of the rest, so that presently there was too little to keep himself fully busy here, just duties enough that he wasn't free to go about such hound and hunting work as he could have otherwise.

Dissatisfied with almost everything, he left the kennel and, vaguely minded to go to Mass, circled the stable and saw, when he reached the road toward the church, that the two nuns were ahead of him, bound the same way, their black gowns and veils dull against the morning's late summer green-and-gold. Hugh wondered, not for the first time, if Ursula would choose that life. He hoped not. He couldn't imagine her a nun, shut up for the rest of her life. But then he could not imagine her married, either. She was just his little sister.

On the other hand, the sooner a husband was found for Lucy, the better. Tom had said something once about asking Master Wyck if he knew anyone in Banbury who might be suitable. That was likely the best way to go about it and he would, once the harvest was done and he had talked with Mother about it.

By then this trouble with Master Selenger and Sir William might be settled, too – another thing off his mind.

Ahead of him the nuns went into the church. A few village folk were going in, too, and Father Leonel would be making ready to begin the Mass, and in his mind Hugh could see it all, familiar all of his life. The short, windowless nave; the chancel hardly big enough to hold the altar; the small sheen of candlelight on the silver altar goods given by the widow who had held Woodrim before Sir Ralph bought it; the green altar cloth that Hugh could remember his mother embroidering with vines and wheatsheaves when he was small; the small, plain-glassed window high in the east gable end of the roof letting in so very little light that gray shadows filled all the rest of the church. And suddenly Hugh knew he could not go in there, to the shadows and the prayers, and already in the churchyard, halfway between gate and door, he turned aside, onto the little dirt path that curved through the churchyard and around the church.

He would sit awhile with Tom, he thought.

They had made Tom's grave on the other side of the church and just outside the chancel, as near to the altar as could be without being buried inside, and the heaped earth of his grave-mound was still raw under the turfs of green grass laid over it at his burial's end.

Sir Ralph was buried across the churchyard, almost against the churchyard wall, the hump of his grave already well-settled, its green turfs melded together by the summer's rains. He had made no provision in his will for where he should be buried. It had been Lady Anneys' choice and she had pointed there, a place that would be easily lost among the other graves and grass if no one bothered to mark it with more than the plain wooden crosses that marked the village folk's graves. Those, being wood, decayed and the graves were lost along with them as folk who might remember died in their turn. No one had known whose bones were dug up when Sir Ralph's grave was made; their bones were simply added to the other bones piled in the small charnel house screened by yew trees at the far corner of the yard, where someday Sir Ralph's bones would go and maybe sooner than some because no one was minded to mark his grave with even a wooden cross, let alone visit or remember it.

Hugh meant somehow to find the money to lay a stone graveslab over Tom, though. Even if it were only flat to the ground and carved with no more than a cross, it would be something, would mean Tom would maybe sleep undisturbed in his grave until Judgment Day.

Hugh had no clear thought why he was going to Tom's grave. To pray for him maybe, or just to be somewhere no one else was; but as he came around the church's corner, he saw Miles at the churchyard's far end, standing near the yews around the charnel house. Miles had his back to him and Hugh paused. He knew Miles came here sometimes – possibly more often than Hugh knew – to where his mother was buried.

'There's not much I remember of her,' Miles had said once. 'She had black hair, very long. She'd let it down at bedtime and hold me on her lap and wrap it around me and tickle my ear until I curled up laughing. I remember walking somewhere with her, too. On a sunny day. Picking flowers out of the wayside grass to make a flower crown. Not much else.'

Not much at all but enough that he still came to her grave, and Hugh's half-thought to leave before Miles knew he was there; but Bevis lying beside Miles raised his head to look at Hugh, and Miles turned around like someone not wanting to be taken unaware from behind.

But seeing Hugh, he waved and started toward him and Hugh waited where he was, beside Tom's grave. Father Leonel had begun the Mass, his old voice faint from inside the church, and Miles, joining Hugh, cocked his head, listening, and asked, 'You came too late to go in?'

'Found I didn't want to, once I was here.'

'You were out and about early, gone when I awoke. Where've you been?'

'To see the hounds. I'm thinking to have a hare-hunt at Beech Heath tomorrow, to give them a run and bring in some fresh meat. Bevis ought to come. Will you?' Before Miles could answer, Hugh felt bound to add, 'I'm going to ask Sir William if he wants to join us.'

'Why?' Miles asked, more rude than curious.

'Because we can't afford to have him angry at us.'

'What about our being angry at him?'

'We can't afford that either. Not when there's no point to it.'

'There wasn't any point to Tom's death either.'

'That wasn't meant, Miles. I was there. I know.'

'Tom is dead, whether it was meant or not,' Miles said bitterly.

Hugh abruptly sank down on an old grave's low green mound across the path from Tom's unweathered one, drew up his legs, wrapped his arms around his knees, bent forward to press his forehead onto them, and said miserably, his eyes tightly shut to close out the world, 'God's mercy. I'm so tired.' He didn't mean 'tired.' He meant 'in pain' but he didn't know how to talk about pain, or about the fear or the wariness or the darkness in him. When Sir Ralph was alive, he had known what the pain was for, had known from where all of it – the pain, the fear, the wariness, the darkness – came. Now Sir Ralph was gone and all of those things should have gone, too. But they hadn't. They were all still with him.

The difference was that he no longer knew the reason for them.

And he was afraid to find out.

Miles sat down beside him on the grave-mound, briefly touched his shoulder, and said with the rare gentleness that was always a surprise from him, 'I'm sorry. I shouldn't have done that to you.'

Without lifting his head, Hugh rolled it from side to side, refusing Miles' guilt. 'You didn't do it. It's me. Everything is wrong since Tom died and I doubt I can ever make it better.'

'You're doing well at it,' Miles said. 'Give it time.'

'I'd rather give it away. All of it.'

'Not until you've married Lucy and Ursula off, and by then your own wife, whoever she is, won't let you.'

Hugh raised his head and looked at Miles. "Whoever she is"?' he echoed, and was pleased he matched Miles' light touch on the words. 'You mean you've decided not to make me marry Philippa?'

'I don't think I'd like what she'd do to either one of us if we tried.'

'Then you'll marry her before you leave for Leicestershire?' Hugh pressed.

'If I marry her, I'll *have* to leave and it won't have anything to do with Leicestershire. It will be because Sir William is after me.'

Hugh let go the lightness, said seriously, 'Have you thought that once Philippa is married, Sir William loses one of his reasons for trying to take over Sir Ralph's will? Then I'll find a husband for Lucy as soon as may be and someone for myself, and with only Ursula left, none of it will be worth Sir William's bother anymore and Master Selenger will give over troubling Mother.'

'Selenger had better give over troubling her before then,' Miles said. 'And how are you going to protect her in the meanwhile?'

'She's doing that, by seeing to it she's never alone. That's why she brought the nuns back with her, I think.'

'You can't keep them forever.'

'When they leave, I'll do something else. Meanwhile, the thing is to get you married to Philippa.'

'Leave it, Hugh. For now, just leave it,' Miles said amiably. But firmly. He slid down to lie on his back, his head pillowed on the grave. Bevis, who had been sitting patiently this while, promptly lay down and nudged his muzzle into Miles' side to remind him he was there. Miles obediently began to play with his ears.

Hugh held silent. Silence was better than making a quarrel where he did not want one, and although the sun was well up now and the dew already dried from the grass, warning the day would be hot later on, just now it was good simply to sit here in the warm, heavy sunshine. He pulled at the grass beside him until he had a handful, then let it fall in a small scatter, listening to Father Leonel without making out the words, while the quiet drew out between him and Miles, until he said, 'You still mean to go to Leicestershire come Michaelmas?'

Miles made a wordless, assenting sound.

Hugh plucked more grass and let it fall. 'I've thought of another reason you should marry Philippa.'

'Hugh . . .' Miles started warningly.

'Just think how angry it would have made Sir Ralph.'

That took Miles enough by surprise that he laughed, choked, began to cough, and had to sit up. Hugh cheerfully beat on his back, helping not at all. Bevis, looking confused about whether he should worry or not, sat up, too. Miles, fending off Hugh's blows with one hand, put his other arm around Bevis' neck and croaked, 'Let be, you dolt.'

Hugh let be and stood up out of reach before Miles recovered enough to repay him. 'Mass seems done,' he said. 'I'm going in to talk to Father Leonel before going back to the hall. Will you come?'

'May as well,' Miles said, and together they circled back to the other side of the church. The village folk were already out, spreading homeward down the village or to work, but as Hugh and Miles reached the broad, round-topped door of thick planks and heavy ironwork standing open into the nave, Hugh heard Father Leonel, inside, saying to someone, 'Go on then,' not sounding pleased about it.

'The day Sir Ralph was killed . . .' Dame Frevisse said.

Hugh stopped in midstride. So did Miles beside him.

'. . . why did whoever went looking for Tom Woderove have such trouble finding him? I understand he'd come back to the manor well before his father's body was found, but he couldn't be readily found when he was looked for.'

Crisply, in a way that made Hugh think she had been asking other questions and the priest was not happy about it, Father Leonel answered, 'Tom took so long to be found because no one thinks to look first thing in a church for a young man. That's where he was. He'd come to me to talk off his anger and make confession of it. Why is knowing that of any help to Lady Anneys?'

Hugh and Miles looked at each other, each silently asking if the other knew what this was about, both of them shaking their heads that they did not.

And Dame Frevisse was ignoring Father Leonel's question to ask, 'Was he worried that Sir Ralph was going to find out what you both had been doing with the accounts?'

'There was nothing to worry about that way. We always made certain there was money enough for his hounds and Sir Ralph cared nothing about the rest. Dame, be advised – let all of this go. Let it rest with the dead. It's better there than being raised up to plague the living.'

Hugh could not make out her murmured answer to that. Maybe she had bowed her head and was accepting the priest's order, because the next that Hugh heard was Father Leonel blessing her in farewell. Beside him, Miles drew back a step, making to leave before they came out. Hugh was ready to retreat with him but they had waited too long. Nor was it Father Leonel who came out but both the nuns, and there was nothing either Hugh or Miles could do, caught flat-footed and in the open, except bow, wish them good-day, and move to go past them into the church. But Dame Frevisse, quicker than they were, said, 'Master Woderove, we were just talking to Father Leonel, trying to understand matters better, so we can maybe better help your mother.'

'Help her how?' Miles demanded.

'She's in deep grief,' Dame Frevisse said.

'For Tom,' Hugh said stiffly. 'We all are.'

'For Tom, yes,' Dame Frevisse agreed. 'But she's in grief for her own life, too.'

'In grief for her life?' Miles echoed, sounding as if he understood no better than Hugh did.

'For her life,' Dame Frevisse repeated. 'We gather that Sir Ralph was not . . . kind . . . to her.'

Miles gave a short, harsh laugh. Hugh said only, 'No. He wasn't.'

'Or to any of you,' Dame Frevisse persisted.

'Or to anyone,' Miles snapped.

'And to you most especially,' Dame Frevisse said to him evenly; but she returned to Hugh with, 'You got on the best of anyone with him, didn't you?'

'For what that was worth,' Hugh said, 'and only because of the hounds and the hunting. He probably got on best with Sir William.'

'Since they were both of a kind,' Miles said, not hiding his raw dislike of that 'kind.'

'Does Lady Anneys ever talk about Sir Ralph's murder?'

'We've none of us talked about it,' Hugh answered sharply. 'Ever.'

'Not at all? Not even when it happened?'

'Not then and not now,' Hugh said almost harshly.

'We were too glad that he was gone,' said Miles.

Dame Frevisse fixed a suddenly narrowed look on him. 'Somebody wanted him gone badly enough that they killed him.'

Miles met her look with his own and answered, 'Yes. And blessings on them for it.'

'Don't you care who?'

'Not greatly, no.'

'Whoever did it,' Hugh put in, 'is long gone and not likely to be found. So there's no point in caring.'

'What about Master Selenger?' she asked them both.

Hugh traded quick, questioning looks with Miles, who did not look as if he understood the question either, before Hugh answered, 'Master Selenger didn't kill him, no more than any of us did.'

'How do you know he didn't? He was there that day. And he's made plain his interest in Lady Anneys.'

'He's only interested because Sir William told him to be,' said Miles.

'Or was Master Selenger interested before,' Dame Frevisse asked, 'and it's Sir William who's being led, rather than the other way on?'

Hugh and Miles traded looks again, and this time it was Miles who answered, somewhat slowly, thinking it out as he went, 'Because if one of them murdered Sir Ralph, it would be the one who first thought of how they could gain by his death. Master Selenger because he wanted Lady Anneys. Or Sir William through the will.'

'Yes,' Dame Frevisse said.

He and Hugh looked at each other again.

'That,' said Miles, still slowly, 'could be worth the finding out.'

But Hugh said, 'My lady, please leave it alone. Please.'

'The day Sir Ralph died . . .' she started.

Worried and puzzled, Sister Johane said, 'Dame . . .' at the same moment Miles burst out, 'Hugh said let it lie, my lady! So let it!'

Hugh, still pleading more than demanding, held out a hand to silence Miles and said, with more quiet than he felt, 'Dame Frevisse, please believe this – that we're all far the better off with Sir Ralph dead than we ever were with him alive. His death is neither a trouble nor grief to anybody here. If there's any grief over Sir Ralph, it's for the wasted years he was alive.'

And there was the terrible truth. That was what Sir Ralph's life had been and it was what he had made of all their lives while he lived. A waste. His life had been a waste, and Tom's death was a waste, and the grief of both those truths suddenly choked Hugh. 'So let his death go, my lady,' he forced out. 'We've grief enough and don't need more.' And because he could not trust himself beyond that, he turned away from her and the other nun and Miles. Turned away from them and everyone and everything except his grief and tangled thoughts. Turned and went out of the churchyard and across the road, blindly headed toward the forest's edge across the pasture there, wanting the sanctuary the forest always gave him. Sanctuary and time to think. Sir Ralph's life had been a waste of all of their lives and none of them talked of his death because no one wanted to know . . . who among them had done it.

Because, very surely, one of them had.

And Dame Frevisse knew it as well as he did.

Chapter 20

With Hugh almost to the woods, Miles broke the startled silence left behind him, saying, 'If you'll pardon me, too, my ladies,' and went the other way, across the churchyard, not even to the gate but bracing one hand on the low wall when he came to it and swinging over. His hound cleared it in an easy leap after him and they disappeared together into the village.

When Frevisse looked back toward the woods, Hugh was out of sight. Beside her, Sister Johane said softly, 'Oh my,' and when Frevisse looked at her, her eyes were large with pity and unease.

'Oh my indeed,' Frevisse agreed.

'Do you think one of them did it?' Sister Johane almost whispered, though there was no one to overhear them.

Slowly Frevisse answered, 'There's nothing that says so.'

'Nor anything that says not,' Sister Johane said, her gaze fixed on Frevisse's face.

'No. There's nothing to say that either. In truth' – and the truth came hard – 'I've not yet learned anything that tells against anyone more than another. Anyone at all.'

Hopefully, Sister Johane asked, 'Then you're going to let it go?'

Staring downward at the grassy edge of the graveled path, Frevisse said slowly, 'I don't know what else I can ask or where else I can look for answers. But to leave it like this . . .'

'If it's the only place you can leave it, you have to,' Sister Johane said.

Frevisse lifted her head with a sigh somewhere between accepting that and impatient at herself, her heart and mind heavy with more than the day's growing heat.

Hugh was afraid and Miles was angry, and she understood

Miles' anger. Sir Ralph had done enough to him to fuel a lifetime's anger. But what was Hugh afraid of?

Of being found out for his father's murder?

Or of finding out who *had* done it?

Or did he know who had done it and was afraid for them?

Or afraid *of* them.

She stood staring at the woodshore where Hugh had disappeared. It was the weather, she told herself. It was too hot for her to think clearly. But the woods' rich greens of high summer were already dulled toward the dusty beginnings of autumn. The year was on the turn.

'This weather can't hold,' she said. 'There'll be a storm before long.'

'Shall we stay here for Tierce and say it in the church?' asked Sister Johane.

'No,' Frevisse said, finding she did not want to meet Father Leonel again just yet, with his burden of knowledge about the Woderoves. Had Sir Ralph's murderer confessed to him yet? Did he know who it was? Or maybe, with his deeper knowledge of everyone here, did he at least have too true a suspicion? 'No,' she said again to Sister Johane's question. 'Let's go back to the manor for it.'

The day passed somehow. The heat grew worse, weighing on everyone, stilling even Lucy's chatter. Neither Hugh nor Miles came in to midday dinner and for once Lady Anneys was impatient at them, saying, 'They could at least say when they're not going to be here.'

At her order, a double share of ale was sent out to the fields for the harvesters' midafternoon rest-time. Later, Helinor came into the garden to tell her, 'Alson brought back word Master Hugh and Master Miles are both in the field, helping to harvest. Thought you'd want to know,' and afterward Lady Anneys was a little farther away from the edge of her ill-humour. She even had supper delayed until nearly dark, waiting for their return, and buckets of water set on the bench outside the hall door to the foreyard to warm in the afternoon sun, with towels and a bowl of soap and clean tunics laid beside them, so that when Hugh and Miles finally walked wearily into the yard, they were able to wash there, stripped to the waist and scrubbing each other's backs, Ursula reported, hanging out the tall window to watch them.

'Well, tell them to hurry. I'm starved,' Lucy said irritably from the table.

'Not so starved as they surely are,' Lady Anneys said curtly. 'You've done nothing all day except moan about the heat while they've been out working in it. Ursula, come here and sit down. They don't need your help to wash themselves.'

They came in, in their clean tunics and with their hair slick to their heads from dunking in a bucket. Baude, wide with her whelps, heaved up from beside the hearth and waddled to meet them, she and Bevis circling each other with waving tails. Talk through the meal was of how the harvest went and whether the weather would break in a storm sooner rather than later.

'Gefori says sooner,' Hugh said. 'Late tomorrow maybe. If it holds off to late afternoon, we'll have most of the wheat safe.'

'What of the beans and peas?' Lady Anneys asked. A storm that battered them into the ground when they should be drying on their plants could ruin the crop and mean much of the manor's food for the next year was gone.

'Father Leonel is praying,' Hugh said.

'Do you still mean to hunt tomorrow?' Lady Anneys asked.

'The hounds need it, if nothing else,' Hugh said. 'But I'll make it short and be done early.' Taking great care at spreading butter on a piece of bread, probably so he did not have to look at her, he added, 'I asked Sir William if he'd join me.'

Suddenly no one except Lucy was looking at anyone else, until after a moment Lady Anneys said with careful quiet, 'And is he going to?'

'He sent back his thanks but said he'd not.'

'Another time, then.'

Lady Anneys spoke as if hardly interested one way or the other; and Hugh with relief said, 'Yes. Likely later.'

The message had been passed between them that, when the time came, she would accept it.

Because they had dined so late, there was little time for staying up and by the last fade of twilight they all went to their beds, before there was need to light candles to see their way. Shut into Lady Anneys' bedchamber, Frevisse freed her head from veil and wimple with a relief matched by Sister Johane's sigh of pleasure as she rubbed at her bared neck. While Sister Johane settled onto their truckle bed, Frevisse moved to close the window shutter but Lady Anneys said, 'Pray, leave it open.' She was sitting on one of the chests with her hair already loosed and falling to her waist, Ursula combing it with long, slow strokes in which both she and her mother seemed to be taking pleasure. 'I'd rather risk the night vapors,' Lady Anneys said, smiling, 'than smother the way we surely will with the window shut.'

So would Frevisse and she willingly left it open, but it made small difference. The hoped-for evening coolness did not come and sleep was hard to reach, no matter how much it was wanted. And Frevisse wanted it very much, because otherwise she lay thinking when there was far too much she did not want to think about because there was far too little she knew.

But without sleep, she found herself considering, in the quiet darkness after Lady Anneys had gone to her bed and Lucy and Ursula to theirs, how comforting it would be to believe Tom Woderove had killed his father.

Found herself likewise thinking how unfortunate it was that she believed Father Leonel when he said Tom had been with him.

If she believed that and refused to believe there had been an unknown someone there or that one of the women or girls could have done it without being bloodstained, she was down to the four men and Degory for the murderer. Or three men if she accepted that Miles and Philippa had been together – and hadn't themselves killed Sir Ralph. Because it might have been planned between them, to go off together but Philippa wait somewhere alone while Miles stalked Sir Ralph and killed him, with her to claim afterward that they had never been apart. It would have been a very quickly made plan, though, and if they were going to kill someone, wouldn't Sir William have been the better choice? His death would have made Philippa sure of her inheritance, setting her and Miles free to marry in despite of whatever rage Sir Ralph might have against it.

Perhaps Philippa had balked at plotting her father's murder. But killing Sir Ralph was purposeless for them. Or maybe not so very purposeless, because Sir Ralph's death freed everyone from him. Which was the trouble. Everyone had that reason to want him dead.

But if Tom was left out of it, who had had best hope of profit from Sir Ralph's death? Sir William if he thought he could take control of her children's marriages from Lady Anneys. Master Selenger if he wanted Lady Anneys and thought he could win her once she was widowed. Hugh if it mattered enough to him to have the hounds all for himself . . .

Sleep was finally starting to come, her mind drifting loose of connected thought . . . and into the thought that maybe they were all lying. That they had all killed him and were all lying. That Hugh and Miles and Sir William and Master Selenger and even Degory had all planned his death and done it, and everything any of them said was lies for the sake of protecting each other . . .

Frevisse found she was stark awake again, staring angrily at her thoughts.

She was like a hen scratching in the dust, throwing bits of everything around at random in hopes of finding a stray fact to feed on, she told herself. And if that was all she could do, she would be better putting her efforts into prayer for peace for the souls of everyone here, that they might come to God's mercy, since it looked unlikely anyone would come to Man's judgment.

The familiar ways of prayer brought her slowly toward sleep; but when it finally came, she found herself in a troublous dream where a man that she knew – in the way one knew things in dreams – was Sir Ralph was struck down and killed and stood up to be killed again, first by Tom – again, in the way of dreams, Frevisse knew who he was, though she had never seen him – and then by Hugh, and then by Miles, and then by Sir William and Master Selenger together, and finally by Lady Anneys, – who unlike the others – beat and beat and beat on him after he was down, making sure of his death and that he did not rise again.

Frevisse awoke from that with a start that wrenched her upright in bed, gasping for breath, certain something terrible was happening. And heard, not in any dream, the high-pitched scream of someone in mortal agony or fear.

Beside her, wrenched equally awake, Sister Johane sobbed, 'Holy Mary, Mother of God, protect us now and in the hour of our death!' But from the bed above them Lady Anneys said, 'It's Baude. She's begun to whelp and is frighted by it. She always does this.'

'Are you sure?' Sister Johane gasped.

'I'm sure,' Lady Anneys said with a calm that could only come from complete assurance. A plaintive voice called from the girls' room and Lady Anneys called back, 'It's only Baude. Go back to sleep.'

Reassured along with Lucy and Ursula, Sister Johane lay down with a relieved sigh. Frevisse lay down less quickly, her mind still tainted by her dream. Baude gave one more agonized howl before Hugh must have reached her and begun to soothe her because the night's quiet came back and in it Frevisse tried to say some of the prayers she should have awakened to do at midnight. A slight stir of air had cooled the room a little and she soon slept again, but not deeply. The ugly tendrils of her dream still strayed through her mind and she was fully awake sometime later when Lady Anneys rose restlessly from her bed.

The darkness beyond the window had thinned to the blue-gray of coming dawn. In the dimness Lady Anneys groped for her bedgown where she had laid it aside before going to bed, found it, and slipped it on before – so quiet-footed that she must have had every squeaking floorboard held in her memory – she went out and down the stairs. Frevisse, having pretended to be as asleep as Sister Johane was, settled herself determinedly for a last small sleep before the household stirred awake and the day began, but there seemed to be no more sleep in her and impatience took over, and rather than resort to pillow-pummeling in the hope of finding a shape both cool and sleep-inducing, she rolled warily off the bed. The ropes stretched under the mattress squeaked slightly the way ropes stretched under mattresses always did, but Sister Johane did not stir, and Frevisse dressed by feel and pinned on her wimple and veil blindly but with practiced fingers before going down the stairs. Lady Anneys had probably gone to the garden for the early morning's coolness. So would she.

Faint lamplight shining around the shut door at the stairfoot somewhat surprised her, and she was more surprised when she opened it to find Hugh and Miles and Degory all there in the hall, crouched near the hearth around a heap of straw where Baude lay on her side, looking far flatter than she had last evening. Hugh and Degory barely glanced up as Frevisse circled them, careful not to come too near. It was Miles who looked up, a wholehearted smile on his tired face, to explain, 'She was too frantic. We didn't want to move her to the whelping shed. So Degory brought straw and we've done it here.'

'All's well?' Frevisse asked softly.

'Five so far and we don't think she's done.'

Craning her neck to see without coming too close, Frevisse saw the little bodies lined along Baude's belly, suckling mightily. Baude looked the least pleased of anyone about the whole business, lying still but with her eye rolled sideways and fixed rather desperately on Hugh, who was crooning to her, telling what a brave, good girl she was.

'You won't be hunting today,' Frevisse half-whispered to Miles.

'We won't, no. The hares will live to another day,' he agreed.

The long, hard surge of a contraction rolled down Baude's length. She tried to flounder to her feet in protest against it, setting Hugh to talking more earnestly to her and Miles to handing the whelps to Degory to put tenderly into a wide, waiting basket nested with rags. Frevisse quickly departed, most definitely not needed there.

At the hall's far end she found Bevis stretched out across the doorway to the rear passage, his great head resting on his outstretched forepaws and such a desolate look on his face that she stopped to tell him comfortingly, 'It will be done soon and you can have Miles back.' He regarded her solemnly but not as if he believed her, then pushed himself up on his pony-long forelegs, clearing the doorway for her. She thanked him because his dignity seemed to require it and, when she was past him, heard him lie down again behind her with a heavy, patient sigh and slight thud.

She likewise heard people early-morning mumbling among themselves in the kitchen as she passed and the rustle of straw-stuffed mattresses being put away for the day. Ahead of her the door to the garden stood open, the morning's coolness flowing in, and she stopped on the threshold to breathe it in with relief. The morning birds were chirruping welcome to the new day, though the sunrise sky was a sullen red along the horizon that warned the threat of storm to come was real.

But overhead the sky was still clear and brightening to rich blue, the last stars washed away by the swelling daylight that showed Lady Anneys standing at the gate, facing outward toward the red sunrise, her arms wrapped around herself as if her bedgown was not warm enough in the morning's cool. From where Frevisse stood, able to see only her back and the long fall of her hair, she looked more a young girl than a husband-wearied wife and mourning mother. There was such peace in her standing there that Frevisse held where she was in the doorway's shadow with a sudden ache for the moment's perfection: Lady Anneys quiet here in her garden; Hugh and Miles intent and content in their work together over Baude and her newborn whelps; Lucy and Ursula safely sleeping; the household servants setting about their everyday early work. This was how lives were supposed to be lived – with pleasure and work and rest in fair amounts all around. Not in the tangled ugliness of angers and fears Sir Ralph had made of it for everyone here, nor the torn, painful mess of secrets, broken hopes, distrusts, and doubts there had been through these past weeks.

Slowly, sadly, Frevisse crossed herself, praying better would soon come.

At the gate Lady Anneys startled and her head flinched sideways, to look leftward along the cart-track toward the stable and other manor buildings. Frevisse's view that way was blocked by the garden's fence and the arbor but the next moment she heard the soft hoof-fall of a slowly ridden horse and had just time to wonder who it could be at that hour and place before Lady Anneys opened the gate and stepped out onto the small bridge across the stream there, saying, wary and worried together, 'Master Selenger. Is there something wrong? Has something happened to Elyn?'

He rode into Frevisse's view. Beyond him the sun had just begun to rise, throwing the shadow of him and his horse sharp-edged and black across Lady Anneys still at the gate as he said, 'Everything's well. There's nothing's wrong.'

'Then why are you here?' She put a hand behind her, to the gate, ready to retreat. 'Sir William said he wasn't going to hunt today.'

Master Selenger swung down from his horse, stood holding his reins but very near her now. 'Lady Elyn has said you always rise to see her brothers and Miles off on a hunt. I thought this would be a better time than most to see you alone. To hunt Beech Heath they'd have to leave before full light and they have. I came around by the kennels to be sure and all's quiet there. But you see.' He gestured at his high riding boots and old, forest-green hunting doublet. 'I came ready with my excuse. If they'd been still here, I would have simply joined them on the hunt. But I've won my chance and here you are alone.'

'They're still here. They didn't go on the hunt,' Lady Anneys said. She was fumbling to clear the folds of her bedrobe from around her feet, trying to back away but hampered by them and kept by the bridge's narrowness from turning around. 'Baude's whelping. They . . .'

Selenger dropped his reins and moved toward her with abrupt purpose, caught her by the arm, and drew her to him, off the bridge and away from the gate.

Lady Anneys tried to pull free, protesting, 'Let me go!,' and Frevisse stepped out of the doorway's shadow, demanding in a clear, carrying voice, 'Master Selenger! Have done!'

He sent her a single, swift, dismissing look, pulled Lady Anneys – now outright struggling to be loosed – against him, put an arm around her waist, and took hold of her other arm, pinioning her to him. She was struggling desperately now, beginning fully to believe what was happening, and Frevisse – her skirts caught up, away from her feet – began to run toward them, but thinking even as she did that oddly Selenger was neither forcing Lady Anneys back into the garden or toward his horse but only out into the middle of the cart-track. He had even let his horse go and it was drifting away to crop grass along the track's far side. What . . .

Sir William's voice cracked whip-sharp into the morning air. 'Lady Anneys!'

Both Selenger and Lady Anneys froze and Frevisse came to a stop in the gateway. Scarcely fifteen yards away, from the same way Selenger had come, Sir William sat on his black palfrey, frowning at Selenger and Lady Anneys. He cast Frevisse only a short look that dismissed her as completely as Selenger had done before he said with dark displeasure, 'What have I caught you at, Lady Anneys?'

'Nothing!' Lady Anneys said shrilly. 'Tell him to let me go!'

'Master Selenger?' he demanded. 'What was happening here?'

'As you see,' Selenger said. He pulled Lady Anneys more tightly to him.

It was wrong. Where he should been defiant, even angry, or coarse with laughter and satisfaction, he sounded sullen, the words and gesture made almost more by rote than will; and then he let Lady Anneys go except for a hold on her near wrist.

An ugly suspicion awoke in Frevisse, made more ugly by Sir William saying with a flicker of what could only be pleasure across his face, 'What I see is that you've been at the man-woman sport together.'

Lady Anneys started a strangled refusal of that. Over it Frevisse said strongly, 'I've been with Lady Anneys since before Master Selenger came. Nothing has passed between them except her refusal of him and his seizing of her against her will.'

'It's good of you to say so, Dame,' Sir William said coldly at her. 'But this has openly gone past your lies being any use. I saw them embracing and how willing she was to it. And in her bedgown for worse measure.'

Lady Anneys cried out in wordless protest and wrenched her wrist free of Master Selenger's hold, but Sir William pointed an accusing finger at her. 'You've violated your husband's will, my lady. You are unchaste and thereby have lost the right to control your children's marriages. I fear that—'

'*I* fear,' Miles said, his voice barely recognizable with fury, 'that you're wrong, Sir William.' He pushed past Frevisse and crossed the small bridge to the cart-track and Lady Anneys' side, Bevis stalking beside him, both of them undoubtedly brought by the angry voices. Raw with anger, he said, 'No woman affairs with a man in the presence of her grandson and a nun, and that grandson and nun will testify we saw nothing between her and Selenger save his ill manners.'

'Don't waste your time with perjury, Miles,' Sir William said scornfully back. 'It'll do no good against my word and Selenger's.'

'My word won't be perjury,' Frevisse said and found she was as angry as Miles.

Sir William's look at her was cold. 'One woman defending another. Worthless.' He urged his horse forward at Lady Anneys. Caught now between outrage and tears, she pulled loose from Selenger's slight hold and tried to retreat, but Sir William rode nearer, looming over her, saying with thick satisfaction, 'No, my lady. Even Selenger will say you've been willingly his. His word and mine against yours. You—'

'*You*,' Miles said. '*You* set him on to this. He's to perjure himself to ruin her for your gain, you miserable . . .' He sprang forward and seized Sir William by belt and sleeve. '. . . *cur*!' And hauled him from his saddle.

Sir William's horse shied violently away, adding to the force of Sir William's fall; he hit the ground hard enough to jar every bone in his body and Miles, his grip torn loose, staggered backward, momentarily off balance. Selenger, who might have come to Sir William's aid, instead caught Lady Anneys by the shoulders from behind and drew her backward, away from the two men and toward Frevisse. Miles caught hold of Bevis' rough-coated back and regained his balance while Sir William rolled over and crawled to his hands and knees, then lurched to his feet, gasping for breath and red-faced with fury.

'You damned whelp,' he panted. 'I'll hang you with my own hands for that. You tried to kill me!'

'If I'd tried,' Miles snarled back, 'you wouldn't be getting up.'

Bevis moved forward, putting himself in front of Miles, trying to push him away from Sir William with a wolfhound's instinct to keep his master out of danger.

'Miles,' said Hugh, suddenly at Frevisse's side. 'He's armed.'

Sir William was, only with the kind of belt-hung dagger that men wore most of the time but he was drawing it and neither Miles nor Hugh had anything at all, dressed only in the loose shirts and hosen they had pulled on while seeing to Baude. Bevis was still pushing against Miles but his dark eyes were fixed on Sir William and he began to growl, the hackles rising the length of his back as Sir William, too blind with fury to heed him, moved toward Miles.

Miles, as able as Bevis to read Sir William's fury, stepped back as Sir William thrust at him. Sir William was just far enough away that the thrust was probably meant more in threat than actually to stab – but Miles stumbled sideways as if his foot had caught in a trackway rut, throwing him off balance, unable to defend himself, and that made Sir William's move too much a threat for Bevis, who – so swiftly there was no chance to stop it or guard against it – twisted sideways between the two men and reared on his hind legs to his full wolfhound height, forequarters and head towering over Sir William for the bare instant before his forepaws hit Sir William on chest and shoulder, driving him backward, snapping his head back to expose his throat that Bevis seized from the side in his jaws with all the intent to death that he had ever seized on a stag in the hunt. Sir William stabbed at him once but then was being shaken and flung from side to side like a barn-killed rat. There was a gurgling that must have been his last attempt to cry out and then blood was spurting from his flopping body and Hugh and Miles both yelled, 'Drop it!' at Bevis, who – well-trained hound that he was – immediately did, letting blood from Sir William's ripped-out throat fountain red into the red morning light, spraying wide and over everything.

Chapter 21

In the instant that Bevis seized Sir William, Selenger swung himself in front of Lady Anneys, between her and sight of what was happening but not enough blocking Frevisse's own view, everything happening so fast that she had time to see but do no more than throw her hand up against the spraying blood, and then Lady Anneys was screaming and Selenger was pushing her at Frevisse, saying, 'Get her away!'

'Carry her!' Frevisse ordered back at him, that being the surest way to have Lady Anneys away, turning from them back into the garden herself as she said it. And Selenger obeyed, caught Lady Anneys into his arms and followed Frevisse as Lady Anneys broke off her screaming and began to struggle against Selenger's hold, crying, 'Hugh! Miles! I can't leave . . .'

'Ursula,' Frevisse returned sharply. 'Lucy. You can't let them come out to this. And the servants. They shouldn't see it.'

They were to the door but, 'Put me down,' Lady Anneys ordered at Selenger with such sudden angry certainty that he stopped and did but kept hold on her, which was as well because she swayed, looking either about to faint or be ill; but she steadied, straightened in Selenger's hold, and shoved his hands away, saying, 'The girls. Yes. And Father Leonel. We need him,' as if air were hard to find but rigidly in control of herself again. 'And the servants.' Who were only now – it had all happened so fast – coming out of the kitchen in answer to Lady Anneys' screaming, both women with a knife or heavy pan in their hand, looking uncertain whether they should be angry or afraid.

Lady Anneys, her bedgown caught up and gathered to her in both hands – a way to hide their shaking as well as clear her feet –

went forward to turn them back from going out, assuring them that, yes, something terrible had happened but that Hugh and Miles were seeing to it, no, they were unhurt but it was better that everyone else stay inside.

'Go with her,' Frevisse said at Selenger. 'See to it she has something strong to drink. Wine, if there is any. And you, too.' Because his face was the same ashen gray as Lady Anneys'.

And so was her own, Frevisse supposed as Selenger nodded with full understanding and followed after Lady Anneys shepherding her servants into the hall ahead of her. Frevisse, wishing she were going with them, turned back because Lady Anneys was right – Hugh and Miles should not be left alone. Though going back to the cart-track was among the last things she wanted ever to do. Part of her was even trying to believe it had not happened, but her hand was sticky with blood and there must be blood on her and when she went through the garden gate into the golden-slanted morning light of the newly rising sun, scarlet droplets of Sir William's blood were falling from the leaves where the arbor's vine overhung the fence; and there was red brightness on the fence and in the grass, and dark red pools and streams across the beaten-smooth earth of the cart-track, spreading out from the ruin that had been a man bare moments ago.

Both Sir William's and Selenger's horses had startled away along the track. Near Sir William's body were only Hugh kneeling and Miles crouched, both soaked with blood, beside the equally bloodied Bevis, who was standing very still, panting, his neck stretched out, his head lowered, Sir William's dagger hanging out of a red, blood-welling gash along his side.

The removed, assessing part of Frevisse's mind judged that the dagger must have raked shallow over bones from the hound's shoulder to almost his flank rather than been thrust deep, and now it was stuck into a rib, not buried in the hound's side. Otherwise he would be dead instead of standing there.

But even as she thought that, Miles jerked into movement, grabbed out the dagger with a cry of pain and rage, and spun around, his arm rising with his clear intent to stab down into Sir William's sprawled body. But Hugh cried out, 'Miles!' and lurched forward in time to catch his arm and force him around, putting them face to face as he cried again, 'Miles!' and let go his arm to take hold of his face with both hands, saying desperately, 'Don't! Don't make it worse!'

And Miles shut his eyes, shuddered, let his arm fall and the dagger drop, then bent over, to slide forward onto his knees and cover his face with both hands.

Hugh, with the wide eyes and stark paleness of someone hit too hard but not yet crumpled to the blow, wrapped an arm around his shoulders, looked up at Frevisse, and asked hoarsely, 'What . . . do we do now?'

By morning's end the sky had clouded to gray and in the early afternoon the rain began.

At least it wasn't the battering storm they all had feared, Hugh thought, watching it through the parlor window. The light, steady pattering would likely hold up the harvest no more than a day. But maybe it would be enough to wash away Sir William's blood, dried and darkened now on the cart-track, the grass, the fence, the leaves. Enough to wash away the sight of it, the smell of it. Wash away everything except Hugh's memory of it.

He could still hear his own hoarse voice asking Dame Frevisse what they should do and her crisp answer, 'Tend to the dog. Miles, get up and go find men and canvas to cover and move the body.'

Miles had pulled himself to his feet and gone. Dame Frevisse had helped Hugh tear his shirt and bind it around Bevis, the wound covered by the time Miles came back with Gib and Duff and a long piece of canvas from the stable. There was pause while Gib threw up in the ditch and then they spread out the canvas where the track was unbloodied, and Hugh and Miles – already bloodied past more blood mattering – carefully lifted and shifted Sir William's body onto it, troubled most by the head. It had so little still holding it on . . .

Not until the body was safely wrapped and out of sight did Miles go aside and throw up in his turn.

Father Leonel came through the garden then, disheveled and with more haste than a man his age should have made. Clutched to his chest he had his box of things needed to give the last rite to the dying but the canvas-wrapped bundle and all the blood told him they were past use and he only said, 'Best bring him to my house.'

Hugh moved to help Gib and Duff with the burden but Father Leonel said, 'Not you or Miles. You need to clean yourselves. And you, my lady,' he had added to Dame Frevisse, who was still standing beside Bevis, a quieting hand on his head.

Only then did Hugh realize she was bloodied, too – nothing like so badly as he and Miles, soaked as they were, and her black nun's gown hiding more than it showed, but bloodied enough, her white wimple spattered and her face smeared where she had wiped at it. But as Father Leonel led Gib and Duff bearing Sir William's body away, she only said, 'I'll order water heated in the laundry shed and someone to bring you clothing. Clean yourselves before you come in,' to him and Miles before she went away toward the house, leaving them to take Bevis to the kennel, to the corner kept for hurt or sick hounds.

Together they cleaned his wound, medicined and bandaged it, and in all that while Hugh said nothing and Miles no more than, 'It's a shallow cut. He should heal well.'

It wasn't much to bring out of the wreck of the morning, and against a man's death, a wounded dog maybe should not count for much; but there were a good heart and faithfulness in Bevis. Sir William had had neither.

'I'll stay awhile with him,' Miles said when they were finished, and Hugh had left him and gone around to the far side of the kitchen yard to the laundry shed, where both Helinor and the two large laundry kettles full of heated water were waiting for him. Helinor's stark stare at him told him he looked as ghastly as he felt but she said nothing, only bustled at having him out of his hosen – nearly all he was still wearing after ripping up his shirt for Bevis – threw them into one kettle to soak, and left him to wash as he would, saying as she went out, 'Don't forget your hair, too.'

He had scrubbed thoroughly, beginning with his blood-matted hair, then dressed, and all the while felt that everything was being done by someone else. Most of him was not here, was hiding behind what needed to be done, rather than facing everything it was not yet safe to feel or think.

He found the hall empty save for Selenger sitting on the end of a bench behind the high table, head bowed and hands hanging between his knees, and Degory still with Baude beside the hearth. Hugh paused to ask how she did, counted the heads nursing heartily along her belly, and said with surprise, 'Eight? There's eight of them?'

Degory nodded happily. 'They came right quick after you left. Strong ones, all of them.'

Very briefly Hugh thought that Degory was probably the only happy person here this morning. The hounds were the center and circumference of his world, and if all was well with them, all was well with him. Hugh, remembering when his own life had been almost that simple, dropped a hand on the boy's shoulder in acknowledgment that he had done well and moved on to Selenger, who looked up, haggard-faced, and said, 'Your mother is upstairs with the nun to help her. She was spared most of the blood and seeing too much. She . . .' His voice shook and he stopped.

'That was your doing,' Hugh said, remembering what he had hardly seen at the time – Selenger putting himself between her and . . . the death. 'Thank you.' Then added, hearing the words come in the strange, removed voice that did not sound like his, 'And you? How are you?'

'I don't know.' Selenger seemed truly bewildered by the question. 'He's dead, isn't he?'

'He's dead. Should I send word to . . . to Lady Elyn? Or do you want to take it?'

'I'll take it. In a little while. I'd like . . . I'd like to see Lady Anneys before I go.'

Hugh did not have it in himself to say that Selenger had seen enough of Lady Anneys. Instead, the words a little thick in his throat, he said, 'Your back, it's all soaked with blood.'

Selenger shifted his shoulders inside his shirt and doublet, stiff and sticking to him with dried blood. He must not have noticed it until then because sickened horror began to spread across his face and Hugh said quickly, 'Go and wash. Someone in the kitchen will show you where. I'll find you something else to wear.' And added, when Selenger started to refuse, 'You can't go back to Lady Elyn and Philippa like that. Leave your clothes in the laundry. We'll see to washing them.'

Practical things. Small things to set against the enormity of death but no less needing to be thought of, needing to be done, and small things were what saw Hugh through the rest of the morning. Small things and Dame Frevisse. It was by her doing that, by the time Master Selenger returned to the hall, clean and in some of Tom's old clothing Hugh had found for him, Lady Anneys was waiting there, dressed in her black mourning clothes, with Ursula on one side of her, pressed close to her and clinging to her hand, and Lucy on her other with tear-blotched face and a packed bag at her feet, Sister Johane standing behind her in a quelling sort of way and Dame Frevisse to one side of them all as if making certain they stayed where she had put them. With some part of his mind determined to note things without feeling them, Hugh saw she, too, was no longer bloodied.

Without other greeting, Lady Anneys said to Selenger as he and Hugh approached her, 'Lucy is going back with you. She can be a comfort to Lady Elyn.' Not mentioning the comfort it would be to have Lucy away from here. 'Sister Johane is going with her, to help them all.'

Selenger accepted that with, 'Yes, my lady,' and went down on one knee in front of her, his head bent low, his voice choked but clear enough as he said, 'I have to beg your pardon, my lady, for the wrong I tried to do you. It was not willingly done, I swear to you and by any saint you ask of me.'

For a startled moment no one moved or said anything, until Lady Anneys asked uncertainly, 'Not willingly done?'

Head still bowed, Selenger said, 'Sir William told me what was in Sir Ralph's will and that he wanted you out of his way. He set me on to do it. If you could be brought to marry me, fine and well and good because that would be enough; but if not marriage, then whatever else I could manage that would ruin you.'

'So everything you did was at his orders?' Lady Anneys said coldly.

Selenger raised his head to look at her and let her see his face. 'By his orders but by my choice, too, because he meant to ruin you. If not by me, then by a rougher way.'

'A . . . rougher way,' Lady Anneys echoed.

'He would have hired someone to . . . do whatever was necessary. To take you by force if need be, so you could be declared unchaste and no longer fit to be executor of Sir Ralph's will. Rather that let it come to that, I agreed to . . . what I did.'

'And this morning?' Dame Frevisse asked. 'What was this morning supposed to be?'

'It was a trap,' Selenger said. 'Sir William was impatient to have the matter settled. You weren't giving way to me, my lady, and I wouldn't . . . force you the way Sir William wanted me to. With Hugh and Miles gone hunting this morning, I was to find a way to be alone with you and Sir William would come on us and accuse you. Just as he did.'

Selenger bowed his head again, away from Lady Anneys' stare into his face. Lady Anneys went on staring, now at the back of his bent head, until finally she said, 'And if you hadn't done this, he would have done something worse to me.'

'Yes, my lady.'

Lady Anneys bent forward and touched his shoulder. 'Then you have my thanks, John Selenger, and . . .' She paused, then brought herself to say, 'And my forgiveness.'

Selenger raised his head. For a moment their eyes held, before he stood up and bowed low to her.

Not until Hugh turned then to see him and Lucy and Sister Johane to the yard where their horses waited – Dame Frevisse had given order for that, too – did he see Miles standing in the doorway, the look on his face telling he had heard it all.

Selenger, Lucy, and Sister Johane left. Duff was sent with word to the crowner. Lucas the reeve was summoned and told what had happened so he could report it to the manor's folk and slow whatever rumors were surely starting. Baude and her whelps were moved to the whelping kennel for Degory to keep watch on them and Bevis. One thing and then another was seen to, and somewhere along the way Hugh had the sudden discovery that he had had no breakfast and was starving. If he had thought about it beforehand, he would have thought he would never have desire to eat again, sick as he was inside himself, but hunger came on him and there was bread and cheese and – at Lady Anneys' order – wine for him and Miles that she said Miles must drink, whether he ate anything or not.

That had been somewhere around midday. The clouds closing across the sky by then had made it hard to know the time, but soon afterward Philippa alone rode into the foreyard. She said she had been at Father Leonel's to pray beside her father's body and she did not want to go home where Elyn and Lucy were wailing pointlessly on each other's shoulders. Could she stay here a time before she faced them again?

She had been crying herself but was calm then. Too calm, Lady Anneys maybe thought, because she gathered Philippa to her and took her into the parlor alone and a while later, when Hugh went in, Philippa had been crying more. 'It cleanses,' Lady Anneys said to him, though he'd said nothing. 'Crying cleanses the weight of grief and makes it easier to bear.'

And he remembered how she had cried not at all after Sir Ralph's death.

Soon after that, when somehow there was nothing else to be done for the while and the rain had started, bringing coolness with it and the autumn smell of rain-settled dust, Dame Frevisse and Miles came into the parlor, too. Ursula was gone off to be with Baude and her whelps and that was good, because she should not be here in their silence, so many things going unsaid and all of them sitting apart from each other. Lady Anneys was on one end of the chest below the window, Dame Frevisse at the other end, both of them with their hands folded into their laps, their eyes down. Philippa, sitting very straightly in one of the chairs, her hands gripping its arms, was staring out the window, the marks of her tears still on her cheeks though she was dry-eyed now. Miles was not with her but on one of the joint stools, leaning forward with his arms resting on his knees and his hands tightly clasped, his gaze toward the floor. Hugh, able neither to sit nor pace, leaned against the wall near the door, watching the softly falling rain, its light pattering the only sound in the room.

Afterward Hugh thought how that should have been enough. To listen to the rain and be simply quiet for a while before having to do whatever came next.

But into the quiet Miles said, 'It had to have been Sir William who killed Sir Ralph.'

Heads lifted and turned toward him, no one saying anything and Hugh silently begging him not to start this.

But, 'It makes sense,' Miles said, looking around at them all. 'He killed Sir Ralph and set Selenger on to ruin Lady Anneys. Maybe Tom's death was an accident or maybe it wasn't, but he surely murdered Sir Ralph.'

'Miles,' Dame Frevisse said softly, barely louder than the rain.

Miles looked toward her.

She met his look and said, still softly, 'Not once since I came here have I heard anyone care about Sir Ralph's death. No one has cared who did it or why. Now, suddenly, you're accusing Sir William. Why? Why now this need to accuse when there was no need before?'

Miles straightened. 'Because I didn't know before. Now it's all of a whole. He killed Sir Ralph and then tried to ruin Lady Anneys, all as a way to have control over the marriages so he could profit from them.'

'It was a savage murder done on Sir Ralph,' Dame Frevisse said, her voice still soft and careful, her gaze still fixed on Miles. 'He wasn't hit only once. He wasn't simply killed. His head was smashed in, struck, and crushed again and again and again. That wasn't murder merely for profit's sake. It was murder done from hatred, and I've heard no one say Sir William hated Sir Ralph. But you did. You still do.'

Hugh straightened away from the wall and said, 'We all hated Sir Ralph. That makes it likely for any of us to have done it. Me as much as Miles.'

'Yes,' Dame Frevisse agreed without looking away from Miles. 'Except you didn't deliberately murder Sir William. Miles did.'

Lady Anneys stood up, protesting, 'He didn't!' as Hugh exclaimed, 'You're wrong,' and Philippa said, '*No!*'

Only Miles said nothing and Dame Frevisse looked away from him to Hugh to ask, 'You know what happened to make Bevis attack Sir William?'

'Miles stumbled and while he was off guard Sir William went for him,' Hugh answered without hesitation. 'Went for him with the dagger. That's enough to set any wolfhound from defense to attack when they're defending someone the way Bevis was defending Miles then.'

'I know,' Dame Frevisse said. 'I've had to do with wolfhounds before this.'

Hugh went wary, hoping his face was as blank as he meant it to be. Most nuns were of gentry if not noble families; any of them might well have had to do with hounds before entering the nunnery. But the way Dame Frevisse said it warned him there was something more than that.

'Wolfhounds,' she said, 'except when on the hunt, are the

gentlest of dogs. They're bred to be.'

'Except when on the hunt or defending someone,' Hugh said.

'Or when they *think* they're defending someone,' Dame Frevisse said. 'You could see what happened even more clearly than I did. Miles didn't truly stumble, did he?'

A swift denial of that would have been best; but Hugh, fatally, froze and Dame Frevisse returned her look to Miles. 'You *seemed* to stumble as Sir William came at you with his dagger. Bevis was defending you, and because you seemed thrown off your balance and off guard, he did what he had been warning he would do. He attacked.'

'He was defending Miles,' Hugh said fiercely – the more fiercely because Miles was saying nothing.

'Sir William knew wolfhounds, too,' Dame Frevisse said. 'He must have known how far he could push what he was doing. His dagger thrust wasn't meant to come anywhere near to Miles and it didn't. It was because Miles seemed to stumble just at that moment . . .'

'Did stumble,' Hugh said sharply. 'Not seemed. *Did*.' Said it too sharply, too desperately, willing Miles to say nothing, to let things lie where they were, leave the denying to him.

Maybe Miles would have, but Philippa stood up and said, 'It wasn't my father killed Sir Ralph. I did.'

Chapter 22

In weary, protesting grief Lady Anneys said, 'Oh, Philippa, no,' at the same moment that Miles stood up, saying, '*Philippa!*'

Ignoring them both, Philippa said at Dame Frevisse, 'Anyone can tell you I'd left the gathering place and wasn't there when Sir Ralph was killed.'

'You left the gathering place with Miles and you came back with him,' Dame Frevisse said.

'He . . . we didn't stay together. He went off one way and I met Sir Ralph and . . . killed him.'

'That's feeble,' Miles said at her angrily.

'It's the truth,' Philippa returned, refusing to look away from Dame Frevisse.

Miles caught her by the arm and turned her roughly toward him. 'Stop it!'

Philippa looked down at his hand on her. He looked, too, then jerked his hand away from her as if burned and would have turned away except Philippa now caught him by his arm, holding him where he was before she moved closer to him, took his face between her hands, and said up at him, intensely tender, 'Never think it, my heart. He never cared what he did. You do. You're not him in any way.'

Hugh held back from any word or movement, until after a long moment of staring down at Philippa, Miles closed his eyes and let out a shaken breath, accepting what she had said. She put her arms around him and his arms went around her and they clung together. Hugh breathed again. If they could hold like that – together and silent – then there was chance . . .

'My guess would be,' Dame Frevisse said evenly, 'that Sir Ralph did indeed come on you in the wood, Philippa, but you were with Miles, and Sir Ralph went into a rage. He did something or said something or both, and Miles killed him.'

Philippa turned around, out of Miles' arms, to face her. 'No. It happened like I said.'

'That can't have been the way of it, Philippa,' Lady Anneys said. 'You had no blood on you when you came back to the gathering place. I know. I looked for it on everyone and there was none on anyone. Not on you or Miles or anyone. You don't have to tell this lie.'

'It's not a lie. It's no more a lie than saying Miles set Bevis to kill my father!'

And Miles did the one thing Hugh had hoped he would not do. He turned his head and looked at him – a long meeting of their eyes – and Hugh knew that everything he was feeling was naked on his face for Miles to read there – beginning with the sickened certainty that Miles had indeed deliberately set Bevis to kill Sir William.

Hugh had had that dark knowing with him all day, since he had wrenched his eyes away from Sir William's torn corpse and seen, instead, Miles' face triumphant with raw pleasure.

Then Bevis had staggered and they had realized he was hurt and had both gone to him, and when Miles saw how bad the wound was, he had grabbed the dagger out of the rib-bone where it had stuck, and made at Sir William's corpse. Only when Hugh had grabbed him and they had stared into each other's faces did Miles seem suddenly to understand what he had been about to do – maybe saw Hugh's horror at him, too – because his raw savagery had turned to something close to that same horror and he had dropped the dagger and hidden his face.

Since then Hugh had taken care not to meet Miles' gaze. Until now. When very surely Miles could see his certainty that it wasn't only Sir William he had killed.

And still Dame Frevisse went on, now at Miles, saying, 'Philippa will lie for you for as long as she has any hope it will save you. She'll lie and you'll lie and others will believe your lies or pretend to believe them and lie for you, too, until neither you nor anyone else knows when you're telling the truth and when you're not. You won't know what the truth is anymore, even between each other.

You know too well how long-lived anger can corrupt and darken lives. Do you think living in lies won't do the same?'

Miles was heeding her. He had turned his head away from Hugh and was listening to her, and Hugh searched desperately for something to say, anything he could say to keep Miles or Philippa from answering her.

But it was Lady Anneys who said with quiet force, 'Leave it, Dame Frevisse. All of it. Sir Ralph's death. Sir William's death. Leave them as they are. And you, Miles, you will be quiet. You'll say nothing else. Nor you, Philippa. Leave it, Dame Frevisse. Here and now it's done.'

'It can't be left where it is,' Dame Frevisse insisted. 'You can't—'

'We can.' Lady Anneys did not raise her voice. 'We're broken pieces of what should have been a family. Sir Ralph's cruelty kept us from ever being whole and we've had too little chance to mend since he's been dead. We need that chance. We'll never be as we might have been if we'd been always whole, but mended is better than broken, healed wounds better than unhealed wounds. If we start searching for "justice" now, everything will only be made worse, broken into pieces so small we'll never mend. Leave it as it is. That Sir Ralph was killed by someone unknown who will never be caught. That Sir William brought his death on himself. Leave it and leave us to make what we can of what we have left. Please.'

That last was as much command as plea.

'The truth—' Dame Frevisse started to answer.

Lady Anneys cut her off. 'The truth is that between them Sir Ralph and Sir William tore us all into pieces and broke us, and if ever we're going to mend, the truth of things here is no one's business but our own.' Her voice hardened into plain command. 'So leave it.'

Dame Frevisse stared at her. She stared back. No one moved. No one spoke.

Then Miles drew breath as if to say something, and more sharply than Hugh had ever heard her speak, Lady Anneys ordered at him, '*No*.'

And Miles held silent.

Dame Frevisse rose abruptly to her feet and went toward the door. Hugh barely gathered his mind enough to open it and stand aside before she reached it, and without even glance at him, she left, leaving silence behind her save for the soft fall of the rain outside the window.

It was a long silence. Then finally Lady Anneys drew an unsteady breath and was no longer rigid but only sitting, her shoulders a little bowed, and that released the rest of them. Miles gently seated Philippa in her chair again and stayed standing beside her while Hugh crossed to sit on the chest under the window where Dame Frevisse had been, and reached a hand toward Lady Anneys, who gave him one of her own, holding to him tightly as she said softly, 'It would have maybe been better, Philippa, if you'd said nothing.'

'I was afraid,' Philippa said. 'I was afraid that if she went on saying . . .' She stopped but the unsaid words were there, no need to say them. If Dame Frevisse had gone on saying what she had been saying about Sir William's death, Miles might have admitted what none of them wanted to hear. 'I was afraid,' Philippa repeated and left it there.

'Unfortunately,' Lady Anneys said, her voice oddly empty of feeling, 'what she said about lies and their corruption is true. And it's a pointless corruption here among us, because, lie how we may, we know the truth. That one of us did kill Sir Ralph.' She looked at Miles, who looked back, his face as empty as her level voice going on, 'We've all known from the very first that it was one of us who killed him. It's only been desperate pretense that it wasn't.'

In silence again, she and Miles looked at each other. Then he said, 'I killed him. Yes.' He straightened. Weight seeming to slip from his shoulders. A weight that had been crippling him, Hugh realized. And now that those few words were said, Miles said the rest, pouring it out with a hatred-tainted anger oddly mixed with raw grief. 'Sir Ralph came on Philippa and I alone together. It was too apparent why we were together and alone. He flew into one of his rages. He was so angered he choked on it. He couldn't even yell he was so furious. He backhanded me in the face and swore he'd see Philippa locked up until she was married to Tom and that he'd geld me if I tried to see her again. He grabbed Philippa by the arm. He hurt her and I hit him.' Miles stopped and looked at Hugh. 'The way one of us should have done years ago, because all the years when I hadn't hit him were in that blow. I knocked him down and before he could get up I kicked him in the head and then I took up a rock that was there and . . . finished it.'

Hugh had dropped his gaze to the floor before Miles finished, unable to look at him, remembering what Sir Ralph's head had been like. As if all the beatings he had ever given had been returned to him in one. And maybe they were all thinking that because for a long moment no one said anything. Only finally, with no particular feeling except curiosity, Lady Anneys asked, 'How did you do that and stay unbloodied?'

Perhaps because she asked it so evenly, Hugh was able to look up and watch Miles as he answered evenly back, 'I had my doublet off when Sir Ralph found us together. It was my shirt and upper hosen that took the blood. I washed the shirt . . .'

'We washed it,' Philippa said, claiming her part in it.

'We washed it,' Miles agreed. 'We went away from Sir Ralph's body, back along the path we'd taken from the gathering place to where there's a small stream. We were there when you found him, Hugh.' Miles looked at him and this time Hugh met his look, accepting it because his mother and Philippa were accepting it. 'That's why we were so long coming back to everyone. I had to put the shirt back on wet, but the doublet is thick. By the time it was soaked through, it passed for sweat if anyone noticed at all. I don't think anyone did. Not with all else that was going on. And the doublet is long enough it hid most of the blood-spattered part of my hosen and they were dark enough the blood didn't much show after I'd rubbed some dirt over them. By the time I gave them over to be washed here, the blood was so long dried there was no telling it wasn't from the hunt.'

'Then all we had to do was keep quiet,' said Philippa. 'Pretend to know nothing more than anyone else did.'

She said it simply but then shuddered, her hands suddenly gripping each other in her lap, and she began to cry. Miles dropped to his knees in front of her, taking her hands in his own and looking up into her face, saying, 'I'm sorry, Philippa. I'm sorry it came to this. I'm sorry.'

Philippa fell into greater sobs and bent forward to put her arms around him and her face against his shoulder. He put his arms around her waist, his face pressed against her hair; but behind him Lady Anneys said, 'Now admit the rest,' and Miles jerked back from Philippa.

Without rising, he pivoted to face Lady Anneys and said, barely above a whisper, 'The rest?'

'The thing Philippa kept you from saying to Dame Frevisse.'

'No.'

Lady Anneys leaned toward him. 'It has to be said.' Her voice was low and steady, her look at him unwavering. 'It's leaving it to rot in the dark will poison your life and Philippa's.'

'He doesn't have to say it,' Philippa said, laying her hands on Miles' shoulders from behind. 'There's no need!'

But there was need. If Hugh had not seen Miles' face after Sir William's death, he might well have failed to understand that, but what he had seen in Miles then should not be left in silence where the rot of it would only spread. The only hope Hugh had came from the horror that had swept though Miles afterward, because it meant he was not dead inside himself to what he'd done. But it had to be said. Whatever damage the truth would do among them, lies – or even a silence that was the same as lies – would do worse.

'Miles,' Lady Anneys said. 'Philippa already knows. We all know. It's for you that you have to say it. Admit to it. Accept it. Leave no room to lie to yourself about it. It's how I survived those years with Sir Ralph. By never lying to myself about what I felt or what I thought. It's by truth and whatever penance goes with it that we stay strong and grow. Not by darkness and lies. You have to say it.'

'No,' Philippa sobbed.

'Philippa, you have to accept it as fully as he does,' Lady Anneys said relentlessly. As she must have been relentless with herself all of her years with Sir Ralph. 'You have to accept it or else reject him because of it, but don't think you can ignore it or deny it. It can't be left to twist and go foul in the dark between you. Miles.'

Miles stood up, turned to Philippa, took her by the hands and drew her to her feet, then let go her hands and said, 'I killed your father. I seemed to stumble because I knew that would set Bevis at him. I meant for Bevis to kill him.'

And now it was Philippa who had to choose but her choice had been made before ever Miles said anything and she drew close to him, whispered something in his ear that no one else heard, and then, as Miles sank to his knees in front of her, his body shaken with sobs, she sat quickly down, and took his head on her lap, her own tears falling on him as she leaned over him, holding him.

'How often I wished,' Lady Anneys said softly, maybe for only Hugh beside her to hear, 'through the years, that I could have cried. Instead of simply hating.'

But she had not simply hated, Hugh thought. She had loved, too. Loved strongly enough that they had not been destroyed by Sir Ralph's dark-heartedness. They had all been tainted by it, yes, but not so destroyed that, now, they couldn't face the darkness and fight it instead of giving up to it.

Not so destroyed that they couldn't love.

The rain had stopped and the cool, gray afternoon was drawing on when Sister Johane found Frevisse in Lady Anneys' arbor. The thick leaves had kept off most of the rain; the benches were dry enough and in the while that Frevisse had been there only Alson from the kitchen had come out once, to ask if she wanted anything. Frevisse had not and otherwise she had been left alone; had tried to pray but not much succeeded; had tried to make peace with her thoughts and utterly failed. So she welcomed the distraction Sister Johane might be.

But Sister Johane sat on the facing bench, still a little unsure of her welcome, and explained, 'Lady Elyn has come to cry on her mother for a while. Lucy and I came back with her.'

Frevisse nodded to that, would have listened to more if Sister Johane had offered it, but she did not, and Frevisse had nothing to say either and for a while the raindrops' drip from the leaves was all there was, before Sister Johane made a small movement of her head toward the house and said, 'It's very strange in there. Among all of them. It felt like something other than grief.'

'Yes,' Frevisse said. 'It would.'

And maybe she would have been the one to say more but a footfall on the path gave brief warning that someone was coming before Hugh appeared outside the arbor. His look went uneasily from Frevisse to Sister Johane and returned to Frevisse before he asked, 'My lady, if I might speak with you?'

'Alone?'

His eyes flickered back and forth again. 'Unless she knows, unless you've told her . . .'

Sister Johane immediately stood up. 'I'll walk the far side of the garden for the while,' she offered.

'If you would,' Frevisse said. 'Thank you.'

Hugh stood aside to let Sister Johane leave and Frevisse moved one hand, letting him know he should sit where Sister Johane had been. He did, and Frevisse, her hands tucked into her opposite sleeves and resting quietly on her lap, waited for whatever he had come to say.

He very obviously would rather have not been there to say anything at all and said, to have it done, 'My mother sent me. She wants you to know what passed after you left.'

That was not what Frevisse had expected. A plea for her silence, or assurance she had misunderstood what she had heard, or a veiled or even unveiled – threat against her if she ever spoke of what she more than suspected. Any of those had seemed possible. But to tell her of what had happened after she left? Unless, of course, he had come to lie to her, in hopes of deceiving her into silence.

'Why didn't she come herself?'

'She said it would be too hard for her. She said it would be better for me to do it, who doesn't know you so well.'

Frevisse slightly bent her head, accepting that, and waited, regarding him with a steady gaze while he readied himself and finally said, 'We talked after you left. Miles admitted to Sir Ralph's death. Philippa was there when it happened and knew why and helped him hide the signs he'd done it.'

'And Sir William's death?'

'He admitted that, too.'

'With Philippa there to hear him?'

'Yes.'

'And?'

'She loves him.'

'He's twice committed murder.'

'Any of us could have killed Sir Ralph at almost any time. The time happened to come to Miles first.'

'And Sir William's death?'

She heard the coldness in her voice and so must have Hugh and he held back his answer, before saying at last, slowly, 'Sir William's death was a mistake. Miles was angry at him. Rightly angry. I think Miles thought that because killing Sir Ralph came so . . . easily, that killing Sir William wouldn't matter to him either. Afterwards . . . he found out it did.'

'And you? Does or doesn't it matter to you.

Her question startled him. 'Matter to me?'

'That he killed your father. That he killed Sir William.'

Hugh paused over his answer, then said slowly, 'I'd rather have him free than paying for those men's deaths with his own.'

'So you'll lie for him and go on lying.'

'Yes.' Hugh did not hesitate over that but then paused again before adding, his eyes locked to hers, 'We'll all lie. But not to each other anymore. And none of us, anymore, to ourselves.'

They stayed staring at one another for a long moment more before, slowly, still meeting his look, Frevisse nodded, accepting that as something better than nothing.

Hugh dropped his gaze, stood up, bowed to her. 'Lady Anneys simply wanted you to know. That's all.'

He made to leave but Frevisse asked, 'Where's Miles now?'

'He's gone to Father Leonel. To confess and take whatever penance he's given.'

That was something, too. But there was one more thing and she asked it before he could leave as he so openly wanted to do. 'Are you still Miles' friend?'

She had startled him again. He stopped, eyes widened with surprise, and said, 'Yes,' plainly never having thought *not* to be Miles' friend. Then he left.

Sister Johane did not come immediately back to the arbor when he was gone and Frevisse stayed where she was, watching a last few rain droplets fall from leaves. Over the hall's roof a waterish gray and yellow sunset trying to happen through the westward clouds gave some hope that tomorrow would be clear. A hope but not a certainty.

Frevisse had been haunted after she left the parlor by the thought of the reckoning that had come – a reckoning as vile as everything that had gone before it, however long it took to come – if Lady Anneys, Miles, Hugh, and Philippa refused to face the depth of wrongs there had been done here. If they tried to ignore what they all knew, the corruption of it would destroy them, heart and soul. Of that she had been sure, and that fear, at least, Hugh had taken from her. They had ended their lies to themselves and to each other.

For the world's authorities to know – crowner and sheriff and all – Sir Ralph's death would go unsolved and Sir William's be seen only as a fearsome mistake. For Miles there was the hope that penance might finally cleanse his heart and spirit of hatred's ugly dross and bring, in God's eyes, absolution for his sin of murder. And Frevisse found she could live with the law's justice not being done if a deeper justice was being answered, if payment was being made – payment of maybe a deeper and more healing kind than the law's justice would have exacted. Penance and love might well save Miles: the others' love for him and, as important, his love for them.

Sister Johane came hesitantly back and sat again, watching her for a silent while before saying, 'Something is better?'

'Something is better.'

'But not well?'

'Not well. Not yet. But now there's hope.' Where, before, there had been none.

'It has to do with the deaths, doesn't it?'

'Yes.'

'But you can't tell me?'

'No.'

Sister Johane thought on that, then said, 'But I should pray for all of them because of it, shouldn't I? For Hugh and Miles and Lady Anneys.'

'And Philippa,' said Frevisse. 'Yes. For all of them.'

Sister Johane accepted that in silence, before saying, sad with longing, 'May we go home soon?'

Something tight-coiled around Frevisse's heart began to ease at simply the thought of that. 'Yes,' she said. 'Soon we'll go home. For now, though, shall we say vespers?'

Author's Note

As always, so many sources studied over so many years have been drawn on for this book that there is no way to detail most of them, but very specifically used this time were John Cummins' marvelous *The Hound and the Hawk* – a gathering in and explaining of a number of medieval hunting treatises – and *The Master of Game* by Edward, second duke of York (died 1415 in the Battle of Agincourt) – a Middle English rendering and extension of Gaston Phoebus, count of Foix's famous *The Book of Hunting* from the 1300s – and *The Hunting Book* by Gabriel Bise for its reproductions of full-color pictures from a 1400s manuscript of Gaston Phoebus' work. For a discourse on modern open-field coursing, *Gazehounds and Coursing* by M.H. Dutch Salmon was invaluable.

Medieval breeds of dogs were not necessarily the same as modern ones, and terms from then may have different meanings now or be totally unfamiliar. Rather than explain the differences and specifics of lymers, raches, alauntes, kenets, harriers, spaniels, mastiffs, greyhounds, and more, I have kept, for the most part, simply to 'hound,' lest I end up writing my own treatise on medieval hounds instead of a novel.

The time of grace – when some animals could be hunted but not others – mentioned here differs from dates given in some sources because times of grace differ from one medieval source to another, dependent on author and place. I used what seemed most likely for where the story is set.

The 'picnic' in Chapter 3 is not an anachronism but so much a part of medieval hunting that Chapter XXXIII of *The Master of Game* is given over to describing how it should be done, including,

'And the place where the gathering shall be made should be in a fair mead . . . beside some running brook.'

The story of the herdboy shifting the cows with a slingshot was my father's story from his own boyhood – though, almost needless to say, the type of slingshot differed.

Specific and particular thanks must go to Cheryl Tregillis of Wyndfal Irish Wolfhounds for urging me to write a book with hounds and hunting in it and then providing me not only with information on wolfhounds but several chances to spend time with some of her own gentle, beautiful, charming Irish wolfhounds, successful in the show ring and fleet of foot in the field.

Thanks are likewise due Dr Carol Manning, who advised on how a small wound in the throat could be sufficient to kill. An author has ideas but needs authorities to tell her what's possible.

Now I pray unto every creature that hath heard or read this little treatise . . . that where there is too little of good language that of their benignity and grace they will add more, and there where there is too much superfluity they will also abridge it as may seem best by their good and wise discretion.

[from the end of *The Master of Game*]